Book *of* Shadows

Also by Alexandra Sokoloff

The Unseen

The Price

The Harrowing

Book *of* Shadows

Alexandra Sokoloff

St. Martin's Press ❈ New York

BOOK OF SHADOWS. Copyright © 2010 by Alexandra Sokoloff. All rights reserved. Printed in the United States of America. For information, address St. Martin's Press, 175 Fifth Avenue, New York, N.Y. 10010.

www.stmartins.com

Library of Congress Cataloging-in-Publication Data

Sokoloff, Alexandra.
    Book of shadows / Alexandra Sokoloff. — 1st ed.
        p. cm.
    ISBN 978-0-312-38471-5
    1. Police—Massachusetts—Boston—Fiction.   2. Murder—Investigation—
Fiction.   3. Occult crime—Fiction.   I. Title.
    PS3619.O425B66 2010
    813'.6—dc22
                                                                    2009045731

10 9 8 7 6 5 4 3 2

For my family: Alexander, Barbara, Elaine, and Michael

Book *of* Shadows

Chapter One

September 22

It was a vision of hell.

A dismally foggy day over stinking heaps of refuse—a city land-fill, the modern euphemism for an old-fashioned dump. Caterpil-lar trucks and front-loaders crouched with metal jaws gaping, like gigantic prehistoric insects on the mountains of trash, an appalling chaos of rotting vegetables, discarded appliances, filthy clothing, rusted cans, mildewed paper: the terribly random refuse of a con-sumer society gone mad. A lone office chair sat on the top of one hill, empty and waiting, its black lines stark against the fog.

And below it, tangled in the trash like a broken doll, was the body of a teenaged girl.

Stiffened . . . naked . . . bloody stumps at her neck and wrist where her head and hand used to be.

Homicide detectives Adam Garrett and Carl Landauer stood on the trash hill: Garrett, with his Black Irish eyes and hair and tem-per, hard-muscled, impatient, edgy; and chain-smoking, whiskey-drinking, donut-eating Landauer, a living, breathing amalgam of every cop cliché known to man: middle-aged spread, broad sweat-ing face, and bawdy, cynical humor—a lifer who used the caricature as a disguise. The partners were silent, each taking in the totality of the scene. The landfill was a succession of hills and pits and carefully leveled ground. Rutted roads wound up the slopes to the fresh dumping mound on which they now stood. A strong, cold wind whipped at their coats and hair, swirling plastic carrier bags across the trash heaps like ghost tumbleweeds and mercifully diffusing the stench. On a hot day the smell would have been beyond bearing.

On one side of the summit a forest stretched below, startlingly green and pure against the chaos of human waste. On the other side the city of Boston was a hazy outline, like a translucent Oz in the bluish fog. Far below, at ground level, were smaller hills of gravel, sand, broken chunks of concrete, logs and stumps, wood chips, various earthy colors of mulch, a black pile of tires. A corrugated tin roof sheltered an open-walled recycling center.

A row of BPD cruisers lined the dirt drive up to the landfill's main office trailer. The temporary command post had been set up beside the trailer, and two dozen mostly African-American and Latino workers huddled beside it, waiting to give statements to a couple of uniforms, while other patrolmen walked the periphery of the fence. A long line of city sanitation trucks was stalled at the front gate, being diverted by traffic control. The first responders had done their best to establish a perimeter, considering the crime scene was a joke: how do you begin to process a mountain of refuse a hundred yards high?

Landauer looked over the reeking heaps of garbage, shook his head gloomily. "Shit." He spat the word. "I don't know if he's the smartest perp I've ever seen or the dumbest."

Garrett nodded, keeping his breathing even, trying not to suck in too deep a breath of the sulfurous stink. Smartest—because any trace evidence would be completely lost in the junk heap. Dumbest—because the unsub must have driven straight in past the office trailer and paid the attendant for the privilege of dumping his terrible cargo. Garrett lit a mental candle, half thought something like a prayer. *Please let there be a record.*

The partners turned away from the dismal panorama and climbed over trash to where Medical Examiner George Edwards, a stocky

Irish banty rooster of a man, stood looking down at the body. Seagulls circled sullenly high above, their breakfast taken from them.

Two crime-scene techs were extracting and bagging one piece of garbage at a time from around the corpse, meticulously preserving as much evidence as possible in the hope that the refuse in which she lay might yield some personal connection to the killer. A videographer documented the original placement of each piece. All three technicians stood and moved back in solemn simultaneity so Garrett and Landauer could approach.

It was Saturday, which meant Garrett was the lead on the case. Department protocol was that partners alternated leads, but Garrett and Landauer had found through long experience that if they took regular days of the week and flipped for Sundays, it all evened out anyway. Garrett nodded to Dr. Edwards and crouched beside the body.

The young woman was as stiff as a Barbie doll—still half-buried and splayed on her stomach; a handless arm, a curve of buttock, one leg visible in the bed of trash. Garrett's face tightened as he stared down at the jagged red stump of the neck, the gleaming white nubs of cartilage, the black stream of ants swarming over the gaping wound. The gulls had also been at it. But there was shockingly little blood; none at all on the trash below the severed neck and very little congealed around the stump—a small blessing: the decapitation had occurred after she was dead.

Garrett pulled a micro-recorder from his suit coat pocket and clicked it on. "Killed elsewhere and dumped," he said aloud. "Decapitation was postmortem." Above him, the M.E. grunted affirmation, before Garrett continued. "Head and hands probably removed to prevent identification." It happened more often than anyone would want to think.

Garrett studied the visible arm and leg. Despite a fashionable slenderness and gym-enhanced muscle tone the girl's limbs were rounded, and silky smooth, the heartbreaking plumpness of baby fat. Garrett felt hot and cold flashes of anger. He spoke aloud, biting off the words.

"Eighteen, nineteen years old. Twenty-five at the most, but I doubt it."

Landauer shifted behind him grimly. "Yep."

Garrett swallowed his fury and continued his visual inspection. He was fighting his assumptions, fighting to keep his mind clear. A naked young woman on a trash heap; so often these miserable victims were prostitutes. Sex killers notoriously trolled highways and rough neighborhoods for these easy, anonymous targets. But there was not that sense about this one.

Okay, why?

He looked her over, looking for the facts. He gently used a latex-gloved hand to lift a stiffened forearm. No track marks, no cuts or bruising, no ligature marks—although telltale abrasions might have been cut off with the hand. "No defensive marks, and it doesn't look like she was bound." *Someone she knew? Or just someone with the element of surprise?*

Garrett was about to set the arm down, then noticed a trail of six black dots along the partially exposed shoulder, about the diameter of a pencil eraser. Hard, smooth, shiny, irregular . . .

Scabs?

He used a fingernail to dislodge one of the drops and examined it on his thumb, held out the dot to Landauer, then Edwards. "Wax, I think."

"Black wax? Kinky," Landauer commented.

Garrett nodded to a tech, who crouched with an evidence bag to take samples of the dots.

Garrett turned his gaze to the exposed leg—not just smooth, but hairless—a salon wax, and fresh pedicure. The skin was healthy and blemish-free.

This was not a runaway, not a heroin addict, not a prostitute.

"Not a hooker," Garrett muttered.

"Not any I could afford," Landauer agreed.

Garrett stood, and the detectives watched as the techs resumed clearing the trash around the body like archaeologists uncovering an ancient skeleton, painstakingly removing trash one piece at a time, placing beer bottles, fast-food wrappers, orange rinds, a stained lampshade, into various sizes of labeled paper evidence bags. Garrett turned to the medical examiner.

"What do you say, Doc?"

"Livor mortis is fixed and she's in full rigor. I'll have to wait for the vitreous potassium tests to confirm, but given the temperature I'd put the time of death at no more than twelve to sixteen hours."

The techs cleared several more pieces of refuse to reveal her back. Between her shoulder blades there was a single stab wound, in the vicinity of the heart. The slit was narrow and practically bloodless.

"Could be the fatal wound," Edwards said neutrally. The photographer clicked off photos.

Garrett's attention was suddenly drawn to the right arm, still mostly buried. "Look at that." He crouched beside the body again, lifted a wet clump of coffee filter and grounds so the other men could see. The right hand was still attached to the right arm, intact.

The detectives looked at each other. "He takes the left hand but not the right?" Landauer said, perplexed. "'S the point of that?"

Garrett stood to let the techs back in. "Maybe he was interrupted. Didn't get to finish." But it sounded wrong as soon as he said it aloud.

With enough trash now removed from around her, the techs rolled the stiffened body onto its back.

"Holy shit." Garrett heard Landauer breathe out behind him, as all the men stared down.

There were dark streaks of blood on her thighs, and the sight was a sick stab, though hardly unexpected.

The true shock was higher, in the pale flesh of the girl's chest.

Someone had carved into the torso with a knife, cruel red cuts against the young skin, the number 333 and a strange design, three triangles with the points touching.

Looking down at the crude slashes, Garrett felt his stomach roil with apprehension, even as his investigative mind registered details.

No bleeding from the cuts; they were done postmortem. So why the looseness in his bowels, the tightness in his scalp, the overwhelming impulse of fight or flight?

Landauer was speaking, the hoarseness in his voice hinting that he was struggling with a similar reaction. His eyes were fixed on the bloody carvings. "Is that supposed to be satanic?"

Garrett found his own voice, tried to breathe through the constriction in his throat. "Or someone trying to make it look that way."

"Three-three-three?" Landauer blustered, some of his panache returning. "The fuck is that? The Devil Lite? Satan can't count? I say someone's messin' with us."

Garrett stood slowly, an anvil in the pit of his stomach. It didn't feel like a game. Not at all.

The three men, and the techs behind them, stood looking down at the girl's corpse, puzzling over the design. The three triangles were maddeningly familiar, and ominous. Garrett was fighting a creeping dread, a feeling of imminent danger. All of the men had moved slightly back from the body. Garrett realized what he was thinking at the moment that the M.E. spoke it.

"Radiation," Edwards said suddenly.

The three crime-scene techs drew back, more noticeably this time.

"That's it. The radiation symbol," Landauer said, his voice thin.

"It's not exactly, though. There's something different about it. The fallout shelter symbol?" The M.E. frowned, thinking.

"Do you think she's hot?" Landauer said. For once the morbid double entendre was completely unconscious. The wind gusted around them. All the men shifted slightly, uneasily.

"I don't think so," Garrett said, only half-aware that he spoke. *The whole damn thing is weird enough already.*

"I doubt it," Edwards agreed. "I'll call HazMat, but I don't see any burns or inflammation."

Radiation or not, this was a bad one. And the acid feeling in Garrett's gut told him it was going to get worse.

Chapter Two

The men split up to do other work until a Hazardous Materials team could arrive to take readings. The detectives left the crime-scene techs behind to walk the grid, and unhappy uniforms to start the odious process of sorting through refuse looking for the missing head and hand. An exercise in futility, Garrett was sure, but it had to be done.

Landauer lumbered down toward the trailer set on blocks that served as the landfill's office to question the attendants, lighting up a Camel nonfilter as he went.

Garrett shouldered the backpack he carried at crime scenes, filled with the bags and flags and miscellany of evidence-gathering, and took off in the opposite direction, along the road, walking the curve the killer must have driven to access the dump site. The road was gutted and gouged, a bitch to drive even in a heavy truck. On one side there was only the flimsiest of fences between Garrett and a sheer drop to the valley below, thick with green trees. On the other side of the road, gripping the hill, was a wide shoulder of startlingly luxuriant weeds. There had been a full week of rain just days before and now ferns and grasses and golden black-eyed Susans and feathery white Queen Anne's lace rippled in the wind, which still carried a surprising chill—a fall day with the underbite of winter.

Garrett shivered slightly, found he was wishing for a cigarette himself. The carvings in the body disturbed him. Ritualistic elements almost always meant multiple killings. And if he really analyzed his feelings about it, there was an unease that went deeper, back to childhood, to the huge and dark mysteries of the masses that were an unquestioned part of childhood, the enforced service as an altar boy.

But along with the disquiet there was a thrill: the strong sense that this was a big case, huge, maybe *the* case that cops dream about, with all the mediagenic elements that made careers. Along with the shifting uncomfortable memories, Garrett felt the stir of ambition.

He stopped at a turnout to look out over the entire dump, the consecutive hills of refuse. The property was circled in fencing, and patrolmen had already been all around the perimeter; nothing had been cut, making it likely that the killer had driven straight in through the gated entrance to dump her.

Why would he risk it? Why not dump her out in the forest somewhere?

He. Another assumption. But the chances of a woman doing this to another woman were microscopic.

Garrett took in the scene again, and couldn't help feeling that the unsub had chosen the setting deliberately, had reveled in the filth and chaos and ungodly waste, had sought the ugliness like a civilized person seeks beauty.

He turned back toward the road and was startled by movement in the sand right in front of him. A horned beetle the size of his kneecap was creeping across the road, shiny black carapace gleaming. Garrett felt a shudder of revulsion, moved sharply aside to avoid the thing.

As he circled the creature at a good distance, his eyes were drawn to a bare patch in the green shoulder beside him. He moved closer to the clump of weeds, staring over the small field.

There were irregular oval brown marks in the wild grass, the size of footprints. The wildflowers around the marks were shriveled and blackened, as if by fire. Through his initial confusion, Garrett thought immediately and oddly of the three triangles.

Could it really be? Radiation?

What in God's name would make footprints like that?

A feeling of dread rose up through him, from his legs through his groin and spine, up to the top of his head. The hair was standing up on his scalp and arms.

He gasped in, sucking breath, inhaling a rotten egg smell . . .

Sulfur.

He wheeled in place, staring around him.

Nothing but piles of gravel and crushed concrete, tangled heaps of rebar. After a long moment Garrett turned back to the dead flowers. He fumbled his digital camera from his backpack and snapped a few shots, then took a plastic evidence bag from a side pocket of the bag and broke off several of the burned flowers, slipping them into the plastic sheath. He stepped back and scanned the dirt road. It was crisscrossed with tire tracks, an amorphous mess, but he pulled a handful of colored flags from the pack and flagged the brown scorch marks in the grass, and the multiple tire marks in the sand of the road.

On his way back toward the body, Garrett stopped a tech beside the parked crime-scene unit van and pointed out the flags he'd placed. "Get impressions of the treads in that area. And there are some burn marks in the grass—get some photos of those, too."

Landauer met him on the road, his big face flushed red with heat despite the chill, and sucking smoke from probably his fifteenth Camel of the day. "See no evil, speak no evil," he grumbled, exhaling and jerking a thumb back down the road toward the office trailer. He lit a second cigarette from the one he had burning, carefully dropping the butt into a metal Band-Aid box he carried around at crime scenes for that precise purpose. "These bozos don't record names or plates, only vehicle size and classification of load. 'Sanitation Truck, Pickup, Trailer, Truck, Dump Trailer.' 'Refuse, Stumps and Brush, Concrete, Rebar, Dirt/Asphalt, Brick.' The attendant doesn't even leave the trailer—just eyeballs the load through the window, weighs the truck on the in and out, and collects the cash. Next time I got a body to dump, I'm a comin' here, too."

"How many customers today?"

Landauer grimaced. "They average 2,250 a day."

Garrett's heart sank. "So this morning . . ."

"Over nine hundred by noon. Got a patrolman getting Closed Mouth Mary to write down every make, model, and color she can remember, but we're not talking rocket scientist here. And yeah, she collected a few checks, but it's mostly a cash business. I don't think we'll be pulling devil-boy's name and coordinates off one of those stubs."

The big detective paused, puffed in smoke. "There is something, though." He exhaled a noxious cloud and nodded up the trash mountain in the direction of the body. The sun was sinking in the sky, throwing long shadows over the hills. "That whole area was scheduled to be capped this morning—they bulldoze dumploads of dirt, cover it up, level it off." He indicated a high heap of dirt on the flat road above the trash pit. "Thing is, this morning the front-loader broke down, threw the schedule off." He pointed to the gigantic vehicle next to the pit.

"So she would have been completely covered if there hadn't been that glitch," Garrett said slowly. *She wasn't meant to be found. And that meant carving the numbers and symbol was a private ritual, not meant for anyone else to see.*

"He's familiar with the operation and schedule of this particular landfill, then," he said aloud with cautious excitement. "A worker, or landscaper or contractor."

"That's the best case," Landauer said with a nod. "The catch is, a lot of these loads that get emptied are from Dumpsters that get picked up all over the city. Someone coulda just tossed her in the nearest one of those—it gets picked up—and she gets dumped out with the rest of the trash. The Dumpster trucks back up to the pit and are emptied hydraulically, so the driver wouldn't even see what he was dumping."

Garrett fought a wave of disappointment. "What about the guy who found her?"

"Worker who came up to repair the dozer."

Garrett's eyes immediately traced the distance between the

bulldozer and the body far below. *A hundred yards, minimum.* Landauer watched him calculating.

"Guy's got good eyes," Garrett said slowly.

"Says he saw seagulls fighting over something," Landauer offered, his voice flat.

Garrett glanced at his partner sharply. "You don't believe him?" In fact, the gulls were still circling above, hoping to return to their interrupted meal.

Landauer spat. His face was neutral. "Guy's skittish, that's all."

Garrett found the mechanic in the office trailer. He sat in front of a raggedy corkboard bristling with invoices and flyers, his hands tearing apart a whitefoam coffee cup, a precise quarter inch at a time. He was short and built like a bull, with dark copper skin and an Aztec nose. He hunched in the metal folding chair as if trying to disappear into it.

Garrett's Spanish was serviceable, but the bilingual version of Severo's story was identical to what Landauer had related in English. Landauer was right, though; the Mexican was decidedly jumpy—eyes shifting around the room, sweating profusely even in the cold of the underheated trailer.

"*Tienes calor?*" Garrett asked. *Are you hot?* The lone space heater was on the other side of the room; Garrett couldn't feel any heat coming from it at all.

"*Poco,*" the mechanic said, and his eyes shifted away again. His fingers found the cross at his neck.

"*You seem nervous,*" Garrett remarked in Spanish.

The mechanic half shrugged. "*It is a terrible thing,*" he answered.

"*It is,*" Garrett agreed. "*Una infamia.*" An outrage. It was one of the first Spanish words he'd learned on the street and it seemed to express what he felt better than any English word that existed.

"*Pero—es todo?*" Garrett pressed. *Is that all?* The mechanic dropped his eyes. Garrett looked at the litter of white chips at the man's feet. "*I think you are afraid,*" Garrett challenged.

The mechanic stiffened, but said nothing.

"*Porque?*" Garrett demanded. *Why?*

The mechanic glanced toward the screened front window, in the direction of the trash hill. The sun was a bloody crimson ball on the horizon.

"*Bruja*," he mumbled, and Garrett's flesh rippled again.

Witch.

Chapter Three

It was dark by the time they arrived back at police headquarters, One Schroeder Plaza, in Lower Roxbury. The neighborhood's dirty sidewalks and barred windows and shady denizens were living, blighted proof that not all of Boston had been transformed by gentrification.

Garrett had put in a call to Lieutenant Malloy from the landfill office, requesting a conference with Dr. Frazer, the forensic psychiatrist, in attendance. If they could make a convincing case that the killing had the earmarks of a serial, it would expedite lab tests and move their Jane Doe (who was not, as it turned out, irradiated) to the head of the autopsy line. The lieutenant's office had called on the ride back informing them that Dr. Frazer would not be available until the next day, and with the order to meet the lieutenant in the conference room as soon as they returned.

Garrett and Landauer headed across the lobby, an expanse of polished stone that had earned the relatively new, glass-and-granite building the nickname "the Marble Palace." Just before they stepped into the elevator, Garrett got the call: the State Police responding that there were no females of Jane Doe's age range reported missing in the state in the last week. Garrett punched off, shaking his head at Landauer, who mumbled an expletive.

Lieutenant Malloy was already in the second-floor conference room, seated rigidly at the head of the table as the detectives walked in. Garrett as always braced himself as he stepped across the threshold; relations between Garrett and the lieutenant had become increasingly strained as Garrett's solve stats climbed.

He took a breath and stopped at the end of the table. "Lieutenant, I just need five minutes to put out a wider Missing Persons search—"

"We know who she is," Malloy cut him off.

The older man slid a printout of a scanned photo across the table. Garrett stepped to the edge of the table and looked down. The photo was a high-quality portrait of a girl with shining blond hair and blue eyes, the face and figure and clothes of a prom queen. A society girl. "Erin Carmody," the lieutenant said, and waited for the name to sink in.

"Carmody," Landauer repeated. "W. P. Carmody? Aw, hell."

Hell is right, Garrett thought, and wondered briefly why this should be any more distressing than the killing of any young woman, a waitress, a prostitute. W. P. Carmody was the corporate and family name of a major Boston office supply company that the original William Carmody had started in the 1860s as a rubber stamp company, offering free delivery by horse and wagon. The modern corporation was the official paper goods supplier of the Boston Red Sox, the Philadelphia Phillies, and the New York Yankees, sponsored the postgame show after Red Sox games, and had built a state-of-the-art gymnasium at the current William Carmody's alma mater, Amherst.

They weren't going to have to worry about expediting any lab work, now. But everything had just gotten a whole lot more complicated.

"She was a sophomore at Amherst," Malloy said, his spit-and-polish formality seeming even more brittle than usual. "Her roommate called her parents this afternoon to say that Erin didn't come home last night and she hadn't seen her all day. Carmody called an hour ago. The daughter is eighteen, five-six, 116 pounds."

"Hell," Landauer said again, in confirmation, staring down at the photo.

The lieutenant didn't say so, but Garrett imagined Carmody had called him directly. Either the lieutenant, or maybe the police commissioner himself.

Malloy was speaking. "Carmody's on his way over to the M.E.'s office to do the ID." He looked across the table at Garrett grimly. "How bad is it?"

Garrett shook his head. "As bad as it can be."

There was a heavy silence in the room. They all knew how bad it could be.

"Rape?" the lieutenant asked, tightly.

"Blood on her thighs and pubic region," Garrett said. "But the kill looks quick." That, at least, was a relief to say. "A single stab wound at sternum level, from the back. The decapitation was postmortem. There were . . . ritualistic aspects."

"Ritualistic how?" The lieutenant's voice had an ominous edge.

Garrett and Landauer exchanged a glance. Malloy was a devout Catholic, the protégé of a highly religious former mayor, and Garrett knew the mere suggestion of satanism was going to chafe. "There are symbols carved into the body," Garrett said. "We'll have to research it, but it looks occult." He reached for a pad of paper and drew a rough approximation of the three triangles, the number 333.

The lieutenant looked both outraged and skeptical, and with good reason. In truth, crimes with "occult" elements rarely had anything to do with satanism or witchcraft. Despite a wave of purportedly satanic crimes in the 1980s, and another rash of "satanic ritual abuse" cases in the nineties that were exposed as mass hysteria, so-called occult crimes generally turned out to be clumsy postmortem attempts to mislead investigators and disguise the much more mundane motives of the real killers or, in a few infamous cases, were misidentified as occult by overzealous authorities.

"It wasn't done for show," Garrett clarified. "We think he didn't expect the body to be found. This was his own private deal. And he's definitely organized; there was planning here. He's not going to present as a raving nutcase. I'll set up a psych consult with Dr. Frazer ASAP."

The lieutenant sat back, and his face was stony. "This is going to be as high profile as it gets. Everything you do will be under scrutiny." The look he gave Garrett fairly shouted that he didn't think Garrett was up to it.

Garrett suppressed a surge of anger, kept his tone neutral. "We're on it." He hesitated for a fraction of a second. "Lieutenant, this kind of sex killing . . . there are probably going to be more. If there haven't been already."

"Don't speculate," the lieutenant snapped. "I don't need to hear any hunches, and I don't need any creative ideas from you, Detective Garrett. I want this by the book—textbook."

"Yes sir," Garrett said, fighting an urge to deck his superior officer.

"Meet Carmody at the morgue. With kid gloves on." Malloy stood, dismissing them.

"Yeah, he loves your ass," Landauer said sardonically as soon as they were out the door.

"Wants me bad," Garrett agreed. Landauer flipped him an affectionate bird and ambled off for a smoke break while Garrett headed back toward the homicide room, brooding.

Malloy was the kind of Catholic Garrett had always despised: prudish, self-righteous, a Bible-thumper. *Probably thinks I'm headed straight for hell.*

Then again, Garrett all too often had that effect on older authority figures.

He knew it was his own ambition that rankled; he wore it on his sleeve. But he couldn't help himself. It was something about Boston, the city itself, that inspired greatness, that demanded greatness, something beyond the ordinary. The gleaming gold of the State House dome, the cathedrals, Faneuil Hall, the ever-present ghosts of giants: Revere, Adams, Thoreau, the Kennedys—the history of extraordinary human achievement was thrust in your face from the time you were a kid: sports heroes, political heroes, authors, philosophers, presidents.

Being a beat cop had been enough for Garrett's father. It was not enough for him.

He turned a corner and slowed. A blonde in a Givenchy suit was striding toward him, with the devastating legs of a runway model and the confidence of a CEO. She was all the way down the hall but he could feel a wave of heat, seeing her: Carolyn Davenport, assistant DA for Suffolk County. Male heads swiveled in her wake and Garrett was hit with an uncomfortable wash of pride, possessiveness, and unease.

He couldn't quite believe he was with her: heiress, star prosecutor, on a lightning track to a political career, following in her senator father's footsteps. She and Garrett had fallen into bed (actually, against the wall) one night after a case he'd headed and she'd prosecuted, a triple homicide. He'd had more than his share of cop groupies and was aware of his own appeal to women: a cop's rough-edged masculinity tempered with vestiges of altar-boy innocence, a fair education thrown in to sweeten the pot. And Carolyn had clearly been looking for a little walk on the wild side, which Garrett, no fool, was more than happy to provide, but he'd never expected her to stick. Her family money and pedigree put her way out of his league—he'd thought. But she'd seen something in him, a diamond in the rough, a restless drive that would take him out of the streets. On good days Garrett didn't even feel like a project, but that maybe, just maybe, it was possible to grab the brass ring and ride the carousel all the way . . .

She reached him, stopped a few paces in front of him, a professional distance away, feet planted, accusing. "You didn't call me," she said, lovely, pissed off.

"We caught a case today—" he started.

"You didn't call me about *the case*."

It hit him what she meant. She wanted it.

"We didn't know what we had at first . . ." he said lamely. A lie. The truth was that he hadn't thought of her at all.

She fixed him with a cool blue gaze. "It's a serial, isn't it?"

"Probably."

"Well, I'm on it. The school connection." It took Garrett a second to remember that Carolyn had gone to Amherst, Erin's college, before Harvard Law. "And of course, a woman's touch." She smiled at him, but he could see she was still put out about not getting the call directly from him.

"You think it's going to be kosher for you to take it—even though—"

"Even though what?" There was a warning note in her voice.

"Us," he said, holding her eyes.

She gave him a tolerant look. "Don't you worry about the office. That's my job." He felt a flash of irritation at her certainty. It was inbred, a birthright . . . no one had ever denied her anything.

There was no actual rule against cops and prosecutors fraternizing, but any hint of impropriety could be risky on a big case like this, and he felt a sharp reluctance to jeopardize this one in any way. But Carolyn had pull, to put it mildly.

He glanced away. "I'm meeting the father."

Carolyn nodded, already briefed. "I'll see him after the ID. The family needs to know we're going to do everything, here."

He gave her a strange look. "Of course."

Her voice dropped without her face or posture changing, and he felt a thrill at her sultry tone. "Call me tonight, then."

"It'll be late." He tried to keep his voice even.

She half smiled. "Of course."

Chapter Four

How do you show a father his headless child?

It was obscene that anyone should witness a parent's private grief in this abomination of a circumstance, but no detective was naïve to the fact that in this world there are fathers who kill their children, who sexually assault them, mutilate them. And so Garrett and Landauer stood stoically against the wall of the autopsy lab, breathing in the astringent bite of formalin and the stench of decaying membranes, while the morgue attendant lifted the sheet from Erin Carmody's savaged body, and their eyes never left William Carmody's face as he looked down on his ruined daughter. Garrett had seen faces that seemed to age overnight. Carmody's face aged in a single, agonized second.

He hadn't brought his wife, but his lawyer (which earned an eyebrow raise from Landauer). The lawyer waited in the hall while Carmody confirmed the ID, pointing silently to a crescent-shaped scar on Erin's arm. When Carmody stepped back out into the corridor he looked ravaged, gray with shock, his lips a thin hard line, but his control was impeccable. He said nothing, no "Get him," no "Avenge my little girl," not a word.

He gave terse, controlled answers to their questions. Erin was a sophomore at Amherst, a business major who'd been an honor student at her prep school; she had a basketball-star boyfriend from a good family, she'd talked to her parents on Friday afternoon and gave no indication whatsoever of something troubling her.

Good girl, from a prominent family . . . even in the face of the father's grief Garrett was painfully aware it was a nightmarish scenario from the press standpoint. Every single move they made would be under a microscope.

The lawyer spoke just one sentence: "What are you doing?"

Carmody sat stoically silent as the detectives outlined the facts as they knew them—until the mention of ritualistic elements. The businessman looked from one detective to the other in dazed incomprehension.

"Those—cuts—are satanic?"

"We don't know, sir. Someone seems to be trying to make it look that way. We'll know more after the exam." Garrett carefully avoided the word "autopsy."

Carmody was quiet for a long moment, and the detectives remained still, their gazes lowered to the polished linoleum of the hall. Somewhere a fan whirred. Then Carmody's voice broke for the only time, as he asked, "And her head?" His whole body seemed to palsy as he said the word.

"We don't know, yet, Mr. Carmody." Garrett felt a twist of fury in the core of him. "We will find him, sir. We will get him."

And for a moment, staring hard into the father's eyes, he felt he had helped.

Carmody and his lawyer left; the detectives stayed. The autopsy had been expedited.

"The perks of power," Landauer said as they gowned up in the morgue anteroom with its long observation window into the autopsy lab. Garrett was silent, thinking of Carmody's tortured face. The man certainly had assumed he had power, until today's stark proof of what an illusion human power really is.

The detectives returned to the refrigerated lab, now gowned and masked, wearing latex surgical gloves on their hands and paper caps on their heads and paper booties over their shoes. Edwards was waiting for them, looking like an oversized elf in his green surgical scrubs.

Merciless overhead lights blazed down on the table, and Garrett flinched inwardly at the sight. The headless torso was on its back, the slashed neck raw and exposed, providing a gaping view of ragged tissue and severed windpipe. The corpse had begun to pass out of rigor mortis and lay less rigidly against the polished steel.

Edwards adjusted the microphone attached to the collar of his scrubs, snapped on a pair of sterile latex gloves, then picked up Erin's chart and began to dictate. "This is case number 10-3760, Erin Carmody, a well-developed, well-nourished eighteen-year-old Caucasian female. The head and left hand of the victim are missing. The remaining torso is fifty-nine inches long and the weight is 104 pounds."

Edwards nodded to Hernandez, the slight, delicately featured morgue assistant, who turned on the X-ray board to light up several rows of film. Edwards studied the ghostly images, then turned from the light board and moved to the head of the table. He bent over the corpse, examining the stump of the neck through the magnifier. "The severance plane is located between C-4 and C-5, the fourth and fifth cervical vertebrae. There is a single slice across the neck, cleaving completely through the thyroid cartilage, through the arteries, across the vertebral column. The wrist amputation shows the same kind of cut." The M.E. paused, his deceptively jovial face knotted in concentration as he studied the muscle fibers. He spoke more slowly. "This was a highly sharpened blade, and long enough to cut cleanly across the entire expanse of neck. There are no hesitation marks, no sawing motions; the blow was delivered with extreme force. This was not accomplished with a knife or a hatchet. My guess would be a sword."

Garrett felt a shock of unreality as he stared across the girl's headless body at his partner. "A *sword?*"

Landauer's returning look above his surgical mask was equally unnerved. He cleared his throat, glanced to the M.E. "How often do you see that?"

"I haven't," Edwards said shortly. "I'll have to research types and variables."

Garrett's mind was racing. *Ritual . . . ceremonial?* "We'll get the details into VICAP." VICAP, the FBI's Violent Criminal Apprehension Program, maintained a database of details of violent crimes from across the country, which law enforcement officials could search for similar, possibly related crimes.

Edwards continued. "Decapitation was not the cause of death. The fatal wound was here, at the breastbone." He indicated the knife wound in the chest, then stepped to the light board to the chest X-ray. "The knife blade entered the chest cavity in an upward thrust and severed the aorta, as you can see by the pooled blood in the thoracic cavity." He traced a pen above a large shadowed area of the chest. "She would have been dead within minutes.

"The decapitation took place well before rigor mortis, probably no more than two hours after death. There are no defensive wounds, and the free histamine levels in her bloodstream indicate that there was no heightened trauma before her expiration." Edwards paused and looked at both detectives in turn. "She was not tortured or unduly stressed before her death."

There was a palpable relaxation in the room. The sound of cooled air blowing through the ventilation system seemed amplified.

Edwards looked over his clipboard and continued. "Furthermore, lab tests indicate that the blood on her thighs, and in her vagina, is menstrual blood." He looked up at the detectives, waiting.

Garrett frowned. *No undue stress . . . menstrual blood . . .*

He spoke aloud. "So . . . there was no rape?"

Edwards nodded toward him. "There is no bruising and no tearing of the vaginal wall, which counterindicates sexual assault, although it is not conclusive. There was sex: semen was present in the vaginal canal and in the pubic region. Bear in mind the sex could have taken place postmortem. The semen samples have been sent over to Schroeder for DNA testing."

Finally, some good news, Garrett thought. Again, the relief in the room was tangible.

"So with any luck we get a ding on CODIS." Landauer exhaled.

Let it be so.

"There are no defensive wounds, and no ligature marks." The M.E. picked up one arm, then the other, as gently as if the murdered girl had been his own daughter, displaying each arm for the detectives. He did the same with her legs and feet. "There are no track marks, either. But . . ." He looked up from the body, nodded toward his clipboard again. "The tox screen indicates significant levels of atropine in her bloodstream."

The word was vaguely familiar, but Garrett couldn't immediately call it up. The back of his neck was tingling, though.

"Atropine is a chemical used by the military as an antidote to nerve gas, and as a means of resuscitation," Edwards continued.

Garrett frowned. *Resuscitation? Antidote?* That wasn't why the word was familiar. "I don't understand—"

Edwards lifted a finger. "Atropine is naturally occurring in belladonna, or deadly nightshade." Now the tingling escalated to a buzz. Garrett could see Landauer struggling to place the reference, too.

"Isn't that some—ritual thing?" Landauer asked. "Is it satanic?"

"Belladonna has been used throughout history in witchcraft rituals," Edwards confirmed. "It's a toxin and hallucinogen that reputedly induces the sensation of flying."

Unbidden, the Mexican mechanic's voice whispered in Garrett's head: *"Bruja."*

The men stared down at the carvings in the girl's torso. *Are we seriously standing here talking about witches?* Garrett thought.

"More fucking rituals. Shit," Landauer muttered. "You think he fed it to her?" All the men knew it was a rhetorical question—it was not the M.E.'s place to speculate, just report the facts.

Garrett tried a more specific question. "Is belladonna hard to get?"

"It's a weed," Edwards answered. "It grows domestically in this region. The berries are sold in those witch shops up in Salem. And it gets used as a recreational drug, mostly by teenagers, into the Goth scene." Garrett could almost see the quotation marks around "Goth" as Edwards said the word.

"What about the carvings?" Garrett asked.

"Postmortem," the M.E. said. "There are no hesitation marks. The characters are distinct and the proportions fairly regular, which might indicate that these are not improvised marks, rather, the person who did the cutting is very familiar with these symbols." Edwards looked at the detectives. "And the knife is unusual. The regularity of the edges of both the stab wound to the chest and the carvings indicate the use of a double-edged blade with a needlelike point." The M.E. paused. "A dagger."

Another jolt. Garrett looked at Landauer, who was startled enough to stop fiddling with the unlit cigarette he held nervously in his fingers.

Edwards continued grimly. "And another thing. The lab identified the black substance on her shoulder." He gave a nod to Garrett again. "You were right. It's beeswax, with a common dye. Candle wax."

Black candles and belladonna. A dagger and sword.

Laundauer exhaled. "Well, shit on a stick. If it's not satanic, it's a damn good fake."

Chapter Five

It was, as always, a relief to take the elevator up from the basement lab, to escape the whine of bone saw and queasy sight of exposed organs. The smell, of course, remained. Garrett and Landauer left the brick building on Albany Street and stopped at a liquor store for a lemon, squeezed juice into their nostrils, tearing up at the acid bite—but they were looking at a long night and the sting of lemon was better than the stink of death.

The Homicide Unit of Schroeder Plaza, with its new computer terminals and desks grouped into work pods, always looked to Garrett more like a law firm than a police station, especially at night when there were fewer detectives to break the illusion of corporate order. Landauer immediately took his Camels and cell phone outside to set about tracking down Erin's roommate and boyfriend. Garrett threw his jacket over a chair and jumped on his computer to fill out the VICAP form to check the national FBI database of violent crimes for similar murders. He was sure in his bones that this was not a onetime killing, and there were so many distinctive signature aspects that there was a chance—a chance—they could get lucky and find a documented trail of crimes. The problem was, Garrett wasn't feeling very lucky.

The night hush of the detectives' room settled around him as he called up the VICAP database. Typing the details of the murder into the computerized form made his skin prickle uncomfortably again. Decapitation, removal of the left hand, black candle wax, ritualistic carvings, belladonna . . .

And consensual sex?

Garrett frowned at the incongruous piece of the puzzle, and sat, staring past the computer, wondering. Then, only half-aware that he was doing it, he picked up a pen and scribbled notes.

Not raped? Someone she knew? Willing participant in ritual?

He paused and looked down at the luminous senior portrait of Erin Carmody on top of his case file . . . then threw down his pen, shaking his head.

A prom queen like that, involved in black magic? You're dreaming. Edwards is right—the sex was probably postmortem.

A hundred and eighty-eight gruesome questions later (*Was the binding excessive, i.e. more than necessary to control the victim? Were objects inserted into body orifices?*) he finished the VICAP report by typing in a request for a profile evaluation and sent the document, then pulled up the NCIC database to generate a list of missing persons. There were twenty-six females between the ages of sixteen and thirty recently reported missing in the Commonwealth of Massachusetts. Erin Carmody was the logical primary focus of the investigation, but if they could not pick up a trail around Erin, they might be able to find someone else missing under similar circumstances.

Garrett printed out the Missing Persons list and added it to the murder book, the binder that would hold all the official reports and photos and notes on the Carmody case, then sat back in his creaky chair for a minute, looking down at the enlarged crime-scene photo showing the carvings in Erin's torso, the numbers. The deep feeling of unease swept over him again.

He sat abruptly forward toward the computer and called up Google. He typed 333 into the search box and looked over the list of entries that came up:

- *The Year 333*
- *333 BC*
- *House Resolution 333*
- *Precinct 333*
- *The Trans 333 foot race*

He started to scroll, speeding through pages and pages of 333 addresses and phone directory listings interspersed with links to various university classes:

- *History 333*
- *Philosophy 333*
- *English 333*

In a word: nothing. Garrett clicked back on the search box and tried:

- *333 Satanic*

This time the search results were cryptic, but more promising:

- *The Use of 333 by Freemasons in American Building*
- *Illuminati: Satanic Numerological Code*
- *Satanic Meetup*

Garrett hunched forward and started clicking through links, only to be confronted with a mind-numbing series of Web sites, newsletters, articles, and message board forums, some graphically illustrated with demonic images, pentagrams, borders of crackling flames; some complete with ominous mood music; all laced with unfamiliar terminology: *Chaos Magic, Golden Dawn, Aleister Crowley, Sigils.* Bizarre bits of text jumped out at him as he skimmed the sites:

- *Research into Satanic Coven activities has revealed that 333 is being used as a New World Order hypnotic keyword . . .*

- WARNING: *Can such noble aims and desires be thwarted by Satan? Why would the Abyss then have a gematria number of 333 and the man have a number of* . . .
- In certain Black Magick Satanic rituals, a key participant is often heard chanting "333—333" at the end of the ritual . . .
- Satanic 333 Skyscraper Looks Down on Useless Feeders and Slaves
- Erstwhile Satanic Master, I am sent into the 333 current for Choronzon to use against the Paradigm . . .

Garrett sat back, feeling as if he needed a serious shower.

A voice above him barked, "Hey. Dreamboy." Garrett started, looked up to find Laudauer grinning down at him. "Talked to the roommate up in Amherst. She says Erin was on her way out to a club on Kenmore Square last night." Landauer gave him a look of sly triumph. "Get this. The club's called Cauldron."

835 Beacon Street, Kenmore Square. The neighborhood was shady, with junkies and crack whores lurking in the shadows of the three-story building: a warehouse, with its few windows painted black from the inside and no identifying signage. An enormous bouncer hovered at the door with beefy bare arms crossed, dressed in a black hood and studded leathers like a medieval executioner. Garrett and Landauer flashed tin at him and walked past the DRESS CODE ENFORCED sign into the castlelike gloom of Cauldron. They stood in the black-lit entry hall with the pulse of synthesizers throbbing through them, blinking as their eyes adjusted to the dark. The walls around them were a bloody red; the ceiling two stories above was crisscrossed with ghostly lengths of white cheesecloth. Black leather booths and a few counters with high stools ringed the walls; the booths were framed in iron with heavy crimson drapes, some of which were already drawn across the entrances, creating cocoons of privacy. Four huge black columns sectioned off the packed dance floor; dozens of heavy linked chains hung from the ceiling, surrounding the dancers in a cagelike cube. The dense crowd of young patrons was costumed to the hilt; makeup

ran down their sweating faces like black tears as they undulated inside the chains.

The two detectives moved through the roar of the crowd, reeling at the assault of pulsing music, lasers, and flickering silent German Expressionist films projected on several walls, with their crooked buildings and monstrous shadows. Young people dressed in leather, chain mail, even dragon wings, milled and drank and slouched on large black cubes. A stocky long-haired blond man at one of the tall tables was completely naked, his entire body painted bright blue. A young woman with candy-apple red hair sidled by them, wearing only strips of wide red vinyl tape across her breasts and pelvis.

Garrett heard Landauer mutter beside him, "Freak, freak, freak-azoid . . ." Garrett looked at his partner and saw equal parts of lust and loathing on his face. He himself could feel the throb of the music through his body, down to his pelvis, an insistent, sexual pulse.

His own taste in music ran to classic rock, on the Irish side: U2, the Pogues, Van the Man, of course the Stones, who were Irish in spirit. But he'd always been drawn to the haunting music of The Cure, whose dark and driving "M" he recognized playing now.

As he paused to listen, the pounding of the music turned into something else, a feeling of . . . import, almost of being watched. Garrett turned in the crowd, staring through the flashing lights and flickering projections . . .

Landauer nudged his arm, breaking the spell, and nodded toward the long oval bar. The partners split up, moving to opposite sides. Garrett stepped between two bar stools, his eyes taking in a banner above the mirror advertising an upcoming *SAMHAIN PARTY—Bands All Night, Costume Contests*. The corseted magenta-haired barkeep gave him a bold and appreciative once-over before Garrett leaned across the bar and flashed his badge, forcing himself to keep his eyes well above her pushed-up breasts.

"Boston PD," he shouted, and put Erin's photo on the glossy wood. "Did you see this girl in here last night?"

The bartender squinted with raccoon eyes, shrugged. "Wearing what?" she shouted back.

Garrett looked over the room, the wildly costumed patrons. The bartender had a point; their own parents wouldn't know them. He glanced down at the blond girl in the photo and had a moment of disconnect. *What was a girl like Erin, a textbook preppie, doing in a place like this to begin with?*

It seemed highly unlikely, yet he knew well enough that teenagers and college students had worlds of secrets they kept from their parents, and even the closest families might have no clue what was going on with their progeny.

Another thought occurred to him as he looked back at the corseted bartender, her lush breasts lifted and displayed as if on a plate.

Was Erin also dressed in some kind of fetish wear last night? Did the killer mistake her for a prostitute, an easy victim? Hookers and runaways were the number one choice of target for sexual predators and serial murderers; they were easy to grab and almost never missed. And Cauldron was in a notoriously bad neighborhood, the perfect stalking ground for an opportunistic killer.

Or was the killer right here in the club with her?

As Garrett thought it, he felt again the unmistakable sensation of eyes on the back of his neck, someone watching him. His whole skin prickled, and he whipped around to stare into the undulating crowd.

Dozens of alien-looking faces gazed back at him expressionlessly, a congregation of the damned.

The sense of presence was strong, but any watcher was perfectly camouflaged in the masses; everyone in the room looked capable of ritualistic murder.

Garrett shook his head and turned back to the bartender, who shot him another lazily inviting look. He ignored the look, and with more difficulty the breasts, as he took back Erin's photo, then turned and scanned the room more slowly, his head vibrating with the music. His gaze stopped on the DJ booth and the shadowy dreadlocked figure working in the cold blue light of an overhead spot. The black-haired young man behind the turntables was half Johnny Depp, half vampire, with an Elizabethan shirt open to his waist and a silver pirate skull around his neck. His cool mascaraed eyes didn't miss a trick as he surveyed the dance floor from the elevated booth.

Garrett started across the floor, and the music segued into an eerie set of guitar chords, with ghostly lyricless vocals layered on top . . . the haunting opening of "Gimme Shelter" . . . as familiar to him as a prayer and as incongruous and as fitting in the setting as any song he could imagine. The dancers around him slowed their feet, swaying hypnotically to the dreamlike spell of the music. After a moment Garrett kept moving, weaving through writhing couples who turned slowly to look at him with pale, painted faces as he made his way forward. He approached the stairs and lifted his gaze to the sound booth. The booth was plastered in band flyers and posters; Garrett's eyes flicked over unfamiliar names: Incus. Scissorkeep. Nitzer Ebb. Rasputina. There were a few he recognized: Siouxsie and the Banshees, Christian Death, Sisters of Mercy, Ministry.

DJ Depp's eyes grazed over Garrett, and though it was more than clear Johnny Boy knew a cop when he saw one, Garrett gave him the obligatory "Boston PD" and badge routine, shouting over the music. The DJ nodded, and looked over the photo that Garrett extended. Garrett gave him a beat to take Erin in, and asked, "Was she here this week?"

The DJ didn't hesitate. "Last night. Vanilla, but good dancer."

Garrett felt a rush of anticipation at the sudden, unexpected break. "Was she with someone?"

The DJ's hands moved over the sound board in time to the music, making several minute adjustments to the sound levels as he spoke. "Yeah. A regular. Guitarist. Prepster gone bad."

"Got a name?" Garrett found himself holding his breath. The DJ paused, then turned to the wall of posters behind him, pulled a glossy flyer down. Garrett took it, stared down at the photo image of four sullen, black-haired, black-clad musicians, shot from above in distorted fisheye, posed close, with faces raised skyward under a large inverted cross.

The DJ pointed to one of the pale, upturned faces. "Moncrief. Jason."

Chapter Six

Garrett made a quick phone call from the relative quiet of the restroom corridor. The DMV check gave Jason Moncrief's address as Morris Pratt Hall, Amherst College. Erin's dorm. The throbbing music segued into another dark piece with a ghostly Irish influence as Garrett found Landauer in the Cauldron crowd and filled him in, shouting over the banshee wail of violins and harmonica. He watched Landauer's eyes take on a sudden gleam in the dark.

"What do you think?" Garrett shouted into his partner's ear.

"Hell, yeah, let's go," Landauer shouted back.

Garrett looked up at the massive, Gothic clock face on the wall. It was already half past midnight and a good hour and a half drive up to Amherst, and it was too much to hope (*Too easy* floated through his brain again) that they could make an arrest that night. But if there was even a remote possibility, they would do whatever it took. College students were apt to be up at all hours on a Saturday night, anyway, and there was much that could be useful about questioning a witness/potential suspect who had been awakened from a sound sleep.

The partners wound their way back through the gyrating crowd and ordered large coffees to go from the corseted bartender, who flipped Garrett a suggestive "Come again," before they turned away from the bar and headed for the road.

The road to Amherst was a dark and misty highway, the thick forest an oppressive tunnel around them: nothing but the dark silhouettes of trees and the occasional roar of a big rig at this hour. At the wheel, Garrett swilled coffee and stared out the windshield at the reflecting center line, his only guide through the drifting fog. Landauer smoked cigarette after cigarette; Garrett could feel lung cancer taking root from the secondhand smoke, and thought for the ten millionth time that he had to put a stop to it, somehow, soon . . .

But not tonight.

He hit the window button and let the cool night air blow against his face.

Garrett had lived in Massachusetts his entire life, but had never been to the town of Amherst until a month ago, on a weekend trip with Carolyn when she'd been a guest speaker at the summer session. He remembered uncomfortably that the trip had not gone well. Amherst was Carolyn's alma mater, one of the most prestigious and elitist institutions in the country. Garrett admitted to a chip on his shoulder about his education: a BA in Criminal Justice at the truculently blue-collar U Mass, Boston, and he was the first of his father's side of the family to finish an undergraduate degree at all. Amherst was U Mass's opposite in every way, a rarefied world Garrett had never been part of, and it grated on him to see Carolyn so obviously in her element, speaking as an intimate to the sons and daughters of the richest men in the state, taking her privilege as a God-given right. Garrett had made unfortunate quips about blue blood and silver spoons and consequently there'd been "no dancing," as Elvis Costello used to snarl euphemistically, that supposedly romantic weekend.

Garrett suddenly remembered that Carolyn was expecting him sometime that evening, and grabbed for his cell phone. He got her voice mail and left an update that was more professional than personal, but utterly failed to fool Landauer, who waggled his tongue lewdly and pumped his hips like a spastic sixteen-year-old before lighting up yet another Camel and dropping his head back against the headrest, closing his eyes as he smoked.

Garrett punched off the phone and drained the last of his coffee, watching the signs for the Amherst turnoff and brooding about Carolyn and Erin. Both blond and beautiful, children of wealth—and now it seemed their best lead was, too.

Landauer suddenly spoke. "You know the part I don't want to think about?" He crushed out his cigarette, stared out the passenger window into the rush of dark. "What's he doing with the head and one hand?"

Garrett felt his stomach tighten. He didn't want to know.

Sprawled on a hill overlooking the tiny, pastoral town, the college offered a breathtaking, panoramic view of blue sky and the Holyoke mountain range by day. But by night the campus was decidedly ominous, with turn-of-the-century lampposts beaming diffuse light through swirling fog, and footpaths gleaming in pale ribbons down the steep hills, under ghostly twisting trees.

Morris Pratt Hall loomed over a moonlit circle of lawn, a four-story nineteenth-century brick building. Farther up a hill a church spire stood oddly alone, a vaguely dangerous-looking needle with no church attached.

The detectives got out of the car and looked up through tree branches at the tall facade of the dorm. It was 2:00 A.M., but more than a dozen rooms on the side of the building they were facing were still lit up. Garrett started to shut his car door, then at the last moment, even though he was already armed, he reached into the backseat and grabbed the Taser that BPD issued all its officers, but which Garrett rarely carried. Landauer looked across the car roof questioningly and Garrett shrugged as he clipped it to his hip.

The dorm entry was startlingly opulent, with a three-story-high recessed archway over sweeping front stairs and a marble porch. The partners' footsteps echoed under the archway as they climbed the steps. A sleepy hall coordinator in a flannel robe answered the buzzer. Garrett's badge opened his eyes.

Jason Moncrief's room was on the fourth floor, and according to the nervous, round-faced H.C., he had a private. The carpeted stairs smelled strongly of beer, as did the darkened fourth-floor hallway. Garrett and Landauer walked past closed doors, caught a whiff of pot from one room. Landauer rolled his eyes and feigned taking a monster toke, then pulled out his badge, lifted a meaty leg, and mimed the start of a kick to break down the door.

Garrett shook his head, but he understood that his partner was blowing off steam. There was a lot riding on the next few minutes.

They slowed as they approached the closed door of 410, Moncrief's room.

He was up.

There was music coming from beneath the bedroom door. It was dark and screeching with unearthly violins and harmonica, and someone was playing live guitar along with the track. Garrett was startled to recognize the same music that had been playing when they'd left Cauldron. Immediately he dismissed the thought; the music was similar, that was all. But the eerie feeling of continuation remained.

Landauer leaned forward and rapped on the door. "Boston PD," he called loudly. The partners listened as the guitar stopped midphrase. There was a quick soft scuffling in the room before the door was pulled open.

The young man facing them was musician-slim, with longish dyed black hair and an indolent and slightly androgynous sensuality—a languor that was possibly drug-related. He looked the partners over with an insolence that stiffened Garrett's spine, but he forced down the reaction; the kid's arrogance might well work in their favor.

"Boston PD. I'm Detective Garrett, this is Detective Landauer. Homicide Unit."

Moncrief didn't have any visible reaction to the "Homicide Unit" identification, but then again, his eyes were black basketballs. High on something, for sure. And that was useful, too.

"We'd like to ask you a few questions," Garrett continued. Moncrief shrugged and pushed open the door.

Garrett and Landauer immediately stepped into the darkened room, unable to believe their luck. It was a small, typical dorm room, with a bed that was larger than usual for a student room; Garrett guessed it was two single beds pushed together; plus dresser, bookcase, institutional desk and chair. The only light came from thick candles burning on the desk and windowsill; Garrett noted with a start that they were made of black wax. He saw from the careful stillness on his partner's face that Landauer had noticed, too.

They were at a dangerous crossroads. They were not at this point legally required to read Moncrief his Miranda rights. He had not been taken into custody, the door was open, he could walk out at any time. And technically they were only interviewing him as a witness. But he was becoming more of a suspect by the second. If they Mirandized him, most likely he would snap shut like a clam, and they would be no farther along than they had been before. On the other hand, if they let him keep talking, un-Mirandized, he might well say something crucial that would then be inadmissible in court.

Moncrief slumped down on the bed beside his guitar. The bedspread was black, as were the curtains at the windows.

Garrett decided to walk the tightrope for another minute or two, if only to get a better look at the room. He glanced at the sound system. "Mind turning down the music?"

Moncrief shrugged, made no move from the bed. Garrett stepped to the shelf that held the sound system and pushed the volume off, then turned back to Moncrief. "We're here about Erin Carmody. Do you know her?"

Moncrief looked at them as if they were imbeciles. "She lives here. Second floor. Killer ass," he added slyly.

Garrett's eyes subtly raced over the sparse contents of the room. A poster that was a larger version of the flyer from the club was prominent on one wall. The ceiling shone with glow-in-the-dark stick-on stars, not randomly applied, either; Garrett could see Orion, Cassiopeia's Chair, and an odd, uneven pattern that he recognized as Scorpio. Astronomy had been one of the classes that had made him stick with college, that rough freshman year.

"How do you know Erin?" he said aloud, in what he hoped was a conversational tone.

"Class. Astronomy," Moncrief said, his eyes slanting sideways at Garrett. "My favorite," he added with exaggerated enthusiasm. Garrett felt a jolt of surprise, then narrowed his eyes. *What fucking game is this?*

He shifted slightly toward the desk to get a view of the bookcase. It was crammed with textbooks and what looked like required reading for class. But one entire shelf was quality hardcovers— what looked like expensive editions, some of them leather-bound and obviously old. Garrett scanned the titles and was electrified to see names and titles he recognized from his hasty Google search. Aleister Crowley was the author of several: *The Book of the Law* . . . *The Vision and the Voice* . . . *Magick in Theory and Practice* . . .

A CD case lay on the shelf as well, and Garrett froze as he took in the title: *Current 333.* The cover photo had a design of three fiery triangles with points touching, on a black background.

Garrett made a quick, instinctive decision and fixed his stare on the kid. "Jason, I'd like to keep talking. But before we go any further I'm going to advise you of your rights." Garrett reached into his suit coat pocket and withdrew his micro-recorder, to which Moncrief had no reaction. Garrett turned on the recorder and began: "'You have the right to remain silent. If you give up that right, anything you say can and will be used against you in a court of law . . .'"

Neither Moncrief's posture nor his expression changed during Garrett's recitation. He looked about to nod off.

"Do you understand these rights as I've explained them to you?" Garrett finished.

"Suuure . . ." Moncrief drawled.

Garrett glanced at the CD case again and made sure Landauer saw where he was looking. Land's eyes registered the title and triangle image.

"Jason, what's Current 333?"

The kid was staring at the green-glowing stars on the ceiling. A secretive smile spread across his face. "Choronzon."

The partners looked at each other. The word was familiar to

Garrett; he was pretty sure it had come up in his online searching. He eased out a notepad and wrote it down, guessing at the spelling.

"*Corazon?* You mean, 'heart'?"

"Hardly," the boy scoffed. "Choronzon," he repeated, with maddening articulation.

"I don't know what that means," Garrett said. "Can you explain it?"

"The Lord of Hallucinations," Moncrief said, his voice dreamy. Garrett and Landauer exchanged another glance. It was possible Moncrief was simply high as a kite.

"Really. You mean, a drug?" Garrett asked pleasantly.

"I mean the Master of the Abyss," Moncrief shot back, his lip curling in disdain.

"I see. The Abyss," Garrett repeated, writing it down. "You know, I think it would help if you started from the beginning—"

"Do what thou wilt shall be the whole of the Law," the kid intoned. *Definitely high.*

Garrett decided to try another tack. "Jason, where is Erin?"

The kid suddenly lunged up from the bed and spat. His eyes had gone totally black, his face feral and twisted. "Zazas Zazas Nasatanada Zazas!" he snarled.

Out of the corner of his eye Garrett saw Landauer flinch back in surprise. Garrett stood his ground, staring at Moncrief. The boy's skin was stretched tight over his skull, his lips were drawn back from his teeth like an animal's, and a strange, foul smell rolled from his mouth. Garrett could feel every hair on his scalp and arms lift, a feeling of primal terror.

His mouth was dry as dust as he croaked out: "Where is Erin?"

Horribly, incredibly, that stretched-taut face smiled . . . a smile so tight to the skull Garrett thought wildly that Moncrief's lips would split open.

"In hell," the thing in front of them hissed, and then it lunged at Landauer like a coiled cobra striking. Fast as that snake he had sunk his teeth into Landauer's bare forearm. Landauer let out a window-rattling yell.

Garrett catapulted forward and grabbed Moncrief's arms, jerking them behind his back. He felt an unbelievable surge of power in the struggling young body and for a moment doubted he could hold him. He twisted Moncrief's arms higher and grabbed at his belt for his handcuffs with his right hand, wrestled them onto the boy's wrists. In their struggle they crashed against the bookcase holding the sound system and the music suddenly blasted. Landauer was shouting, swearing a blue streak; Moncrief's jaw was still clamped around his arm. Blood seeped from between the boy's teeth. With his left hand Landauer snatched the Taser from Garrett's belt and shoved it into Moncrief's neck.

The screaming violins filled the room as Moncrief's eyes rolled up into his head and he crumpled to the bed, jerking horribly for an interminable moment . . . and then was still.

The partners stood above him, Garrett still feeling the slithering power of that slight body, Landauer dripping with his own blood.

Chapter Seven

The Taser had only stunned the boy, Moncrief was conscious, but groggy and docile as the partners led him, one gripping each arm, down the hall, down the beer-soaked stairs, out the grand entrance to the car, jostling past wide-eyed half-dressed students who'd been awakened by the shouting. Garrett saw several cell phones pointed in their direction and, not for the first time, cursed whatever moron had invented the camera phone.

Landauer insisted that they drive straight back to Boston rather than stop at the campus infirmary, and Garrett was secretly relieved; the sooner they got Moncrief into a cell, the better, as far as he was concerned.

Once shut inside the back of the car, Moncrief dropped instantly into a deep sleep. Landauer turned from the passenger seat to look at their collar. "Look at that," he said with disgust. "Guilty as they come." Garrett got what he meant. Any seasoned cop knew that an innocent man falsely accused will not be able to sleep a wink in custody, while a guilty one has not the slightest problem dozing off.

The ride was uneasy, the partners feinting around the real questions while Landauer treated his arm with hydrogen peroxide and

Neosporin from the car's first-aid kit. "Think all that will count as a confession?" he asked, low.

Garrett glanced warily in the rearview mirror, but there was no mistaking the authenticity of the adenoidal snoring coming from their suspect. "I don't know about confession," he said, sotto. "But we've got probable cause nailed."

"Lunatic, right?" Landauer said. "Complete fruitcake." His voice was uneven. Garrett didn't speak. They were both thinking of what they had seen in that room.

Crazy was the only sane word.

Landauer had managed to reach Dr. Frazer, the BPD's regular forensic psychiatric consultant, on the drive back, and the pasty, balding doctor was there to meet them in the predawn at the Suffolk County jail intake for an emergency evaluation. The detectives filled out arrest reports while Frazer examined Jason Moncrief.

Moncrief had by then regained at least some consciousness or savvy—or the physical fact of being in jail had snapped him back into reality. As the detectives led him from the car into intake he'd asked for a phone call and an attorney and refused to say anything more. All Dr. Frazer could do was expedite the normal psychological tests, and do the physical exam.

And when that was done, as the guard led their suspect off, Jason Moncrief suddenly turned and looked at Garrett, dark hair and dark eyes and translucent face under the stark glare of the fluorescents. And Garrett felt his heart stop for a fraction of a second.

He was looking at a teenager. A slight, scared, shaking teenage boy.

And then the guard yanked him forward and Jason stumbled on.

With Moncrief safely locked away in a single cell on suicide watch, the detectives and the psychiatrist reconvened around the big table in the conference room back at Schroeder Plaza, joined by Lieutenant Malloy and Carolyn, at 6:00 A.M. looking so fresh and polished that it hurt Garrett's eyes to look at her. He himself had gone beyond five o'clock shadow to predawn beard and felt his skin would have to be scraped and sterilized even before he could shower and crawl into bed, if that was ever going to happen this century.

The big news was, Moncrief wasn't crazy.

"No history of psychiatric problems, no dissociative symptoms, response to preliminary testing was normal," Dr. Frazer reported, his eyes gleaming behind wire-framed glasses that were just a touch too big for his pale, diminutive face. Garrett found the psychiatrist annoying, fastidious to a fault, and prissily condescending—shrink was far too apt a word—but he was the department's favorite forensic consultant, with a résumé as long as Garrett's arm. Garrett reached for his coffee mug to avoid looking at the good doctor as Frazer continued his report. "But urine and blood tests showed the presence of atropine in his system."

Garrett and Landauer looked up from their coffees, which by now were not optional.

Frazer started to elaborate. "Atropine is a hallucinogen found in—"

"Belladonna," both detectives finished. Frazer looked surprised, possibly annoyed. He nodded stiffly.

"The lab found atropine in Erin Carmody's system, and partially digested belladonna berries in her stomach," Garrett briefed the others, sliding copies of the M.E.'s final report across the table. "It's used as a recreational hallucinogen—and in witchcraft rituals."

Carolyn's eyebrows arched. She scribbled quick, neat notes on her legal pad.

Garrett took a moment to focus and started a recap. "Moncrief lives in the same dorm as Erin Carmody. We have a witness who puts them together last night—Friday night—at a Goth club in Kenmore Square called Cauldron. Moncrief plays in a band called Shriek, with a satanic theme going on: inverted crosses, a CD titled *Current 333*, the same number that was carved into Erin's torso. The CD cover has the three-triangle symbol as well. I've just started researching it, but it looks like 333 is a number used in satanic rituals."

He looked to Dr. Frazer, who frowned back. "I'm not familiar with it." The doctor jotted it down.

Across from him, Garrett saw Carolyn write "333" and a question mark.

Landauer leaned forward. "The kid is definitely into this shit. His room is black everything. Bedspread, curtains—"

"—candles," Garrett finished. "Black candles. And the lab found black candle wax on Erin Carmody's body."

"We've also got semen from Erin's body," Landauer supplied. "All we need is a DNA test and a match—"

Carolyn tapped her Cross pen on her pad. "There's definitely enough here to hold him and get a semen sample."

"We need a search warrant for the room, and his car." Garrett heard impatience and sleeplessness grating in his own voice. "I'd like to get a look at the books on his shelf." The others looked at him. "I think we're going to find some of this 333 stuff, the triangles, in those books. The titles came up on my Internet search."

"So you need a search warrant for his room and car, and you need a court order for samples for DNA testing," Carolyn summed up, writing as she spoke. When she looked up, her eyes were bright and predatory, a quality Garrett had found sexy when he first met her, and now . . . was not entirely sure how he felt.

"Preferably before someone ponies up bail." Landauer agreed, and Garrett nodded.

"I can do that," Carolyn said, and closed her file. She leaned back in her chair, pen balanced between two fingers, taking control of the room. "Moncrief's got a public defender for the moment. His father's in the military, a colonel; Moncrief specifically didn't want him called. His mother's apparently in Europe, on vacation with the current husband: number four." Garrett and Landauer raised eyebrows at each other at that as she continued. "I'm going to move on this before the family can be reached."

She slipped her pen and pad into her Coach briefcase and stood. The men all rose automatically, something Garrett knew they would never have done for any other woman in the building. Carolyn gave them all a ghost of a smile, as if acknowledging the fact. "Gentlemen."

As the door closed behind her, Dr. Frazer cleared his throat and glanced to the lieutenant. "Before the detectives called me this morning I was putting together a preliminary profile on Erin Carmody's killer. I think it's of use for you to hear what I had compiled before my intake examination of Jason Moncrief."

Malloy nodded for him to proceed. Frazer removed several files from his briefcase and opened one, passing photocopies of a report around the table to the other men.

"As we all know, true satanic crime is extremely rare. The 'satanic' crimes that have been identified have never involved organized or official covens. There are two types of these satanists identified by forensic profilers: 'self-styled' satanists, and 'youth subculture' satanists."

The psychiatrist passed another set of photocopies around the table: a collection of mug shots and some instantly recognizable newspaper photos. "The most well-known 'self-styled' satanic serial killer is Richard Ramirez, a.k.a. the 'Night Stalker,' who was convicted in Los Angeles in 1989 of thirteen counts of murder."

Garrett stared down at the famous photograph of Ramirez in court, with his black hair, flat eyes, and vulpine cheekbones, holding up his left hand to flash a pentagram inked on his palm.

"Ramirez identified himself as a satanist, and was indeed involved briefly with the Church of Satan; he boasted of having felt 'the icy touch of Satan' during a ritual conducted by Church of Satan founder Anton LaVey. But in actual fact Ramirez was a lone practitioner and used the concept of satanism to justify his fantasies of rape and murder. The murders he committed were not part of any ceremony or tradition. He was taking the minimal knowledge he'd picked up about satanic practice and using it for his own purposes."

Frazer opened the next file, and passed around another photo. Garrett looked down on a black-and-white of a smiling man in a suit, vest, and tie, with a wide brow and receding hairline. He looked more like a Rotarian than a serial killer.

"Clifford St. Joseph was convicted of first-degree murder in San Francisco in March 1988. His never-identified homeless male victim had been kept in a cage and sexually abused by St. Joseph. The autopsy report states that a pentagram had been carved in the victim's chest. His genitals were slit, his body drained of blood, and candle-wax drippings were found in his right eye."

Garrett and Landauer both started and looked at each other across the conference table with a shock of recognition at the similarities. The psychiatrist glanced up, nodded to acknowledge their reactions, and continued.

"St. Joseph owned several books on the subject of satanism and the occult, but he was not part of any cult or organized tradition; the 'ceremonies' he performed on his victim were ones that he had created on his own. The murder, just as the Night Stalker killings, was not part of any recognized occult ritual; it was rather a sadistic sexual homicide, with trappings of satanism."

The psychiatrist paused, and reached for his third file. "And now, Detectives, if you'll bear with me, I think you'll find the next case particularly interesting." Garrett and Landauer exchanged a glance across the table. As if they both hadn't been riveted for the last fifteen minutes. Garrett could tell Landauer was having trouble refraining from making some comment that would undoubtedly get him suspended without pay for a week. Garrett fixed a look of intent focus onto his face and turned back to Frazer.

"The second pattern we find in these homicides is the 'youth subculture' murder. A prime example of a youth subculture satanic murder case is the 1995 murder of Elyse Pahler. Fifteen-year-old Pahler was raped and stabbed to death in a eucalyptus grove in Arroyo Grande, California, by her high school classmates Royce Casey, Joe Fiorella, and Jacob Delashmutt. These teenage killers were from middle-class homes, and of above-average intelligence, but according to their teachers lacked any real interest in school. The boys were in a band together and discovered the occult through heavy metal music. They began networking with practicing satanists in Internet chat rooms and collecting books on the topic of satanism. Joe Fiorella, in particular, had a growing library of satanic literature, including books and pamphlets by renowned satanist Aleister Crowley."

Garrett felt a sharp stab of recognition at the name: the author of at least three of the books he'd seen on Jason Moncrief's shelf. Across the conference table Landauer was equally transfixed. Garrett leaned forward, listening in building excitement as the forensic psychiatrist continued.

"As you know, serial killers are driven by fantasy; they obsessively play out their violent desires in their imaginations until they try the fantasy out on another human being. As a group, these three boys created fantasies about human sacrifices, specifically the sacrifice of a virgin." Dr. Frazer looked up from his notes to emphasize his next point. "When interrogated, the boys claimed that Satan had required a human sacrifice of them to fulfill their request to make their band successful."

Now Garrett was positively tingling. *It was textbook. Was it really going to be this easy, this time?*

Then he had a sudden flash of Moncrief, with his skin stretched over his skull, the insane fire in his eyes, before he lunged at Landauer, bared teeth gleaming . . .

Garrett forced himself back into the room, forced himself to focus on Frazer's words. "But it should also be noted that Joe Fiorella had an obsession with the victim, his classmate, Elyse Pahler. So again, despite the outward presence of satanic elements and influences, this murder was consistent with the behavioral pattern of sexual homicide." Frazer glanced down at the bottom of his report, and added, almost as an afterthought, "The three young men ultimately pled 'no contest' to the rape and murder charges and were sentenced to twenty-six years to life in prison."

Frazer put aside his notes, stacking them neatly. "You can see from these examples that so-called satanic murders are committed by dabblers, either 'self-styled Satanists'—who are lone occult practitioners; usually adults; or 'youth subculture Satanists'—teenagers involved in a group exploration with the occult. Both types of perpetrators have some foundation in satanic practices but are in actuality simply using the surface details of satanism and the occult to satisfy their own sadistic fantasies." He glanced at Garrett. "Detective Garrett is right that the killer will in all likelihood own reading material that details rituals, specifically satanic rituals, and quite possibly ritualistic pornography; killers like these use print and other media images to fuel their fantasies. Adult serial killers overwhelmingly choose vulnerable victims such as homeless runaways and prostitutes. They troll neighborhoods frequented by these types and choose their victims opportunistically. And such a killer will often attempt to insert him or herself into the police investigation.

"In the 'youth subculture' model, the behavioral pattern will include a young white male or males from a middle- or upper middle-class background with an above-average IQ, though it's likely the killer's grades will not be good. There will be a history of drug abuse, particularly the use of hallucinogens, and indications of cruelty to animals or animal killings. The perpetrator will have participated in satanic activity as part of a peer group rather than as a lone practitioner, and will likely choose a victim he knows personally and harbors a sexual interest in . . ."

The psychiatrist continued, but Garrett no longer heard him. His head was buzzing; he was off in a world of his own.

This is it. A perfect case. My ticket to anywhere.

Chapter Eight

Morning light glimmered around the edges of the buildings outside the glass corridor as Garrett and Landauer headed back from the conference room to the detectives' room to catch up on their reports. They were both gravel-eyed and snappish from overdoses of coffee and sleeplessness . . . but they were also in hyperdrive. They were close. So close . . . and well within that golden forty-eight-hour window, when it was most likely that a crime would be solved.

Lack of sleep be damned, they were going to have to get back up to Amherst right away, this time with a warrant, as soon as Carolyn could get back with it, to search Jason's room and Erin Carmody's room and question Erin's roommate and boyfriend and other kids in the dorm and teachers and whoever the hell they could get to talk about Erin and Jason Moncrief.

In the work pod opposite Garrett, Landauer was positively gleeful, despite his stubble, despite the adrenaline crash, despite his bitten arm. "For once it looks like that cream puff Frazer might actually earn his keep. Didja hear all that? Satanic books, satanic music, praying to Satan to make the band successful . . . we are home free, homes. Slam-fucking-dunk," he exulted.

It did seem like a dream come true, a perfect solve.

But now that they were out of the conference room Garrett was feeling alarm bells going off all over the fucking place.

Something wasn't right.

The kid was seriously wrong, that was a fact. Violent *and* weird and into drugs that were off the charts even for a seasoned junkie. Opportunity and means, check. Into the occult, check. The numbers added up, and the number was 333: Current 333, to be precise, whatever the hell that was. But . . .

But.

Jason Moncrief might be a nutcase, but he was nineteen years old. Nineteen. For a moment Garrett recalled the look in Jason's eyes as the guard led him away.

A kid. A terrified kid.

For all its grotesque crudeness, the murder of Erin Carmody was a sophisticated crime. A man's crime, not a boy's, even if that boy was wealthy and prestigiously schooled. The decapitation, the carvings, the disposal of the body—all were precise and controlled. Mature.

Which meant—what?

"He didn't do it."

The voice came from above him, female, and Garrett had drifted so far off into his own thoughts that he wasn't sure he'd heard it, or that he was even awake.

When he did focus, he was startled to see a woman of perhaps thirty standing in front of his desk, tall and willowy, dressed in a longish skirt over high boots, and a fitted blouse, all of a vaguely equestrienne style that was perfectly fashionable, but on this woman the effect was palpably sensual, with a hint of Victorian perversity. She was as Black Irish as the Black Irish come: eyes and eyebrows and long thick hair like coal, a pale yet still slightly olive-tinged complexion, sculpted cheekbones and full dark mouth, lips berry red, almost purple, like lush grapes, like wine . . .

Garrett pulled himself back from highly inappropriate thoughts and tried to concentrate.

"I'm sorry, what did you say?"

"I didn't," she said curtly. She was very edgy, holding herself stiffly. "I'm looking for the detectives handling the Erin Carmody killing."

"That would be us," Landauer offered, eager to get in on this. Garrett could see Palmer and Morelli, who had just arrived for the 8:00 A.M. shift, eyeing the woman from the coffee counter as well.

The dark woman looked the detectives over, one then the other, taking their measure, and Garrett felt her look go straight through him.

"I have information that might be pertinent to the case," she said, finally. Garrett's mind scanned through possibilities. *Was she from Amherst?* She was older than a college student, he was sure, but she might be a graduate student. She also looked like she could be a regular at that club, Cauldron; in fact, he had a nagging sense that he had seen her before—though surely he would have remembered.

"What information is that?" he said aloud.

"There are others."

Garrett's pulse spiked as he felt the pull of a real lead, real insight. "And how would you know that?" he asked drily, careful not to betray any excitement.

Again she hesitated; he sensed a strong reluctance to speak. "I dreamed it."

Garrett's excitement deflated. *A loony toon.* Out of the corner of his eye he saw Landauer untensing in his chair as well.

"You dreamed the murder," Garrett said.

"I dreamed three," she said, and loony toon or not, the tone of her voice compelled him. A weary look crossed her face. "Look, it's what I do."

"You dream," Landauer said, insolently innocent.

She turned to look at him. "Among other things," she agreed, without expression.

"So you're a psychic," Garrett said, to deflect the storm he could feel brewing. The department had used the input of psychics in the past; the concept wasn't unheard of, but certainly Lieutenant Malloy had never approved that kind of input, and Garrett had never seen or heard of any particular success, himself.

This time the woman didn't pause. "I'm a witch. That's with a W," she said pointedly to Landauer.

Again, Garrett heard the Mexican mechanic's hoarse voice in his head: *Bruja*. And again, he felt a prickling at the back of his neck.

The woman was watching him. Garrett realized that she was still standing. He rose and indicated the chair that she had been ignoring. "Please sit down—let me get some information here," he said, reseating himself and reaching for a report form. After a moment she sat, her back straight as a dancer's.

"Your name?"

"Tanith Cabarrus." Garrett could feel Landauer's eyebrows raising across the aisle. She spelled it and Garrett wrote the alien-sounding words.

"Address and phone?"

"411 Essex Street, West, Salem, 01970."

Garrett sat back in his chair, trying to keep his face neutral. Salem. It figured. All the New Age loons in the state congregated in Salem, milking tourists looking to be titillated with gruesome stories of the town's famous witch trials. Garrett was feeling his lack of sleep as a building irritation, coupled with the increasing doubt that anything constructive would come out of this odd interview. Still, it wasn't hard to look at Tanith Cabarrus.

"And occupation is . . ." he trailed off, reluctant to say the word. She looked fleetingly amused.

"You can put down that I own a bookstore."

Garrett glanced up at her. "Do you?"

"Yes, I do."

She was young to own her own business and Garrett had to admit it gave her a bit more credibility. "So why don't you tell us what you know?" he suggested. He was expecting her to describe vague details from a dream, so what came next threw him.

"It was a ritual killing. The killer cut something into her body, here." She put her hand on her abdomen, under her breasts.

Garrett and Landauer were wide awake, now. In fact, they were speechless. Garrett's mind was racing: had details of the crime scene been leaked? *But by whom? A worker at the dump, a cop, the family?*

Then she added, "And I think . . ." She paused and her eyes went distant and cold. "He took her head."

"You got a name for us? Address? Identifying details?" Landauer drawled, feigning boredom.

She looked at the big man. "Do you dream addresses, Detective? That's a pretty advanced technique, as dreamwork goes. I'll have to get your secret out of you, sometime." She turned back to Garrett before Landauer could muster a response. "I didn't see him. Just a shadow."

"How do you know it was a *him*, then?" Garrett asked sharply.

She gave him a withering look. "Surely you know women don't do this kind of thing, *Detective*."

She happened to be right, but he didn't care for the imperious tone. "Anything else?" he asked, his voice brittle.

"Yes." She looked across the desk, directly at him. "That boy you arrested didn't do it."

Again he felt as if the earth had shifted under him. "How do you know we arrested someone?"

She arched her eyebrows. "It's all over the morning news."

Garrett remembered the students with their damned camera phones. These days onlookers couldn't wait to sell their footage to CNN. They'd have a circus on their hands, now. And the main act was sitting right in front of him.

"So if he didn't do it, who did?"

Her gaze grew cloudy. "Someone older than that boy. And powerful." Her dark eyes rested on his. "And sick," she said bleakly. "Very sick."

"You dreamed all this." Garrett's voice sounded thick to his own ears.

"I had three dreams. Actually, one dream, three times. On these dates." She took a pocket calendar from her bag and removed a Post-it, which she handed across the desk to him. She had written three dates:

June 21
August 1
September 21

"It was the same each time. A man in a ritual triangle, lit by fire, using a dagger to cut into the body of a—young person. And then picking up a sword . . ." She swallowed, looked away.

Garrett was unnerved. *The dagger, the sword . . . it's all so specific.* He fought for objectivity. "So if you 'dreamed' this before, why is this the first time we're hearing about it?"

"It's not," she said. There was ice in her voice. "The first time, I hoped it was just a dream. The second time I knew it wasn't, and I called here—the police station. I was told no such killings had occurred. This time—when I saw the news—I came in."

Garrett frowned and made a note on his pad to check tip calls made around the date she had listed.

"I wrote down the dreams each time. I made copies, if that's of any use." She reached into her large tooled leather purse and removed three photocopied sheets of paper. He took them, glanced through them. Short phrases, images, impressions: *Fire. A shadow moves in the triangle.* There were sketches, too: a triangle drawn in red, scribbled flames.

Garrett looked for a time at the triangle, and felt his stomach roil. *A triangle.* He didn't like it. Not at all.

She was speaking and he looked up, was struck again by the startling blackness of her eyes.

"You need to know this. The dates are significant. They're Sabbats—holy days in the pagan calendar. June twenty-first—the summer solstice. August first—Lammas. Friday night, September twenty-second, was Mabon, the autumnal equinox. The next Sabbat is five weeks away, and it's the most powerful of the year . . ." She paused and said a word that sounded like "Sowwen."

Garrett frowned. "Spell that?"

A look that might have been irritation crossed her face. She leaned over the desk and wrote on his pad. He smelled apple musk in her hair and heat shot through his groin. She straightened, turned the pad around to face him. He forced himself to look at the page in front of him. The word was *Samhain*—the word he'd seen on the banner at Cauldron.

"Halloween, to you," she said drily. "It's the festival marking the end of summer and the beginning of winter. The Sabbats are power days, best for working rituals. And Samhain is the most powerful night of the year. So if he's conjuring, which I think he is, whatever he's doing will have the most powerful effect on that night. And that's not good."

Garrett felt his sleeplessness like an undertow. None of this was sounding real at all. He had a sudden wave of paranoia that the dark woman was just playing with them . . . and then another wave that there was something huge that he was overlooking, something dangerous.

At the other desk, Landauer suddenly leaned forward, with exaggerated interest and what Garrett recognized as an ominously friendly tone in his voice.

"So . . . you're in a coven?"

The dark woman—Tanith—glanced at the larger detective. "No. I don't like people much. I'm a solitary."

"A solitary . . . witch."

"Yes."

Landauer leaned back in his chair, and it creaked under his weight. "Show us."

She turned and looked at him full on, and her eyes were ice. "Show you what?"

The big detective spread his hands jovially. "Show us some magic. Put a spell on me."

Garrett was about to protest, break it up, but something in the witch's face kept him quiet. She was so still Garrett found he couldn't breathe, himself. Then she walked three steps to Landauer's desk and picked up his left hand. Landauer was startled, but quickly forced a neutral look onto his face. She turned his hand over and stared into his palm. Something unreadable flickered in her expression. She picked up his other hand and examined that one. Garrett was amused to see his partner squirm.

She released both of Landauer's hands, then reached into the front of her blouse and drew out the long silver chain she wore around her neck.

The chain held a perfect, handmade three-inch silver dagger, with gemstones glittering in its hilt.

Tanith pulled the chain over her head in one smooth gesture. She stared down at Landauer, her eyes locked on his, and used the dagger to slice open her left middle finger. Blood dripped from the slash. She extended the finger to Landauer—a classic, deliberate *fuck-you* gesture—and said, "Suck it."

Landauer looked up at her, stupefied. "Wha . . ." He didn't move. Garrett felt himself riveted.

"You heard me," she said with an uneven smile, and in that moment Garrett thought she did not look quite sane. "Are you afraid?"

Landauer recovered his bravado. He took her extended hand with a smirk and lewdly closed his mouth around her finger, used his tongue to lick sloppily at the blood. Garrett felt himself bristling with a jealous possessiveness that he couldn't have explained to himself. Across the room, Palmer and Morelli were frozen at their desks, openly gaping at the sight.

Tanith stood with her legs braced until Landauer had completed his big show of sucking off her finger, and released her hand. She let her arm drop to her side. "You're done," she said flatly.

Garrett didn't miss the brief, jolted look on his partner's face. He felt distinctly odd, himself.

Tanith wiped the bloody dagger off on the waistband of her skirt, put the chain back over her head, and dropped the knife back into her shirt, between her breasts. She turned to Garrett. "I take it we're finished, here."

"Thanks for coming in," Garrett fumbled, still not sure what in Christ's holy name had just happened. "I—we'll call you if we have questions."

Her smile twisted. "Of course you will." She gathered her bag from the chair . . . then she turned back, and her eyes met his for a brief, veiled moment.

"Do you believe in evil, Detective?"

The question so startled him that he answered honestly. "Yes, I do."

She touched her finger to the triangle sketch she had given him, and held his gaze. "This is evil."

She turned and walked out through the work pods, with every detective's eyes following her.

Chapter Nine

No sooner had the door closed behind her than Landauer threw back his head and wolf-howled. "She can ride my broomstick anytime."

Morelli and Palmer chuckled lewdly from behind their desks, and the tension was broken. Garrett fought down irritation, shook his head. "I have two words. Blood test." Predictably his tone had no effect on the others; they continued to comment obnoxiously. Garrett tuned them out and looked down at his desk. The weird word stared up at him from his legal pad: *Samhain*.

Five weeks away . . .

He was tired . . . too tired to process what had just happened. But without thought he turned to his computer and typed "autumnal equinox" into the Google search box. He didn't even have to click through a link to see that Friday *had* been the equinox, just as the—witch—had said.

But he went no farther than that. His phone buzzed, and it was Carolyn. The search warrants were ready.

The partners stopped briefly at the crime-scene lab to order a team with a van to meet them up at Amherst to process Jason's and

Erin's rooms. In the elevator going down, both detectives slumped against the wall; Landauer closed his eyes. Garrett spoke aloud. "It *was* the equinox. Friday night."

Land didn't open his eyes. "I know, G. It was in the paper on Friday, on the Calendar page. That New Age shit always is. She coulda gotten it from there. She coulda gotten the details about the head and carving from the news, already—fuck knows what's been reported. We had three dozen dump workers tellin' their wives all about it last night. Everyone's out to make a buck."

Garrett was silent and Landauer finally opened his eyes. "You really want to go back up there and tell Malloy we just got a hot tip from Stevie Nicks?" He didn't have to describe the scenario. Garrett could picture it just fine on his own. "We got a live suspect in custody, bro, so let's never mind the spooky shit. We work the case—we nail this fucker."

The media was in full force outside the building: television vans with their microwave dishes and camera crews unloading equipment on the sidewalk while Armani-suited reporters and their scruffier print and radio colleagues hurried up the stairs, en route to the press conference. Garrett and Landauer took a quick left toward the back entrance of the building. At least they weren't required at the briefing. The chief himself was sitting in on this one, with Malloy. Garrett wondered for a second if Malloy's order to stay away from the press was partly to keep Garrett himself out of the limelight, and immediately thought, with some shame, that he himself would scathe any other detective unmercifully for that kind of self-serving arrogance. Land was right: work the case.

They swung the Cavalier by the courthouse to pick up the warrants at the lobby desk, and then got back on 90 West toward Amherst. Thankfully the wooded road was nearly deserted on Sunday morning. They'd agreed to split the drive in two in order to get a nap apiece; at this point even forty-five minutes would be saving. Garrett won the coin toss and fell into a black hole of unconsciousness within seconds; he'd always been able to sleep in a moving vehicle. The motion was lulling, and he thought he did not dream, until he bolted out of sleep with the image of Jason's stretched-taut face grinning at him from the dark.

Landauer glanced at him from the driver's seat. "Yeah," he said. The radio was on; he was listening to a local news station. *"Police spokesmen would not confirm the presence of satanic elements in the brutal slaying of Erin Carmody, daughter of the CEO of W. P. Carmody and Company. The headless body of the eighteen-year-old Amherst sophomore was found at a city landfill yesterday morning—"*

Garrett rubbed his stubbled face, trying to wake up. Land turned down the radio. "So far looks like no one's spilled about the carvings. But they are on this satanic shit like white on rice."

Garrett licked his dry lips; his mouth and brain felt stuffed with cobwebs. "You want to pull over? I'll drive."

Landauer gestured toward a road sign with an unlit cigarette and Garrett saw the turnoff to Amherst was only a few miles away. "You should've stopped," he said, guilty.

"Nah, you looked so pretty sleeping there, Rhett." Landauer grinned at him. "Don't sweat it, you won't be thanking me on the drive home."

They drove through the stone gates of campus and stopped at the unmanned information kiosk. Garrett jumped out to grab a campus map, which they studied on the dashboard, locating the campus police building. Malloy had made the calls to the chancellor's office to ask for cooperation and assistance from the campus police force. Of course with Carmody being a celebrity alumnus and a major donor, the school could not have been more obliging.

The college was roughly divided into thirds: the academic and residential buildings, the athletic fields and facilities, and a plot of open land that housed a wildlife sanctuary and a forest. In the daytime the Victorian creepiness had retreated; the lush green knolls were dotted with large trees just starting to come into their autumn brilliance. The detectives motored the Cavalier past the Campus Center, a sprawling building with outdoor terraces, a campus store, and a coffeehouse. Farther on, original nineteenth-century red-brick buildings were interspersed with everything from a pale yellow octagonal structure to the latest garishly modern dorm. There were few students out yet, on Sunday morning; it was still just past eleven.

The campus police building was a low brick structure across the lot from the back of the Campus Center.

Not the head of the campus cops, but clearly his man in charge, Sergeant Jeffs, was there to meet the detectives and had obviously been instructed to bend over backward to accommodate the investigation. Jeffs was young, fit, and alert, which Garrett immediately appreciated; they'd be able to trust him with the secondary interviewing of potential witnesses. He ushered them into a meeting room in the bright and orderly six-room campus security building.

Jeffs already had a file out on the table that turned out to be the answer to Garrett's first question: "Did Jason Moncrief have any record of behavioral problems, any incidents?"

The young sergeant passed them the file. "We had an anonymous tip two weeks ago that he was dealing drugs. We entered and did a search of his room."

Garrett quickly scanned the file. "No warrant?" he asked.

"Not required for dorm rooms. According to campus policy the students' rooms are school property and we only need permission from the dean's office to search, not from the individual students. It's part of the student housing contract."

"Sweet," Landauer murmured.

"It's common for university campuses," Jeffs explained. "The school is in loco parentis. We didn't find anything illegal, so no action taken . . ." A shadow passed over the sergeant's face. "But this kid is no boy next door. He's got a weird way about him."

"Got that right," Land said fervently. Garrett nodded without speaking, and there was an uneasy silence in the small room. Garrett finally broke it.

"You didn't find any weapons in the search?" He was thinking of a dagger, the murder weapon.

Jeffs tensed. "No. That would be automatic grounds for expulsion."

Garrett closed the file and sat back. "He's a sophomore—no problems last year?"

"Nothing that ever got reported. He was totally off our radar. And I checked the hospital, too, to see if there was anything medical or psychiatric we should know about." Jeffs shrugged briefly, and there was frustration in the gesture. "Nothing. But after we talked to him we flagged his file. I have to say I've just been waiting for something ever since. You know, after Virginia Tech . . ." The sergeant's face was troubled. "But I never in a million years thought it would be something like this."

Garrett met the young sergeant's eyes with what he hoped was reassurance. "How could you?"

Responding to Malloy's request, Jeffs and the campus cops had sealed Erin's room for processing as a crime scene, and Jason's as well. Garrett asked Jeffs to take whatever men he had on duty and clear all students from the floors of the dorm where Erin's and Jason's rooms were located so the CSU could start on the rooms as soon as they arrived. The students would be held in the lounge and questioned individually.

"And try not to let them bring any laptops or cell phones with them," Garrett instructed as they got back in their car to follow Jeffs over to Morris Pratt Hall.

In the car, Landauer glanced at the list on his legal pad and turned to Garrett. "Who's it gonna be, Kemosabe?"

They had a choice now: question Erin's boyfriend, who lived in campus-owned housing a few blocks from the school; question Erin's roommate, Shelley Forbes; or search Jason's and Erin's rooms. Garrett was itching to get into Jason's room, but it wasn't going anywhere and their witnesses might, and the crime-scene van was still en route.

"The roommate," he decided. "I want to see if she has anything to say about Erin and Moncrief before we talk to the boyfriend."

While Jeffs and his officers rousted students out of their rooms and secured them in the downstairs lounge of the dorm, Garrett and Landauer met Erin's roommate, Shelley, in a downstairs suite of Morris Pratt, where she'd been moved when the campus police sealed off the girls' room. The wide window had a view of the oddly churchless steeple. Shelley Forbes was preppily pretty, but nowhere near Erin's league, despite some obvious surgical enhancements: a nose job and breast job, at least, Garrett thought, on top of expensive corrective orthodontia. That kind of early plastic surgery was always unnerving to him. *Braces, sure, but what kind of parent buys their teenage kid a boob job?*

Shelley was presently red-eyed, shaken, and crying copiously in the way that only teenage girls seem to be able to cry. Garrett's micro-recorder was rolling on the coffee table in front of her. They were going to have to do a lot of fast-forwarding later.

"It's s-so h-horrible," she sobbed. It was, in fact, horrible, but Garrett could see Landauer straining to keep a semi-compassionate look on his face.

"Shelley, when Detective Landauer talked to you on the phone, you told him Erin had gone to the Cauldron club on Friday night. How did you know that? Did she tell you specifically?"

"She had a flyer for some party she left on her desk," she sniffled.

An equinox party, Garrett thought. *And Samhain is next,* his mind continued, unbidden.

Shelley's face crumpled. "It was him, wasn't it? He killed her. That freak Jason."

Garrett kept his voice neutral. "Why would you say that?"

"They said on TV it was satanic. He's into all that."

The damn media. It's going to be hard to get any kind of uncorrupted version of the story.

Now that Shelley was wound up, she kept going. "And he was always hanging around. Following her. Texting her."

The partners exchanged a glance. *Nothing about that in the campus security file.*

"Did she report this to the hall coordinator, or school officials?"

Shelley shook her head, sniffling. "I told her to. Erin never wanted to make waves, you know? That's just not how she w-was . . ."

"Can you tell us what any of those messages said?"

She shook her head again. Garrett made a mental note to comb through Erin's and Jason's e-mail, not that he wouldn't have.

"Shelley, did Erin say she was going with Jason on Friday, or did you see them leave together?"

"No, but why else would she go to a Goth club like that?" The partners looked at each other, not following. Garrett raised an eyebrow, and waited. Shelley's voice rose, defensive. "That's where his freak band plays."

Garrett was trying to reconcile a massive logical contradiction. "But—if he was stalking her, why would she go at all?"

Shelley's voice rose. "It was like—a spell. She was upset after she broke up with Kevin, and he just moved in on her, that's all."

Now Garrett was completely confused. He latched on to the most obvious point. "Erin broke up with Kevin?" Kevin Teague was the boyfriend.

"It was crazy. She wasn't acting like herself at all." Shelley uncrumpled an already soggy Kleenex, blew her nose.

"When was this?"

Shelley shrugged listlessly. "A couple weeks ago, I guess."

"And did Erin start seeing Jason before or after the breakup?"

Now the girl flared up. "She wasn't *seeing* him. He was hanging around, okay?"

Garrett increasingly felt lost in a miasma. "Did she tell you she felt threatened? Did she seem afraid?"

"Well, of course she was afraid. He's a *freak*." She dissolved into sobs. " I told her he was bad news . . ."

"I understand, Shelley," Garrett said soothingly, tamping down his impatience. "We just need to know what actually happened. Did Erin go to Cauldron often?"

"*No*. Never." She folded her arms on her chest for emphasis.

"But you think she went with Jason on Friday night."

"I could tell she was because she wouldn't talk about it. She knows I can't stand him."

Garrett's strong sense was that there was something more voluntary going on between Jason and Erin than Shelley wanted to admit. He sat back, trying to process, and looked at Landauer, who raised his hands and shot him back a look that clearly said, *This one's yours.*

Garrett remembered his passing thought about fetish wear. "Was

Erin dressed up when she went out to the club? Anything unusual?" He could see Landauer frowning his puzzlement on this one.

Shelley frowned, too. "Unusual?" Her voice registered disdain. "You mean Goth? That wasn't Erin."

Garrett wasn't thinking Goth so much as leathers, fishnets, corsets. Despite what they already had on Jason Moncrief, he was fighting to keep his mind open to all possibilities. If Erin had been dressed like other patrons of the Cauldron club, it would have been easy to mistake her for a prostitute, and that could have made her a prime target for a trolling sex killer.

"How was she dressed, then?" he tried.

"I didn't see her before she went out."

Garrett thought for a moment, and suddenly threw a curve ball. "Did you know she was doing drugs?"

Through the tears, Shelley was immediately more alert—and evasive. "Not that I know of." To the side of her, Landauer all but rolled his eyes. "*He* was, though," Shelley said ominously.

"You mean Jason?" She nodded emphatically. "How do you know?" Garrett pressed.

"He was *always* high. Laughing at things that weren't funny . . . looking at you without ever talking. His eyes were weird all the time." She shivered. "He just wasn't *right*."

That's looking like a consensus, Garrett thought bleakly.

"Shelley, have you seen Jason since Friday night?" he asked aloud. She shook her head. "He hasn't come by the room?"

Shelley's eyes widened in alarm at the thought. "No. He's arrested now, though, isn't he?"

"At the moment, yes, he's in jail. Why? Did he ever threaten you?"

Her face darkened. "He *looked* at me. He knew I could see what he was, and he didn't like it." She crumpled into sobs again. "I told her. I told her . . ."

Garrett and Landauer were silent as they walked through the front entry of the dorm, onto the portico outside. Landauer lifted quizzical eyebrows, looked back toward the room. Garrett shook his head. "We'll have to get a look at Erin's text messages. Maybe there are e-mails. I wouldn't buy into the stalking angle just on the roommate's say-so. There was a lot of hedging going on there."

Landauer tapped out a cigarette, brooding. Garrett stared across the campus green. His eyes stopped on the isolated church spire. It bothered him, for no reason he could name; some inescapable Catholic imprint, no doubt. "But I think she was being straight about Erin breaking up with the boyfriend. Wonder what he's going to have to say about that?"

The boyfriend, Kevin Teague, lived in a campus-owned upperclassman house on nearby Overlook Drive.

Amherst had officially banned fraternities and sororities on campus in the eighties in an attempt to attract a more diverse student population, but no one would know it from looking at Campbell House. The sleek and sleepy young men who lounged on the deck chairs and tables on the front patio were classic preppies: jocks and business majors and future captains of industry. *Or future felons*, Garrett thought darkly, feeling the weight of the chip on his shoulder.

His eyes took in a litter of half-empty glasses and an abandoned kegger, remnants of what had obviously been a night of hard partying. The young men were quick to put together the presence of detectives with the morning's headlines about Erin; Garrett and Landauer's entrance caused a stir of whispers and stares.

Kevin Teague met them on the back deck, which was cluttered with a motley assortment of lounge chairs and more party detritus, including the faint smell of vomit toward one clump of bushes.

Teague was a type Garrett knew too well from his own high school and college sports days: genus jock asshole bastard. He was dark-haired, square-jawed, and sullenly handsome, his body sculpted by steroids no doubt pressed on him by a zealous daddy or coach or both, and he looked more hungover than grief-stricken. He slumped in a lawn chair, sipping coffee from a mug Garrett suspected was laced with some hair of the dog. Land took out his pack of Camels, but didn't light up.

Garrett looked Teague over surreptitiously, noting a certain bru-tality in the linebacker hands, the square jaw. *No way this guy would have been happy about being dumped*, Garrett thought. *Even though he probably had plenty of his own on the side.*

He opted for a formal, subservient approach. "I'm sorry for your loss, Mr. Teague." As he'd expected, Teague didn't bother to offer his first name instead.

"I can't believe it," he said, and looked over the lawn. "I can't believe it."

"You don't mind if we tape this, do you?" Garrett took the micro-recorder from his jacket pocket. Teague's eyes flicked at him warily, but he nodded assent. Garrett turned it on and identified himself and Landauer and the witness.

"Mr. Teague, when was the last time you saw Erin?"

Teague frowned. "Maybe Monday or Tuesday."

"Not on Friday?"

"We had an away game. Connecticut."

"I see," Garrett said. "What about the last time you talked to her on the phone?"

Teague shrugged. "I don't remember. "

"This week? Last week?"

"Season just started. Doesn't give me a lot of free time."

"I see," Garrett repeated. "And Jason Moncrief?"

Teague looked at him sharply. "What about him?"

"You didn't know him?"

"No. I mean, everyone knew who he was. He was kind of hard to miss." Teague's lip curled as he said it. Garrett silently noted the past tense.

"Hard to miss in what way?" he asked pleasantly.

"In a dipshit psycho way."

Landauer and Garrett looked at each other. Land nodded some-thing that looked like agreement. He held an unlit cigarette in his hand.

"So when did Erin break up with you?" Garrett asked, still pleas-antly.

Surprise, then anger, flared behind Teague's eyes. "It was mutual," he said sullenly.

"I asked when," Garrett said, not so pleasantly.

"Two weeks," Teague ground out, and his gaze was murderous.

Two weeks. About the time Jeffs got an anonymous tip about Jason, Garrett noted to himself. "And she was seeing Jason Moncrief at that time."

"Yeah. She was *seeing* him." Teague's tone added, *"Bitch."*

"Odd that she didn't tell her parents," Garrett mused. "Her father was under the impression that you two were still an item."

Teague smiled without humor. "I don't know anything about that. I wasn't keeping track of her."

"Did you ever go to the Cauldron club, Mr. Teague?" Garrett asked. At the deck railing, he could see Landauer frowning at him— *What gives?*

"Why the hell would I go there?" Teague looked from one detective to the other.

"You weren't there on Friday night?"

Teague stood, knocking over his coffee mug. "Look—you said you had questions about Erin. It's shitty that she's dead. But I'm not going to sit here and get interrogated. I was at a game with a whole team of guys. Talk to them. Talk to the coach. Erin was out with that freak and he killed her. If you have any more questions for me, you can ask my lawyer."

"Pretty fast to lawyer up," Garrett said softly as they walked back out to the car past the growing front-patio audience of ersatz frat boys.

Landauer looked at him. "A, these prep mommies and daddies teach their baby preps to scream for lawyers before they can walk. And B, you were coming at him like a suspect. 'Sup with that?"

Garrett didn't know himself what he was trying to prove. "All I know is, that is not a guy who would be happy to have his girlfriend stepping out with a musician. And I don't think the timing of that anonymous tip was a coincidence. I bet you a hundred right now, Teague made that call."

"So then Teague kills Erin and carves satanic mumbo jumbo into her to frame Moncrief?" Landauer was skeptical. "I got a twenty says his alibi's bulletproof. Asshole does not equal murderer."

When the partners got back to Morris Pratt Hall, the white crime-scene van was parked outside. Inside the dorm, wide-eyed students stared from where they were corralled in the lounge as the detectives walked by the open double doors toward the elevators.

The lead criminalist, Lingg, a wiry, bespectacled scientist of mixed Asian descent, met them on Erin's floor, with his young, tomboyish assistant—*Jenny? Jerri?*—hovering behind, pulling a wagon filled with boxes and equipment. Lingg informed them that the team had already photographed and lasered for prints and vacuumed for hair and fiber that might tie Jason to Erin, then he indicated the open door of a room halfway down the hall. "It's all yours. Flag anything you want us to bag, and we'll start on the suspect's room."

The partners donned paper booties at the doorway and surveyed the room. Shelley was right about one thing: there was nothing remotely Goth about anything in Erin's clothing or belongings. It was a college girls' room, overwhelmingly decorated with floral linens, sparkly pillows, cute knickknacks, all of the highest quality without reflecting anything particularly unique or artistic about the taste of the inhabitants. Garrett and Landauer moved into the room like giants into a dollhouse, snapping latex gloves onto their hands.

"Make a wish," Landauer said, meaning: *What would you most like to find in this search?*

Garrett thought for a moment. "The cell phone."

Landauer snorted. "Good luck." Of course Erin would have had it with her; it had likely been dumped by her killer, and it would take them days to get phone records.

Landauer gravitated toward the closet. There were two of them, both surprisingly large for the size of the room. Garrett's eyes grazed the dresser and bed table. There was a stuffed school mascot, a jewelry tree, family photographs in both elegant silver and novelty frames. Garrett felt anger rising. This life, Erin's life, had just begun. She never had a chance.

He forced down the emotion, forced himself back into processing mode, continuing his survey of Erin's belongings.

Along with the family shots there was still a photograph of Kevin Teague on her dresser, which Garrett noted with interest. *Keeping up appearances? Unwilling to let go? Or had she been involved with both boys at once?*

He moved for the desk, zeroing in on the main thing he was looking for: Erin's laptop. Of course, it was also top of the line. Garrett sat down at the desk to turn it on. These days, the key to a teenager's life was in text: the text messages on smart phones and the e-mails and AIMs and Facebook and Twitter and MySpace pages. This generation was in constant communication with itself, and that could be of enormous help in this case. But as Garrett hit keys, he found the laptop was password-protected, and did not have an automatic log-on programmed in, meaning they'd have to get Erin's password from AOL, or have a tech break it. Garrett guessed Erin would not have wanted to risk her roommate snooping; he got the distinct feeling that would not have been an unreasonable concern with Shelley.

He flagged the computer for Lingg to take and got up from the desk to scan the bookcase. The books on the shelves were mainly business textbooks and about a dozen classics from what was clearly an Intro to English Literature class. But Garrett also noted an *Introduction to Astronomy* textbook. *So Jason wasn't lying about that: they had a class together.*

The CDs were predictable, sweet and lightweight pop: Snow Patrol and The Fray and John Mayer and Jack Johnson and Natasha Bedinger, but Garrett scanned through every title until he found what he was looking for.

Current 333. Jason's CD.

Garrett stepped over to the closet, where Landauer was scanning Erin's clothes with a slightly lost expression, and showed him the CD case. "On her shelf," he said, nodding toward the bookcase.

Landauer raised an eyebrow. "Okay, so what are you thinking?"

Garrett paused. "Let's say he gives this to her. If he's stalking her, she's going to throw it away, right? Or turn it in to the hall coordinator, or the school. But apparently she never contacted any authorities to complain."

"Or—he left it for her without a note, and she stuck it on the shelf. Or the roommate did."

Garrett turned the CD case over and frowned, feeling the weight in his hand. He flipped it open. There was no disc inside.

He turned in the room, focused on the sound system, on a shelf beside the desk. He walked two steps to the shelf, punched on the CD player, and pushed the EJECT button. The five-disc tray slid out. The *Current 333* CD was in one of the slots.

Landauer lifted his eyebrows again, nodded thoughtfully.

"So what—he sneaks into her room and puts the CD in?" Garrett asked, with an edge.

"Not all that likely, " Landauer conceded.

Shelley's disjointed account was running through Garrett's head. Despite a lot of denial from Erin's friends, Jason and Erin seemed closer than anyone wanted to admit. Garrett was about to say so aloud when his cell phone buzzed. The number on the screen was Lingg's, and it was followed by the number 911.

Urgent.

Chapter Ten

Upstairs on the third floor, the black curtains were drawn at the windows of Jason's room and the room was dark as night, with only an ultraviolet light on to illuminate the space. Garrett had to suppress a shiver as they stepped into the dim room; the memory of their disturbing encounter with Jason was too close to the surface. The distorted white faces of Jason's band glowed eerily from the poster on the wall.

Lingg's moon face gleamed at the detectives in the dark as he filled them in with a morose optimism. First, he lifted the Luminol-sprayed sheets from the bed. Irregular splotches glowed green in the UV light. "Definitely semen. Hardly surprising to find in the room of a college male. However . . ."

Lingg stepped to the closet in the purple-tinged darkness and indicated a massive pile of dirty clothes on the closet floor. "We took these jeans from the top, there."

He held up a pair of pencil-leg black jeans. There were a few luminous dots on the outside of the pants legs (matching the now brilliantly glowing stick-on stars on the ceiling above them) but when Lingg turned the top of the pants inside out, the whole crotch area lit up with shining streaks.

"Blood and semen, both." Lingg's face was lit up as well, with a faint purplish tinge.

Garrett and Landauer looked at each other in the spooky glow of the light. Landauer said what they all were thinking. "Twenty says we get his and hers DNA. Proves he fucked her."

"Fucking isn't killing," Garrett said, almost to himself. He added, more loudly, "We're going to need more. Everything we can get. There's something else—" But he never got to complete his sentence. As he turned in the dark room, he saw red, malevolent eyes glowing from a corner, and a blur of movement, some huge shape poised to spring—

Garrett yelled. Landauer and Lingg spun in the darkness, Landauer grabbing for his weapon. Garrett lunged at the window curtains, ripped them open. Sunlight blazed into the room, dazzling them.

Garrett turned and stared toward the corner, blinking against the sudden light. There was nothing, no one there: just a narrow, full-length mirror on the wall.

"Jesus Holy Christ, Rhett," Landauer gasped. "What the fuck?"

Garrett gazed at the mirror. His pulse was still going a mile a minute. *What the fuck is right.* "Sorry," he said finally. "Sorry. I thought I saw . . ." But there was no describing what he thought he'd seen. *Great. I'm hallucinating now. That's helpful.*

"Some sleep would be good," he managed.

The other two men stared at him, then Landauer reholstered his weapon. Lingg diplomatically turned away and crossed to the door, where a crate of evidence bags was set in the hall outside, to bag and tag the jeans. Jenny-or-Jerri slipped back into the room with her camera slung over her shoulder, while Landauer stepped to the closet, scanning the shelves and floor. He pointed for the assistant's benefit. "Take all his shoes . . . let's see if we can get a match to soil from the dump."

Garrett looked around the room, letting his heartbeat return to normal. He saw black fingerprint powder dusted on surfaces, and felt a sudden certainty that they were going to find Erin's prints in the room.

A cell phone was on the bed table, plugged into a charger. The guitar still lay on the bed, where Jason had put it down the night before, and Garrett realized with a slight shock that it was just twelve hours ago, now.

He picked up the phone and flipped it open. The screen photo was the cover image of the band's CD, with its ominous triangles. Garrett punched up *Contacts* and scrolled down. There was an **E** listed, and he recognized the number programmed into the address book as the one he had for Erin Carmody. Next he punched up the list of recent calls and found several calls to Erin over the last week, mostly at night, some of twenty- and thirty-minute duration.

So she wasn't hanging up on him.

The last call was Friday at 8:08 P.M. Garrett flipped over to the text message record and again found scattered messages to Erin's number, in text shorthand: some messages that he recognized and others that were more obscure. Maddeningly, it was not a brand of phone that showed the entire conversation; they would have to subpoena Erin's phone records for her responses, if there were any.

Garrett scrolled down. The first several texts were brief and innocuous; variations on YT? And WU? *You there?* and *What's up?* And WAN2TLK, which he assumed translated as *Want to talk.*

He moved on to one he didn't recognize: BOOMS, and for a moment simply felt old. He scrolled farther and paused at one of the messages, startled.

Tuesday 12:01 A.M.: GNSD.

He recognized the combination of letters from some old interdepartmental memo on Leetspeak and texting abbreviations: *Good night, sweet dreams . . .*

He frowned, and scrolled more slowly, now. On Friday at 8:08 P.M., not long before Erin and Jason were both seen dancing at Cauldron, there was a message that read simply: BRT, which he knew meant *Be right there.*

There was also one message on Saturday: YT? *You there?*

That last message was time-stamped 1:23 P.M., approximately twelve hours after Erin's murder.

Garrett stood beside the desk in a fog.

"You are not looking happy," Landauer observed from across the room. Garrett stepped to him, showed him the phone, watching him as he scrolled through the received calls.

"GNSD?" Landauer frowned.

"'Good night, sweet dreams.' I don't know BOOMS." He looked at his partner. "I gotta say. This is looking more like dating than stalking."

"Could be, Rhett. But that kid is not right." Landauer glanced toward the bed—held up his bandaged arm for emphasis. "Erin wouldn't be the first one to say yes to someone she shouldn't have. However it started out, what happened at the end there weren't no date."

"But look at the last message," Garrett persisted. There was a knot in his stomach that wouldn't go away. "He texted her at 1:23 Saturday afternoon, looking for her."

Landauer glanced at the message. "Yeah, or he wanted to make it look that way. The kid is weird, but so far no one's saying he's stupid." Garrett looked at him. Laudauer shrugged. "Playin' devil's advocate. So to speak."

Garrett handed the cell phone to a patiently waiting Lingg to enter into evidence. Landauer drifted back to the closet while Garrett stepped to the bookshelf to look at the books, scanning over the odd names: *Magick in Theory and Practice. The Vision and the Voice.* He turned to Lingg and pointed at the books. "These are going with me. This shelf. I'll sign for them."

"Sure," the criminalist said, nodding.

While Landauer busied himself with the closet drawers, Garrett tried the computer, a Dell laptop. The screen saver dissolved up, a field of black with a single line of white text:

There is no grace, there is no guilt. This is the Law: DO WHAT THOU WILT!

Garrett stared at the rhyme, recognizing "Do what thou wilt" as something Jason had said to them last night. The phrase was no less disturbing in the daylight. After a moment he tried clicking into the

My Documents files, but the files were password protected, as were Moncrief's online accounts.

He motioned to Jerri-Jenni-whoever-the-fuck to take the laptop, then stopped and looked into the young woman's fresh face, and it clicked. "Jenna," he said.

"Yes?" She cocked her head toward him, surprised.

"What does BOOMS mean in text?" Garrett asked.

"Bored out of my skull," she answered promptly.

Garrett looked at her. "Would you text that to someone you planned on killing?"

Jenna's eyes widened slightly. "Um . . . depends on how bored I was. I kinda doubt it, though."

Garrett nodded, frowning. "Yeah." And his thoughts were swirling again, and the knot was back in his stomach.

After a moment Jenna turned away with the laptop. Garrett moved back to the desk and opened the long top drawer to look down on a mad scatter of pens, pencils, club tickets, band postcards, legal pads, batteries, pills, Jolly Rancher candies, Dubble Bubble gum. Nothing eye-catching at first glance, and Garrett was inclined to move on—then he spotted an antique-style metal key. He reached with a gloved hand and picked it up, examining it.

"You find a lockbox in the closet?" He spoke aloud to his partner.

"Nope," Landauer answered. He'd started on the bureau drawers.

Garrett turned from the desk with the key and scanned the room. His eyes stopped on the black-quilted bed. He crossed the room and crouched beside it, picking up the black comforter to look below. In the dark space under the bed, amid an unnerving collection of dust mice, was a battered, antique-looking box. "Hey. Land."

Landauer stepped over from the dresser while Garrett lifted the box onto the bed and unlocked it, opened the lid. They looked down on a startling collection of objects: black candles, a tarnished silver hand mirror, an oil lamp, a cup, a bell, a jar of salt, a vial of oil, a hexagonal metal container with punched-out holes that Garrett recognized from his altar-boy days as a censer, for burning incense—and a thick book of photo album size covered in bloodred leather. Garrett lifted the book, curious . . . but his attention was immediately drawn to the two long, thin objects wrapped in black silk, lying beneath the volume. He picked one up and unwrapped it. In the folds of the silk lay an intricately carved red hardwood wand with a large cloudy crystal at the tip. Garret rewrapped the wand and replaced it in the box, then picked up the other black-wrapped object. He could tell what it was instantly. He lay it carefully down on the bed and folded back the silk. The detectives looked down on a gleaming silver dagger.

Landauer exhaled above him and Garrett realized he'd been holding his breath as well. There was a quiet thrill in Land's voice as he spoke.

"Now we're cooking with gas."

Chapter Eleven

They drew the curtains and Lingg moved in with the Luminol.
The UV light revealed no obvious traces of blood on the dagger.
There were more sensitive tests to be done in the lab, but suddenly
Landauer looked up at Garrett in the purplish dark.

"You thinking what I'm thinking?"

Garrett nodded slowly. "We've got it."

There were still dozens of witnesses to question—dorm residents, professors, advisers—and countless personal belongings to
sort through, not to mention e-mails, phone records, and Jason's
car to be processed. But with the semen and blood on the jeans, if
the DNA matched Erin's, and the presence of a dagger in Jason's
room, plus the CD case with its symbols corresponding to the carvings in Erin's body, and the testimony of the roommate and the DJ
at the club, they likely had more than enough circumstantial evidence to charge Jason.

"I'm thinking we want to get home and try to talk to this kid before he's lawyered up to the gills," Landauer said, his voice faraway.
"We've got a shitload here, G-man. If our luck holds he might just
cop to it all."

"Okay," Garrett said, feeling both electrified and hazy from lack of sleep. They could go through Moncrief's personal effects back at Schroeder, while they waited for results of lab tests, and their IT expert could get into Moncrief's and Erin's laptops. "Let's think. What do we still need to get done, here?"

"Moncrief's car. Check with Jeffs if there's any student interviews we should know about. And we're out of here."

Garrett nodded. "I want to talk to the other members of the band, too," he said abruptly. But they were not Amherst students; he'd already run DMV checks.

He turned to survey the room again. The red leather-bound book was still lying on the bed beside it, unopened, and he made another move to reach for it—

"Detectives." Both of them turned toward the terse voice behind them.

Sergeant Jeffs was standing in the doorway, an intent look on his face. "I've got someone you're going to want to talk to."

Chapter Twelve

Garrett recognized the round-faced, curly-haired hall coordinator from the night before (*God . . . just the night before . . .*). The partners sat in Kurt Fugate's one-bedroom apartment on the ground floor, his perk for managing the building and all its student residents. Jeffs stood against the wall, watching.

Fugate was a senior, older than their other interviewees, but so far the most nervous; he was mature enough to be suitably shaken by Erin's death. He sat in an armchair, relating what he'd told Jeffs. "All these rooms are supposed to be double occupancy. Jason only had a single because his roommate requested a transfer. Urgently."

Seated uncomfortably on the futon couch, Garrett had a sudden flash of Jason's stretched-out face, the wolfishly lolling tongue . . .

Fugate swallowed coffee from a school mug and continued. "Bryce came to me to request the transfer. He wouldn't give any specific reason—he really didn't want to talk about it at all. But he said he didn't want to stay another night." He glanced at Jeffs, back to Garrett. "If you ask me, he was scared."

"Scared how?" Garrett pressed.

Fugate looked at him straight on. "He had a suitcase with him when he talked to me. He really wasn't going back up there."

Garrett glanced at Landauer. "But he wouldn't give any details."

The hall coordinator shook his head. "No. Sorry. He didn't want to talk about it."

"No problem. We'll be speaking to him." Garrett made a note, then looked up. "Did you know Jason yourself?"

"Only by sight. There are 120 kids in the hall, it's a new school year . . . I just hadn't gotten to know everyone."

"Did Erin Carmody ever complain to you about being stalked?"

The young man looked horrified. "God, no. I would have—done something."

Garrett nodded thoughtfully, and met Landauer's eyes, while he said aloud to Fugate, "Thanks. You've been a huge help."

They were in luck: Bryce Brissell was on campus, working in the scene shop in the theater building, just a few buildings away. There was building going on in the dim space backstage, muffled hammering and sanding and sawing from the scene dock and the costume shop, and the smell of paint.

Bryce was tall, pale and gangly, almost two-dimensionally thin, with a long shock of diagonally cut, dyed auburn hair that kept falling into his startlingly green eyes. *Contacts*, Garrett thought. The boy wore his sexuality on his sleeve. He even gave Garrett a furtive look as he folded himself into a battered armchair in a grouping of sprung sofas and davenports in the curtained wings backstage. It didn't take much prodding for him to open up about Jason. He pulled out clove cigarettes, prompting Landauer to dig out his own Camels, and articulated for the micro-recorder, everything with a dramatic delivery and fluttering hands that Garrett could feel grating on Land without even having to look at him.

"I left because I couldn't live with him," Bryce said, taking a nervous drag on his cigarette. "It was the black magic. At first I thought he was just posing—the whole death metal thing, yada yada, scary scary. But he just got more and more into it. I knew he was doing rituals in the room. At first I could tell because of the candles, nothing but black. He got into using different bizarro oils, I think for spells. He had all those creepy books—I swear, I didn't even like sleeping in the same room with them." Bryce looked off toward the curtained wings. A single ghost light on a tall pole shone on the stage like a torch, a halo of light. "And then things started to go really weird," Bryce said softly.

"Weird how?" Garrett prompted.

Bryce paused, and the reluctance suddenly seemed genuine. "There were these smells in the room, even when he wasn't there," he said slowly. "Like, burning. I could feel these—drafts—even when the windows and door were closed. And sounds. I would wake up in the middle of the night because there was this whispering." He stopped, frowned. "Babbling. Like a lot of voices all at once, on top of each other. But there was no music playing, no TV, no iPod, nothing. He'd be sitting cross-legged on the bed, just him, staring into space . . ." Bryce shivered, and Garrett thought of Jason's black, dilated eyes. "And then he'd look at me . . . and his eyes . . . his eyes were so empty."

Despite himself, Garrett felt a chill. Bryce exhaled smoke and touched his lip before he continued.

"Okay, and I do props, right? And I'd been collecting some stuff for a bill of one acts: Pinter, Beckett, Ionesco. Well, one night I was studying alone in the room and I heard a phone start to ring behind me. Not a cell phone, but one of those old-time phones, a Sultan?" He looked at the detectives and lowered his voice.

"It was the prop phone. It was ringing in the closet. But it was a *prop phone*. No cords. No wires."

Garrett and Landauer eyed each other, and Bryce stiffened at their obvious skepticism. "I swear to God, it's true. That's when I packed up, right then and there. Whatever he was into, I wasn't going to live in the same room with it."

"So you felt in danger?" Garrett suggested.

"*Yes*, I felt in *danger*," Bryce said, affronted. "What do you think I've been saying?"

Garrett tried to steer the interview back to something solid. "Did you ever see Jason with Erin Carmody?"

Bryce shook his head, hair flopping.

"She never came to the room?"

"Not that I knew of."

"Did Jason ever speak about her?"

"No. It's not like he talked a lot, though. Mostly he acted like I wasn't there. He was always off on his own trip." Bryce stared off toward the stage and shivered. "My dad was batshit that I moved off campus and lost the whole semester deposit. But look what happened." He looked at the detectives with wide eyes. "What if I'd stayed?"

As they walked out the dark hall toward the red light of the EXIT sign, Garrett looked to Landauer, who was tapping out a cigarette. "What do you think?"

Landauer grimaced. "Drama queen. Literally." He widened his eyes like an ingénue. "'The phone was *ringing* in the *closet*,'" he said, fluttering his hands as he mimicked Bryce's voice. He dropped the lisp. "The phone is definitely the only thing in the closet."

"If you're finished—" Garrett began.

"I'm makin' a point, here," Landauer growled, holding up a warning finger.

"Which is?"

"Moncrief doesn't like having a gay roommate and he hazes Tinker Bell till he leaves. Moncrief's a musician. Sound effects: babbling voices, ringing in the closet."

Garrett stopped and looked at his partner, who stood with the unlit cigarette in his hand. He had the strong feeling Landauer was trying to explain away something he didn't want to look at. *But we both saw it, Land: Jason's stretched-out face and black basketball eyes. We heard that rasping, inhuman voice . . .*

Garrett suddenly felt the hair on the back of his neck rise, the same absolute sensation of being watched that he'd experienced at Cauldron.

He turned sharply and stared into the dark of the hall.

They were alone, nothing in the corridor with them but the glowing red patches of the EXIT lights.

Get a grip, he told himself. *Get some sleep.*

Land was staring at him, and he shook his head. "Maybe you're right. Maybe Jason was hazing him. I don't know what to think. I think I'm too tired to think."

"You and me both," Landauer admitted. He looked back toward the stage with a frown. "But something's hinky about that story and I don't like it. I don't like any of it."

Outside the theater building, they saw the media had found them. Microwave-dished vans from different news stations dotted the campus, shooting atmospheric footage. Jeffs's officers had established a no-media zone around Morris Pratt Hall, but news choppers hovered above, shooting from the air what they could not get from the ground. Garrett stood and watched as a suited reporter with a fresh haircut and a mike chased down a couple of back-packed students. *Everyone in the continental U.S. knows Jason Moncrief killed her, by now. Signed, sealed, delivered.*

The partners met Lingg and Jenna in the parking lot at the side of the dorm, where they were processing Moncrief's car, a black late-model Mustang hardtop convertible. The kid was no pauper.

Lingg turned away from the car with a grin. "Happy New Year, Detectives. We found Erin's phone. Under the passenger seat. And more semen and blood traces in the back."

Slam dunk.

In his oddly maternal way, Lingg suggested that Jenna drive the Cavalier back to Boston so Garrett and Landauer could catch an hour's nap in the CSU van, and the partners gratefully accepted, each taking a piece of the floor in the back. Garrett folded his suit coat under his head and lay back with his eyes shut. He was nearly dead, yet his mind was racing, cataloguing.

- *An eyewitness putting Erin and Jason together mere hours before her murder*
- *Blood and semen on Jason's jeans*
- *The ceremonial objects under his bed, including a dagger like—if not identical to—the one that killed her*
- *Erin's phone in Jason's car*
- *Blood and semen in Jason's car*

- *The leather book with its ominous and incriminating symbols*
- *Eyewitness testimony that Jason was disturbed and disturbing*

At this rate the lab would find traces of Erin's blood on the dagger, Moncrief would give them a full, voluntary confession and agree to a plea, and they'd be closing the book on this one within the week. A dream case. All the glory and none of the hassle. *And what was so wrong about that?*

"There is no grace, there is no guilt . . ."

Garrett spoke aloud to his partner from where he stretched on the floor of the van. "I was wrong. You were right. It's the kid."

For a moment he thought Landauer was already asleep. Then his voice came, disembodied, from the other side of the van. "This is a weird one. It baffles the fuck out of me."

Garrett said slowly, "Yeah."

And then they were out.

Chapter Thirteen

The nap was lifesaving, and both detectives were able to shower and change into spare clothes in the locker room of Schroeder before once again convening in the conference room with Malloy and Carolyn. Normally Malloy would not have shown hide nor hair on a Sunday, his church day, but apparently the Carmody name trumped God, and of course time was of the essence.

As Garrett began to list the evidence, he knew they had the charges nailed just by watching Carolyn's and Malloy's faces.

"The DJ at Cauldron puts Erin and Jason together just hours before her death. Erin's roommate says Jason was obsessed with her and was out with her that night. Erin's missing cell phone was found in Jason's car. We have a pair of jeans taken from Jason's room which have traces of blood and semen that we believe DNA tests will match to Erin and Jason, confirming they had sex that night, and there are similar traces in Jason's car. We have a CD from Jason's band that contains the symbols and numbers that were carved into Erin's torso. We have three student witnesses willing to testify to Jason's unbalanced mental state. And we have a whole collection of occult ritual objects from a lockbox under Moncrief's bed, including a dagger like the one used to kill Erin.

It's being tested for blood residue right now. The rest of it—well, none of it looks good." He passed out photos of the ceremonial objects.

The silence was electric as Carolyn and Malloy looked over the photos. Garrett and Landauer held each other's eyes over the table.

"This is very strong," Carolyn declared, looking up. Her face was shining. "Very strong. We should have zero trouble getting a grand jury to hand down an indictment. When will we have DNA results?"

Garrett was the complete professional as he answered her. "The lab will be able to tell us unofficially within two days. The full report will take a couple of weeks because of corroborative tests. But we can match blood type, and the semen taken from Erin's body was from a secretor, so we have the blood type on that as well."

"That'll work," she said, writing. "How soon can you get me a charging package?" She looked to Malloy, and Malloy raised his eyebrows at the detectives.

Garrett and Landauer looked at each other, calculating. A charging package was a daunting document: a presentation of all the evidence, lab reports, witness testimony, photos, and evidence lists that the DA's office needed to file charges. It would also be used in negotiations with Moncrief's attorney, to show them how strong the case was and apply pressure for a plea. The partners were painfully light on sleep to begin with, but the nap in the CSU van and the shower had helped.

Landauer was already thinking out loud. "All the lab tests have been expedited. We should be getting results throughout the evening—print matches from the car, the blood screens . . ."

Garrett added, "The phone records will take a while, but we've got the call logs from the cell phones, and the IT guys should be able to open the computer files on both laptops . . ." Then he frowned. "I'd like to be able to talk to the other band members, too."

"Do you really need those witness accounts to make a preliminary case?" Malloy interrupted, with an edge.

Garrett weighed it, conceded, "Probably not. But, Lieutenant, if we could get in to see Moncrief tonight, we might just be able to get the whole thing out of him. Especially with the stuff we found under the bed—"

"It's not going to happen," Carolyn said. "Moncrief's family has hired Merrill James."

There was no need for her to elaborate. James was one of the two top defense attorneys in the state, a celebrity lawyer for celebrity cases.

"Obviously they know we're going to be charging Moncrief with Erin's murder," Carolyn continued. "James has already gotten a technical restraining order stating that no law enforcement official can question Moncrief unless James is present. And James hasn't been returning calls today—I've tried."

They all sat, absorbing this news.

Malloy narrowed his eyes toward the detectives. "We have twenty-eight hours left on the initial forty-eight-hour hold for the assault on a peace officer arrest. Can we get a charging package together in time to arrest him again for Erin Carmody's murder before he's released on bail?" His voice seemed curtly challenging, but then again, it always did.

"We can do it," Garrett said.

"You got it," Landauer agreed.

"There's another thing, and this is important." Carolyn put her manicured hands flat on the table. "The office has directed me to go for a no-bail hold, and of course I agree. So we need the charging document to reflect that Moncrief is either a flight risk or a danger to the community, preferably both." She nodded toward Landauer. "Now, the attack on Detective Landauer goes a long way toward 'danger to the community,' but can you build from there?"

Garrett felt a wave of fatigue, and forced himself to focus. "Flight risk, I don't know," he said slowly. "We didn't get anything from anyone we talked to that would make a case for it. Erin's roommate Shelley Forbes will testify that she felt threatened by Moncrief, and so will Moncrief's ex-roommate, Bryce Brissell, but he's not the most credible witness."

"Anything that goes to premeditation would help. E-mails, threats," Carolyn said encouragingly. "See what you can put together.

I'll start on my end with these notes so far, and fax me what you've got as lab results come in. I'm totally available to you," she finished, looking at Garrett without a hint of double entendre.

Malloy pushed back in his chair. "I've called in a couple of typists to transcribe tapes and reports. They'll be at your disposal for as long as you need them," he said, but he avoided eye contact with Garrett as he said it. "I want this done."

Chapter Fourteen

As the partners spread their reports and notes and tapes out over the long table in the back of the detectives' bureau, the reality of the mountain of work they had ahead of them sank in. Since their arrival at the landfill yesterday morning, they had worked the case nonstop, without enough of a break even to do more than file the most preliminary notes in the murder book. They were starting from scratch.

They began by setting up the two typists Malloy had provided (not for the detectives' convenience, Garrett knew well enough) with the witness interview tapes to transcribe.

Back at the long table of files, Garrett looked over the clear plastic evidence crates and spotted the maroon leather-bound book in a top crate.

He reached for a box of latex gloves and slipped a pair on to take the book from the crate, then sat at the table with it. It was heavy, the blood-colored leather soft to the touch.

He opened the cover of the book. The pages were fibery, document quality, giving the volume an antique feel, and the writing was completely hand-blocked, in black calligraphy pen—and completely incomprehensible: a twiglike alphabet that looked vaguely familiar, but was no language that Garrett could name.

Garrett carefully turned the pages with gloved hands. Amid the writing there were drawings as well, including sketches of pentagrams . . . and on later pages, the number 333 and the triple triangle design that had been carved into Erin Carmody's torso.

He spoke aloud to Landauer. "He's got those triangles and 333 in this book, too, but the writing's in some kind of code." Landauer glanced up from the witness report he was detailing, stood, and came around the table to look.

"Is that a language?" Garrett asked him.

Landauer frowned down at the stick letters on the page. "It looks familiar, but I can't place it."

Garrett sat back against his chair, in a fog of sleeplessness. The logo he'd seen on Moncrief's laptop screen ran through his head again, like a mad chant:

There is no grace, there is no guilt. This is the Law: DO WHAT THOU WILT!

He was suddenly aware of the weight of the book in his hands. The thick pages, the look of the lettering, the whole feel of it—all made him profoundly uncomfortable. He realized that even with latex gloves on, he had no desire to be touching it.

He shoved back his chair and stood. "I'm going over to the lab to see if they can translate this thing."

Landauer nodded distractedly, already moving back to his witness reports. "Get an ETA on the prints and blood."

The crime lab was a short walk down a connecting corridor that overlooked the dim and sickly lights of the Lower Roxbury hood. Garrett brooded on the notion of premeditation as he walked with the heavy book. The volume had an odd feeling in his hands that he couldn't identify but which he didn't like, a sense almost of malevolence. That, of course, was nonsense. *But what if Jason had plotted Erin's death in the book?* If he had written anything down, that would go to premeditation.

Garrett walked faster, and turned in through the door of the lab.

"Hello, young Garrett! Thanks for the OT!" A cheery voice called out from a desk as Garrett stepped through the gate at the counter.

Criminalist Warren Tufts was a veteran, nearing seventy but wiry and spry and perpetually delighted with his job. He tipped precariously back in his swivel chair and eyed the book in Garrett's hands. "Bearing gifts, I see. What new treasure do you have for us this fine evening?"

"I was hoping you could tell me. It's the suspect's, but it's in some kind of code." Garrett opened the book randomly on Tuft's desk. "Need to get it translated."

Tufts scowled down at the twiglike letters. "I'm no good with code. It's all Greek to me! Henderson's in Alaska. I'll have to outsource this. There's a guy at MIT we use. Is it a rush?"

Garrett paused. It was as far as he was concerned. "Yes," he decided. As he handed over the book, he felt a strange reluctance to part with it. "And can you make a copy for me? I'd like to take a look through myself, tonight."

"Right you are." As Tufts got up and moved toward the file room, Garrett looked over the rows of steel counters at the back of the lab. Two counters were crowded with individually bagged pieces of trash, and Garrett recognized the refuse taken from the landfill. He frowned, remembering something.

"Hey, Tufts. We took some burned flowers from the landfill. Did you get anything on those?"

The criminalist stuck his head out the file room doorway. "Don't think they've been processed yet. Burned flowers?"

"Yeah. Scorched."

"What've they got to do with all this?"

"I don't know," Garrett said, and shook his head. "I don't have a clue."

Twenty minutes later he was back in the homicide room, with a thick pile of photocopied pages and the original book. He'd prevailed on Tufts to make a second copy so he could take the original with him in case he needed it—for what, he had no particular sense, only that it could be important.

Landauer sat at the long table, hunched over a laptop, a stack of reports in front of him. He looked up at Garrett with a glazed look in his eyes. They both contemplated the piles of files and random pages stacked all over the table. A thick silence fell.

Garrett cleared his throat. "I'm thinking my place. Order porterhouse and Caesars from Dino's. Eat, write, nap. Eat, write, nap."

Landauer exhaled. "I am so with you, Rhett." They both reached out and started packing boxes of documents.

Garrett's house, north of Logan Airport, was the house he'd grown up in, his parents' house, in a crowded lower middle-class neighborhood that had gentrified in the precrash housing boom. Garrett was the fifth son in an Irish Catholic family, the late-in-life mistake, conceived when his mother was forty-nine and his father fifty-five. Garrett was ten years younger than the next youngest of his brothers, who had always been more like uncles to him than siblings, and he guessed he could thank the papal ban on contraception for his very existence, but with what he saw daily as a cop he was the most fervent advocate of birth control he knew. If there was a way to put it in the water he would vote for it, no questions asked.

His parents were dead, now; his father from complications from alcoholism just over four years ago, and his mother simply followed in her sleep a mere three months after. Some people would call that love.

Garrett's brothers and their families were long gone out of state: New Hampshire, Connecticut, Maine—and rebel Paulie to Fort Lauderdale. Garrett had inherited the house, and after the obligatory mourning period he'd slowly rehabbed the place, discarding furniture untouched since the sixties and revealing clean lines and antique moldings and gorgeous hardwood floors under his mother's wallpaper and fussy Irish lace and religious bric-a-brac.

Just having his own walls around him now was rejuvenating. The delivered meal and another round of showers had energized both detectives, and three hours into it they had made real headway on the charging document, using the murder book and their notes from Amherst to draw up a complete chronology and fill in about a third of the reports they needed. Tufts called in with another nail in Jason Moncrief's coffin: some of the fingerprints in Moncrief's Mustang were a match for Erin's. However, the lab had found no blood residue on the dagger they had taken from Moncrief's room.

The partners took a break for cannoli and channel-surfed through the news. The stations were falling all over themselves to profile Jason: rich kid, young mother, older father high ranking in the navy. Young mother did *very* well in the divorce and had husband-hopped ever since, every time doing better, while Jason was shuffled from private school to military school, his behavior deteriorating with each successive transfer.

Poor little rich kid. Garrett had no sympathy. Still, he was hearing nothing that would necessarily indicate a budding young psychopath.

"He did a Jim Morrison," Landauer summed up, and when Garrett looked at him, he said, "Moncrief. Rebelled against a colonel father. Got into all that spooky shit. Classic Apollonian-Dionysian conflict."

"Land," Garrett said blandly, hiding his shock; his sometimes Neanderthal partner never failed to surprise him. "I didn't know you could even spell Dionysian."

"Who said I could?" Landauer said. He stood and stretched and then retired to the spare bedroom for a nap. Garrett took their plates into the kitchen, and after a hesitation, decided to allow himself a beer. When he returned to the living room he could hear wall-shaking snores rumbling from down the hall.

The descent of night had given Garrett his second wind. He pressed on, with a Guinness in front of him and case files and crime-scene photos spread out around him on the long dining table he always ended up using as a desk. It was tedious work but strangely satisfying to him, building a case. He usually enjoyed the process, watching links emerge. But there were contradictions here: he was seeing two conflicting tracks to the evidence, and that was troubling. It seemed clear from the phone logs on both cell phones and the text messages that Erin had gone with Jason voluntarily to the Cauldron club on the night of her death. Still, Garrett knew not just from police work but from personal experience that young women have a terrible blind spot for what they think are bad boys, and a frightening naïveté about the dangers of experimenting with the wild side. As a musician Jason would have a certain troubadour allure, but there were dark currents there, an apparently fatal undertow.

Next he considered Jason's roommate. Bizarre as Bryce Brissell's story was, there was a ring of truth to it. *Excuse the pun*, Garrett thought grimly. And Landauer might not be so far wrong about Jason faking scary effects.

Garrett reached for the copy of the tape he'd made of Jason in his room, and rewound it to listen from the beginning again. He fast-forwarded through his own recitation of the Miranda warning.

"Do you understand these rights as I've explained them to you?"

"Suuure . . ." Moncrief drawled.

"Jason, what's Current 333?"

"Choronzon."

Garrett frowned at the word. He rewound the tape and listened again. Jason's voice was slow and slurred.

"Choronzon."

"Corazon? You mean, 'heart'?" Garrett asked him on the tape.

"Hardly." Jason's voice mocked. *"Choronzon."*

Then Garrett sat up in his chair, listening more intently. There was a faint whispering in the background. At first he thought it was just the hiss of tape, but the sound increased. Whispering. Not just one person, either, but an overlap of voices behind his own and Jason's voices.

"I don't know what that means. Can you explain it?"

"The Lord of Hallucinations," Moncrief said in that dreamy, slurred voice.

"Really. You mean, a drug?"

"I mean the Master of the Abyss."

The whispering was louder now, and Bryce Brissell's story came back to Garrett. *"I would wake up in the middle of the night because there was this whispering. Babbling, actually, like a lot of voices all at once, on top of each other."*

This is crazy, Garrett thought. *The stereo must still have been on. The whispering was on the CD.*

He'd turned it off himself, though.

I must have turned it down, not off. But even as he thought it, he clearly remembered punching the POWER button.

On the tape, his own voice continued:

"You know, I think it would help if you started from the beginning—"

"Do what thou wilt shall be the whole of the Law."

Garrett stared at the recorder as Moncrief's voice intoned the words, and the whispering sped up in the background. Garrett could feel the hairs on his forearms raising.

"Jason, where is Erin?"

And then Garrett's whole scalp buzzed, as that horrible, guttural voice blasted from the recorder:

"Zazas Zazas Nasatanada Zazas!"

He heard his own voice croaking: *"Where is Erin?"* And that snakelike hiss: *"In hell."*

Then pandemonium. Landauer yelling, cursing, and Moncrief's feral snarling, all over the wail of the—*impossible*—music, and the frantic, escalating babbling of voices . . .

Garrett quickly punched off the tape and sat back, as rattled as he had been the night before.

Whatever had been in that room with them was certainly capable of murder.

But what had been in that room?

He got up and paced the floor, staring toward the recorder. He suddenly crossed to the table and reached for the murder book, flipped pages until he found the interview form he'd filled out on Tanith Cabarrus. The orange Post-it she'd given him was still stuck to the report, with its ominous list of dates:

June 21
August 1
September 21

Garrett found himself suffused with an almost paralyzing agitation and dread. He remembered his intention to check Missing Persons, forgotten in the sudden rush to Amherst. Now he dropped into a chair and ripped through pages in the murder book to find where he'd filed the Missing Persons lists, under *To Be Checked*. He scanned the pages for the dates: *June 21, August 1 . . .*

There were no MPs listed under either date.

He pushed back his chair and stood, catching his breath. *All right, then. Nothing there.*

But his heart refused to slow. He was in the grip of a certainty that whatever was going on, it was imperative to keep Jason Moncrief off the street.

He paced in a circle, with an agitation he couldn't contain. *Premeditation*, Carolyn had said. If they could prove premeditation, she would be able to ask for a no-bail hold.

And then he knew. The book. He seized the volume bound in blood-colored leather and crossed to his favorite easy chair.

Fifteen minutes later he stood, with a rock in his stomach as he stared down at a drawing on a page. He was no closer to understanding the strange writing, but the illustration needed no interpretation: it was a crude sketch of a severed left hand, with a lit candle burning in the stiffened clutch of fingers.

Erin Carmody's killer had taken her left hand.

Garrett reached for his phone and speed-dialed Tufts's number at the lab . . . but before the connection went through he abruptly punched off, thinking.

He turned to his own book, the blue binder of the murder book, open to the witness report labeled *"Tanith Cabarrus,"* and looked down at the phone number under her name on the first line. After a long moment he picked up his cell phone again and dialed, only half-aware that he was holding his breath.

She answered on the second ring and the smoky voice electrified him. "Book of Shadows."

So it was the bookstore number. He glanced at the clock. Nine-thirty. "Ms. Cabarrus?" he asked, though he knew it was.

There was a long pause and then she said, "Detective Garrett, is it?"

He was entirely startled. "How did you know?"

This time the pause was distinctly amused. "That's my job, isn't it?"

For the life of him he could not think of a response.

"What can I do for you?" she asked, finally, and he tried to focus.

"I know it's late, but I have a piece of—evidence—that I think is important. And I thought, with your expertise, you might be able to tell me what it means."

Another silence. "You mean, now?"

A vision of Tanith Cabarrus, with that tumbled hair around her face, those dark, lush lips against the phone, inflamed him.

He cleared his throat, blocked the thought. "If that's at all possible."

"What is this evidence?"

"I'd really prefer to show you and have you tell me." He felt his words sounded vaguely obscene, and hoped she wasn't thinking the same.

There was a very long silence. "Where are you?"

He could not at all gauge her reaction. "Near Logan."

"You know I'm in Salem," she pointed out.

"I do. But it's not so far, this time of night. I could be there in forty minutes." He waited through the silence.

"I'll meet you halfway," she said. "Do you know the Lamplighter, in Lynn? It's right off 1A."

Lynn was an older industrial center in the North Shore, halfway between Boston and Salem. Garrett began, "You really don't have to do—"

She cut him off. "I'd prefer it."

He was silent, awkward, wondering if she felt in some way threatened. "If you're sure—"

"If it will help."

"Half an hour, then," he said, and the silence felt thick, intimate. "Thank you," he added, formally, he hoped.

"Half an hour," she said, and clicked off.

Garrett closed his phone. His stomach and groin muscles were taut, and he breathed out to settle himself. He stood and looked toward the hallway, the bedroom where Landauer was sleeping, with world-class snores, and he thought of Tanith again . . . the curves of her body, the silver dagger between her breasts . . .

Let him sleep, Garrett thought, and knew the thought had nothing to do with charity. But he'd never claimed to be a saint.

Chapter Fifteen

For the third time in twenty-four hours Garrett found himself driving out of town on a dark and largely deserted highway, through eerily drifting fog. The book was on the backseat, in a briefcase, wrapped in plastic. Above the trees the moon was high and bright, with Venus glimmering beside it, and Garrett felt wide awake, impatient, and adrenalized. An old rhyme ran through his head that he hadn't even remembered knowing:

> *Lynn, Lynn, city of sin.*
> *You never come out the way you went in.*
> *Ask for water, they give you a gin . . .*
> *The girls say no and then they give in.*
> *It's the darndest city I ever been in.*

To silence the taunting rhyme he reached for the stereo dial and flipped around to talk radio, trying to catch up on how the case was being played in the media. He hit a weird kind of jackpot with a call-in talk show about youth and satanism. There were the requisite holy rollers and career Catholics claiming the devil's work and the corruption of the younger generation. One nut job was really starting to foam at the mouth, quoting in an increasingly psychotic whine: *"And every spirit that confesseth not that Jesus Christ is come in the flesh is not of God, and this is that spirit of Antichrist, and even now already it is in the world—"*

Garrett had had enough of the Bible in his youth to last a lifetime. He was reaching to switch stations when a new caller came on and a familiar word caught his attention. *"Do you know what Halloween really is? All Hallows Eve, All Souls Day? It's a Sabbat, a pagan festival. It was held to honor the Samhain, the "Lord of Death."*

Garrett leaned forward and turned up the volume. *"Samhain is the day when Satan himself comes to fellowship with his followers."*

Despite himself, Garrett felt a chill. *Thirty-six days to go . . .* a voice whispered in his head.

On the radio, the caller had worked himself into a high dudgeon. *"And this is what we're helping our children celebrate. Oh, we do it in the name of fun, but what is the real meaning? Is it still the same as in the old days? I say the answer is YES—"*

The talk-show host had had enough and abruptly moved on to the next caller, who was irate. *"You people don't even know the difference between Wicca and satanism. It's ignorance like yours that led to real witch hunts. Witches don't even believe in the devil. That's a Christian superstition. That one's all yours . . ."*

The devil, Garrett thought. *Jesus Christ. The whole world's gone batshit.*

He punched off the radio and made the turn off the highway into Lynn.

The Lamplighter was exactly as Cabarrus had said, right off 1A, in the warren of streets that was downtown Lynn: an old-fashioned inn in the style of a hunting lodge, with beams and stonework and wide windows and a broad porch. The moon was high and silvery white above. Garrett got out of his Explorer and looked around at the half-full lot. He had no idea what kind of car she would have driven, and thought briefly of Landauer's broomstick joke.

He walked up the steps and pushed through the doors.

Beyond a lobby with gleaming oak floors, a few stairs led down into a spacious lounge, with low tables around a towering river-rock hearth with a crackling fire.

He saw her instantly; she sat alone at a table near the fire, the flames flushing her face. She wore a silver blouse and black skirt, and her dark riot of hair was for the moment pulled severely back. His memory had not exaggerated—she was heart-stoppingly beautiful.

He was unable to do more than register a too-brief glance; she looked up almost immediately, directly at him. He moved down the stairs to cross to her table. Strangely, though half a dozen businessmen were scattered at the tables and at the bar, no one else in the room seemed to be looking at her. Garrett would have thought that no one would be able to look at anything else.

He took the chair across from her, though he disliked having his back to the door, and edged a little sideways to give himself more of a vantage of the rest of the room. "I appreciate your meeting me. I'm sorry to disturb you so late."

"It's not so late," she said, without smiling.

A waitress appeared by Garrett's side with a coffeepot and he nodded for her to fill his cup. "Have you eaten?" he asked Cabarrus.

"I'm fine," she said. "Another tonic," she told the waitress.

So no drinking, he thought, and felt an unprofessional stab of disappointment.

Tanith looked at him, narrowing her eyes, and he had a sudden sense she had read his thought. He cleared his throat and reached down to remove the original bloodred leather book from the briefcase, carefully unwrapped the plastic. "I can't give this to you—I brought it so you could look at it."

She was staring across the table with a completely unreadable expression. He opened the book, using the plastic wrapping as a glove, so she could see the odd writing. "Have you ever seen anything like this before?"

She focused down on the writing for a moment, then glanced up at him as if suddenly realizing he was there, and frowned. "Of course. It's a grimoire. A spell book. Of ritual magic. Where did you get it?"

"I can't tell you that."

She looked at him knowingly, and he had to shift his gaze. "The point is, it's in some kind of code, and I—we need to break it, as soon as possible." He put the book back in the plastic and handed over a few photocopied pages he'd selected before he left home. None of them had the number 333, the three triangles, or the sketch of the severed hand. He only hoped there was nothing sensitive in what he was giving her that could compromise the case.

She glanced down at the pages, and an amused look flickered over her face. He sat forward. "What? Do you know what it is?"

"The root of all evil." He tensed, and she shook her head. "It's a money spell. Get rich quick." She held the pages between her fingers dismissively. "This really is amateur hour."

"But you can break the code?"

She shrugged. "There's nothing to break. It's a straight-ahead substitution."

"What alphabet is it?"

"They're runes," she answered.

Runes. The name, as the letters, was vaguely, maddeningly familiar. "Isn't that—some kind of a game?"

"It's a Viking alphabet. Rune stones are thrown for divination—to tell fortunes."

"Can you give me an index?"

She turned over a photocopied page and took a silver pen from her bag, then swiftly wrote the alphabet from A to Z in a column on the left side of the page.

A
B
C
D
E

Then she started again from the top and began to fill in the corresponding letters in the twiglike alphabet, which was obviously something she knew well, because she did it unhesitatingly, without having to stop and think. He watched her as she wrote it out. The silver chain glimmered in the V of her neckline and he thought of the dagger between her breasts . . .

He pulled his eyes away, cleared his throat. "So you see this kind of book a lot?"

She continued writing without looking up. "Any practicing magician keeps a grimoire."

"In code?"

"It's always preferable. The more effort you put into a spell, the more effective it will be. The extra concentration and work of writing in code focuses intent, and makes manifestation more likely."

At the bottom of the page she added six double letters: NG, GH, EA, AE, OE, TH—and wrote the corresponding symbols beside them, then handed the sheet across the table.

"That's it?" he said, staring down at the simple index with a sense of unreality.

"That's it. Oh, and most of these letters can be reversed, so anytime you see a mirror image of one of these symbols, it's really just the same letter."

He looked up from the page, across the table at her. "Thank you. I—this is incredibly helpful."

She looked down at the remaining pages in front of her. "I have to say, all of this is strictly Ritual Magick 101. That's not the book of an accomplished magician; it clearly belongs to an acolyte. A dabbler. Anyone can get this stuff off the Internet." She looked up at him. "It's his book, isn't it? Jason Moncrief."

"I'm sorry, that's confidential."

She looked at him, then suddenly leaned across the table and slid her hand into the plastic sheathing the grimoire so that her palm lay flat on the leather cover. Garrett was so startled he didn't have time to react. Her eyes were black and unfocused. Then her face cleared and she sat back, withdrawing her hand, before he could do or say anything.

She pushed back her chair and stood, pointing down at the book with one finger. "This one has killed no one. Others have died. More will die. And you have the wrong man. And you know it."

She turned without another word, and walked across the gleaming wood floor, up the stairs, and out.

Chapter Sixteen

THE HAND OF GLORY

To make a Hand of Glory, you must acquire a corpse no more than twenty-four hours dead.   Sever the left hand at the wrist with a sharp knife.

Take a winding sheet and squeeze out the blood of the hand to dry it. A pound of flesh should be cut from the corpse and rendered down to produce a bowl of fat.   Preserve then the hand for two weeks in an earthenware jar filled with salt, saltpeter, and black pepper—all well powdered and mix't.

Remove the hand and dust off all of the powder. Place the hand in a hot oven that is fired with vervain and fir. Leave it for an hour and then remove. Mold the drying hand into a fist, with space in the center to take a candle.

Fashion a candle from the previously rendered corpse's fat and virgin wax. The wick should be made from freshly spun flax.   Coax the candle into the curled fingers, and squeeze them tightly, gripping the candle firmly in position. When complete with the candle fixed into the mummified fist, you have a Hand of Glory!

With a Hand of Glory, you have a power. You have magic! As you light the candle, you cast your spell: "Hand of Glory, Hand of Glory, put my foe to sleep, in a sleep that is fast and deep!"

Your intended victims will not be able to rouse themselves . . . you will be free to do whatever mischief you wish to do.

Do what Thou wilt shall be the whole of the Law. Zazas Zazas Nasatanada Zazas!!

Landauer lowered the translated page, shook his head to clear it, and looked over to where Garrett sat on the windowsill, nervously drinking coffee.

The dawn light was gray behind him, and Landauer's face was gray as well. Garrett suspected it was not entirely because of the lighting.

"Jesus."

"Yeah," Garrett said quietly.

Landauer dropped the page down on the table, and was probably unaware that he wiped his hands on his pants after he did so. "So . . . this was in that—book."

"Grimoire."

"And you seriously think he took Erin's hand to make a fucking candle out of it?"

"There's the drawing of it, right there." Garrett nodded to the grimoire, open to the page with the sketch of the Hand of Glory. "And the spell calls for a left hand . . ."

Landauer pushed the grimoire away from him at the table with a queasy expression that Garrett found painfully familiar; he remembered his own trouble touching the book. "This is some seriously sick shit we're talking about, G."

"Yeah." Garrett stood, and walked around his living room restlessly. "But it's a direct link between Moncrief's grimoire and Erin's murder: her left hand was cut from her body. And less than a month before her murder, Jason Moncrief wrote out a black magic spell that called for the left hand of a dead human being. I'd call that evidence of premeditation."

"Yeah . . ." Landauer said. He looked down again at the open grimoire. "That's some good work, there," he said, finally.

"God bless Google," Garrett said, keeping his voice even as he lied.

He had been back home just under two hours after he'd left, to find Landauer still sleeping hard in the bedroom. Garrett had stood in the hall feeling both as if he'd gotten away with something and as if he'd never been gone at all, that he'd simply fallen asleep in his chair and experienced a quickly fading but disturbing dream.

He'd spent most of the rest of the night using the code sheet Tanith had written out for him to translate the candle spell, and then the titles of the other spells in the grimoire to see if there was anything else that deserved immediate attention. Then he stashed Tanith's code sheet in a desk drawer, looked up a rune substitution code online, and printed it out, to explain how he had been able to break the code. Tracks covered, no need to elaborate. And as long as it got done, what difference did it make how it got done?

Landauer looked at him appraisingly, but after a minute looked away. "Well, if it wasn't a slam dunk before, it sure as shit is looking like one now."

They finished the charging package together, with the Hand of Glory detailed under the section titled "*Motive*," and at 10:00 A.M. they were in the conference room on the second floor of Schroeder, drinking more coffee as Carolyn and Lieutenant Malloy read through the evidence at the long table.

"Spells," Malloy muttered, with a tone of biblically righteous anger. "Black magic."

Carolyn looked up from the charging package with that gleam in her eyes. "Gentlemen, this is very impressive. This is a solid suggestion of premeditation. We may very well be able to force a plea."

Malloy hesitated, then nodded acknowledgment. "Fine work," he said gruffly, and Garrett felt a sharp stab of victory.

Take that, tight ass.

———

As Garrett walked back toward the homicide room, he heard a female voice behind him. "Detective Garrett." For a split second, as he turned, he was sure he would see the witch.

It was Carolyn, of course.

She stopped at a formal distance, and looked him over. "You must be dead," she said, but there was a suggestive warmth in her voice.

"I got a few hours," he said, dismissing it.

Her eyes shone at him. "It's a huge case, Garrett. Huge. You'll get national attention, and you deserve it."

He was annoyed at the thrill that gave him. "You may be right. Right now I just want to make sure it's all lined up."

"Well . . ." She glanced to the side to see if they were still alone. "Call me."

"You know it," he said automatically, but for once the thought didn't give him an erotic charge.

He drove home on autopilot, and didn't even remember how he got to the bedroom. The last image in his mind, before he fell into a comatose sleep, was the yellow flame of a lit candle clutched in a severed human hand.

Chapter Seventeen

Garrett jolted awake, and not because he was finished sleeping.

There was someone in the house.

It was dark, but he had no conception of what time it was. He heard nothing, could see nothing, but knew beyond doubt there was another person in the house with him. It was an unmistakable sense of presence.

He grabbed for the Glock in the top drawer of the bed stand, discarded the idea of clothes. Instead he threw off the bedcovers.

Naked, he eased into the hall, his heart pumping hard. It was dark, but there was a light at the end of it, dimmer than the living-room light would have been. *In the kitchen, then . . .*

He stopped at the end of the hall, pressed against the wall, and steadied his weapon as he strained to hear.

There was a soft, hydraulic swish. *Refrigerator?*

He carefully stuck his head around the wall of the hall to survey the dark living room. No one. Then he crossed the hardwood floor in swift steps, stalking barefoot, holding the Glock in a double grip before him, and peered around the separating wall into the kitchen.

Carolyn stood at the refrigerator, blond hair cascading around bare golden shoulders. She wore nothing but a clinging cream silk teddy and held a dripping bottle of Cristal, and looked as out of place in his little kitchen as a runway model in a trailer park double-wide.

She swiveled on showgirl legs, surveyed Garrett's Glock and his nakedness, and smiled a cat smile. "I hope you got some sleep. We have celebrating to do."

She poured champagne into the two flutes she held carelessly in her left hand and walked barefoot and pedicured across the kitchen tiles to him. She stopped in front of him and gently pushed the gun aside. "Sorry," she said briefly, barely glancing at it. She put a glass in his hand and clinked her own against it, then drained the flute as she leaned forward against him. There was nothing but the thinnest silk between his now aching hardness and the warm wet of her. Garrett ground himself forward as he drained his glass, then pushed her against the counter, pushed the silk aside, and eased the length of his shaft into her. Carolyn laughed deep in her throat and wrapped one sleek thigh around him as he bent her back on the counter, tearing the silk of her teddy down, exposing lush breasts that he pressed his palms into, feeling hard nipples against his hands as he thrust; spearing, slamming, into the wet suction of her cleft. He moved his mouth to her breasts, sucking greedily as he clutched the globes of her ass and his aching cock plunged deeper and deeper and she gasped into his ear. And as he ground himself into her, he had a flash of dark hair spilling on creamy skin and a gleaming dagger between perfect breasts and the thought made him explode in molten, volcanic waves, with an inarticulate cry as he collapsed into Carolyn's heat.

Chapter Eighteen

He woke again, this time to full and painfully bright sun. He knew from the angle that it was way past dawn; it was not the shiny brightness of morning, but used daylight, afternoon daylight.

Waking more, he realized he was alone in bed. Carolyn was long gone, leaving a lingering scent of Dolce & Gabbana on the sheets. Her last words, before he'd dropped into a black abyss of sleep, had been, "I think you should meet my father." And exhausted as he had been, Garrett had registered the words with an electric thrill.

Now, turning the idea over, he understood that he had passed some test, had graduated to a new level. *Meet the family.*

He lay back on his pillow, marveling. This was turning into a hell of a fall. Even though all of this—the high-profile nature of the case, the apparently quick solve—was partly just luck. Then again, luck was possibly part of the ongoing test, with Carolyn. He suspected luck was toward the top of Carolyn's internal list of non-negotiable requirements.

The thought gave him a twinge of discomfort he didn't want to look at, so he glanced at the clock instead. 3:00. That was P.M., which meant he'd slept nearly thirty hours, minus, of course, their little interlude.

But for once he didn't feel any jolt of tension, of urgency to be somewhere. He stretched, savoring the feeling—and the warm fragrance of perfume and sex.

It's not that they could stop working, never that. But the investigation had entered a new phase, a slower phase. Now they had to build an airtight case (unless the charging package proved to be enough to force a plea, which neither Garrett nor Carolyn thought was likely).

And they had time. Justice was slow. Realistically, after the arraignment, Jason Moncrief's trial would not be for months. There was no longer that urgent rush . . .

The word *Samhain* flickered briefly in Garrett's mind, spiking his pulse.

But he immediately shut down the thought. He would prove Jason did it, beyond a shadow of a doubt, and that would be that. There would be no replays, no more killing. Their suspect was in custody. The world was safe.

He threw back the bedclothes and stood.

It was 5:00 P.M. before he rolled into Schroeder, and Landauer had barely preceded him. The big man looked him over knowingly. "You look *relaxed*, this fine evening, Rhett."

Garrett allowed himself a small indiscretion. "Yeah, I just about got myself relaxed into a coronary." He grinned at Landauer, the cat who ate the canary.

"Wild women," Landauer said. "Rich, connected wild women," he added. He looked pretty relaxed himself. Land didn't talk much about his wife except the obligatory marital bitching, but there was no bite to the barbs. Garrett knew that—except for the smoking—Bette kept the big man in line, and that was saying a lot.

The newly relaxed partners headed for the lieutenant's office, and not even the prospect of facing Malloy could take the swagger out of their steps.

"What's on the agenda for tonight?" Malloy began coolly, without preamble. So much for that brief flash of goodwill. Garrett reined in his thoughts, kept his face carefully neutral.

As Carolyn had predicted, there would be no getting in to see Jason, and his high-powered lawyer had also denied requests to interview the family, not that there was much of one. The gag order was frustrating, but it made sense to Garrett. No lawyer with a single brain cell in his head would want anyone questioning that kid.

He answered Malloy, his voice level. "We interview potential corroborating witnesses: Moncrief's bandmates. I want to establish an ongoing threat to Erin Carmody." *I want someone to give me incontestable proof he did it*, he thought to himself silently. *I want to hear someone say, "Yeah, it was him."*

I want to believe it.

"Good," Malloy sniffed, shuffling files so he wouldn't have to meet Garrett's eyes.

Fuck you, Garrett told him silently. *I'm on the rise, and you know it. You can kiss my shapely Irish ass, and sooner than you think. You keep that chair warm for me, L.T.*

"Yes, sir," he said aloud, and followed Landauer out.

Garrett had found regular band rehearsals listed on a calendar taken from Jason's desk drawers. Instead of calling ahead the partners decided to just show up; the element of surprise had worked in their favor before.

The rehearsal space was in a warehouse near Kenmore Square, on a dicey side street just a stone's throw from Cauldron. Jason's bandmates were far less eerie in person than they appeared in the poster and on the cover of the CD, really just eighteen- and nineteen-year-old kids with dyed hair and black clothes—and none had Jason's feral charisma. The long-haired keyboard player, Todd Hartlaub, was cute in a puppy-dog way that probably netted them a sizable number of young female fans, and he did the talking for the other two: a bassist who was a good six and a half feet tall, with black-rimmed glasses and huge hands, a cross between Ray Manzarek and Tommy Tune; and a spaced-out drummer, mop-haired and clearly, hopelessly stoned.

"When was the last time you saw Jason?" Garrett began.

The boys looked around at each other. "Two weeks," the keyboard player answered. *Front man*, Garrett thought.

"Can you be any more specific than that? A day?"

Hartlaub assumed a serious and deferential expression, but those big brown eyes were watching the detectives carefully. "Yeah. nine-eleven."

Garrett frowned. Something already sounded off. "So two weeks ago today. Don't you rehearse more often than that?"

"Hell, yeah," Hartlaub said, resentment plain in his voice. "He just wasn't showing up. Then he fucking missed a gig. We were always hauling ass to cover for him. So—we voted, and he was out."

That's interesting, Garrett thought. *I bet Jason wasn't happy about that.* He looked over at Landauer, who nodded slightly, tapping his unlit cigarette against the edge of a speaker. Garrett pulled out a pocket calendar and looked back to the keyboardist.

"You told him he was out that Tuesday, then? September eleventh?"

"Right," Hartlaub said heavily.

Garrett made a note on the calendar. "And?" he prodded.

"He lost it. Totally. Broke things." The kid's eyes were oblique. "Kicked in a drum." Behind him, the drummer roused himself from his haze to nod vigorous assent. "He did that." Hartlaub nodded toward the wall, where there was a hole in the Sheetrock the size of a fist, with cracks radiating out from it in the plaster—a brutal punch. Garrett saw Landauer raise an eyebrow, and Garrett himself had a flashback to the feeling of Jason's uncanny strength when he'd attacked Land in the dorm room.

"Would you say that was typical of Jason—that kind of temper?"

"No," the bassist suddenly spoke. Danny Coyle.

"Last few months, though . . ." Hartlaub looked away.

"What?" Garrett prodded.

Hartlaub shrugged. "He was different."

"How long have you known him?"

"We've been playing since eighth grade." That was the tall bass player again, in a quiet voice.

Hartlaub shot him an oblique look and continued himself. "Last year we were really going, you know, getting some serious gigs. But this summer he started fucking up, big time."

"Where were you all on Friday night?" Garrett asked without any change in tone. He had not forgotten Frazer's profile of the "youth subculture" killers: the bandmates who had sacrificed their classmate to the devil.

Hartlaub started to answer, then his eyes widened, and he spoke slowly. "We had a gig at Man Ray. It was big—the equinox party."

Another equinox party.

The bandmates were nodding assent. "From when to when?" Garrett queried.

Hartlaub answered again. "Got there at nine to set up. We went on, like, eleven . . . did three sets, broke it all down after."

They would check that alibi, but Garrett didn't think Hartlaub would be stupid enough to offer it if it wasn't true. "Was Jason supposed to do that gig with you?"

"Oh, yeah," Hartlaub said, and his voice was tight. "Why do you think he was so pissed?"

"Have any of you heard from him or seen him since that rehearsal two weeks ago?"

"No," Hartlaub said, and the other boys echoed him.

Garrett suddenly shifted focus. "Did you know Erin Carmody?"

"No," Hartlaub said. Garrett looked to the other two boys, who shook their heads.

"She never came to any rehearsals?"

"No."

"How about performances? Gigs?"

"No," Hartlaub said. Again, the bassist shook his head in agreement, and a beat behind, the drummer mirrored him.

"Are you sure?" Garrett pulled out a photo of Erin, the radiant senior portrait, and moved around to each of the musicians in turn, so all the boys could see. He was watching their faces carefully. Again, universal head shaking, more seriously sober than Garrett was expecting. The bassist turned his head away from the photo in what looked like genuine emotion. He spoke, and his voice was tight.

"She didn't. But her asshole boyfriend did."

Garrett stared at the bassist. "Did what?"

The tall young man didn't look away from him. "Came to a gig. That jock."

"Kevin Teague?" Garrett demanded. The bassist nodded. "Which gig was that?"

"It was at Cauldron."

Garrett looked at Landauer. Teague had said he'd never been to Cauldron. Garrett felt his pulse speeding up. "When was that?"

"About . . ." The bassist stopped, thinking. "September seventh. He stood in front of the stage the whole time just staring at Jason, real asswipe stuff. And then followed him out to the parking lot and beat the shit out of him."

"Teague," Garrett repeated.

"Yeah. Teague."

"Did you guys report it?" Garrett asked, even knowing there was no way.

Hartlaub rolled his eyes. The bassist lifted his shoulders, resigned. "We weren't there. The pussy just jumped him. Split his lip, broke a rib. What do you do?"

I knew that arrogant shit was up to no good, Garrett thought to himself. *But killing Erin to get back at Jason? That's a stretch.*

He circled the rehearsal space, trying to collect his thoughts. He spotted a stack of flyers on the low, burn-scarred table, reached, and casually picked one up. "So what does this mean—'Current 333'?"

The keyboardist shrugged. "I don't know."

Garrett stopped, looked at him. "You don't *know*? It's the title of your CD."

Hartlaub looked uncomfortable. "That was Jason's trip. Something about entropy." He glanced toward the bass player. "'Chaos magic,' he said. It sounded—you know—edgy. He wrote a couple of songs about it—Choronzon, the Master of Hallucinations."

Choronzon, again.

Garrett realized with a start that he hadn't yet listened to the CD they were talking about, though he'd been meaning to all along. He mentally kicked himself for the oversight. There could be any number of emotional or virtual clues in the music or lyrics.

"So what is that, satanism? Black magic?" Garrett asked aloud.

"Jason called it ceremonial magic," the bassist said. "He was reading Aleister Crowley, especially." Garrett thought again that Hartlaub might be the front man, but formal education or not, it was this bassist who had it going on.

"But ceremonial magic wasn't something you practiced or believed?" Garrett asked the bassist.

"No," Hartlaub scoffed.

"Hell, no," murmured the bassist. And the drummer shook his mop of hair.

"Do you know if he attended any group ceremonies, or hung out with other practitioners?"

The bassist and Hartlaub looked at each other. "Nothing like that," the bassist answered. "It was just a slam at the colonel—you know, his father—the whole military/religious thing. The old man's a fascist, always trying to force Jason into ROTC, used to not let him play, that shit. So what was guaranteed to piss him off the most?"

Hartlaub jumped in. "But then it started getting whacked."

"Whacked how?" Landauer asked.

Hartlaub just shook his head. The bassist answered slowly. "We'd be laying a track and he'd start chanting in the middle of a song and go on and on, we couldn't get him to stop. It was like he was gone." The young man, who towered over Garrett by four or five inches, grimaced in what looked very much like revulsion. "And when we played it back—"

"Shut up, Danny," Hartlaub warned.

"Come on, you know it's—"

Garrett stepped between them. "This is a murder investigation," he reminded Hartlaub coldly, and the keyboardist backed down instantly. Garrett turned to the bass player.

"When you played it back, what?"

The bassist's voice dropped. "There were other voices on the recording. Not ours. This—babbling—river of voices, all at once."

Garrett was aware of Landauer tensing in recognition just as he did. And Landauer didn't even know about the voices Garrett had discovered on Jason's interview tape; Garrett hadn't remembered to tell him. *That's three times, now, the babble of voices. What the fuck is that about?*

"Freaked me the fuck out," the drummer mumbled, off in his own world. There was a distinct chill in the room.

"So—what?" Landauer suddenly said, too loudly. "You thought he was pranking you? Fucking with the sound?"

The three musicians were silent. "Yeah," Hartlaub finally said, flatly. "Sure."

There was a long silence, which Garrett finally broke. "When you heard Erin Carmody was dead and Jason was arrested, what did you think?"

"Complete freakout," the drummer muttered from the drum set.

Garrett glanced to him. "You were surprised?"

"Whoever thinks that shit is going to happen?" Hartlaub said.

"Did you think it was possible?" Garrett said, looking around at all the boys.

The bassist glanced toward the hole in the wall, but said nothing.

Hartlaub shrugged . . . then for a moment, he looked bleak, older than his years. "Something wasn't right."

"Ever get the sense this kid wasn't right?" Landauer said as they walked over dirty sidewalks back to the Cavalier, with traffic blowing by them on the industrial street. "At least now we know why. His daddy was a sumbitch. Explains everything. My daddy was a sumbitch, too. Whose wasn't? Nowadays that's supposed to *mean* something." Land waggled his fingers like a distressed drag queen. "Boo fucking hoo."

Garrett let all that pass. "Teague lied about never going to Cauldron," he said.

Land shook his head. "You know, Rhett, I knew you were gonna be all over that. Why don't you just admit you have a hard-on for that guy?"

"I'm just saying—he lied." *He's an asshole, with a temper, he's a lot stronger than Jason, and he was pissed.*

"Bottom line, his alibi's gold," Landauer reminded him. It was true. Kevin Teague had spent the night of Erin's murder on a basketball court in full view of hundreds of sports fans, then on a bus full of his teammates plus four coaches and assistant coaches, and then in a hotel suite in Connecticut with five other people. Unless he had hired someone to kill Erin, he had had nothing to do with it.

And Garrett had to admit, everything else the band had said pointed to Jason, not Teague. It was all starting to sound like a broken record. A disturbed kid, possibly psychotic. A perfect match for Frazer's profile. But there were some things that didn't fit, that twisted and poked at Garrett like broken glass.

They had reached the Cavalier, and as Landauer stepped off the curb onto the street, Garrett suddenly spoke. "You catch that about the babbling voices?"

Landauer's face tightened. "Kid is a musician. Sound technician," he reminded Garrett.

"It was on our interview tape, Land." Garrett put his hands on the top of the Cavalier and looked across at his partner as cars raced by behind him. "I played it back and I heard it."

Landauer looked back at him for a minute. "The stereo was on, remember? Don'tcha think that might account for any—babbling?" He shook his head. "Don't let all this freak you out, G. Kid's in jail. What's he gonna do?" He pulled open the passenger door and lowered himself into the car. After a moment, Garrett did the same.

Inside, as Garrett started the engine, Landauer leaned forward and switched on the radio.

"In our top local news, the district attorney's office will seek charges of first-degree murder for Amherst sophomore Jason Moncrief in the killing of W. P. Carmody heiress Erin Carmody. Carmody's mutilated body was found in the Pine Street landfill on Saturday morning. Both students were residents of Morris Pratt Hall on the Amherst campus; authorities are investigating rumors that Moncrief may have been stalking Carmody."

"Sounds like Shelley's been talking," Landauer grunted. Garrett frowned; he'd been thinking the same thing.

The female anchor continued. *"Sources speculate that there were satanic aspects to the killing."*

"Look what you learn on the radio," Landauer said with exaggerated delight. "There are satanic aspects to our killing."

The radio anchor continued, in that oh-so-serious news voice. *"Assistant District Attorney Carolyn Carver announced the charges on the courthouse steps."*

Carolyn's smooth, silky voice replaced the announcer's. Garrett felt himself start to harden, even hearing her on the radio. *"The state is certain that the grand jury will hand down charges of murder in the first degree in this incomprehensible crime."*

Landauer glanced toward Garrett. "She's a star."

"Yes, she is," Garrett agreed without inflection. In his mind he could see Tanith Cabarrus leaning across the table to put her hand on the grimoire, see her black eyes, hear her voice.

"You're wrong. And you know it."

He reached and turned up the radio, letting Carolyn drown out the voices in his head. *"We are confident that we will win justice for Erin Carmody and her family."*

Garrett made the turn downtown, hoping to God that she was right.

Chapter Nineteen

The grand jury hearing went off without a hitch.

Garrett and Landauer spent a day testifying in the stifling conference room at Three Pemberton Square, the high-rise courthouse. Jason did not appear; the defendant's attorney does not put up a defense for grand jury hearings, and all the state had to show was probable cause. Carolyn smoothly and expertly led the detectives through their recounting of the witnesses' testimony, and after just an hour of deliberation the grand jury had handed down a true bill of indictment: murder in the first degree.

The detectives decided to take a well-deserved night off, but Garrett pled exhaustion to Carolyn and took a rain check on her offer of a debauched celebration. The real truth was that his gut was gnawing at him. His grand jury testimony had been an honest presentation of the facts as he knew them, but all his doubts about the case were raging. Most people they arrested were so obviously, patently guilty that Garrett never had any qualms. Even in the highly unlikely circumstance that the suspect was not guilty of what they'd arrested him for, he was without a doubt guilty of *something*.

But this case—there was nothing that felt right about it.

Now as the sun set outside his dining-room window, Garrett sat at the table that was never used for dining, surrounded by stacks of Jason's belongings: the magic books, the bloodred leather grimoire, the file boxes containing the contents of Jason's desk drawers and bookshelves.

Garrett pulled the grimoire toward him and opened the cover. The pages were dated, almost as if the book were a diary of sorts. Garrett stood and retrieved the substitution code Tanith had written for him from the desk drawer where he'd hidden it, then sat back down with it to translate the first date. Jason had begun the book in May, May 14. And according to his friends, his personality had changed radically over the summer, and not for the better. His behavior had become bizarre, he had violent outbursts, he was scaring people around him. Then on September 21, a girl he had known and likely dated, and had been with that night, was murdered.

How does that happen?

Garrett reached for a plastic evidence crate, the books and other items he had requested from Jason's dorm room, and rooted around in it until he found the *Current 333* CD. He rose and put the disc in his sound system, then stood in his living room, listening. It was death metal but with some sophisticated musicality going on (undoubtedly coming from the bass player, and possibly Jason himself). Garrett could hear the influence of The Cure, U2, R.E.M. The word "Choronzon" stood out immediately. *"The Master of Hallucinations,"* Jason had said, and now, listening to the music, Garrett caught the words *"My Master"* and *"Mighty devil"* and something that sounded like *"Sacrifice to your will,"* but Jason's voice was little more than a growl and Garrett couldn't be sure what he was hearing. He checked the CD for liner notes, but there were no lyrics.

He stared into space and thought for a moment, recalling the words of the tall bassist. *"He was reading Aleister Crowley, especially."*

Garrett turned back to the box and lifted out the books, separating out the volumes written by Aleister Crowley. He sat with them and turned to the index of the first, *Confessions*, looking in the C's for Choronzon and Current 333, and flipped to an inner page to read:

The name of the Dweller in the Abyss is Choronzon . . . The Abyss is empty of being; it is filled with all possible forms, each equally inane, each therefore evil in the only true sense of the word—that is, meaningless but malignant, in so far as it craves to become real. These forms swirl senselessly into haphazard heaps like dust devils, and each such chance aggregation asserts itself to be an individual and shrieks, "I am I!"

Garrett shook his head. Disturbing . . . but incoherent. He took another book from the pile, *The Vision and the Voice*, used the index again, to find:

And whoso passeth into the outermost Abyss—except he be of them that understand—holdeth out his hands, and boweth his neck, unto the chains of Choronzon. And as a devil he walketh about the earth, immortal, and he blasteth the flowers of the earth, and he corrupteth the fresh air, and he maketh poisonous the water; and the fire that is the friend of man, and the pledge of his aspiration, seeing that it mounteth ever upward as a Pyramid, and seeing that man stole it in a hollow tube from Heaven—even that fire he turneth into ruin, and madness, and fever, and destruction.

Garrett pushed the book away from him, feeling a churning in his gut. That sentence: *"He blasteth the flowers of the earth."*

The burned footprints and scorched flowers.

"And as a devil he walketh about the earth, immortal . . ."

Garrett immediately stood to shake off the thought, and walked the floor of the room. *We don't need to get caught up in any of this demon stuff.*

"Sacrifice to thy will . . ."

He turned and looked back toward the pile of books on the table. *But what if it goes to motive?* Did Jason kill Erin as a sacrifice to this "demon," Choronzon? Just as the three boys in Frazer's psychological profile who killed their classmate as a sacrifice to Satan?

Garrett circled the table, tensely. He was no closer to understanding what Choronzon was; if anything he was more confused.

And it seemed to him that there was more than a little mental illness going on with this Crowley.

I need an interpreter, he thought, and immediately Tanith Cabarrus was in his mind.

He leaned across the table to pick up the last Crowley book again . . . then he froze, looking down.

There was a silver bookstore label on the back of the book, with an address:

Book of Shadows
411 Essex St., West
Salem, MA
978-555-0728

Book of Shadows. Garrett heard a feminine voice saying it. He turned to the table and grabbed the murder book on Erin Carmody. He turned to the police reports section and looked down at the page for his initial interview with Tanith Cabarrus. The address and phone number were the same as on the label.

Jason had gotten those books at Tanith's shop.

She knew him.

Chapter Twenty

The wind was high that evening, frantic and gusting, and the moon fat and nearly full over the waving branches and rustling leaves, as Garrett drove into Salem Town.

Landauer had not picked up when Garrett called him, and Garrett had debated with himself less than ten minutes before he headed up to Salem on his own. For the first half of the drive he had wrestled with half a dozen ways to justify himself: it was their night off; Landauer had made it cheerfully clear that if Garrett called him for any reason whatsoever he was a dead man; Malloy would never approve of consulting with a professed witch so Garrett was forced to hide his activity; he didn't want to rope Landauer into a wild goose chase, he didn't want Land to catch shit from Malloy if he found out they were considering information given to them by a witch . . .

Then he gave up and admitted to himself that every one of his excuses was bullshit. He simply wanted to see the witch alone.

Miraculously he found a parking spot on Essex, and started off through the rippling wind, trees and bushes stirred into green frenzies around him, and onto the cobbled street of the pedestrian mall, the center of town. Entering the warren of narrow streets was like stepping back through time; the tight rows of colonial buildings were carefully preserved, with wrought-iron lampposts lining the walkways and antique signage hanging from hooks and chains above the shops. The town's theme was inescapable: Essex Street and the town square were crowded with witch supply shops, psychics and tarot readers, and witch history museums, complete with soundtracks of howling winds and creaking doors piped out onto the sidewalks, enhancing the naturally atmospheric colonial storefronts and autumn wind rustling through the trees.

Garrett had learned the story in sixth grade, and it all was coming back to him now: the witch trials of 1692 that started with the "possession" and accusations of a handful of supposedly bewitched teenage and preteen girls and ended in the execution of twenty accused witches, and the imprisonment of 150 accused, five more of whom died in Salem Town's wretched jail. It was a chapter in American history that had left a lasting impression on him, laced as it was with repressed sexuality, voodoo, magic, torture, execution, and the strong possibility of hallucinogens: Garrett remembered one theory that the witch hysteria was the result of the whole town being high on ergot, a psychedelic mold that grows on rye. And then with a ripple of unease he recalled that lurking in the shadows of the tale, documented in the court transcriptions, was the devil himself, to whom the accused witches had supposedly promised their souls.

The story hit every hippie, punk, Goth, Dionysian, counterculture pleasure center that humans possessed, and modern Salem's tourist board took advantage of every creepy, erotic, haunting, bloody detail of it.

Already Halloween decorations were everywhere. Women in black clothing walked the streets around Garrett; he even passed some people in full costumes: zombies, pirates, and the ever-present vampires. The whole place had always given him an unsettled feeling. Tonight it didn't help that he had the dissonant sounds of the *Current 333* CD and the strange descriptions of Choronzon working on his ganglia. And even as he thought it, his heart gave a sick lurch . . . as he spotted a statue of a decapitated man holding his own bloody head in front of the Salem Wax Museum. Garrett walked quickly by, turning his face from the sight; it was too grim a reminder of Erin's real-life fate. And he felt a flash of anger as well. He himself had fallen away from Catholicism long ago, but this deliberate courting of the dark side still felt to him dangerous and wrong. He was far out of his comfort level in every way. *Going to see a witch about a satanic killing.*

He had reached the 400 block of Essex, the heart of downtown: rows of walk-in shops with the worst of touristy excess. He began checking the addresses for 411. He had not called ahead, so that he could see Cabarrus in her element but without any warning.

Now he realized even though he'd been watching the numbers above the shops, he must have missed it; he was already at 413 Essex. He walked back to the last shop he'd passed, and found himself staring up at the number 409.

There was no 411 Essex.

Garrett turned in the street, frowning, as he tried to push down an uneasy feeling. Across the street two women . . . *witches* . . . in capes and long black skirts turned to look at him as they passed, and Garrett had a sudden sense of reality wobbling. *Get a grip*, he told himself.

He looked around him for some sign of the shop. Up ahead was a wooden sign hanging by chains depicting a witch figure hunched over a crystal ball and the lettering: **Which Witch?** Fog rolled from the doorway onto the sidewalk.

Garrett walked up and through the open door. Mist swirled around his feet from the fog machine set just inside. The shop was dim and the music was Hollywood eerie. Amid the shelves of crystals and ceramic objets, a sharp-faced woman in her early forties sat at a round table, dressed in a gypsyish purple skirt and a black fishnet shawl. She looked up from the table and a flicker of interest crossed her features as she took Garrett in.

"May I help you?" she purred.

"I'm looking for a shop called Book of Shadows."

The gleam in her eyes dulled. "You want Essex West. This is East. But you don't want *her*, believe me."

"Why is that?" Garrett asked automatically.

She smiled, and there was something predatory in it. "Believe it or not, our profession attracts some unstable people. Best to steer clear of *that* one." She paused suggestively. "But if it's a reading you want, I can do one for you. You won't be sorry." The glitter was back in her eyes, an unmistakable invitation.

"Thanks anyway," he said, and moved out of the shop.

Garrett found his car again and breathed easier as soon as he was off the main drag. Essex West was a few blocks off the downtown center, a quiet residential street. The house at 411 was a two-story Victorian and well maintained. A discreet hand-carved and painted sign on a column of the porch read:

BOOK OF SHADOWS

Books, Herbs, Readings, Psychic Healing

There were lights in the big picture window downstairs and the columns of the porch were crossed with dried cornstalks, which Garrett had seen on many of the lampposts, street signs, and porch pillars while driving into town. Some witch thing, no doubt. Otherwise, the outside of the shop was devoid of the usual flamboyant Halloween paraphernalia, and there was no fog machine. That, at least, was a point in Cabarrus's favor.

Garrett cruised by the shop and then parked his Explorer half a block down the street so he could approach the house on foot. A small, lit sign in the window said OPEN and so he reached for the knob and walked in.

A tinkling bell announced his presence, and a white cat curled on the counter beside the cash register lifted its head to regard Garrett with green-glass eyes.

Aside from the cat, the shop was empty and very still, but there was—there was no other way to say it—an *energy* about it. Candles flickered in wrought-iron candelabra, diffusing a subtle and intoxicating fragrance.

It looked to be four downstairs rooms: the one Garrett was in, two book-lined rooms to either side of it, and a back room with its doorway concealed by a deep blue velvet curtain embroidered with glittering stars and planets. Glass jewelry cases displayed hand-wrought ornaments of silver, and gemstones on velvet stands. A wall of shelves behind the counter was lined with herbs and powders in glass jars. Another case held an assortment of card decks, variations of the Tarot; silver wands set with crystals, mysterious lumps in velvet pouches—and gleaming silver daggers. Garrett felt his pulse jump at the sight.

And still no one emerged from the back room. *Very trusting,* Garrett thought. *Or maybe there's some kind of spell on the place.*

Since he was alone, and curious, he stepped into the next room to peruse the shelves.

He took a book out of a shelf at random and looked at the back cover—sure enough, the silver *Book of Shadows* sticker was on the bottom right corner. Then he gave the room an appraising glance, and stepped to a bookcase labeled "MAGICK" and a shelf labeled "C," where he quickly located the same books he'd found in Jason Moncrief's dorm room: Aleister Crowley's *The Book of the Law* . . . *The Vision and the Voice* . . . *Magick in Theory and Practice* . . .

He heard movement in the main room, and low voices. He turned, walked quietly toward the doorway. He stepped to the side of the door and looked carefully around the door frame.

Tanith stood in front of the silver-starred velvet curtain with a petite young woman, college age at most, dressed in black tank top and jeans, with a punkish blond pageboy, and ear and nose and eyebrow piercings. The gold glitter eye shadow on and under her eyes was marred by streaks of tears . . . she was still crying as she turned impulsively to Tanith and threw her arms around her, hugging her hard.

Garrett barely heard her whispered, "Thank you." Tanith took her hand and tucked what looked like a small drawstring bag into her palm.

"Blessed Be," Tanith said, and stroked her cheek.

The girl took a step back, then walked toward the door shakily.

She turned to give Tanith an ambiguous glance before she pushed quickly out the door. Tanith stood with her back to Garrett, watching the girl leave . . .

Then without turning, she spoke aloud in that velvety voice, "Detective Garrett."

Garrett felt both a shock and a rush of heat at her words. Tanith Cabarrus turned slowly to face him. She was backlit by the starry lights decorating the store, which emphasized the fall of her dark hair and the tiny tightness of her waist. She was corseted, he thought mindlessly, she must be; he could have spanned her waistline with his hands. The thought and sight did not improve his disposition in the least.

"What a surprise," Cabarrus said, her eyes on his face and her voice dripping with irony.

"You didn't see me coming?" he shot back, without thinking. "I thought that was your job."

He saw the curl of a smile on her mouth. "It's been a slow day," she said. "Perhaps it will improve," she added, and it was all he could do not to shove her against the wall and take her there. Her eyes gleamed at him. "And what can I do for you?" she asked in a sultry drawl, as if she knew exactly what he was thinking.

"Who was that girl?" he demanded.

"A client," she said, and did not elaborate. They locked eyes, staring at each other in the glimmering dark.

"I had some more questions about the case," Garrett said evenly. "I'm sorry to drop in unannounced."

She smiled with bitter amusement at the lie. "What questions would those be? You've indicted your man. You've closed the case. What more do you want?"

Garrett answered patiently. "All an indictment means is that we have probable cause for a trial. I'm still building the case."

"But your mind is made up," she challenged him.

He hesitated. "I have questions."

She looked at him sharply, then something changed in her face and she smiled at him, but he noticed it didn't reach her eyes.

"Will you have some tea, then?"

His face must have betrayed him because she glanced toward the racks of herbs and added with exaggerated innocence, "Nothing exotic. Just Earl Grey, if you like."

She turned and stepped through the silver-studded curtain at the back of the room. Garrett stood still in the doorway, then crossed the polished wood floor and moved through the curtain, feeling velvet brush against his face. He found himself in a small, dark-painted room lit only by standing candelabra. Two ornate, high-backed Victorian chairs were set on opposite sides of a round table; a deck of Tarot cards lay in the center of the table. He smelled incense and patchouli.

Cabarrus crossed to the table and folded the cards into a dark piece of silk, then set them on a shelf. She turned to a hot plate on a narrow table and removed a teapot, from which she poured amber liquid into two cups. She brought the cups to the table and set them down before she sat, with that perfectly straight back, and indicated the opposite chair.

Garrett sat, and in all his experience as a cop, all the weirdest places he'd been, he couldn't remember ever feeling so out of place and uncomfortable. He had the distinct sense that that was the point.

Tanith smiled at him, dark eyes shining, and answered his thought. "I'm sorry. Not exactly your style, is it? But it is more private." She sat back in her own chair and crossed those endless legs.

Garrett cleared his throat. "I'm a little out of my league with this magic stuff. You were a great help the other night and I was hoping you might be willing to clear some things up for me."

Her smile died as she stared across the table at him. "I'm more than willing to do whatever it takes to help catch the real killer."

"I appreciate that," he said without expression, while thinking: *She's covering for this kid. Why?*

Aloud he said, "Are you familiar with this design, or what it means?" He took his notebook from a coat pocket and drew the pattern of three triangles, pushed it to the center of the table between them.

She looked down at the drawing and frowned. "It's a sigil: a symbol used in ritual magic. This is the sigil of the demon Choronzon."

Garrett felt an electric thrill, the feeling of puzzle pieces falling together. "Choronzon," he repeated carefully. "So what would it mean to have this—sigil—written somewhere?"

She looked disturbed. "It depends on where it was written. But it would probably mean that someone was trying to summon the demon. Writing the sigil is a way of calling it."

It wasn't written, it was carved into Erin Carmody's body. The memory made his skin crawl. But that wasn't information he was willing to share.

He shook his head in real bewilderment. "Why would anyone want to summon a demon?"

A dozen conflicting feelings passed over her face, like the rippling of water on a lake. "To use its power. To make it do your bidding," she answered.

For a moment he could only stare at her. *She actually believes all this.*

He shifted in his chair. "This is probably a stupid question, but why would a demon do anything a—human—wanted?"

"It wouldn't," she said. "You would have to bind it." Before he could ask, she answered, "Not with ropes. With a spell."

This is totally insane, he thought, and forced a neutral tone. "And then it would do what you wanted it to?"

Again, that conflicted look. "If you were a powerful enough magician to control it."

It was probably the weirdest conversation he'd ever had in his life. "It sounds kind of risky." *Not to mention batshit crazy.*

"You are right about that," she said flatly.

"Are demons stupid enough to let that happen?"

She looked at him in the wash of candlelight. "The demon would have its own agenda, of course." She sighed, and answered his unspoken question. "Since they have no corporeal form themselves, demons can only do their work through human agents. And they covet our life. Demons are drawn to human life. They envy us desperately."

A phrase from the Crowley text popped into Garrett's mind: *It craves to become real.*

"That's how they're able to be lured," Tanith said, as if she'd heard him. "Of course, arrogance has something to do with it. Thinking they're too powerful to be bound."

She glanced at his face and leaned forward slightly, startling him. "Detective Garrett, you might be more comfortable with this conversation if you thought of it as a metaphor."

"Did I look uncomfortable?"

"Just a bit," she said drily.

Once a Catholic, always a Catholic, he thought. But the idea of wanting to summon a personification of evil was incomprehensible to him.

"Do you think of demons as metaphors?" he asked her.

She narrowed her eyes. "We're not talking about me. Why do you want to know about Choronzon?" she said, with obvious tension in her voice.

He ignored the question. "Do you do that kind of thing—summoning demons?"

A strange look flickered over her face in the candlelight. "Regardless of what you may have seen in the movies, witches don't have anything to do with demons." She pushed back her chair.

Afraid he'd lost her, he half rose and said quickly, "I'm sorry, this is all new to me."

She stared at him across the table, and then relented, sinking back into her seat. "I understand that."

He grappled with his thoughts. "How many demons are there, exactly?"

She looked bleak. "Legions."

He felt a twinge at the ancient word. "So what do you know about this one . . . Choronzon?"

She paused before she spoke. "Choronzon is not one of the host of more well-known Solomonic demons. He's in a class by himself. He was made famous—relatively speaking—by the magician Aleister Crowley."

Garrett kept his face still and wrote on his pad. "Aleister Crowley," he repeated, with no expression. "Can you tell me about him?"

She looked at him stonily in the orange light. "You know of him."

He blinked. "Why would you say that?"

She glanced at his pad and he realized she had been aware of what he wrote all along. "You spelled his name correctly. It's not a common spelling. In fact, Crowley made it up himself."

"I've only seen the name," Garrett said stiffly, annoyed at being caught. "Jason Moncrief had quite a few books by this Crowley on his shelf."

She looked amused. "What a surprise."

"What do you mean? Do you know Jason Moncrief?" he demanded, perhaps jumping the gun.

She frowned. "No. I know the type."

He felt a twinge of disappointment—and anger. *She's lying. Unless . . .* He glanced out toward the shop. "Do you have any employees helping you here?"

"No. I work alone."

And I doubt you'd not remember Jason Moncrief buying a set of books on Crowley. I doubt you miss much of anything at all. But he kept those thoughts to himself. *Don't confront her. Not yet. Better to see what else she might let slip.*

"You said this magician, Crowley, made the demon—Choronzon—famous. Can you tell me about that?"

She studied him warily. "What do you need to know?"

"Everything."

Her eyes held on his face . . . and Garrett suddenly found it hard to move. Then she got up and left the room, pushing the velvet drape aside. Garrett sat in the flickering dark of the velvet room, his heart beating faster than it had any right to. After a prolonged moment, she returned carrying several large volumes and he felt himself breathe again.

She sat back in her chair and opened a book, turned it toward him to show him a black-and-white portrait of a man with a handsome but dissolute face and burning, compelling eyes. "Crowley was an early twentieth-century magician and author of numerous occult books on spiritualism and magick practices. He was a Cambridge graduate, a chess master, a voracious drug user and voracious bisexual, and some say a British spy. His father was an English gentleman and a preacher, but from an early age Aleister Crowley sought what he called 'Satan's side.' He had a lifelong obsession with the nature of evil and with Satan particularly. At first he joined and studied with a group of magicians called the Hermetic Order of the Golden Dawn, but when he began studying the demonic system known as Abra-Melin, a higher magician in the Golden Dawn accused him of dabbling in malignant forces beyond his control. So Crowley left the Order and founded his own magical order: Astrum Argentium, the Silver Star. And at some point . . ." She paused, her face going blank for a moment. "Crowley started to go off the deep end, indulging in sexual sadism and fetishism, abusing absinthe and other drugs. He was infamous for orgiastic parties and bizarre sexual exploits, and became known as 'the Great Beast,' 'the Wickedest Man in the World,' and even 'Antichrist.'"

Garrett stared at her. "You know a lot about it for someone who has no interest in demons."

She stared back into his eyes, and hers were like onyx. "I didn't say I had no interest. I don't work with them, myself. But any student of magic knows Crowley. He casts a long shadow."

Garrett backed down, glanced at his pad. "So—Choronzon."

"Choronzon is a demon from Enochian magic—a system supposedly dictated by angels to Renaissance occultists John Dee and Edward Kelley. Dee and Kelley called Choronzon 'that mighty devil,' and 'the deadliest of all the powers of evil'; they equated him with the serpent in the Garden of Eden."

She turned the pages of another book to reveal illustrations that chilled Garrett's blood: spiny, bestial, deformed, reptilian creatures, with split tongues and lizard hands, eyes like black holes and jagged rows of spikes for teeth. Garrett had to suppress a shudder of revulsion; they were creatures from the hell grimly detailed by the nuns who had taught him, in stories that had given him screaming nightmares as a child. *Superstitious crap*, he told himself, but the thought was hollow.

He glanced again at the twisted things in the illustrations. "You said demons have no corporeal form."

Cabarrus nodded to him, impressed. "Very good, Detective.

This is merely how we see them. A projection of evil and bestiality. Choronzon in particular is said to cause madness, chaos, and decay, by his very presence. He is variously described as the Lord of Hallucinations, the Dweller at the Threshold, the Demon of the Abyss, the Demon of Dispersion, 'He who causes mental chaos,' 'He who blasts the flowers of the field.' "

Garrett sat up at this. "The flowers." Tanith looked startled, and he realized he'd nearly shouted. "I'm sorry. Tell me about the flowers."

She answered slowly, studying him. "It's a quality associated with the demon—that it scorches the flowers where it walks."

Garrett sat still and didn't like the swirl of sensations he was feeling. "What else?" he asked tightly.

She gave him a strange look, but resumed. "The story is that in his later years Crowley, along with Victor Neuberg, a male initiate who was also Crowley's lover, tried to summon and bind Choronzon in a magical triangle during a ritual in the Sahara Desert. The demon manifested in the triangle but was more powerful than Crowley anticipated and it took control of his body. It's unclear what happened, but contemporaries said Crowley's mind was never whole after the attempt. He became a slave to drugs and died in disgrace. And Choronzon . . . developed a taste for humans."

Garrett sat back with his mind reeling. "That's—quite a story." It was a more coherent narrative than what he had read on his own, but no less disturbing. He sat in silence for a moment, then something occurred to him. "Do the numbers 333 mean anything to you?"

She stared at him. "It's another sigil for Choronzon. Three-three-three is the number of the demon. What does Choronzon have to do with this investigation, Detective?" she asked tensely.

"I'm not at liberty to say—"

Tanith put her hand out and pointed at the page where Garrett had drawn the triangles. "Was this sigil what was carved into that girl's body?"

Garrett looked at her with a jolt—and knew he had betrayed what he was thinking.

Tanith stood in agitation, smoothing her hands on her skirt. "So whoever killed her is trying to summon Choronzon. You don't want that to happen, Detective Garrett."

He stood as well. "I don't want any of this to happen. It's my job to prevent it from happening, and I'm good at my job, Ms. Cabarrus."

Her dark eyes flashed. "I have no doubt. But in this case the killer is playing to your weakness, because you're going to ignore evidence that you don't want to believe." Her words struck Garrett with a cold shock of truth.

"You're right, I don't believe in demons," he answered her. "I think that's a bullshit way of excusing the evil that people do all on their own, all the time. We have free will. We always have the choice."

"I agree," she said instantly, surprising him. "Demons may well be no more than concentrated and projected human desires."

He looked across at her, trying to understand. "So you don't think they're real?"

"*Real* isn't the question. Demons *are*, Detective Garrett."

Her eyes went to the tabletop, to the page with the three triangles, and she began to pace the room. The candlelight gleamed off her silver and crystal jewelry. "If the killer carved that sigil into Erin Carmody's body, he is using human sacrifice to summon the demon. For your purposes, it doesn't matter if the demon comes or not. What you need to know is that the killer believes it, and he won't stop killing until he gets what he wants."

"We have a suspect in custody—"

She whirled on him, her eyes blazing. "You know a *boy* didn't kill those three people—"

"I don't know there are three, either," he lashed back. But even as he said it, he was remembering his initial certainty that Erin's murder could not be a first killing.

"Because you haven't looked."

"Are you sure you're not covering for Jason Moncrief?" Garrett demanded.

She made a scornful noise in her throat. "Why would I do that?"

"You haven't been straight with me, Ms. Cabarrus. Moncrief had numerous books by Crowley on his shelf. He got those books from your shop."

She stared at him in what looked like genuine bewilderment. "That's not true."

"The stickers are on the back," Garrett said.

"Then he shoplifted them. Crowley's books are expensive, and they tend to walk away on their own. A certain kind of teenage boy . . ." She trailed off, staring at him. "Do you think I'm *involved* in this, somehow?" Her face was so incredulous he faltered.

"I think you're a pretty staunch defender of someone you don't even know," he said flatly, and stood his ground.

"I don't *know* him. I know what happened," she flung back at him. "I understand what happened," she amended, and there was a tremor in her voice.

"What happened?" Garrett demanded.

"He opened a door," Tanith said. Her eyes were bleak. "And something reached through."

Garrett stared at her. She must have realized she'd lost him, because her next words were deliberate and rational. "He's a teenager who dabbled in something he doesn't understand. But he didn't kill her—"

"What are you saying, then, a demon did?" Garrett scoffed.

"Maybe," she said seriously. "Or someone under its power."

Garrett had an unwelcome flash of Jason's coal-black eyes, that stretched-taut face. "Everything you're saying about this 'demon' still points to Jason Moncrief. He had the books, he wrote songs about it, he had all the ritual items in his room—"

"Items *any* magician might have—"

Garrett's eyes fell again on the book open on the table between them, the reptilian forms, and suddenly understood what he'd been trying not to think about.

"I saw it," he said violently.

She stopped, stared at him, into him. His heart was pounding as if he had run a mile. "What did you see?" she asked softly.

He struggled with himself. "Something," he said, with effort. "I saw . . . something." *In the mirror in Jason's room* . . . "I heard something . . ."

She moved a step closer, searching his face. "Tell me."

"Voices. Layered on top of each other. On our interview tape." The words were out of his mouth before he realized he was saying them. Across from him, her eyes were dark and still. "What does it mean?" he demanded.

She bit her lip. "It's an early sign of demon infestation."

"Possession?" he asked, incredulous. "You've got to be—"

"Isn't that what you've been thinking?" she asked quietly.

"*No*," Garrett exploded. "What I see is a disturbed young man with a history of antisocial behavior and what looks like a hell of an obsession with this—Choronzon. Whose 'sigil' just happened to end up carved in Erin Carmody's chest. All the evidence points to Moncrief, Ms. Cabarrus—"

"Then why are you here?"

The truth of that froze him. Then he reached out and grabbed her wrist and it was like an electric shock between them, a shock he felt through his entire body. "All right. All right. Then give me something," he said, and his voice was harsh.

She wrenched her arm away. "I did. The dates. There are three dead. Two other people have been killed on those dates I gave you—"

"There *are* no missing persons on the dates you gave me. Don't you think I've checked?"

"Then you're not looking in the right place." She slammed her hands on the table, startling him. "He's killing on the holy days. And while Jason Moncrief sits in jail—you have less than a month until Samhain."

"Until the *demon* strikes again," he mocked her, to make it less real.

"Until someone does." Her eyes lasered into his. "Unless you do something about it, *Detective*."

Chapter Twenty-one

Garrett woke to the sound of rumbling and a dismal day outside his window: thick black clouds threatening a downpour. And an even more dismal task in front of him.

It was the day of Erin Carmody's funeral.

The last thing Garrett wanted to do was spend the day in a church with a dead girl, but he and Landauer would be there early, suited and shaved. It was standard operating procedure in a murder case; killers were often perversely moved to attend the funerals of their victims, and even when—*if*—the killer was locked securely away, mourners had been known to say things in the throes of grief that they might not ordinarily say, things that could make a case.

And Kevin Teague would be there. Alibi or not, Garrett wanted another look at him.

Garrett was not admitting aloud that he was troubled by Tanith's insistence that there were multiple victims, and he certainly hadn't told Land about his little trip up to Salem—not until he could make some sense of it himself.

But Teague was a loose end Garrett didn't like.

The church was typical New England, a nineteenth-century

stone structure on the outskirts of Boston, nestled in the middle of a thick grove of trees; the gravestones of the cemetery scattered over gently rolling hills. Inside the church, massive flower arrangements were everywhere; the scent was overpowering. The coffin, of course, was closed. The service was standing room only, the church overflowing with mourners, students rubbing shoulders with the crème of Boston society, come to pay respects to the Carmody dynasty.

Even in his best suit, Garrett felt painfully underdressed. Then he felt shame at the thought. *You think the Carmodys give a good goddamn about clothes, today?*

He forced himself to the task at hand, and scanned the crowd from his vantage at the end of a back pew.

Landauer sat on the other side of the chapel, looking as impassively uncomfortable as Garrett felt, and Carolyn was toward the front; not observing, as the detectives were, but present simply because this was her own social circle. By mutual agreement she and Garrett were not communicating while he worked the funeral, which was a relief; he was distracted enough already.

His pulse suddenly spiked as he spotted Shelley Forbes and Kevin Teague taking seats together in the Carmody's pew, up-front.

Okay, then, jocko. We're going to have a little talk, you and me.

Garrett settled back into the pew to wait out the service. These days he felt out of place in any church, but today it was particularly painful. The funeral seemed to him a total lie, the body within the coffin incomplete, missing the part that makes human beings most human.

Erin's life had ended in a dark ritual, and the one going on before him seemed a flimsy and inadequate attempt to counteract the damage done. Whatever God there was had some explaining to do.

Garrett looked up at the stained-glass panels in the slanted ceiling to distract himself . . . only to find himself staring at a pane depicting winged Lucifer tempting a gaunt Christ in the wilderness.

He had a sudden clear image of the reptilian things that Tanith had shown him the night before. *"Choronzon in particular is said to cause madness, chaos, and decay."*

Garrett's stomach twisted. *What century are we in? How can civilized people believe these things?* He looked quickly away from the colored glass, letting the hymn block out his thoughts.

As the service concluded, Garrett caught Land's eye across the chapel and nodded slightly toward Teague. Landauer nodded back and started out the door with the flow of mourners.

Outside the church the day was still dark, with scudding clouds and the threat of rain, a heavy feeling in the air to match the somber proceedings.

Mortuary attendants discreetly herded the funeral party out onto a winding path toward the grove that encircled the graveyard. Garrett walked at the edges of the crowd, following Teague, and when the young man drifted behind the Carmodys, Garrett stepped in front of him, cutting him off from the others.

Teague recognized him instantly; his eyes turned hooded and wary. Garrett indicated a side path with a jerk of his head. Teague glowered under those dark, full eyebrows, but stepped onto the path with him.

"So you've never been to Cauldron," Garrett said flatly, as soon as they were out of earshot of the other mourners.

"No, I haven't," Teague snapped back, hostility seething in his voice.

"So I guess you didn't attack Jason Moncrief in the parking lot there on September seventh."

Teague's lip twisted. "Who says so?"

Garrett paused. The only real witness was Jason; the bass player's story was hearsay.

A smug look crossed Teague's features. "You better watch those unfounded allegations, Detective."

Garrett took an abrupt step toward the young man and the smirk disappeared from his face. "You better watch that mouth, Teague. I have witnesses who place you at Cauldron."

"The night she died?" Teague demanded. Garrett didn't answer and Teague shook his head, disgusted. "You're tripping. If you think I killed Erin you're as crazy as Moncrief." He stepped back from Garrett, clearly knowing that he could. "Like I said. From now on talk to my lawyer."

He strode off down the path, toward the graves.

Garrett felt a surge of anger and had to stand for a few minutes in the quiet circle of trees to compose himself. The wind whispered through the leaves above him.

When he was calm enough to rejoin the funeral party, the mourners were filing past the grave site, putting flowers and gifts—notes, stuffed animals, trinkets—on top of the coffin. A good number of the procession broke down in tears.

Garrett felt a tightness in his chest, a new fury—for Erin's wasted life.

And then his pulse suddenly spiked as he caught sight of a familiar figure, unmistakable: a slim young man with heavy dark glasses who towered a full head over everyone else around him.

The bass player from Jason's band, Danny Coyle.

He paused beside the coffin and lay a white, square envelope on the gleaming surface with the other gifts.

Keeping his eyes fixed on the musician, Garrett stepped into the line of mourners filing by the coffin. When his turn came he stopped on the fresh earth beside the bier and lay one hand gently on the surface of the casket as if in tribute, while he snagged the white envelope with his other hand and slid it into his coat pocket. He bowed his head for a moment longer, then turned and walked quickly away from the grave, following the bassist at a distance, weaving through the headstones and monuments. It was an easy tail, given the dispersing crowd and the height of his target.

As he followed the young man through the graves, Garrett pulled the envelope from his pocket and examined it. It was a CD in a white sleeve, with Erin's name written on it. The CD inside was unmarked.

Garrett strode faster to overtake the bassist. "Danny," he called. The young man turned around, and looked startled to see Garrett. He stopped beside a tomb and waited, with a hunch in his shoulders, as Garrett caught up.

Garrett stopped in front of him, smiled, spread his hands as he glanced back toward the grave site. "I thought you didn't know Erin."

"I don't," the musician began.

"Yet you come to her funeral and you leave her this?" Garrett held the CD up between his fingers.

Danny stared at Garrett, and Garrett saw a mixture of conflicting emotions on his face: confusion, a flash of anger, a hint of what looked like contempt.

"It's from Jason," the young man said.

Now Garrett stared at him.

"He called me and asked me to bring it here, today."

"From where?" Garrett demanded.

Danny gave him an odd look. "From jail."

"I mean, where did you get the CD? We cleaned out his room."

"It was in our rehearsal space," Danny said patiently. "He called me and asked me to get it."

"What's on it?" Garrett was furious with himself for not searching the room.

Danny stared at him stonily. "I didn't play it. It's private."

"Do you not realize that this is a murder investigation and you could be charged with withholding evidence?"

Danny looked startled, then straightened his shoulders and said in a steady voice, "Jason is my friend, man. I can't believe he killed anyone. Whatever he was into, I don't believe that. He wanted her to have it"—he nodded at the CD in Garrett's hand—"so I brought it."

He met Garrett's eyes and did not look away. And then Garrett nodded, dismissing him.

As Danny started off across the grass, Garrett suddenly called after him, "Wait."

The tall young man turned back, impassive.

Garrett stood, for a moment just collecting his thoughts, unsure of what he wanted to say, only that there was something. And then he found himself asking a question that surprised him. "Did you guys do a gig on August first?"

The bassist thought for a second. "Yeah, in Saratoga."

"Saratoga Springs? New York?" Garrett asked.

"Right."

"Was Jason with you for that one?"

Danny frowned. "Yeah."

"The whole time?" Saratoga Springs was at least a ten-hour drive.

Danny looked bewildered. "Yeah. We drove up together, did the gig, spent the night in a motel, drove back. Why?"

Garrett didn't answer, because he didn't quite know himself . . . only that August first was one of the dates that Tanith Cabarrus had given him.

He shook his head, and after a time, Danny turned and continued walking through the gravestones.

The skies opened up just as Garrett got to his Explorer, and he sat back with the rain pounding on the roof and bouncing off the windshield and started the engine, then slid the CD into his player and sat back to listen.

It was completely unexpected, the music, nothing heavy or hard, nothing like the death metal that had been on the *Current 333* CD, but a simple, haunting track, and a single vocal.

Garrett sat back against the seat and listened to Jason Moncrief sing.

Magical, lyrical, princess of light
Guide my way through this starless night.
Moon in your hair and fire in your eyes
Make me worthy to claim your prize.
Forest nymph, my forest queen.
Shining lady of the unseen.

Garrett leaned back against the headrest. *Fuck me.* He stared out at the drenching rain, with blood pounding in his head.

He didn't kill her.

Chapter Twenty-two

The moon was rising through the tall windows of the detectives' bureau. The glass bricks of the lower floors glowed pale green.

Hunched at his work pod, Garrett had been staring at the Missing Persons reports for some time now, as if a name would somehow miraculously appear on the dates he was checking. There was nothing. There simply were no missing persons on or around the dates Tanith had given him.

But her voice kept insisting.

"There are three dead already."

And the sweet, haunting lyrics of Jason's song to Erin refused to go away.

Garrett stood and walked down the back stairs (the DNA stairs, he always thought of them, the double spiral staircase in the back of Schroeder), with the tall clear glass windows looking out onto the darkened adjoining strip of park, and crossed the lobby to the complaint desk, where walk-ins and call-ins could make reports. The desk was generally staffed by rookies or even cadets, and rookies made mistakes.

He was in luck; tonight there was an actual sergeant behind the desk, with a crew cut and handlebar mustache. Garrett leaned in to the counter. "I need to know if any missing persons were reported on or around these dates." He passed the sergeant a Post-it with the dates *June 21* and *August 1*. "Anything around those dates." He paused, then took a shot. "I'm thinking it would be a young woman." Garrett had meant that the report would be *about* a missing young woman, but the desk sergeant misunderstood.

"Yeah, a streetwalker did come in—August one sounds right. Said a friend of hers never came back from a date."

Garrett stared at him, fury building. "Where the fuck is the report?"

The sergeant's guard went way up and Garrett knew he had to contain himself if he was going to get what he needed.

"She didn't fill one out. She came in less than twenty-four hours after this hooker 'disappeared.' I told her we couldn't take a report on an adult until forty-eight hours had passed." The sergeant shrugged, defensive. "She never came back in."

All kinds of bells were going off inside Garrett. Tanith Cabarrus was right—there was another. A prostitute. And he'd initially thought the killer might have mistaken Erin for a prostitute. He felt a building rage that none of this had been recorded and that he had been a breath away from missing it entirely.

"I need a name. A description," he ground out.

The sergeant bristled. "She was a hooker," he said, as if that covered everything. "Eighteen, nineteen. Using, twitchy. Wig and dark glasses, like she was in disguise. Said her and her friend were working Chinatown." Then something flickered in his face. "She had a food name . . ." he paused, thinking. "Bree. She said her name was Bree."

A couple of years back Garrett had dated a vice cop named Stoney—Melissa Stone. Her name conjured a rush of erotic flashbacks: fucking in backseats; up against the rough brick wall of an alley; Garrett standing, shaking, sweating, Stoney on her knees, wide lips wrapped around him; Garrett's fingers up inside her and Stoney shuddering as he pressed against her from behind . . .

She'd been working undercover in the BPD's "Operation Squeeze":

an aggressive series of busts of prostitutes and johns in the gentri-
fying Chinatown district. When Garrett was being honest with
himself he had to admit it gave him an illicit thrill to hook up with
a pretend hooker. Landauer had taunted him unmercifully and
Stoney was no fool, either; she'd called him on it, Garrett was unable to deny the charge, and ultimately Stoney couldn't get past it.
The problem with dating a cop was that they read you too well.

All of that played for a moment on Stoney's face when she
looked up from her desk in the vice squad room and saw him coming. Garrett was selfishly gratified to see an involuntary ripple of
attraction as well, her own rush of erotic memories, quickly covered.

She leaned back in her chair and crossed her arms as he stopped
in front of the desk. "So you finally caught your big one," she said,
as if no time had passed.

"Yeah. And now I'm hoping it's not even bigger than everyone
thinks." He said it bluntly and the change in her eyes made it clear
she understood he wasn't playing. She sat up straighter.

"What's up?"

He stepped close to the desk and lowered his voice. "I need to
find someone. Fast. A streetwalker named Bree, eighteen, nineteen
years old, working Chinatown. Has a hooker friend who went missing in August, probably her same age."

Stoney's eyes darkened. "Jesus. I never heard about it—"

"Wasn't reported."

"But it's connected to yours?" she asked uneasily.

"I don't know yet. I've got to find this girl," he said, and met her
gaze. She looked away from his eyes.

"I'll put the word out," she said. "Your cell the same?"

"Yeah. I owe you, Stoney."

"Yeah—you do," she said. And from the flatness in her voice
Garrett knew that he was not forgiven, and he was only lucky that
Stoney was a good cop and would put that first.

A lead. Maybe a lead.

But the churning in his stomach made him think that this was a
door he didn't want to open.

———

In a ritual triangle, lit by flame, a shadow figure held a dagger up in the wavering yellow light. The voice was low and husky as it intoned the Latin words. "Choronzon, acerbus et ingens! Cede pectares cras nocte sumendus, alere flamman tuam. Do et dus. Date et dabitur vobis! Abyssus Abyssum invocat!"

The robed figure cast a parchment inscribed with the triangle sigils into the fire. Then the figure turned to the altar—to the severed head on the plate. And as the cloaked figure muttered in a building frenzy, the head's eyes snapped open . . . and stared.

Chapter Twenty-three

Garrett fought his way to consciousness, past disturbing images of candles and inscriptions and burning parchment and severed human heads. Somewhere far away a phone was ringing.

He grabbed for his cell on the nightstand and mumbled "Garrett" into it without checking the number.

A husky female voice said, "Did you find her?"

What immediately ran through Garrett's mind was *Tanith*, and he felt himself harden under the sheets in response. Luckily he asked, "Who is this?" to be sure.

There was a silence, then a wary voice. "Bree. Stoney told me to call."

Garrett scrambled up to sitting, reached for the clock. 3:00 P.M. That made it the next day. He rubbed his face to wake up. "Can I meet you?"

It was a wintry afternoon, with high fast clouds and a chill wind whipping through the concrete corridors of Washington Street, a retail district where Boston teens still shopped for cheap Nikes, music, and books. Garrett drove past pushcart vendors selling backpacks and phone accessories and knockoff purses on the sidewalks.

Boston's infamous Combat Zone, the downtown red-light district, was long gone. When real estate prices shot up in the eighties, the sleazy strip where adult bookstores and dance clubs and streetwalkers and dealers once blatantly hawked their wares had been inexorably gentrified and sanitized. Skyscrapers sprouted up, with their condos and office space and doormen and underground parking, and a pristine granite sidewalk had replaced the vomit-and-blood-stained concrete. But despite the surface polish, sex workers still prowled the nearby streets of Chinatown and Downtown Crossing.

Bree ("*Just Bree*," she'd said on the phone) had directed Garrett to meet her at a dim sum restaurant, on a street where brick buildings and colorful awnings and vertical signs in Chinese lettering bloomed under the shadow of a thirty-six-story office tower. In a tight cotton tank top and jeans and platform shoes and tats, the lone young woman at the table looked like a college student—until she took off her sunglasses and Garrett got a look at her eyes. They were colder than December.

"She's dead, isn't she," Bree said flatly.

"Why do you say that?" Garrett asked.

The girl looked at him in disbelief. "Homicide? How stupid do you think I am?" She lit a cigarette shakily and Garrett was surprised to see tears in her eyes. She brushed at them angrily. "So?" she demanded.

"What's your friend's name?" he asked.

"Amber," Bree said, in a voice that dared him to mock it. "Just Amber," she added.

"Amber," Garrett repeated gently, and had a sinking feeling. "I don't know that she's dead. I hope not. That's why I'm here. I need to know what you know." He pulled out a pad. Bree stared at him stonily. He summoned patience, persuasion. "You reported her missing on August one. Why? What happened?"

"Nothing happened. Stupid fucks wouldn't even take the report," she spat.

Garrett understood the anger. "I'm sorry. The desk sergeant was following protocol, but I think he was wrong. If there's anything that you can tell me, I promise you I'll make this a priority."

The girl narrowed her eyes, weighing him, and finally spoke. "She called me the night before. She said she was in the park, and she had a date." The girl's eyes turned bleak. "Then she kind of joked—'If I don't come back you can have my boots.' And you could tell it wasn't really a joke, right? But when I asked her what was up, she said, 'Nevermind, no big,' and hung up." Bree's face trembled and she took a long drag on her cigarette. "She never showed up later that night—I've left about a million messages and she never returned one. No one's seen her." The tears threatened again, and her whole body was shaking.

This was not good in any way. Garrett tried to keep his face impassive. "Did she describe the guy? Anything?"

Bree shook her head, her eyes fixed on the table. "That was all she said. But she was weirded out. I could tell. God damn it . . ."

"All right, the park," Garrett said quickly. "Where is that?"

"Couple blocks away. She went there for her breaks . . ."

"Show me."

It was a sad little park, sandwiched between a disreputable parking lot and a construction site. It was probably the only remains of a long-gone church and no doubt slated for demolition along with every other building in the neighborhood. The scraggly lawns were sunburned and choked with weeds and the cement paths were littered with used condoms, fast-food wrappers crawling with ants, and shattered vodka bottles. A homeless man sprawled on a bench, dead to the world.

But as Garrett looked around him, he saw one valiant tree, with autumn leaves now red and brilliant as rubies, and there was a fountain in the center, long dry, with stone benches around it, and on the top of the fountain was an angel, stained and worn, but there was a ravaged beauty about it. Garrett didn't have to ask Bree why Amber had gone to the park. It may have been small comfort, but there was comfort there.

The afternoon shadows were lengthening and the wintry wind flapped at his coat as he slowly scanned the park. He had no idea what he thought he would find. Amber had disappeared over two months ago, and turning up anything like evidence in a public park was about as likely as finding evidence in a landfill. And yet . . . there was some feeling about the park, almost a sense of déjà vu . . . it felt like a piece of the puzzle. So Garrett walked the littered paths. Bree at first trailed behind him, picking her way carefully around the scattered glass, teetering on her open-toed platform shoes, but she quickly gave up and sat on the lip of the fountain to light up a smoke. Garrett stopped and looked back to ask her, "Did she have a favorite spot?" And of course the girl pointed to a bench in full view of the angel.

Garrett stepped to the bench, scanning underneath and around it, saw piled trash and gum wrappers and cigarette butts, smelled a faint stench of vomit.

He straightened, and slowly sat on the bench, looking up at the angel.

And then he felt a prickle on the back of his neck, as tangible as fingers.

He stood, twisting to look behind him.

He saw a gnarled and dying tree, a crumbling stone wall, the skeletal girders of an unfinished building beyond. No one human.

But the feeling of being watched was overpowering.

Garrett took a few steps on the path, looking toward the skeleton of the building with its open tiers . . . and then froze, staring down to the side of him. Behind the bench were footsteps in the weeds . . . blurred, but unmistakable: scorched, blackened footsteps in the withered wildflowers . . . just like the burned footprints at the dump.

Someone stepped behind him and he spun—to face Bree. "What is it?" she asked him, her face pale and tight.

Garrett looked back at the scorch marks. "I don't know."

She followed his gaze to the blackened prints and frowned. "Freaky . . ." she said from far away.

Garrett got his digital camera from his Explorer and returned to the footprints. He clicked off photos and collected some of the burned flowers in several evidence bags. And again he heard Tanith's voice in his head: *"The demon scorches the flowers where it walks . . ."*

While Bree watched him from the fountain, he stepped back and took several more shots of the park, of the benches, of the dry fountain with the angel, then circled back to Bree and sat on the rim of the fountain beside her. There was a pile of crushed cigarette butts at her feet. Garrett flipped open his notepad. "How old is Amber?"

Bree exhaled smoke from a fresh cigarette. "She said seventeen." Bree shrugged with cynical skepticism.

"Do you have a photo of her?"

Bree's eyes clouded. "Uh uh." She sounded for a moment like a little girl. Then her face hardened again. "You could get a mug shot though."

"Does she have a family somewhere?"

"If you want to call it that. She ran away when she was fourteen. Wanna know why?" Her gray eyes were challenging.

Garrett's face tightened. It was always the same story. What people did to their kids could almost make him believe in demons. "I'm sorry," he said inadequately. "But do you know where her family is?"

Bree crushed out a butt and lit yet another cigarette. "Maine somewhere. What difference does it make? They sure as shit don't care."

She was racked by a coughing fit. Garrett waited, thinking, *Worse than Landauer.* When she had control of herself again, he asked, "Bree, since she disappeared, have you felt in danger yourself?" She looked up, her eyes widening. He continued. "Have you ever felt you were being followed or—watched?" Garrett's gaze went to the perimeter of the park, past the bench where he had been sitting before.

The girl's eyes followed his. "I don't think so," she said warily. "What do you mean?" When Garrett hesitated, she asked raggedly, "Do you know who did it?"

"No, I don't." Garrett took out one of his cards. "But I want you to call me. If you feel—strange about anything, if anyone comes asking about Amber, if you just want to talk." He wrote a number on the card. "And this is the number for Youth Services—"

"Yeah, yeah," Bree said wearily. "Stoney gave me the number." She glanced away from him, up at the angel. "What else am I supposed to do, huh? These days? You tell me."

Garrett's guilt about keeping Landauer out of the loop had reached lapsed-Catholic proportions, so he phoned him from the car. Land sounded grumpy and Garrett guessed he'd pulled him away from his dinner. It was also entirely possible that his partner had spent the whole day in bed.

"Not an emergency," Garrett said quickly.

"Then the fuck you calling?" Landauer grumbled.

"Look, Land, I might have something. I found a missing person. A hooker named Amber. A friend of hers says she disappeared from around Chinatown on August one. Sixteen-, seventeen-year-old Caucasian. She hasn't been seen since."

Land was surly, but his brain was working. "There was no MP of that age range on the list."

"I know. I checked with the front desk and her friend came in on the day after she disappeared. There was never an official report filed."

There was a pause; Garrett could picture Landauer frowning, working it out. "How'd you know to—" he stopped. "August first. That's one of those days Stevie Nicks gave you."

Garrett shifted uncomfortably behind the wheel. He didn't bother to correct Landauer with Tanith's real name. "Yeah."

The silence on the other end was ominous. "What does this have to do with Moncrief?" Landauer asked, finally. Garrett could hear the scowl in his voice.

"I don't know, Land. But maybe there's a witness. I'm going to follow up."

Landauer sighed, martyred. "What time?"

Garrett could hear his reluctance and pounced on it. "Look, go back to your dinner. I can call you if there's anything there."

"You sure?"

"No problem," Garrett said, keeping his voice casual. "I'll fill you in in the morning."

He disconnected, fought down another surge of guilt, and turned onto Highway 1 toward Salem.

Chapter Twenty-four

The sky was dark and the moon was huge in the sky as Garrett parked again on Essex Street outside Book of Shadows. He looked up through tree branches at the shining amber disk, and realized tonight it was full—it looked twice normal size and golden-toned, as a full moon often will do. A strong wind swayed the branches of the elm trees lining the sidewalks. Dry leaves rolled and swirled in the street. *Halloween weather*, Garrett thought to himself, and the thought was ominous. *Three weeks to go.*

He climbed the front steps of the house and walked into the shop to the musical tinkling of bells, and the fragrant warmth of the shop enveloped him. Tanith looked up from the book she was reading at the counter. They were silent, looking at each other under the strings of white lights sparkling like stars, and Garrett felt the charge between them from across the room, felt it through all of his body. Finally she spoke. "Detective Garrett, we really must stop meeting like this." There was amusement in her eyes, and also a challenge that excited him. The white cat rolled over and stretched luxuriously in front of her.

"I'm sorry to keep dropping by," he started.

The look she gave him said she didn't believe him for a second.

"That's perfectly all right," she said languidly. "This time I did see you coming."

He never knew whether or not to believe what she said; it all seemed like a game to her.

"I may have found another," he said, knowing she would know what he meant. Her amusement vanished, and she closed her book.

"Where? Who?"

"I haven't found a body. But a young woman did go missing on August first. A streetwalker."

Tanith's face was still, but she said nothing. He watched her as he spoke. "It looks like you were right, and at this point I don't care how you're doing it. You have some kind of understanding of all this and I need to use it," he said brusquely, without adding "Please."

She stood and moved out from behind the counter, walked across the shop and locked the door, then flipped the OPEN sign in the window to CLOSED. She turned and looked at him expectantly.

Garrett took files out of his binder and spread photos of the park with the angel out on the counter. "This is the last place she was seen."

Tanith moved to the counter beside him and they both looked down at the photos of the forlorn little park. She studied the shots for a long moment. She was wearing a black, off-the shoulder sweater that exposed her long neck and delicate shoulder blades, and Garrett could smell the fragrance she wore, apple musk again, heady and enticing. He had to stop himself from reaching out to touch the curve of her neck. Then he felt an uneasy prickle as she touched her index finger to the photo of the bench that had been Amber's favorite, the bench in front of the angel on the fountain. Tanith looked up at him, her eyes dark.

"What about this park bothers you?"

Garrett hesitated. *Am I really going to trust her?*

Then he drew another photo from the file and put it down in front of her: the photo of the footprints burned into the wildflowers, the shriveled weeds around them. He watched her face as she stared down. "The blasted flowers . . ." she murmured, and sat abruptly on the high stool.

"Have you ever seen anything like that before?" His voice was sharp.

She continued to stare down at the photo. "No. No, I haven't." Her eyes flicked up at him. "But that's what you're thinking, isn't it? Choronzon."

"I'm thinking someone else knows the story you told me and is playing games," Garrett said flatly.

She studied him with an oblique expression. "Did you find these—the footprints—at the other crime scene as well? Where Erin was found?"

Garrett paused, struggling with himself. It was more information than he was comfortable giving her. But she was his only slim lead to something—unfathomable. He gave a brief nod of assent, in answer to her question.

Tanith leaned back on her stool. "What exactly do you want from me, Detective? It's clear you don't believe."

"If there's another victim out there, if this girl was killed, too, then I need to find her. The body." He thought of Amber's booking photo, which he'd pulled up from the system: a stark shot of a waif with a mop of dark hair and burned cigarette eyes. She looked like a junkie, and a child. He didn't want to think about what her short life—and the last few minutes of it—had been like. He stabbed at the photo of the burned footprints with a finger. "This is the only lead I have. If there's something you can do with it, I'm all ears." He knew his voice sounded harsh and strained but it was the best he could manage.

"Did you collect any of the flowers?" Tanith asked, surprising him.

"Yes," he answered warily. In fact, he had brought samples of them with him; he had been toying with the idea of showing them to her.

"And a photo would be good, if you have it. I can do a reading, if you'd like."

A reading? Some witch mumbo jumbo? he thought, feeling like Landauer. "What does that entail?" he asked aloud, uncomfortably.

She half smiled. "All you'd have to do is watch and listen. But if you have something from the scene—both scenes would be best—I can try to see. It's called psychometry, and the principle is that objects retain emotional imprints of the people who touch them." Her face was shadowed in the starry lights. "If you think the killer has something to do with these footprints, if he touched the flowers, they might retain some essence of him. And then . . ." She hesitated. "I might be able to see more from there."

Garrett stared at her, flabbergasted. He had no idea how to answer her.

"No charge," she added, with a straight face.

What have you got to lose? he asked himself. And some internal voice taunted him, *And don't you want to know?*

"I'd appreciate it," he told her, with no idea what he was about to get into.

"This way, then," she said, and started toward the curtain in the back, dark as night, with its weave of silver stars.

Garrett followed as Tanith walked into the inner velvet-draped room with the round table and two chairs. She moved to a cabinet standing against the wall and removed a glass pitcher, a goblet, a plate, and a bakery tin, which she took to the table.

What is this now, a snack? Garrett wondered. While he watched in bemusement she filled the pitcher with water from the sink and set it on the table, then opened the tin and placed several small cakes on the plate. She did not offer him any of what she had laid out, nor did she eat or drink herself. Instead she took a key from the cabinet, crossed the room to the door in the back, and unlocked it.

She took a lit candle from one of the shelves on the wall beside the door and stepped aside to let Garrett in to another dark room. It took him a moment to adjust to the darkness but he could feel immediately it was a much bigger room, longer. Tanith took the candle she held and began lighting candles in the tall wrought-iron candelabra that stood in each corner of the room. Garrett looked around him in the golden wash of candlelight. There were no visible windows. Heavy purple cloth draped the walls, creating a womb-like cocoon. On the bare black-painted floor was inscribed a white circle of about nine feet in diameter, and there was a five-pointed star inside of that, large enough that all five of its points touched the circle: a pentagram. Garrett felt an uneasy jolt, seeing such a huge version of the familiar yet alien design. In the precise center of the pentagram stood an altar draped in dark silk, on which stood a wineglass, a small bowl, a metal box, and a gleaming dagger with crystals set in the hilt, all laid out like surgical instruments.

Jesus Christ, Garrett thought. *What am I doing here?*

Tanith turned away from the last candle. She was dark against the light, black spill of hair, black sweater, and that milk-pale skin.

He forced his eyes away from her and moved to lean against the wall, carefully avoiding the circle and the star. Tanith glanced at him over a bare shoulder, and lifted a tall stool from beside the cabinet. She set the stool just inside the circle. "I'll need you to be inside the circle with me," she told him.

Garrett blinked. "Why?"

"It's for your protection."

He almost laughed, but restrained himself just in time. "Protection from what?"

"The working of magic draws forces of all kinds. The more powerful the ritual, the more powerful the forces, good and bad. I'll begin the ritual by casting a circle of protection. The circle keeps anything—unwanted—out."

"Don't worry about me—" he started.

Her eyes flashed. "You'll need to stay within the circle, Detective, or we're done."

Garrett felt his back stiffening. *Then I'm out of here,* he was on the verge of saying . . . but forced himself to suppress the words. Holding her eyes, he stepped into the circle. She startled him by stepping up close to him, holding out her hand. He stood in consternation until she prompted, "The flowers?"

Garrett reached into a jacket pocket and pulled out the glassine bags containing samples of the flowers he'd taken from the crime scenes: one from the landfill, one from the park. He put them in her hand, and felt a ripple of desire as their fingers brushed. She turned to the altar and shook the burnt fragments out into a silver dish.

"And the photo?" she asked. He reached into another pocket and withdrew the photo of Amber. Tanith took it from him and looked down for a long moment, then she made a sound in the back of her throat and turned sharply to the altar. She placed the photo gently on the silk.

Garrett sat on the stool she had set out for him and watched, fascinated in spite of himself.

She left the circle and crossed to a cabinet against the wall that looked antique, from which she removed five new candles: yellow, red, blue, green, purple. She stepped again to the circle and bent to place a yellow candle on the gleaming white line, then moved a few steps and placed the red candle precisely a quarter of the circle away, then the blue one across from the yellow one, and the green one on the fourth quadrant. The purple candle she placed on the altar in the center of the circle.

She was completely unself-conscious as she worked, as if she were alone in the room, as if she had performed these gestures hundreds of times before. As he watched her, Garrett felt a powerful drowsiness come over him, an involuntary relaxation of his own muscles. In some part of his mind he was reminded of the masses of his childhood: the candles, the altar, the incense, the rituals . . . only then, of course, there had never been a woman at the altar. It occurred to him that perhaps that was part of the point.

She returned to the cabinet again and took out a crystal wineglass and a small bowl. She filled the glass with water from a pitcher inside the cabinet and took a pinch of something white from a glass jar and put it in the bowl. She carried those items to the altar and set them there, then opened the silver cylinder and removed a long fireplace match. She struck the match and used its flame to light the contents of the square metal box: incense, Garrett could smell the pungent fragrance instantly.

She stood silent and still in front of the altar, then suddenly she lifted the wineglass of water in both hands toward the ceiling, a theatrical and surprisingly powerful gesture. She spoke aloud in a clear, resonant voice: "Water, I empty and prepare you to receive the purification of salt."

She set the wineglass on the altar and picked up the small bowl, lifting it in both hands: "Salt, I bless you in your task of purification. May you cast out all that is unwanted so that the light may prevail."

She poured the white crystals into the glass, then moved around the room, sprinkling the salt water with her fingertips, three times around the circle, and Garrett felt as if a rope were tightening around his heart.

When she had completed three rounds she returned to the center of the circle and stood before the altar with her hands down by her sides. She closed her eyes, bowed her head, and just stood, breathing slow, deep breaths. Then at once she opened her eyes, lifted her head, and snatched up the dagger, causing Garrett's whole body to tense. She extended her right arm with the dagger held out, a straight line. Her eyes were unearthly dark and her voice blasted through him. "I conjure thee, O great circle of power! Be for me a boundary between the world of humans and the realm of the mighty spirits, a meeting place to contain the power I will raise herein." Slowly she turned in place, her arm extended, the dagger sweeping the room in a circle, its jewels gleaming in the candlelight, until she had made an entire revolution. And then she turned again, sweeping the dagger up and over her head, down to her feet.

Garrett was paralyzed with fascination and unease, watching her. *This is medieval, it's completely insane.*

"As above, so below. This circle is sealed. So mote it be!" she intoned, and stamped her foot once on the ground. Then she dropped her hands and stepped again to the altar.

She removed another long fireplace matchstick from the silver cylinder, struck the match, and took the flame with her as she moved around the circle again, lighting each candle in the same order that she had placed them. She stepped to the yellow candle, facing out, and called out in a clear, strong voice: "Watchtower of the East, Element of Air, I call thee to witness and guard this circle."

She bent and lit the candle. Garrett started as the flame sprung up and wavered as if in a sudden draft. He saw Tanith's dark, heavy hair ripple in the air current and he felt a breeze against his face.

Did that just happen? What the hell?

Tanith turned and moved across the circle to the red candle, where she repeated, "Watchtower of the South, Element of Fire, I call thee to witness and guard this circle." She bent, with dark curls spilling about her face, and lit the candle. This time it flared up, tall and strong.

At the blue candle she recited, "Watchtower of the West, Element of Water, I call thee to witness and guard this circle." She bent and lit the candle. Garrett felt he was hallucinating by now: the flame of this candle was a pure blue light, and there was a sudden coolness in the air.

She moved to the green candle, facing out, and called, "Watchtower of the North, Element of Earth, I call thee to witness and guard this circle." She bent and lit the candle, and in Garrett's mind, this one burned green, and he smelled loam and forest.

Then she stepped to the altar to light the purple candle and stood with her dark hair tumbled down her slim back as she chanted, low, in a voice like prayer, "Mistress Hecate, Queen of the Night, Goddess of the Dead, Watcher at the Crossroads, guide my sight; grant me perfect vision this night. I humbly ask you now to show what this petitioner seeks to know."

She took up the silver dish and poured the burned flowers into her hand, then stood still, with her eyes closed, cupping her hands around the flowers. The candles flickered at the points of the circle as Tanith stood, breathing, slowly and deeply. Garrett couldn't keep his eyes off her face, as pale and beautiful as carved ivory in the light. Her breathing subtly increased, became deeper: labored, shuddering breaths.

The flowers fluttered from her hand and she jerked her head up. Her eyes were completely dilated as she stared into space . . . her breath was a shallow panting. She whipped around to face Garrett, and stared at him, but her eyes were unfocused as a blind woman's and Garrett had the eerie feeling she did not see him at all.

When she spoke it was in a harsh rasping, totally unlike her own silky voice, a grating that pained the ears to hear.

"The girl you seek is done and she's not the only one. Three more shall he take, ere his craving he will slake."

Garrett found he was on his feet, standing, stupefied. The voice he was hearing did not sound human. It was ancient and sibilant and utterly chilling. She rasped on.

"Samhain is the eve, when those who love the lost will grieve. Three to die to do the deed. Three captured. Three bound." And then a hoarse, guttural shout: *"RELEASE THEM!"*

Her face was contorted into something inhuman. She lurched forward arthritically, her hands twisted into claws. *"Release them,"* she croaked again.

Garrett felt waves of adrenaline pulsing through him. He could smell earth on her breath. Through his shock, the overwhelming sense of otherness, Garrett forced out, "How? Tell me how."

She raised a clawlike hand toward him and stared blackly into his eyes and Garrett felt his mind shudder; his thoughts were swirling in his head as if in a powerful wind. Then he was slammed with a sudden, surreally clear vision of the park. He could see himself there, standing beside the marble bench and staring toward the skeleton of the high-rise. A hulking black figure stood in the shadows of dusk: a huge shape, standing behind him, watching him.

Garrett gasped aloud. Suddenly the crone's eyes opened wider.

"Yes. Yes. There is a watcher," she said in that rasping voice, blank eyes unseeing. *"Speed you and find him. Find the watcher in the park."*

Garrett's hair stood up on the back of his neck and he remembered with nauseating clarity the sensation of being watched. He felt that gaze again, like touch on his neck, so strongly that he turned to look. He saw nothing but blackness beyond the shimmering circle of candlelight, but every nerve in his body was alive with the sense of danger, and his hand moved automatically for his weapon.

Behind him Tanith gasped. Garrett spun again . . . to see her shuddering through her entire body. Her knees buckled . . . Garrett leaped forward to catch her, but she stiffened, caught herself on the edge of the altar, and held up a warning hand.

"No." It was her own voice again, and the contortion was gone from her face. Garrett stopped, holding back.

She straightened and held out her arms. Her voice was hoarse, but her own, as she called out:

> "Elements of East, South, West, and North,
> Return you now as I called you forth.
> Open again this sacred space
> Send all energies back to place."

She moved her arms in a sweeping motion, as if catching and gathering something into her fists, then opened her hands and pushed outward. The candles wavered wildly with the force of the motion. Garrett felt a rush through his body, like electricity.

Tanith's hands dropped limply to her sides and she stood straight and tall in the center of the circle . . . then her legs buckled and she crumpled to the floor.

Chapter Twenty-five

Garrett stood for a paralyzed moment, realizing he was loath to touch her. He fought down the feeling and sprang forward to kneel by her side. She was breathing, and when he felt for her pulse it was fluttery, but present. He scooped her up and lifted her, rising to his feet, only half-conscious that his driving impulse was to be away from the circle, away from the pentagram.

He left the circle with its candles still burning on the quarters, and carried Tanith from the room, through the door into the inner reading room. Her hair was against his face and she was a sweet, live weight in his arms, breathing shallowly against his chest. His heart was pounding out of control. He started to cross to the outer door, but she moved against him and said, "Here . . ."

He looked around him and set her carefully down in one of the high-backed leather chairs, then stood by her side as she put her head down on the table, her breathing still labored, but slowing.

Finally she lifted her head and reached for the pitcher of water she'd left on the table. She was too shaky to lift it and Garrett took it from her and poured liquid into the goblet. She clasped it with both hands and drank greedily, draining the whole cup, then she grabbed for the cakes she'd left on the plate. For the next full minute she ate and drank without speaking, as if she were raven-ous. Garrett couldn't keep his eyes off her; his head felt as if it were going to explode. He was overcome by the impulse to get out, to get as far away from there as possible—and the desire to sweep her up again, crush her to him. Finally she leaned back in the chair, wiping her mouth with the back of her hand and closing her eyes.

After what seemed like an eternity, she opened her eyes and looked at him. "Amber is dead," she said bleakly. Garrett started; he had not given Tanith the name. "Her killer carved three triangles into her body, and the number 333, the sigils of the demon, just as he did with Erin. And there is a third . . ." She faltered, looking into space. "Not like the others."

"Not like the others, how?" he managed.

"I'm not sure. Not . . ." she stopped. "I don't know." Her face hardened. "He took their heads for his rituals."

Garrett felt his stomach drop in horror. "What rituals?"

His face must have reflected his disgust, because she made an effort to speak calmly. "Necromancy. It's a powerful black magic practice. A magician reanimates a corpse to gain information from the nether realm. This one—this man—is probably communicating with the demon through those he has killed, receiving instructions through them—"

Reanimates the dead? Talks to the demon? Garrett's whole mind was rebelling against everything he had seen and felt. All he wanted to do was get out, get as far from all of this as he could go. But he was going to take what he could from her before he left.

"Who is he?" he demanded hoarsely.

Her gaze became distant. "Someone in the middle part of life . . . he has the bulk of a man. He is alone in the world, unstable . . . a lost soul. He is weak, so he seeks power in the dark: has been courting the demon in secret rituals for some time, and his mind has dissipated; it is the demon who drives him now." Her eyes slowly focused on Garrett again, and she shook her head. "I saw from a distance only."

Garrett's whole skin was prickling, but he shoved down the feeling. *Nothing but generalities, useless.*

He spoke in agitation. "You said, 'Three captured, three bound.' Does that mean he has prisoners?" He didn't know what he was saying, who he was asking about. Moncrief was in jail; he'd put Moncrief in jail himself.

Her face shadowed, and he heard anger in her voice. "His three victims are dead, but not free. They are between the worlds. The killer has their heads. He's bound them to him in a ritual and their souls cannot move on."

He felt fury, and doubt, and she leaned forward, with compassion and urgency in her face. "I'm sorry, Detective Garrett, I know this is difficult for you. I know you don't want it to be real. But you must understand this. This man is out there now. He will take another victim on Samhain, when the veil between worlds is thinnest and the demon can come through."

He struggled to block that thought, focus on what was real. "You said *three* more." *But that thing that had been speaking hadn't been her, had it?* Even now that the ritual was over he was finding it hard to believe that that horrible voice had come out of her throat, that the spasms of that twisted body had been her own.

Tanith was staring at him. "She said that?" she asked, stunned.

"Who? Who is she?" he demanded.

"You wouldn't believe me," Tanith murmured. "I don't know what it means." She looked sick, suddenly weak and faint, but he didn't care, didn't want to care. She was right. He didn't believe her. He didn't believe any of it. He just wanted out.

"Please," she said, and reached to touch his arm. He jerked away from her as if something loathsome had brushed him, and felt logic returning.

What were you thinking? Buying into a sideshow performance like that? A few candles, some rhyming mumbo jumbo—it's an act. This is how she makes a living. Just another gypsy con artist.

She caught her breath . . . and suddenly stood from her chair, staring at him. "You aren't going to do anything," she said, her voice shaky. "You really aren't."

He couldn't speak, because he had nothing to say. *Demons? No. Not in this lifetime.*

"Then go," she answered him. "If you're not going to listen, then go."

"I'm going," he said, and shoved back his chair as he stood. "Thanks for the show. I understand how that kind of performance would keep you in business." He turned his back on her, striding toward the door.

"Don't forget your picture," she called to him from behind.

He turned, and saw her extending Amber's photo toward him. He looked down at the image of the lost girl. Tanith moved closer and he reached automatically to take it. Their fingers met with a shock of static, and he flinched back.

"Detective," she said with contempt. "Fare thee well."

He turned and pushed through the curtain of stars.

He stood in the hall of Carolyn's high-rise, ringing the bell.

Inside he heard soft footsteps and the hesitation that he knew was Carolyn putting her eye to the peephole.

After a second she opened the door, and stood barefoot, in a white silk robe. Before she could speak, he had backed her into the marble-tiled hall and kicked the door shut behind him. He pushed her against the wall and bent to kiss her neck, and heard her purr, "Well, well . . ." before he took her mouth, took her breasts, took her, took himself into welcome oblivion.

Chapter Twenty-six

October 15

For Garrett, the next week was a blur. Jason Moncrief was arraigned, and entered a plea of "not guilty" with the judge.

Of course he did, nearly everyone does. It means nothing.

The judge set a trial date, which as Carolyn and the detectives had expected, was three months away, giving them plenty of time to keep gathering real evidence.

The DNA reports came back in, and as everyone in the department, the D.A.'s office, and anyone in the U.S. or maybe the world who watched the evening news or signed on to the Internet had expected, the tests proved that the semen found in Erin Carmody's body was Jason Moncrief's, and the blood found on Jason's jeans and sheets was Erin Carmody's. For the last week Landauer had been positively glowing, and Garrett knew why—it was as strong a circumstantial case as they had ever been a part of.

Garrett himself had been doing a bang-up job of forgetting that night with Tanith Cabarrus, her ritual performance and ominous predictions . . . and the feel of her body in his arms. After all, this was reality, and there was plenty of real police work to be done.

But with every day that passed, the specter of Halloween loomed larger in his mind.

"Three more shall he take, ere his craving he will slake . . ."

And Amber's burned-cigarette eyes stared out of the photo that Garrett had filed away . . .

And the sweet, haunting lyrics of Jason's song to Erin would not stop playing through his head.

So this afternoon Garrett stood outside the Suffolk County jail in a mercilessly cold wind. The sun was sinking and the jail was right off the Charles River. Garrett turned away from the glistening silver water and headed toward the facility.

Suffolk County, where Jason Moncrief had been sent for pretrial detention, was a seven-story brick building with a facade of columns and a triangular piece on the roof that made it look vaguely like a temple. In reality it was a maximum security facility housing nine hundred pretrial detainees in thirteen separate housing units with 453 cells, and 654 beds, making it as massively overcrowded as almost every correctional facility in the U.S. As he passed through security, Garrett tried not to dwell on what Jason's life had been like inside.

On an upper deck of the building, Garrett looked out over the exercise yard. Inmates in their radioactive orange jumpsuits milled in their mostly racially segregated groups, some playing basketball at dilapidated backboards, some pumping iron at the rows of benches and weight machine. The technical restraining order was still in place and Garrett couldn't get in to talk to Jason in person. But he could look at him. And Jason wasn't hard to spot, with his dark hair and eyes and pale skin, so like—

Garrett forced himself away from the thought of Tanith.

Jason was completely alone on the bench of the riser on which he sat. More than alone: there was no one at all in his vicinity; he seemed segregated, himself. Garrett had been watching for fifteen minutes and no one had come near him. Usually a kid that young, with the looks he had, would have all manner of unwelcome attention—or alternately, the scrupulous attention of one large older inmate who had taken him "under his wing."

Jason looked alone in the yard.

Garrett turned to the bulky hack—corrections officer—who

had escorted him up to the observation deck. "This kid Moncrief. How's he been?"

The C.O. looked down on the yard and flicked a hand in Jason's direction. "Just like you see. Complete loner. He's in solitary except for weekly exercise. But it's always the same. No one goes near him."

Garrett raised his hands, but didn't have to ask the question. The C.O. shrugged. "Spooky kid. There's something about him. Maybe Satan's protecting him, like he says." He laughed shortly, but there was no conviction in the sound. "He draws these fucking freaky designs all over himself and sits in his cell and—chants—all day long. Weirds out everyone on his block. And sometimes . . ." The C.O. trailed off.

"What?" Garrett asked sharply.

"Sometimes it sounds like there's other people in there with him."

Garrett felt a jolt. Back to the voices. *"An early sign of demon infestation."* "Crazy," he murmured, without realizing he'd said it.

"Yeah," the C.O. answered. "That's what they keep saying."

Garrett nodded thanks to the C.O. and started down the metal stairs toward the ground floor. In his mind he was turning over the jail screw's remark about "freaky designs" on Jason's body. *Well, that's something, isn't it?* If the kid had been stupid enough to cover himself with

the sigils of the demon Choronzon

the same designs he had carved into Erin Carmody's body— then fuck the pretty song. He'd just hammered another nail into his own coffin.

Garrett was making a note to get a physical search warrant to check out Jason's homemade tattoos when he reached the ground floor. He hesitated, looked through the chain-link fence at the yard.

Jason had not moved.

But as Garrett studied him, he suddenly looked up, straight into Garrett's face. Garrett froze as they locked eyes across the yard.

And then Jason stood from his seat on the riser and walked deliberately toward the fence, toward Garrett: a sinuous, almost reptilian walk.

Garrett stood still behind the fence, in a kind of disbelief, watching his approach.

Jason stopped in front of the fence, staring through the links. "Detective," he said, in that sly, feral voice Garrett remembered. "How good of you to come. Are we going to talk, now? Are you here to have the Mysteries explained? Do you crave an audience with the Master?"

Garrett lunged toward the fence, but stopped himself just in time. He was shaking with rage.

"You murderous little shit. I know you killed her. Her parents put her in the ground without her head, you sick fuck. I hope you burn for this."

Jason shuddered through his whole body, and suddenly someone else looked out through his eyes, someone lost, and haunted, and terrified. "Erin," he whispered. His face trembled. "I didn't touch her. I didn't do it. I swear it."

Two C.O.s were suddenly behind him, pulling him away from the fence as a bell jangled dissonantly through the yard. "I swear it," Jason said miserably, his eyes desperate on Garrett's face. "I swear it."

Chapter Twenty-seven

In the anemic wash of the streetlamps, the deserted park was ghostly and colorless, a stage set of dead trees and shrubs with the dry fountain and angel in the center. The park had that in common with the landfill; there was a brutality about the ruination, a killer deliberately seeking ugliness.

Garrett parked his Explorer around a corner and a block away so his approach would not be as obvious. In the dark car he reached into the backseat for an old White Sox sweatshirt. He crumpled the garment up in his hands, spilled the dregs of his coffee on it for good measure, then stripped off the business shirt he was wearing, strapped on the shoulder holster for his Glock, and pulled on the wrinkled and newly stained sweatshirt over that, to create an impromptu derelict look. Then he opened the glove compartment and removed a Taser and an extra set of cuffs.

You have a partner, he told himself harshly. *What are you doing out here without your partner?*

Jason's voice whispered back to him.

"I didn't touch her. I swear it."

He left the car and walked toward the park.

On this cold and windy night the streets were deserted except for

an occasional disreputable car cruising by. There was a chill in the
clear air and the waning moon was a stark misshapen disc in the sky.
Garrett walked through the brick gateposts of the park and onto the
concrete paths, past the twisted tree with its leaves like blood. He
moved slowly so that he could get a good sense of his surroundings,
and he weaved a little, stumbling on the path as if he were drunk.
The wind whispered in the weeds and bushes beside him.

Garrett didn't know what he could reasonably expect to find
there. But he could not forget the words of whoever or whatever
had been speaking to him that night in Tanith's candlelit circle, the
words that had been tormenting him since that unnerving night:

"There is a watcher in the park."

Is.

He reached the bench—Amber's bench—and half fell onto it,
slumping back as if the walk had been an effort. Although he
couldn't see them he was weirdly aware of the burned footprints
right behind him; he didn't like having his back to them.

The demon blasts the flowers of the field . . .

He stared up through the moonlight at the stained angel, as Amber must have done a hundred times before.

In his mind he saw again the circle in the candlelight, Tanith's bot-
tomless eyes as she croaked at him in that inhuman voice: *"There is a
watcher in the park . . ."*

Then he felt the same prickling on the back of his neck, and every sense suddenly sprang to alert. There was someone behind him.

Garrett stayed slumped in position, barely breathing. And then
in one move he stood and twisted around to look behind him.

A huge dark shadow moved beside the gnarled tree. Garrett's
pulse skyrocketed as he spotted the shadowy figure. Undeniably
real. He reached for his holster and drew his weapon and shouted,
"Police, don't move!"

The shadow took off running—big, bulky, silent. It bolted toward the perimeter of the park, darting through the parched bushes.
Garrett took off running after it. It was a stretch that he had any
cause for pursuit—loitering, maybe, trespassing—but he'd think
about that later.

For the size and bulk of the fleeing man, he was amazingly fast and light on his feet. Garrett was panting by the time he'd dodged through the dry and browning hedges and reached the sidewalk. The hulking shadow had disappeared; there was no movement Garrett could see. He spun around, scanning the dark . . .

. . . and across the street he spotted a black shape squeezing itself through a gap in the green plastic fencing blocking off the front of the construction site, surrounding the skeleton of the building. Now his suspect was trespassing, and that was cause enough. Garrett pulled himself upright and darted across the street in pursuit. As he ran he grabbed for the cell phone in his pants pocket and hit speed-dial for Emergency Dispatch. He barked into the phone, "Detective Garrett in foot pursuit southbound Tremont and Washington." He sucked in air, stopped on the sidewalk, and searched for an address on the curb of the site. "Suspect trespassing at 93 Tremont, wanted for questioning in homicide. Suspect African-American male, six-four, heavyset, dark parka and pants."

He heard the response, *"Copy, Detective Garrett,"* and shoved the phone back in his pocket as he stopped on the sidewalk in front of the green fencing, quickly calculating. He knew units were already on their way, but the watcher could be through the skeleton of the building and out the other side in just minutes.

It was his least favorite type of situation because there was no way of seeing what was beyond the fence; the watcher could be right on the other side of the gap, with any kind of weapon at all.

Garrett gasped in a centering breath and stepped up to the gap in the sagging fence. He grabbed the edge of the plastic and stuck both his weapon and his face halfway through the gap.

His heart was pounding out of control as he blinked rapidly to adjust to the darkness.

He was looking in on the skeletal structure of the building: a raw concrete floor, metal piers, scattered sawhorses, vast empty spaces. There was no sign of the hulking dark shape.

Garrett slipped through the gap in the green fencing, noting that it had been pulled off the pole; someone was using this gap as a thoroughfare. He moved across the concrete floor into the cavernous building.

There was a stark, luminous quality to the space; the ambient light from outside streetlamps caught the pale of the cement flooring and made it glow like marble. Metal slugs were scattered on the floor like silver coins, and the whole floor was coated with white, powdery cement dust. And as Garrett looked at the slugs, he spotted a trail of footprints in the cement dust: huge, blurry footsteps that reminded him queasily of the burned footprints in the wildflowers. He tightened his grip on his Glock and moved forward, following the prints.

He stared into the darkness . . . and saw a large chunk of darkness shift. He had a sudden mental flash of reptilian jaws, scaly skin, basilisk eyes: images from the paintings Tanith had shown him. Nightmare images.

He banished the thought and yelled again, "Police! Don't move!"

The dark hulk scuttled into the shadows again and disappeared.

And before his eyes, Garrett saw the wall in front of him ripple like water. He froze, his mind for a moment unable to comprehend what he was seeing. Then he realized the rippling wall was opaque plastic sheeting, draped from ceiling to floor and blowing slightly in the wind. He clenched his jaw and moved forward, pulled the plastic back to enter.

Garrett smelled him first: a rank stink of sweat, urine, garbage, every combination of filth. He had just a glimpse of a metal shopping cart parked at the wall, filled with white plastic carrier bags, double-bagged and tied around pouches of—stuff. And then he saw his suspect: a huge dark mass barreling straight at him, and raving at the top of his lungs: "Current status in static! Chaos! Chaos in the current! Disperse diverse diversion. Beee-eep. Bee-eep. WHOOO!"

Garrett responded entirely by instinct; as the dark mass hurtled toward him, he stepped aside and stuck out his foot to trip him— and as his attacker stumbled Garrett lunged at him with his full body weight and tackled him. The man fell and Garrett fell with him, landing flat on top of him. It was like crashing into a garbage heap; his fall was cushioned by the man's bulk, but the stink was overpowering. The big man jerked and bucked. Garrett kneed his attacker in the back, wrestled for the man's beefy arms, and managed to slap a cuff on his substantial wrist, then jerked the other arm behind him to cuff the other wrist. The huge man beneath him was howling now, an animal sound, mixed with sobbing. His bare brown feet, blackened with filth, kicked the pavement in helpless rage.

Garrett scrambled to his feet, tried to breathe through his mouth to minimize the assault on his olfactory glands, and planted his shoe firmly on the back of the man's neck. Somewhere on the streets outside, Garrett could hear the wail of sirens. Beneath him, the dirty man continued his raving.

"Don't hurt! Danger! Dragons in the current. Don't look! Don't hurt! Nooo!"

Chapter Twenty-eight

The patrolmen who assisted Garrett in leading his collar to the squad car were no more happy with this particular job than Garrett was; he noticed one of the young uniforms fighting not to gag at the smell emanating from the huge man. The other uniform, stronger-stomached, muttered, "Get the gas mask," under his breath. The collar, an African-American male who looked to be in his early thirties, was six feet four if he was an inch and nearly three hundred pounds, almost certainly schizophrenic at the very least and way off the meds—if he'd ever been on them. Garrett recognized the "word salad" aspect of his speech (and even without that the shoelessness and overall state of filth would have been a pretty good indicator). They had themselves a classic "dirty man," one of the homeless chronic mentally ill who lived out of grocery carts and garbage bags, and more often than not wore their entire meager wardrobe at once, at all times, winter, spring, or summer. The parka and frayed cuffs and blackened feet were pathetically characteristic.

The man was docile as they led him out of the construction site; apparently exhausted by his rush at and struggle with Garrett.

The uniforms had parked their black-and-white at the curb out-side the park. As they led the big man out of the construction site toward the patrol car, Garrett played a hunch and steered the man on the path leading toward the center of the park. "Take him this way," he told the officer holding the man's other arm.

"How come—" the uniform began, then thought better of it. "Sure."

Garrett guided them toward the bench . . . and the footprints. Their captive was completely passive, head down and lumbering along like a child, but as they came closer to the bench the big man jerked his head up. "No!" he screamed, with eyes bulging, the cords standing out in his neck. "No no no no no. Bad bad bad bad bad. Dragonfly demonbite eat her eat her." He flailed in their grasp, all the power in that hulking body suddenly alarmingly apparent.

"Shit!" yelled the younger uniform.

Garrett yelled back, "Take him that way!" He jerked at the homeless man's arm, pulling him away from the burned footprints. And on impulse, he added, "Run!"

Their collar was more than happy to run with them, pounding across the paths.

As they reached the sidewalk Garrett halted, panting. The man had completely ceased his struggling and screaming and stood limply between them as the officers gasped for breath.

Garrett and the officers exchanged a look, then the officers loaded the huge man into the back of the patrol car. He curled up on the seat and burst into tears.

Garrett stood on the sidewalk, still breathing hard as he watched the man weeping in the backseat. Garrett was fighting an adrenaline buzz and massively conflicting feelings. His strong suspicion was that he was not looking at Erin's killer. The man was barely functional; Garrett could not imagine him bringing Erin's body onto the landfill without detection; that was the work of a much more crafty, outwardly sane, and organized killer.

And if the big man had killed Erin the blood would still be on those clothes, Garrett noted, without a trace of humor.

Yet somehow, he was sure the homeless man was a thread of the case, a potential witness at least, and he intended to follow that thread where it led.

The stronger-stomached uniform turned to Garrett, then glanced back out toward the stone bench. "What the hell was all that about?"

Garrett looked back in the direction of the footprints. The streetlamp cast a sickly yellow light around the empty bench; the angel looked down from the fountain. "I don't know," he answered.

But maybe he did.

One of the privileges of rank was that Garrett did not have to be the one trapped in the squad car with this particular cargo as the officers transported him to the nearest BPD substation. Garrett was already at the counter with the desk sergeant when the two uniforms brought the homeless man in. A couple of passing detectives gave them wide berth, turning their faces away from the smell as the uniforms led him down the dingy corridor.

The official "reason for arrest" was "assault on a law enforcement officer."

"But I just want to talk to him," Garrett explained to the desk sergeant. "He may be a witness in a case of mine. If I can just have a room to question him—chances are I'll be releasing him."

The desk sergeant snorted sympathetically. "Good luck with that."

"Yeah," said Garrett.

He called Landauer from the substation, the guilt now perfectly overwhelming. It was pushing midnight. It was an uncomfortable conversation.

"Hate like hell to do this to you, Land, but I might have a witness to that prostitute's disappearance," Garrett began.

"You *might*." Landauer was sleepy and pissed, not a good combination.

"It's not much to go on, but the guy has been hanging out in the park. It's just a hunch, but I'm going to question him and I just wanted to make sure you were in the loop."

Garrett listened to his partner breathe on the other end of the phone. Finally he spoke. "This is hella weird, G. Where you going with this?"

"I don't know. That's what I need you for, pal."

———

Landauer showed up half an hour later, rumpled and disgruntled, and the partners walked the scuffed floors of the substation—an older building, almost medieval compared to the modern, airy halls of Schroeder. They passed a row of vending machines, headed toward the interview room.

"What the hell're you doin' here, G?" Landauer asked pointedly. "We got our guy. Slam dunk, remember?"

"What if there's another one?"

Landauer narrowed his eyes. "On the witch's say-so, you mean?"

Garrett stifled a sigh and tried to avoid thoughts of Tanith in that candlelit circle. "We got a missing girl, Land. Same age as Erin Carmody. Gone missing on one of those—holidays. I don't like it."

They stopped in front of the interview-room door and Landauer looked through the two-way mirror at the hulking, filthy man at the table. "*That's* your witness? Jesus Christ, G . . ."

Garrett was about to answer when his eyes fell on the vending machines across the hall. "Hold on." He shoved his hands in his pants. "Got any change?"

Landauer cursed and dug in his pockets.

They entered the interrogation room and Garrett saw Landauer's face curdle from the smell. He shot Garrett a baleful, *you-so-owe-me-for-this* look. Garrett gave him an apologetic grimace, then sat down in the chair across from the homeless man. Landauer leaned against the wall, as far from the witness as he could get. Garrett cleared his throat and spoke gently to the big man, as if to a child.

"Hello. My name is Detective Garrett. Can you tell me your name?"

The man did not respond. He stared dolefully at the table in front of him, tears rolling down his ample cheeks.

Garrett took a Mars bar out of his coat pocket and set it in the center of the table. The big man's face lit up and he grabbed for the candy. He tore off the wrapper and stuffed it into his mouth like a little kid.

After he'd scarfed the chocolate, Garrett spoke. "Can we be friends now? I have more candy if you'll talk to me."

The hulking man looked at him with red-rimmed eyes and said nothing.

"You're not in trouble, okay? We just want to ask you a few questions." Garrett took Amber's photo out of his pocket. "We're looking for this girl." He put the photo down in front of the man. "Have you seen her?"

To Garrett's surprise the man put his shaggy head down on the table and wailed.

Garrett and Landauer exchanged a glance. "You have seen her," Garrett began.

"Noooo . . . Noooo . . . No . . ."

"I think you have seen her," Garrett said firmly. "Can you tell me what happened?"

"Dragons," the man said tearfully. "Huge! Whoosh!!! Ate her up."

Landauer stroked his chin and looked at Garrett impassively.

"Dragons," Garrett repeated.

"Dragons dragging down down deep." The big man began to rock in his seat. "Dark entropy current formless malformed malfunction . . ." The chair was tipping back and forth, thumping against the floor, faster and faster as he rambled. "Entropic current chaos. Beep . . . bee-eeep . . . bee-eeeep . . ."

The partners stepped out of the interview room, with the big man still ranting behind them.

"Well. Case closed," Landauer said with a straight face. "Dragons got her."

Garrett was silent, standing in the sickly glow of the vending machines. *Chaos. Entropy. Dispersion. Current.* The words were in no order that made sense, but he'd heard them before. On Jason's *Current 333* CD.

Landauer glanced back toward the observation window of the interview room. "So what are you going to do with Dragon Man, drop him off at a shelter?"

Garrett sighed. "Psych intake. I'll see if anyone has a bed open—"

Of course the chances of an empty bed in any mental facility when winter was approaching were next to nothing. Then into Garrett's mind, unbidden, came a picture of the sign on the front of Tanith's shop: *Psychic Healing*. And he fell silent, midsentence. Land looked at him questioningly. Garrett shrugged. "But you know how it goes. He'll be back on the street tomorrow. I'll take him back to his cart I guess—"

Landauer's hand suddenly closed around his arm. "None of my business, bro, but from where I stand you are looking in grave danger of fucking up your fast-track gravy train."

Garrett looked at him, startled. But he didn't have to ask what his partner meant.

Landauer released his hold on Garrett, shook his head. "Ain't no way I see Miz Carolyn putting up with a witch on the side. I would think long and hard about my next move, 'f I were you."

The men locked eyes. Garrett found his whole body tensing, his fists clenching. He took a breath, releasing the stance. "Appreciate you coming out," he said neutrally.

Landauer gave him a cynical smile. "Your funeral, my friend."

Chapter Twenty-nine

The big guy huddled in the far back of Garrett's Explorer as Garrett drove back toward Chinatown, and even with all the windows down and cold wind gusting through the car, he was regretting his decision. Dragon Man was quiet enough, busy with the stash of candy Garrett had given him, but he was just as ripe. Garrett was considering running him through a car wash.

He tried to breathe shallowly and brooded.

He had been keeping deliberately busy since the night Tanith had performed the ritual, blocking the thought of her standing in the circle as that alien voice croaked out insane things. He dreamed it, though, sometimes, and the dreams were never good.

And yet, she'd been right. *Again.* There had been a watcher in the park, and he'd found him just as she—or whatever that voice had been—had directed him. A watcher who responded to the photo of a missing girl, a watcher who ranted about dragons and demons and dispersion and "the Current."

He glanced in his rearview mirror at his passenger and said softly, "Choronzon."

In the backseat, the Dragon Man stiffened, freezing midbite of candy, and raised his liquid eyes to the rearview mirror to meet

186 • Alexandra Sokoloff

Garrett's gaze. Then he dropped the candy bar and curled up in the seat into a tight ball, with his arms crossed over his head.

Garrett reached for his cell phone and slowed the Explorer, steering with one hand as he punched in a number. He was surprised when Tanith picked up immediately. "Book of Shadows."

"You're awake," he said into the phone, startled.

"Night person," she said. Neither of them identified themselves, and Garrett felt a teasing and unwanted heat at the intimacy of that.

"You were right about the watcher," he said, aware that his voice was tight.

"You found him," she said, not a question, and Garrett noticed she'd said, "Him."

"Yeah. There's a problem, though," he said, and when she was silent, he spoke.

The wind had picked up, tumbling leaves in flurries across the moonlit paths of the park, as Garrett pulled the Explorer over to the curb in front of the construction site. Before the Explorer was even stopped, the Dragon Man was fumbling for the door handle and jumping out of the car, his bare feet hitting the sidewalk, running. He was astonishingly fast for the size of him.

Garrett tossed a placard on the dash that stated OFFICIAL BPD BUSINESS and followed.

By the time Garrett had squeezed through the loose plastic fencing, the big man was already halfway across the pale expanse of concrete floor. Garrett followed as he disappeared through the opaque plastic sheeting.

Garrett stepped through the plastic wall himself, just in time to see the Dragon Man throw himself at his shopping cart. He clutched the metal side of the cart, checking over the rows of white bags like a worried mother hen.

"Is there anything in there of Amber's?" Garrett asked aloud. The big man stiffened and made a growling sound in his throat.

"Okay," Garrett said, lifting his hands. "I'm just going to sit right here, all right?" He cautiously took a seat on the floor beside one of the cement columns and leaned his back against it.

The Dragon Man continued his inventory, and then, apparently satisfied, he sighed and removed a stained dark blue bedroll and a folded blue tarp from the cart. He spread the tarp beside the cart and then unrolled the bedroll on top of it, giving Garrett furtive searching looks as he did so.

"I'm going to sleep, too," Garrett assured him. He leaned his head back against the column and shut his eyes, breathing slowly and deeply. He could feel the big man's silent, watching tension across the space, but as Garrett continued his own long, deep breaths, he heard the beginning of deep, rumbling snores.

Adrenaline crash, Garrett thought. He was having one himself; his muscles were relaxing into a near stupor. Dealing with the mentally ill always unsettled him, the specter of the mind turning on itself.

He remained still, propped up against his column, for another minute or two and then as the snoring continued, he opened his eyes and looked toward the shopping cart.

Go through it? Wait? He debated with himself.

Then he eased himself to his feet and moved one quiet step at a time toward the cart. He could see dozens of precisely packed white carrier bags, double layers of plastic, each neatly knotted at the top.

He was just reaching to remove one when he heard the rustle of plastic behind him and froze . . .

Then spun, in one move reaching under his sweatshirt and drawing his Glock—

Tanith stood in the slit of the plastic.

He felt a different kind of rush, seeing her. Slowly, he lowered the gun. "Jesus Christ, I told you to call me when you got here."

"I'm sorry, I didn't mean to scare you."

She sounded amused and it burned him. "You shouldn't be walking around here by yourself."

"I'm fine." Her face was pale, almost translucent, and there were dark circles of fatigue under her eyes. She moved through the plastic and set down the bag she was holding, a large carpetbag made of an expensive-looking patterned fabric. She was in another enticingly fitted calf-length skirt of a deep violet color, and a white blouse with a plunging neckline. Garrett felt his heart start beating faster, which irritated him. *Focus,* he told himself.

"I appreciate you coming," he said, his voice brittle. She didn't answer him; she was already looking past him at the large sleeping lump in the bedroll. Garrett hadn't told Tanith much on the phone; just vaguely that the witness had "mental problems," but seemed to be familiar with the missing girl.

Tanith stepped past Garrett (*that intoxicating scent*) and looked down at the large, dirty man squeezed into the bedroll, snoring in a deep rumble.

"Schizophrenic," she murmured, and Garrett was startled, although of course he'd made the same assumption himself.

"I think so," he answered softly, though there didn't seem to be any immediate danger of waking the man. "Autism, too, maybe, some developmental thing."

She looked down at the sleeping man for a long time, and Garrett had no idea what was going through her mind, but she seemed to be studying something about him. She did not seem bothered by the smell, or even to notice it. She knelt on the concrete and put both her hands at the sides of the man's face, as if cradling his head—except without touching him; her hands were about an inch away from actual contact. She remained in that position for at least a full minute, without moving or speaking, her eyes lowered and her face intent.

Finally, she stood, looked toward Garrett, and gestured to the wall of plastic sheeting. Garrett followed her through the slit into the wide dark expanse of the unfinished building. Tanith kept moving and Garrett trailed her, marveling at her perfect posture; she did not walk, it was more of a glide, like a dancer, like a nun.

She stopped and stood in the middle of the floor; her hands steepled under her chin, brooding. "You think he saw the killer."

"I'm pretty sure he saw the girl. Amber. It's hard to tell what else he saw," Garrett answered. "His sense of reality is not . . . great."

"No," she answered abstractedly. "Very disordered. Extreme mental chaos." Garrett was not sure how she would know that, as she had not spoken with the man at all, though Garrett supposed the state of the man's clothing was somewhat of a tip-off.

Then he remembered uneasily that mental chaos was one of the qualities associated with Choronzon.

"And what would you like me to do?" Tanith asked him bluntly. Her eyes gleamed, and Garrett had the distinct feeling that she knew exactly what he wanted her to do, but was making him say it aloud as some kind of power game. He felt a flare of anger, and also of desire.

"I thought you might be able to talk to him," he said, keeping his voice even.

She studied him without smiling and then said, "That's interesting of you, Detective. Is it a spell you want, then?"

He fought down the anger. "I told you, I don't care how it gets done." *Only that hadn't exactly been true, had it?* "If there's something you can do, then do it."

He stared into her black eyes and she stared back, a long and dangerous moment. Then she lifted her head slightly. "There may be."

She went through the wall of plastic again, and returned carrying the carpetbag. She stood in the midst of the columns, surveying the area, then pointed at a large bare expanse of floor. "I think there. And I think I should be alone with him, but don't worry, I'll cast the circle large enough to protect you," she said with a perfectly straight face. Garret understood he was being teased, but tried to ignore it. He was pretty sure he'd gone off the deep end already, or he wouldn't be here at all.

She knelt on the cement floor beside her carpetbag and opened it. From the angle she had chosen—deliberately, Garrett was sure—he could not see into the case, but he watched as she withdrew a folded purple silk cloth, several purple candles (the ever-present candles), a dagger, a silver chalice, and a smaller, square leather case.

She rose, stepped to the empty floor space, and shook out the cloth, stirring up swirls of concrete dust like smoke. The cloth was round, Garrett saw, and when she floated it down to the floor, it made a perfect circle. She placed the purple candles at the four quadrants of the circle and lit them.

She returned to her carpetbag, and withdrew a large purple crystal, amethyst, Garrett thought, his mother's favorite gem; and an electric light that looked naggingly familiar.

"Black light?" he asked, frowning.

"Ultraviolet, yes. Different colors have different healing properties. Violet is for mental clarity; it soothes mental disorders. The idea is to surround him in violet, like a color bath."

She switched on the black light. The purple light glowed in the vast empty space, and her white blouse instantly turned luminous.

She opened the smaller leather case; it was full of labeled glass bottles with liquids of different colors. She removed several and poured a few drops from each bottle into the silver cup, and placed it at the edge of the silk circle with the knife and crystal.

Finally she looked over at Garrett. "I'll get him, then."

"Do you want me to—"

"I don't think so," she said with unnerving calm, and disappeared through the plastic wall. Garrett waited uncomfortably, debating whether or not he should go after her.

Then she emerged through the plastic, leading the big man by the hand. He was blinking drowsily, looking only half-awake. He shuffled on the floor like a child, and his bare feet kicked up little clouds of white dust.

Tanith led him to the circle of purple silk, and guided him carefully through the lit candles to the center of the circle.

"Just sit down here with me," she said gently, and tugged at his hand as she sunk to the floor. Obediently he folded himself into a crossed-knee position and sat across from her, a hulking shadow in the purple light.

Tanith picked up the large amethyst crystal from beside her and held it up in front of her so that it caught the candlelight. The Dragon Man's eyes widened.

"Pretty, isn't it?" she said in a low, coaxing voice. "Do you like it?" He did not answer, but seemed mesmerized by the sparkling chips of light. She held the stone for him to gaze at . . . and then spoke even more softly. "Here. You hold it." She extended the stone and he took it hesitantly, staring into it. "Close your eyes. You can still see the stone." He shut his eyes, and Garrett could see his breathing slow.

She stood noiselessly and unhurriedly, and moved around to stand behind the Dragon Man. He did not seem to notice her. "Lie down now," she said, and touching her hands lightly to his shoulders, she eased him back to lie on the silk, in the circle of candle-light. He held the crystal clutched to his chest. She smoothed his brow with her fingertips, and then moved around him, gently placing his arms by his sides and leaving the crystal centered on top of his chest, then straightening his legs so they rested together. "You're inside the crystal now, inside the purple. You're inside that shining purple light . . ." Garrett saw the big man's body loosen, growing more limp. "That's good. Relax," Tanith encouraged softly. "And now I want you to breathe in with me—breathe in that purple light. Breathe in . . ." The Dragon Man did not open his eyes, but sucked in air. Tanith breathed in with him. "Now breathe out . . ." She repeated the breathing with him three times.

She stood still and looked down on the big man in the candle-light, then reached into her shirt and drew out the dagger on its chain. Again she extended her arms with the knife pointed straight ahead; again she made a slow, steady revolution in a circle.

Her face was pale in the glowing violet light, her onyx eyes fixed in space.

She completed the circle, slipped the chain back around her neck, and knelt at the Dragon Man's left side. She reached forward with both arms extended, holding her palms inward at the top of his head, about an inch away from actually touching him. She brought her hands smoothly down the entire length of his body, one hand on either side, not quite touching his skin the whole way down.

She repeated the entire gesture six more times, then reached for the silver bowl and dipped her fingertips into the liquid she'd mixed there. She moved to the Dragon Man's head, where she lay her hands gently, one on each side of his head, with her thumbs resting on his temples. She closed her eyes and was still, holding that position. Garrett found himself roiling with envy, imagining her hands on him. He shook his head, forced himself back into focus.

Tanith shifted her position so she was kneeling at the Dragon Man's head and this time held his whole head in her hands as she spoke aloud into the darkness. "I banish chaos, pain, and fear. Mercury, I call on thee: aid his thoughts and words and tongue, that he may tell us all he's done. This watcher now knows clarity. As I say, so mote it be."

She sat again on the floor beside the man's bulk and spoke tenderly to him. "You are within a circle of protection, a circle of healing crystal light. You are safe. You are loved. You can say anything, here, and you will be protected. Do you hear me?"

Garrett found himself holding his breath . . . as the big man on the floor slowly nodded.

"You can speak," she told him. "What is your name?"

To Garrett's utter astonishment, the Dragon Man spoke, a deep, resonant James Earl Jones voice.

"Roland, ma'am."

"Roland what?" Tanith asked, without a trace of surprise.

"Roland Cutler," he said, without opening his eyes.

"Roland, I'm Tanith. I'm very glad to meet you. Are you comfortable?"

"Yes, ma'am."

"That's good. I want to ask you questions about a girl named Amber." The man stiffened on the floor, tensing every muscle in his body. Tanith said quickly, "You're safe. You're safe here." Slowly he relaxed, not altogether, but enough.

"You do know Amber," Tanith said softly.

"The lost girl in the park. She loves the angel," the Dragon Man murmured. Tanith glanced over at Garrett. He nodded tightly. Inside he was reeling, a disorienting wave of paranoia. *Am I being set up? How can this guy have gone from stark raving to lucid because of some purple light?*

"That's right. That's Amber," Tanith said. "We're looking for her, Roland. Can you tell us where she is?"

The big man shuddered. He did not open his eyes, but tears squeezed out from the corners and ran down his cheeks, plopping softly onto the dark silk below him. "A bad man got her. Very bad. Scares me . . ." He paused, and whispered . . . "Evil."

The wind rippled through the empty space, and Garrett felt the chill in his bones.

"Tell us about the man, Roland," Tanith said softly.

"He came in a car, like one of her—like the other men."

"Describe the car," Garrett said sharply. On the floor, Roland stiffened. Tanith glanced at Garrett, shook her head slightly, frowning.

"What kind of car, Roland?" Tanith asked. "Can you describe it?"

Roland squeezed his eyes shut, shaking his head.

"You were in the park, watching," Tanith suggested. Roland nodded his head warily. "But now you're only seeing it as if you're watching a movie. That's all; it's just like watching a movie. Tell me about the car."

After a moment the big man spoke slowly. "Dark blue . . . Camaro. It's not new . . . but not too dinged up."

Beside the pillar, Garrett moved, impatiently, opened his mouth to ask about the plates, but before he could speak, Tanith was asking.

"What about the license plate? Can you see the numbers?"

Roland frowned, moved on the silk circle on the ground. "I can't see it," he fretted.

"You can see it," Tanith said. "Tell me."

"T-O-R," Roland said obediently. "Then there's a nine . . ." He squeezed his eyes tightly closed, as if squinting to see. "That's all I can see. I'm sorry," he added.

Garrett had pulled out his notebook and was writing furiously. *Hypnotism*, he told himself. *Not magic. You've seen it before.*

"That's very good, Roland, thank you." Tanith glanced toward Garrett. "Let's talk more about the man. Can you describe him?"

Roland started to shake his head on the floor, in mute denial.

"It's all right. I'm here with you. Tell us what you see."

"She went to the car and talked to him. Then she got in and he took her away . . ." The big man was crying again, softly sobbing. "Hurt her. Hurt her," he choked out. "Killed her."

There's something wrong, here. Something . . . Garrett shook his head and Tanith looked toward him. After a moment, she spoke aloud.

"Roland, how do you know? Did you see him kill her?"

"He brought her back." He shuddered again with a sob. "She was dead."

Garrett straightened, electrified. He kept his voice low. "He brought her back to the park? The body is in the park?"

"Did he bring her back to the park?" Tanith asked.

"To the Channel," Roland said, through tears.

Tanith glanced toward Garrett. "Fort Point Channel?"

Roland nodded.

"He killed her at the Channel?"

"No, he brought her back," the big man's voice trembled. "She was dead and he put her on a chain and dropped her into the water, down, down, down."

Tanith's face was intent in the glow of the candles and black light. "Was this the same night?"

"The next night."

Garrett wasn't following this at all. "Wait—then what were you doing at the Channel?" he said sharply.

Tanith ignored him. "Where at the Channel, Roland? Can you tell us where?"

"HarborWalk. Binford Park."

Even crazier. Binford is miles away from Chinatown. "How the hell . . ." Garrett muttered. Tanith shot him a black look and he didn't finish.

"Did you follow the car?" she asked the man in the circle gently. "The Channel's pretty far away. Why were you there?"

The man on the floor lifted his hands helplessly. "I went there. And he came and he put her in the water in a big stone on a chain."

"Who is he? Describe him," Garrett demanded.

The candles in the circle flickered as if in a rush of wind. On the floor, the big man stiffened. Then he sat up suddenly and pointed, eyes blank and staring. "There," he said, barely audible. There was pure terror in his voice.

Garrett whipped around, scanning the dark expanse of the building.

Inside the circle, Tanith stood, her body tense as she stared into the purple-lit dark. "Yes, I see."

Garrett stared into the dark, saw nothing. *Demons again,* he thought. *Back to the nut farm.* But he found his arms were raised in gooseflesh.

The big man's face contorted in terror and he started to scream. "No! No!" Around them the candles were wavering wildly in the wind.

Tanith spun, took a step toward the outside of the circle—and suddenly Garrett saw her stagger back violently, as if she had been shoved. He started toward her, but Tanith held both hands out, palms flat, a gesture of holding back. Her voice blasted out a warning: "Hold, intruder, get thee gone. I say this circle will hold strong. With each step your powers thin; you may not, cannot come within. Go!" she said savagely and pushed with her hands. The candles wavered, sizzling. The wind whipped at the plastic sheeting, gusting through the empty building.

Quickly Tanith raised her head and her hands high in a V and called out: "Circle, Elements, Watchtowers hold, with all the magic strength of old. Hear me now and ancients hark, repel the powers of the dark." Her voice was strong but there was a harsh undercurrent in it, almost as if she were in pain.

The wind dropped . . . the wild whipping of the plastic ceased.

The gooseflesh on Garrett's arms faded, and the sense that his heart was enclosed in a vise. He breathed in sharply.

"Blessed be," Tanith murmured.

The Dragon Man was no longer thrashing on the floor, his breath had slowed. Tanith drew herself up, drew a ragged breath. "Roland, I'm going to bring you back into the circle, now. When you open your eyes you will feel rested and at peace. I promise you, we're going to help you. Take a deep breath, now . . . and release it all . . ."

As the Dragon Man breathed out, she stood, extended her arms straight out at her sides with palms up, and made a slow revolution. "I draw up now this circle's power, away to wait for another hour."

She brought her hands together, dropped her head, and remained standing, her body shuddering with her labored breathing. Then she lifted her head and knelt by Roland's side, taking the amethyst crystal from his chest.

He opened his eyes and looked at her hazily. She stared into his eyes, then put her hands on his forearms and helped him sit up.

"There. There." She squeezed his hands reassuringly. "You were wonderful. Thank you."

After a moment, he ducked his head and nodded shyly.

She pressed the crystal into his hand. "Keep it." As Roland looked at her in wonder, she told him, "Detective Garrett is going to take you back to your bed, now." She looked to Garrett. Garrett stood for a moment, staring back at her . . . then he stooped and helped the big man up, and led him through the plastic sheeting to his bedroll. The Dragon Man dropped heavily to his knees and stretched out on the floor, clutching the crystal to his chest. No sooner had he put his head down than he was snoring again, with tracks of tears drying on his face.

When Garrett moved back through the sheeting, Tanith was sitting against a concrete column, her hands over her face. She quickly lowered them and sat up as he stepped in.

"What the hell was that?" he said, low.

"He is being watched," she said bleakly. "I'm afraid the healing drew his attention."

"*Whose* attention?" Garrett demanded.

"You know," she said quietly. "Choronzon. And the one who serves him."

The wind breathed between the columns, stirring the white cement powder into dust devils. Garrett felt another wave of paranoia that this was all some elaborate con, set up by the two of them.

He said in a harsh whisper, "This doesn't add up at all. How could that man"—he stabbed his finger in Roland's direction—"how could he possibly have been both places—just *happen* to be there when the killer is picking up the girl—then again when he disposes of her body, in a whole different place . . . maybe as much as a day later?"

Tanith was silent in the dark. She finally raised her head and spoke. "But that's rational thinking, and we're not dealing with the rational. Roland had—has—a connection with Amber. He was looking for her and he found her. It's not rational. He didn't do it rationally. He did it by intention. He wanted to find her and he did."

Garrett stared at her. "That's . . ." He shook his head, laughed in disbelief.

She smiled tightly. "I know that's not how you think the world works. But the mentally ill are sometimes extremely psychic. They sense, they intuit, they see things that we can't. He's telling you the truth as he knows it."

She stood from the floor and stepped to the silk circle. She stooped to pick up a candle, and as she extended her arm, Garrett had a glimpse of dark stains on the white sleeve that had not been there before.

He strode toward her and seized her arm, turning it over to look at it. The sleeve of her blouse rode up above her wrist with the movement, and Garrett saw ragged dark gashes, fresh blood in her pale flesh.

He had a flash of her staggering backward in the circle . . .

"What are these?" he demanded.

She pulled her arm away. "You don't believe it, do you? So don't believe."

Garrett's mind was racing. The cuts were still wet. *She could have done it herself when I took Cutler back to his bedroll. Classic con artist trick.*

Tanith shook her head as if she understood what he was thinking. She glanced toward the wall of plastic sheeting. "I can't leave him here, it's not safe anymore." Her eyes moved to the darkness beyond the purple circle. "I'm going to take him to Arlington. Even when they have no beds they can sometimes find a bed."

He looked at her, wondering how she would know the policies of a mental institution. She smiled wryly. "This line of work, you need to be able to refer clients to what they need. Believe me, Detective Garrett, I can tell mental illness from possession." Her face shadowed. "But Choronzon causes mental chaos. If Roland chanced to meet the demon, the encounter may well have affected his mind."

Behind her, the plastic sheeting rippled like water in the wind.

Tanith took a step toward him, looking into his face. "Will you go to the Channel?" Their eyes met and Garrett felt the heat between them, felt it in every cell of his body, and for a moment, neither of them moved. Garrett's mouth was dry. Then he nodded.

"Be careful," she said softly.

Chapter Thirty

"He put her on a chain and sunk her down, down, down."

In the dark of night, Garrett strode on the concrete path of the HarborWalk, with the Channel glimmering beside him. His breath showed in the cold, misty air. His emotions were still roiling from the—whatever it was that had just happened—and he felt a powerful drowsiness that he recognized as partly denial.

Tanith's voice echoed in his head. *"Be careful."*

He snapped himself into focus, looked around him to stay alert.

In daylight the HarborWalk was a popular tourist destination, and in warmer months joggers and lovers strolled beside the water in the evenings, drawn by spectacular views of the lights of downtown Boston and their sparkling reflections in the dark water.

But after the restaurants and cafés closed, the area turned ominous, with large parts of it still under construction and detours that jogged through too-deserted streets. A cold wind off the Channel made Garrett pull his coat tighter around himself; the crescent moon was an icy shimmer in the water.

It makes no sense. Why would the killer chance leaving her in such an open area?

The water, he answered himself. In some part of his mind he knew it had something to do with the water. The elementalness of it. *Earth, Air, Fire, Water. He put Erin in the dirt and he wanted Amber in water.*

Garrett wasn't sure what exactly he was looking for, but the good news was Binford Park, the spot the Dragon Man had named, was tiny, just half an acre of landscaping beside the waterfront, with a pergola and an unobstructed view of one of the wider sections of the Channel.

The concrete path along the waterfront was edged by a low concrete seawall, with a chest-high black iron railing. Garrett stopped at the railing and looked over it. The water was ten feet below where he was standing. Waves lapped against the wall.

"He put her on a chain and sunk her down, down, down."

What are you doing here, anyway? he asked himself. *If he dropped Amber's body in the water, then you'll need a dredging crew to find it.*

Garrett knew he was looking at one of the deepest parts of the Channel. Before Binford Park was constructed, almost half a million cubic yards of dirt had been excavated from the area, creating a gigantic casting basin that was used to construct huge concrete sections of tunnel, which were then floated into the Channel and submerged in a trench as part of the "Big Dig."

No, there'd be no finding a body here without a diving crew. *If there's even anything left to find.* Garrett had seen what marine animals do to human remains. There'd be no flesh left by now, and the bones would have separated and been carried out by the tide.

But the Dragon Man's words kept running through Garrett's head:

"He put her on a chain and sunk her down, down, down."

"He put her on a chain."

Garrett leaned out over the metal railing and looked down the blocky stone wall below him. And down by the waterline he saw what he had been looking for, something he had apparently remembered from—he didn't even know what—published photos of the HarborWalk construction, or some previous trip to explore the new pathways.

There were thick metal rings embedded into the stone, every ten feet or so, along the seawall.

Garrett began to walk the path, stopping every ten feet to look at each metal ring. With every step his dread increased.

At least there won't be any burned flowers, he thought, looking around him at the concrete path and stone wall. It did nothing to quell his anxiety.

A dozen rings down the walkway he saw what he was looking for: a chain hooked to the large metal ring below him.

"He put her on a chain . . ."

Garrett felt cold wind on his neck, and he whipped around, looking behind him. Nothing but darkness, the wash of streetlamps.

With bile rising in his throat, Garrett scanned the wall below him. It was constructed of huge rough blocks, which jutted out unevenly, providing narrow ledges and footholds.

Garrett jumped the railing and eased himself down the rough rock wall, feeling for footholds. He stopped on a ledge two feet above the surface of the water and knelt to look down on the iron ring and the chain linked to it. It was not soldered, but attached by a thick, open hook. Garrett reached into the icy, lapping water and pulled up on the chain. There was some give, so he pulled up enough slack to release the hook, then wrapped the chain twice around his wrist and started the climb back up the wall. The chain grew taut as he reached the iron railing. Garrett clamped the hook on the metal handrail, hoisted himself over the railing, and then braced himself on the fence to haul the chain up. It was a sickly, heavy weight and he had to strain at it.

He'd pulled up thirty feet of chain when it finally surfaced: a thick black rubber bag, the size of a small sleeping bag, attached to the chain, with water weight at least two hundred pounds; Garrett was unable to lift it farther.

Then again, he didn't want to. Despite the encasing rubber and the cold air, he could smell it from ten feet above.

Chapter Thirty-one

Fog rolled across the Channel as the men gathered on the concrete walkway in the first gray light of dawn: Landauer, Medical Examiner Edwards, the uniforms securing the scene, all postponing the inevitable. No one likes a floater. Even if this one wasn't technically floating. They knew what they were in for when Edwards unzipped the bag: a nightmarish stew of bones floating in white adipocere, slippery as soap, but with an unsoaplike, unbearable stink.

Edwards stood looking down at the bag. "Can you estimate a date of death?" he said to Garrett, finally.

"August first," Garrett said with certainty. Landauer looked at him, but said nothing.

Edwards shook his head. "Then my strong suggestion is we have the bag transported to the lab without opening it, and freeze it for several hours before we proceed with an examination."

"A-fucking-men," Landauer mumbled.

"There's one thing I need to know first," Garrett said, unable to wait, although he would have staked his life that he knew the answer already. He stepped toward the wet black bag and the other men drew back.

"Hold the zipper up with one hand," Edwards instructed. So nothing would spill out, he meant.

Garrett held his breath as he stooped to unzip the bag slightly.

But one brief and horrifying glance into the grisly soup was all he needed. The liquefied corpse was missing its head.

"So were you plannin' to fill me in, or do you have a new partner, now?" Landauer's voice was genuinely bitter through the sarcasm and Garrett squirmed inside with guilt as they faced off in the detectives' bureau. Out the windows behind them, the sky wept a dismal gray rain.

"It was the Dragon Man," Garrett said. "I stayed with him for a while when I dropped him off. Some of what he said in the car made sense. He came up with Binford Park, and that he saw a man drop Amber in the harbor. So I . . . followed up," he finished lamely.

"That nutball strung enough words together for you to find a body chained up like that," Landauer said flatly. "That's what you're going to tell Malloy."

"There was no head," Garrett said softly. "And Jason was in Saratoga with the band that night. He's got three alibi witnesses."

"Aww, fuck this." Landauer batted one of the rolling desk chairs with one meaty hand; it careened, crashing into a desk. "That's where you're going with this? Moncrief is innocent?"

"What if he is?"

"What if *she's* covering for him?"

This stopped Garrett, and Land moved in for the kill. "Do you not remember Frazer's profile? 'A lone occult practitioner'? 'The killer will often attempt to insert him or *herself* into the police investigation'?" Landauer glared at him like an angry bull. "She came to *us*, bro. You ever asked yourself what she wants out of this?"

Someone cleared his throat from the doorway and the partners turned to see Detective Morelli standing against the jamb. "Lieutenant wants to see you."

———

Garrett stood at the conference table in front of a stony lieutenant and an even stonier Carolyn. He tried to keep his face, his voice, everything about him noncombative.

"Edwards says the pelvic bones indicate the victim was a young woman, in her teens or early twenties," he said. "Amber Bright was reported missing on August second, and she was seventeen years old. She was booked for solicitation in January but the ID and name she gave in intake were false. We are presently attempting to identify her; we have her booking photo in the NCIC database. The decomposition of the body we found is such that it's impossible to fix a time or date of death, but Edwards estimates a month or more. The decomposition is also too advanced for us to know if there were carvings in the torso, but the head is missing, like Erin Carmody's—"

"What about the hand?" Malloy demanded.

"Neither hand was taken," Garrett answered. "But there are three things that tie the two murders together so far: the missing heads, the age and sex of the victims, and the dates of the murders."

"How the dates?" There was an edge in Carolyn's voice.

Garrett turned toward her. "Erin Carmody was killed on September twenty-one, the autumnal equinox, which is a pagan holiday. Amber Bright disappeared on August one, which is also a pagan holiday called Lammas. Both holidays are celebrated in the satanic tradition as well, and we've already established a satanic connection."

Garrett paused, steeling himself internally, before he continued in the most neutral voice he could muster. "On the night of August one, Jason Moncrief was in Saratoga Springs at a band gig. He drove ten hours that day in a car with his three bandmates, then was onstage with them from 8:00 P.M. to midnight; he remained in the bar with the band until closing, and then slept in a motel room with the three other band members before they drove back to Boston the next day."

The silence coming from Carolyn and Malloy was so thick Garrett could feel himself starting to choke on it. Landauer wouldn't look at him.

"I hope you're not suggesting that Jason Moncrief has an alibi for this murder, Detective," Malloy said, and his voice was like ice. "You said the decomposition was too advanced to fix a date. You're only assuming the date, from the word of a prostitute." In his mouth the word had the force of biblical condemnation. "Further, you haven't even identified the corpse as Bright's."

Garrett kept his face and voice steady. "I think there are too many similarities to ignore—"

Malloy spoke over him. "I might add that the witness who you say led you to discover this second body is suspect at best. Quite frankly I'm still unclear on the thought process that led to these conclusions."

Garrett could feel heat in his face. "The witness has been sleeping across from the park where Amber Bright made her last phone call—"

Malloy interrupted him again. "All you have is speculation. Work the cases, Detectives. No assumptions. And I don't want to see any premature speculation in the media. This will not turn into a circus, do you understand me?"

"Understood," Landauer said stiffly.

Garrett escaped the room to the corridor. He felt wrung out by the meeting, but when he heard the clicking of high heels on the floor behind him he knew the ordeal wasn't over. He turned to see Carolyn striding toward him.

"What are you trying to do?" It was rage in her voice—quiet, controlled, checked—but rage nonetheless.

"I'm trying to make sure we have the right guy locked up. I'm trying to make sure the real killer isn't still out there. I'm trying to do my job," Garrett said evenly.

"Don't you dare suggest that I'm not," she said, with that tightly reined anger.

"I would never do that," Garrett said.

She walked a few paces in agitation. "I just don't understand where this is coming from. We have a perfect case."

Garrett summoned all the calm he had. "But what if it's wrong? These are seventeen-, eighteen-year-old girls being killed, Carolyn. All I want is the right guy off the street."

"No matter what it does to us?" Her emphasis was slightly on the "us."

He felt a sick twist in his stomach. "I hope I just heard you wrong," he said softly.

She shook her head in sheer disbelief. "I don't think I know you at all."

"Maybe you just never bothered to look," he said, staring into her face. Her eyes widened . . . and then narrowed in fury. But Garrett no longer cared. He turned to walk away from her. As he reached for the handle of the EXIT door, he saw Landauer standing at the end of the corridor, watching them.

Chapter Thirty-two

A bar was his first impulse. His second impulse came before the third shot of Jameson's, before he was moved to start screaming along with the Drop Kick Murphys on the jukebox, although the raucous soundtrack continued in his head once he'd poured himself into his car.

And once again he was on the road to Salem.

It was dumping rain by then, raining so hard it was difficult for him to drive, and at one point he pulled off the road, staring out past his frantically beating wipers at the downpour, wondering if it was simply madness to continue.

He closed his eyes and had a vision of Tanith's hands on the Dragon Man—so gentle—and so in command.

He opened his eyes and pulled back onto the road.

The shop was dark, as was the second story of the house. He stood dripping and freezing on the porch and rang the bell several times, while rain blew around him in gusts. There was no stirring from within.

He used the excuse of the whiskey to justify to himself what he did next.

He had a passable talent for breaking and entering, and not just as part of his police training. There was a time in his life, as with many teenage boys of a certain neighborhood and from a certain socioeconomic stratum, when he could just as easily have fallen on the wrong side of the law-and-order equation.

He picked the lock in under a minute and was inside the door.

In the dark the shop had a medieval apothecary look, with its thick glass jars of herbs and powders and the cases of crystals and wands. Outside, the rain thundered down, and a crack of lightning illuminated the room for a moment in ghastly grayish light.

Garrett's heart was beating fast, and he felt a rush that he knew was familiar to criminals; the powerful effect of dominance, of conquest. He understood what he was doing was not merely immoral but also stupid in the extreme, but he continued anyway, walking noiselessly past bookcases with their mysterious volumes, on to the starry velvet curtain in the back. He stepped through into the reading room, with its lingering redolence of incense and concentrated darkness.

There was a spread of Tarot cards on the table, the pale cards with their faintly glowing symbols and names below: *The High Priestess, The Lovers, The Devil, Death*. The medieval images gave Garrett a sense of foreboding.

But it was the back room that drew him. He found the key in the standing cabinet where he'd seen Tanith take it from.

He used the key to unlock and open the door and was assailed by more darkness, and the faint phosphorescence of the pentagram within the circle inscribed on the floor. In this space there was no danger of light leaking through to the outside. He closed the door quietly behind him, muffling the sound of the rain, and felt along the wall for a light switch. His hand felt only the thick cloth that covered the walls; there were no protuberances that would indicate a switch. But he remembered there were candles everywhere. He reached into a pocket and switched on his Maglite, the small but powerful flashlight he carried on his key chain, and used the circle of light to guide him to the altar in the center of the pentagram. He lit several candles and then stood while his eyes adjusted to the warm and flickering flames.

He glanced around the room and then back down at the altar—and was startled to see a wide, thick hand-bound book. *Jason's grimoire?* His mind raced. *How did she . . .*

But when he picked it up he realized it was not the same book, just disturbingly similar.

He hesitated . . . then stifled his conscience and opened it.

The pages were the same kind of handmade paper that Jason Moncrief's grimoire had been fashioned of, and the writing was in code, not the twiglike runes, but something more scrolled and feminine, vaguely Celtic.

He paged through the book. The writing was incomprehensible, but there were rough drawings, of him, of Landauer. He turned pages with numb and building disbelief . . . and then stopped, staring down at a page with a sketch: the circle with the three triangles. The sigil of Choronzon.

He felt a rush of nausea, of fear . . . and then the sudden certainty that he was not alone. He whipped around—

Tanith stood behind him in the dark.

He had not heard the door open; it was closed behind her, as if she had passed through it. The thought unnerved him even more than having been caught.

Then the force of her fury hit him, although she said nothing and did not move; it was like hearing screaming in his head. Thunder boomed in the sky outside, shaking the windows of the house.

She strode forward, jostling him hard as she passed him, and slammed the cover of the book closed.

"What is that?" he demanded, without much force.

She turned on him in a rage. "Do you know it could have killed you, to open that without permission? Do you know I could have booby-trapped the house, put a spell on the door against intruders, bound the book with toxins . . . so if you so much as touched a page you would die a slow death, untraceable . . ." Her voice was low and lethal and he had no doubt she was serious.

"Did you?"

Her eyes blazed fire. "It's what you deserve."

That he couldn't argue, but his face burned nonetheless.

"You still have no idea what you're dealing with." There was contempt as well as fury in her voice. "You don't understand and you don't want to understand."

She turned from him, but he stepped in front of her, blocked her from the door. "What is that thing?" he demanded again, pointing at the book lying on the altar.

"That is *none* of your business," she hissed, a venomous sound.

"It is when you have a book just like Jason Moncrief's—"

"You are a fool. It's my Book of Shadows. Every witch keeps one."

"What's in it?"

"You'll find out—"

He grabbed her wrist, twisted her toward him. "Spells," she spat at him, trying to jerk her hand away. "You have *no idea* what you've done—"

He grabbed her other wrist and held her, struggling, against him. He spoke beside her cheek. "I found Amber. Her body was sunk into the Fort Point Channel, on a chain. He has her head."

Tanith stiffened in his arms. In the candlelit silence, their hearts pounded against each other.

"Jason didn't kill her, then," she gasped, in what sounded like triumph.

Garrett tensed. "Why do you say that?"

"You know it—" She tried to pull away from him and he held her firm.

"That won't free him. No one will believe it. There's no establishing time of death. The decomposition is too advanced."

She stared at him in shock and fury. Then she pushed him away with a strength that startled him. She circled the floor in the flickering candlelight, breathing hard, not looking at him.

He watched her, saw her trembling. "What is this kid to you? Why do you care?"

She didn't answer, but suddenly veered to the cabinet against the wall and pulled the door open, to take out a decanter of wine and two goblets.

She set them on the altar and looked at him. "Are we going to talk, now, Garrett? Then why don't we get comfortable?" She poured both glasses full and extended one to him. He stared at her, not taking it.

"Oh, please, you've already had a few, haven't you?"

"Why do you care?" he asked again.

She lifted the glass and drank it down. She wiped the red from her lips with the back of her hand, a gesture that sent flames racing through Garrett's body. She filled the glass again, then picked up both glasses and walked to him deliberately, extending one. He took the glass without drinking.

"Why are you helping him?"

"Because he didn't do it." She drank again, her eyes challenging him, and he lifted his own glass to his lips and drank, too. The wine was spicy and complex, a welcome rush of heat.

He lowered the glass and looked down at her. "Why did you lie?"

"Why are *you* lying?" she answered back, and drank again, then stepped forward to him, extending the bottle. To his surprise, the glass in his hand was already empty. She reached to fill it. "You know it's true. You know he didn't do it."

"You have no idea what I think—"

"I do. Because I read your mind," she flung at him.

"Stop it." He clasped his hand around her arm. "No games."

She leaned forward against him and put her lips to his hair. "No games like breaking and entering, *Detective?*" He could feel her breath in his ear and his cock leapt to life, hardened to stone. "What game would you prefer?" she whispered. And then he was pulling her against him and his mouth was on hers. Her lips were sweet under the bite of wine, and soft, and luscious . . . She opened her mouth under his and sighed and fire shot through him as their bodies ground against each other. She put her hands under his sweater and found bare skin; her fingers moved on his abdomen,

212 • Alexandra Sokoloff

rippling the muscles of his stomach as she touched him, moving lower . . . stroking him . . . his mind was a dark rush of lust. She pulled back from him, gasping, and he seized her again and she jerked against his hold, deliberately off-balancing him so they staggered to the floor. He was on her, then, and her legs were wrapping around him and his tongue was in her mouth and she was pulling off his sweater, ripping at his shirt; he could hear buttons popping and rolling on the floor and then he forgot everything when he felt her hands on his stomach again, pulling open his pants and sliding her fingers inside and down, stroking the hard aching length of him.

He ripped open the buttons on her tight vest and sunk his mouth into her breasts, licking and sucking as she tipped her head back on the floor and shuddered, and he took her mouth again, devouring her. They struggled on the floor, half fighting, half kissing, in the center of the glowing circle, shedding clothes, finding skin.

He was huge, throbbing, as he slid into the hot core of her, and he moaned with the pleasure as she closed tightly around him. They rocked together, writhing naked in the pentagram, bodies locked in fury and ecstasy, waves of heat and cold breaking over them as they slammed into each other until he was shouting . . . searing heat and blinding white light flooding through him . . .

Below him her eyes flew open, dark as night, the pupils huge, and she was murmuring words he didn't understand . . .

And then he saw her not below him, but floating above him, in the air, although he was still lying on top of her—and she reached down her hand and seized him and he felt himself pulling out of his body . . .

He was in the air with her . . . floating above their still and naked bodies.

Before he could comprehend what was happening there was a crack of thunder and a great wind, as if the storm had penetrated the walls, but not blowing at them, rather sucking them in . . .

And they were gone.

Chapter Thirty-three

There were no walls, no house . . . and the rain and clouds had disappeared, leaving only the rush of wind. They were flying: fast, exhilarating speed, with black night and the starkly glowing full moon on their left side and crimson sunrise on the right. The shock of seeing full day and night at once was electrifying. Garrett felt weightless, nothing solid but the clutch of her fingers around his hand.

The sunrise brightened to white, and then the white was clouds in the wind, layers and layers of all thicknesses, cumulus, nimbus, cirrus . . . light and fluffy in the air, then freezing to snow on an ice field, melting to whitecaps on blue waves, then boiling to steam that blew away to reveal pure blinding white salt on a desert plain, with the moon gleaming white in a pale sky above.

The changes made him dizzy, the sensation of flight, a feeling even beyond sex; the top of his head was coming off . . .

The moon sank behind the racing clouds . . .

And they raced after it, plunging into white . . .

. . . Then falling, falling, into dark.

It should have killed them to hit, but suddenly they were on the ground, although he could not feel his feet touching it. *It's a dream, it must be*, he thought incoherently. It was dark, though the moon spilled pale light over the hill on which they stood. Alien, yet familiar to Garrett; he'd been here before, in his body.

He wanted to ask her where they were, but he could not form words in his fleshless existence. As if knowing, she turned toward him in his mind and whispered, without speaking: *Watch. Listen.*

He looked over the bare, earth-covered hills around them, and the familiarity was gnawing, but without the aid of smell and touch, the sensation of air on skin, everything seemed two-dimensional, an alien world.

Tripping. I'm tripping, his mind managed. *The wine. Something in the wine . . . drugged . . .*

He looked up toward the moon . . . and it was the stark black silhouette of the office chair, pitched on the top of a hill that finally oriented him. They were at the landfill where Erin Carmody's body had been dumped.

Shhh, Tanith said in his head, and he turned his attention toward the sound.

A car was stopped on the moonlit ribbon of road, the rutted dirt road where Garrett had seen the burned footprints. A stooped figure turned away from the open lid of the car trunk and Garrett saw it carried a dark wrapped shape slung over its shoulder—the size of a human body, wide on top and tapering at the bottom, wrapped in a black plastic tarp.

The dark figure hauled its terrible cargo toward the lip of the hill, where he stopped at the cliff's edge and transferred the object wrapped in the tarp from his shoulder to his arms. He stood for a moment, then pulled the tarp back and flung its contents over the side of the hill. The figure stood, staring down over the side of the hill as he rolled the tarp into a ball.

Look, Tanith spoke in Garrett's head, and without knowing how he knew to do it, he turned toward the car.

The license plate was visible in the moonlight: TOR 936

And he knew the make of the car: a dark Camaro, navy blue or black. The car seemed drawn in crystal clarity, hyper-real.

Garrett glanced back toward the figure on the cliff's edge. It suddenly stiffened . . . turned slowly . . . its face all in shadow, hooded by its coat. It was still, staring toward Garrett and Tanith with an intensity Garrett could feel even from the distance.

Then it dropped its bundle and shot forward into the air, a black and ragged and virulent shadow, hurtling straight at them, with a shriek of sheer black madness—

Chapter Thirty-four

He woke abruptly to his head pounding more violently than any hangover he could ever remember experiencing, and there had been a few. He was on the bare black floor of a dark room, naked and alone in the center of a pentagram within a painted circle, and for a long and paralyzing moment he had no idea who he was.

Then the dream came flooding back to him.

Flying through the clouds, through ice, through steam, through desert . . . the sensation of flying . . .

His stomach roiled with the memory of motion, and suddenly another image flashed into his mind.

The landfill . . . the dark shadow . . . the blue Camaro and the license plate . . .

Garrett sat up in the dark velvet-lined room, cringing at the throbbing pain in his head. The air was heavy with the smell of apple musk and sex.

A wave of nausea suddenly doubled him over and he dry-retched, over and over again, his stomach spasming. He sank back on his heels, swallowed, and breathed shallowly, fighting the nausea.

Jesus, what did she give me?

Finally the sickness passed enough for him to straighten. He looked around and saw a wineglass on the floor; red liquid had spilled out in a puddle. He crawled over to it and looked at the glass. There was a thickness to the dregs of sticky liquid left in the bottom.

He reached shakily for his clothes and dressed, wincing at every move, every muscle in his body aching. Then he took out one of the glassine evidence bags he always carried in his coat and stooped to scoop the wineglass into it.

He moved out through the doorway into the dark reading room. The cards were gone from the table, and the room was empty, as was the front of the shop; no sign of Tanith.

Moving gingerly, he walked for the door as quietly as he could . . . but as he was reaching for the knob, he stopped. He turned and looked toward the shelves of herbs and powders behind the counter. Then he crossed to stand in front of the shelves. The jars were labeled and alphabetized, and it took him no time at all to spot the jar he was looking for:

Belladonna.

The homicide room was mercifully quiet for a Saturday. Garrett headed straight for the crime lab and handed the wineglass and the glassine bag of belladonna over to Warren Tufts. "The wine in the glass. I need to know what's in it."

Tufts looked him over with a raised eyebrow, and Garrett knew the criminalist was taking in his pallor and bloodshot eyes, his death-warmed-over appearance. Garrett didn't try to explain. He had no doubt Tufts had seen worse.

He went back to the detectives' bureau, ignoring a curious Morelli and Palmer, and slumped in his seat behind his desk, too exhausted to muster even the energy to go to his car and drive home. His thighs ached and he had a sudden memory of Tanith riding him, both of them naked and straining, her black hair spilled over her breasts, her mouth ripe and sweet against his . . . and he felt himself weak with desire again.

He tilted his head back against the chair, and must have dozed, because he was in the dark and watching a shadow figure creep from a Camaro—when suddenly a female voice spoke from above him and he jolted awake.

"You look like hell."

He blinked up to focus groggily on Carolyn, who stood in front of his desk, pristine and unsmiling.

She held a file folder in her hand, which she tossed down on the desk in front of him. "Try doing your own homework next time."

Without a word of explanation about what she meant, she pivoted on one lethally fashionable heel and was striding out of the room.

Garrett didn't even have the words left to call her back. He reached for the file and opened it.

The name in black type hit him from the top of the page. *Teresa Smithfield, a.k.a. Tanith Cabarrus.*

He was looking down at a rap sheet.

It took him two mugs of coffee to go over it all, not because of the length of the file but because of how hard his tired mind was trying to fight it.

A September 1999 arrest for five counts of fraud and grand larceny, for which "Smithfield" received three years and was remanded to MCI Framingham, the state women's prison, where she served nine months before being released on probation.

A June 2000 arrest for disorderly conduct, after which she was institutionalized at McLean State Hospital for four months, then discharged to the care of a Selena Fox.

The file was thick with photocopied official documents. One of them was an intake report from McLean Hospital.

INTAKE REPORT

IDENTIFYING DATA: *The patient is a 23-year-old white female with no known address, arrested by the police on 24 June and brought into the emergency room, subsequently admitted into the locked psychiatric unit as a Section 12: risk to herself and others. She gave her name as Teresa Smithfield. She carried no ID or identifying papers.*

HISTORY OF PRESENT ILLNESS: *Arresting officers received a 911 call from Salem resident Althea Carstairs reporting "a young woman going crazy in the park." Police arriving at Salem Willows Park found Ms. Smithfield in a disheveled condition, covered in blood and brandishing a large knife, which she threatened the officers with, screaming at them to stay away. Officers held their weapons on her and instructed her to drop the knife, at which point she began slashing at her arms and chest, screaming that she had to "cut them out." Officers subdued and disarmed Smithfield using Tasers. Officers conducted a visual examination and concluded the blood on Smithfield was most likely her own, as she had numerous fresh cuts and stab wounds in various parts of her body.*

In the patrol car en route to the psychiatric ward, Smithfield kept up a steady stream of muttering and periodic screaming about being attacked. She claimed there were demons inside her.

On admission the patient continued to repeat her belief that there are demons inside her and that they "tricked her" into letting them in. She begged repeatedly for help and screamed not to be left alone. She would not respond to questions about her perceptions but seemed preoccupied with internal stimuli. It is likely that she is experiencing both auditory and visual hallucinations.

Blood and urine screens for alcohol and illicit drugs are positive for significant amounts of the hallucinogen atropine, which indicates possible drug-related psychosis in addition to an organic condition.

PAST PSYCHIATRIC HISTORY: *Patient has an arrest record for fraud, and served nine months in MCI Framingham. During the first months of her sentence she received numerous official write-ups for fighting and "antisocial behavior." Patient has a series of vertical scars on her left wrist, suggesting at least one past suicide attempt.*

ASSESSMENT AND PLAN: *Patient clearly suffers from a psychotic condition that may prove to be chronic paranoid schizophrenia, quite possibly exacerbated by the use of hallucinogens.*

The use of antipsychotic medication is indicated and will be initiated. We will continue to carefully monitor Ms. Smithfield's safety, given her dangerously self-destructive behavior.

There were more documents, and Garrett had no doubt as to their authenticity; there was no more meticulous researcher than Carolyn. And he, of course, had never bothered to check. He felt sick, betrayed—and more than that, like a complete and utter fool.

The phone buzzed on his desk, and he reached for it. "Garrett," he said, his voice hollow.

"Got that analysis for you, chief," Warren Tufts said on the other end. Garrett sat up straighter, but he knew what Tufts was going to say next. "You were right on the money. The wine in that glass was laced. Atropine."

Landauer met him in the smoky dark of the Hibernian, with its polished and endless bar and Irish soundtrack, and there were no "I told you so's," no recriminations, only the warm and hulking presence of a partner and friend. Of course, Garrett was fairly certain Land had told Carolyn about Tanith to begin with, but that was for his own good, obviously saving him from himself.

"She was running a phony fortune-telling business, swindled people out of their money. Then a complete mental collapse, institutionalization, delusions, schizophrenia . . . she's as loony as Moncrief." Garrett swallowed the rest of his Jameson's, chased it with a Harp, and nodded to the bartender for more. "I've been a total ass." He was aware he was slurring.

"You're always a total ass, Rhett," Landauer said, and Garrett knew he was forgiven. Garrett was not about to be so kind to himself. He spoke harshly.

"She dosed me with belladonna last night."

Landauer looked at him over his beer. "No shit? How was it?"

Garrett gave him a thin smile "I feel like I was hit by a T. But last night . . . it was wild. Hallucinations . . ." He trailed off as memories of sex, of flight, raced through him . . . then the image of the

Camaro, the dark shadow of the man, the shadow's sudden flight. "It felt wicked real."

The bartender brought their next round and Garrett swallowed his whole. The lights blurred to a comfortable haze around him. "Here's the thing," he said slowly, so there would be minimal slurring. "Belladonna. She's working so hard to get this kid Jason out, you know what I'm saying? Do you think she's in on it? He got the drug from her; they're using these girls for some rituals . . ." He suddenly remembered. "There was a girl—same age as Erin—in her shop. Fuck knows what all she's in to." He slammed his hand on the bar.

Landauer looked him over. His face was red from the whiskey, but his eyes were still focused and sharp. "Yeah, she played you good, bro. And maybe her head's not screwed on so tight. But murder? There's a difference between kinky and hinky."

Garrett felt himself swaying on the bar stool. "Dunno . . ." he muttered. Suddenly Landauer's hand was under his arm, and he realized that his partner had just barely stopped him from falling off the seat.

"I'm driving you home, Rhett. You sleep this one off and we'll talk in the morning."

Whiskey on top of belladonna did not turn out to be the happiest of combinations. Sometime during a brutal night Garrett woke from an instantly forgotten nightmare to find himself drenched in sweat, his head and throat burning up. He threw off his sheets and lay back with his head throbbing, feeling as if the bed were rocking.

Flying . . .

He licked sweat from his lips, wondering if he had it in him to make it to the bathroom for water.

And then he heard movement in the living room.

Adrenaline shot through him and he sat up, straining to hear.

Silence . . . nothing but the sense of presence . . .

. . . and then the slow scrape of wood against wood . . .

A window?

Garrett reached to his bed stand, eased open the drawer, and withdrew his Glock.

222 • Alexandra Sokoloff

He stood noiselessly . . . and had to brace himself against the wave of dizziness. He felt weightless, incorporeal. Every muscle in his body was tensed as he moved naked to the bedroom door and put his head against the door frame to look out into the hall.

Pitch-black and no sound.

Garrett barely breathed.

There was no stirring from the living room—only that certainty of presence.

Garrett slipped through the doorway and eased into the hall, one slow barefoot step in front of the other on the hardwood floor. His heart was racing, his mouth dry as dust.

At the end of the hallway he pressed his back against the wall and listened. Nothing.

Slowly, slowly, he peered around the corner . . . and his eyes widened.

The living room was dark and empty—but all the windows were wide open. The curtains billowed, breathing at the frames. Garrett spun to the front door. It, too, was open into the night.

There was a sound behind him and Garrett twisted around again, his weapon aimed in front of him—

Tanith stood on the other side of the room, naked, perfect body gleaming in the moonlight, her dark hair spilled around her shoulders—

She held a large book open in her hands, offering it to him . . .

And behind her in the window, yellow eyes gleamed in the darkness—then leapt forward . . . a dark, thick hulk, hurtling toward him . . . and the leathery shape of wings . . .

Chapter Thirty-five

Garrett jerked upright.
He was in bed, in the dark, in a cold sweat.
Alone.

Chapter Thirty-six

Garrett had never before, in any way, experienced any doubts about reality. The very idea that reality could be in question had never occurred to him. He found himself now in a profound state of unsettlement, something he didn't like at all.

He circled his living room in the subdued light of dawn, checking the windows and door again. They were all locked, as they had been since he'd awakened.

You were drugged. Get over it, he ordered himself as he poured and drank cup after cup of coffee, alternating with whole bottles of water at a time, hoping to flush the residuals of the psychotropic from his system.

And possibly it was more than the drugs. The woman is an expert hypnotist. If she could do what she did with the Dragon Man, she could induce hallucinations. Or memories, even.

So his mind said. His body, though . . . his body felt as sore as if . . .

As if he had flown.

It felt real. It all feels real.

When the night's dream stubbornly refused to fade from his

mind, he sat down at his computer and Googled "atropine" and "belladonna."

After a half hour of clicking through articles, he sat back in his chair, limp with relief. Every personal and medical account he'd read of experiences with belladonna reported the same symptoms: hallucinations of flying so real that at the time the subject was convinced that he or she had actually flown. He had also found an article documenting the use of belladonna in a ritual known as sex magick, in which orgasm was the trigger for hallucinatoric flight.

"Nothing but drugs," Garrett muttered, his voice sounding hollow.

And yet, the Camaro. There was something about it that gnawed at him. It had seemed, in a hallucination of hyper-clarity, particularly real, and significant.

Look, Tanith's voice whispered in his mind, and he felt the sound in his whole body.

He swiveled in his chair, rotating away from the desk. The chair came to a slow stop, facing the dining-room table.

And the murder book.

Tanith standing naked in the moonlight, holding the open book out toward him . . .

Garrett stood and crossed to the book. He opened the stiff blue cover, flipped through pages—and stopped on a witness report from the landfill, the list of makes and models of cars that the landfill's office manager had made.

Garrett scanned the list, and his index finger stopped on a line. *Dark blue Camaro.*

There were no license plates noted; the list was only the office manager's recollection of the cars she had let through the gate that day.

Garrett stared into space, then pawed over the scattered files and notepads on the table. He stopped still . . . lunged forward and seized one battered notebook: his scribbled notes from Tanith's session with the Dragon Man.

He paged back and stopped again—on the partial plate number the Dragon Man had given her: TOR 9.

And he had a sudden, shocking vision of the plate that he had seen in the flying dream: TOR 963.

One call to the DMV later, and one to the Pine Street landfill office, and then Garrett was in the shower, under water as hot as he could get it, trying to steam the cobwebs out of his head.

He dressed, and finally felt steady enough to call Landauer. "I've got something weird," he said into the phone.

"What else is new?" came the inevitable response.

Garrett didn't laugh.

Landauer sighed through the phone. "Ah, fuck."

Forty minutes later Land was slouched on Garrett's sofa, legs sprawled, staring down at a sheet of paper. "Let me get this straight. Dragon Man gave you the partial plate number."

"Yes," Garrett said. He did not mention his own sighting of the plate in the—dream. "And that dark blue Camaro on that page, with license plate **TOR 963**, is registered to a John McKenna, who was employed at the Pine Street landfill until June fourteenth, when he failed to show up for work and never came back." He didn't say it aloud, but if Tanith was right about three victims, that had been just a week before the first killing.

The partners looked at each other silently from opposite sides of the room. "Whaddaya know . . ." Landauer said softly. "He got a sheet?"

Garrett shook his head once. "Not to speak of. A drunk and disorderly last year, pled out; one DUI five years ago. High school dropout. Spotty employment history, mostly manual labor. But a homeowner," he added. "Out in Lincoln. Not married."

Laudauer raised his eyebrows. "So he's got himself some privacy."

They sat with it. Garrett's eyes strayed to the printout of Mc-Kenna's DMV photo: a red-bearded, stocky, hard-bitten man of forty-three. "*A lost soul. Alone in the world*," Tanith's voice whispered in his head.

Landauer rubbed his jaw. "We've got a suspect in custody. Charged."

Garrett lifted his hands. "Could be nothing. We pay him a visit."

Landauer weighed it, nodded. "Okay, Rhett. It's your rodeo."

Chapter Thirty-seven

Lincoln, Massachusetts, was a rural town in Middlesex County, west of Boston. The brilliance of the autumn leaves on the trees lining the highway made the journey feel like driving into a painting. Red and gold and amber and orange leaves swirled across the road in front of the Cavalier, giving Garrett an uneasy stabbing reminder that Halloween was mere days away.

McKenna's employee file contained a note that McKenna had not returned several phone calls made by the office manager to inquire after his whereabouts, and that there had been no machine to leave a message on. There still wasn't, when Garrett tried the number himself. But according to the phone company the bills were still being paid, on auto-pay, as were the other utilities. His phone records would have to be subpoenaed for recent activity, but all indications were that McKenna was MIA.

Landauer drove, as Garrett was still shaky from the lingering effects of belladonna. They did not speak for some time, while Landauer navigated west out of the city and onto Highway 2.

As much as Garrett was trying not to think, the cattails along the side of the road kept reminding him of the crossed stalks of corn bound to the columns of Tanith's store. He felt his face tighten and his gut roil with doubt, and he must have sighed or grunted because Landauer glanced over at him questioningly.

Garrett shook his head. "Maybe this is all wrong. Cabarrus is a con artist. The fraud conviction. You were right: she's been trying to insert herself into the investigation from the start."

Landauer was a beat slow in answering. "Except that we both know women don't kill like that."

"I'm not so sure." Garrett's words tasted as bitter as they sounded. "This isn't an ordinary woman. These weird rituals she does. The drugs. These young 'clients' of hers, coming in for spells. There's no telling . . ." He stopped, staring blankly out at the cattails. "I never had any clue what she was capable of."

Landauer looked out the side window. After a moment he said, "You notice anything about me, last couple weeks?"

Garrett looked at him, not understanding.

Landauer waited. When Garrett said nothing, Land reached forward and slid open the ashtray in the dash. It was empty. It took Garrett a moment to register the significance.

Landauer met his eyes for a moment, looked back at the road. "When was the last time you saw me with a butt in my hand?"

Garrett's mind raced wildly back through the last few days. But he'd seen Landauer with a cigarette, dozens . . .

No, he realized. *Holding* a cigarette. Not lighting it. Not smoking it.

"I haven't had one since she walked into the office that day," his partner said, not looking at him. "Fuck knows I've tried. I just can't."

Now Garrett forced his mind back to the day in the bull pen: Landauer taunting Tanith: *"Show me. Put a spell on me . . ."* Tanith pulling the dagger from her blouse and cutting her finger . . . Landauer licking her blood . . .

His partner was speaking again, his gaze fixed out the windshield. "I never thought anything could make me quit. Now, I don't want it. Can't do it. She says, 'You're done'—and I am."

Garrett stared at his partner. "So what are you saying?"

"I'm sayin' whatever she is, it's not all bad." He shrugged. "I'm never gonna repeat this to another living soul, but she mighta saved my life." Then his face darkened. "If you ever say a word to Bette, so help me, I'll kill you dead."

Garrett sat back against the seat and looked out at the flashing autumn colors of the trees, a blur of reds and oranges and ambers, like fire, like flight.

The isolation of the town was an ominous factor, not a point in McKenna's favor. A quaint Main Street gave way to old farm-style houses along a rural road with the distances between them growing larger and larger as the detectives drove on.

McKenna's house was outside the limits of what there was of the town, which a green-and-white population sign put at 9463. Landauer turned off a paved road to follow a dirt road through a barrier of trees that opened into what used to be farmland. The partners squinted through autumn sun at the house, an old Cape with paint peeling off the clapboards, a sagging porch. A junked car rested on its rims in the yard, and wind rustled through the elms, sending leaves swirling down like golden rain. As the partners got out of the car, Garrett saw a sludgy pond off the side of the house, and a shed with weathered, unpainted siding and double doors padlocked together. There was no sign of the dark blue Camaro.

The grass around them was knee-high and Garrett found himself scanning for . . .

Burned footprints . . .

He shook off the image, wondering what he thought he was doing.

As the partners started up toward the house, no dogs barked to warn of their approach, and there were no signs of any other animals, or people, or a working car or other vehicle, either. Rumpled curtains were drawn at all the visible windows.

The porch steps creaked under Landauer's bulk, a somehow ominous sound. He reached out for the doorbell. Surprisingly, the chime worked. The partners stood in the slight breeze as they waited in silence. Dry grass crackled in the fields around them. Garrett felt his stomach churn again, but it could have been the lingering effects of belladonna. The house didn't feel occupied . . . and yet something was—

Landauer frowned, squinting at the dirty screen door. "What the . . . ?" Abruptly he reached forward and pulled open the screen, to reveal a brown-red handprint smudged on the wood door beside the knob, with lines and whorls of fingerprints.

No question. Dried blood.

The partners looked at each other.

Landauer leaned forward and pounded on the door with a meaty fist. The hollow booming echoed in the house. "Mr. McKenna, this is the police." There was still no stirring, no sound.

"McKenna's missing . . ." Landauer pointed out. "Bloody hand-print. Exigent circumstances. Reasonable suspicion of danger. I say we go in."

Garrett nodded in agreement. Both men unsnapped the holsters of their weapons.

Landauer reached and grasped the doorknob. He frowned.

"What?" Garrett asked, tensing.

"Sticky," Landauer said with a grimace. "And unlocked." He turned the knob, pushed the door open.

They stared into the dark cave of the living room. Then, hands hovering beside their weapons, they stepped inside the door.

The room was dark from the drawn drapes, and there was a musty and slightly foul odor. A few pieces of sagging furniture, with empty beer cans and newspaper sections scattered beside the sofa on the old and dusty carpet. The air was tainted with the faint, sweet odor of rotting food.

There was a fireplace that looked like it was crumbling from the inside. Garrett was sure it was five kinds of fire hazard and he wouldn't have lit it himself for any amount of money, but the still-pungent smell of wood smoke and the half-burned logs on the grate indicated it had been used recently.

"Mr. McKenna?" Landauer called again loudly, pro forma. "This is the Boston Police Department. Are you in the house, sir?"

No response.

As his eyes adjusted to the dark, Garrett scanned the walls, covered in faded flowery wallpaper. His immediate guess was that McKenna had inherited his parents' home; the décor was circa 1940 with a few seventies' touches, and none of it or the furniture were a man's choices.

Garrett nudged Landauer and nodded up to the clock above the doorway to the kitchen. It was a round plastic battery-powered version and it was stopped, the thin red second hand frozen atop the longer hand with the big hands indicating 3:33. Landauer went strangely silent and just then Garrett realized the significance beyond the fact that no one had replaced the battery.

333.

Now Garrett stiffened, too.

The men fanned out, moving slowly. Garrett glanced through pocket doors into a front parlor stacked with accumulated junk: greasy tools, a small disassembled engine on a side table, a dinner table overflowing with newspapers and boxes. There was a hall extending to the back: bathroom and bedroom probably, and a set of stairs to the second floor. The kitchen was to the right, with a closed swinging door.

There was no sound and no feel of any presence besides their own in the house; they could both sense the emptiness, which diffused their tension somewhat. They both relaxed in the same moment, hands withdrawing from the vicinity of their firearms. They exchanged a glance in the dim room, then Landauer nodded toward the hall and moved into it, while Garrett pushed open the swinging kitchen door with the tip of his shoe.

It was as dark and dank as the rest of the house, with a rank, neglected odor. Garrett smelled stale, uncirculated air, garbage not taken out for weeks, long-dirty dishes, alcohol-laced sweat . . .

And something else. Something he didn't want to think about, something naggingly familiar . . .

He was distracted from the thought by the faint sound of Landauer's footsteps clumping from the second floor above him.

Garrett turned in the room, continuing his visual inventory. Dishes were piled in the sink, and the remnants of a meal were still on the table . . . several beer bottles, a fast-food bag, a petrifying half of some kind of burger in an open cardboard carton. There were two closed doors on the other side of the kitchen, one that led to the outside, and the other a solid door, probably to a cellar. (Garrett heard his father's voice in his head: "*Cella*.") Garrett glanced at the outside door, then moved toward the other. He reached for the doorknob . . . but hesitated before grasping the knob.

There was a counter to his right with a dish towel crumpled by the sink, and he reached for the towel and wrapped it around the doorknob. The knob twisted under his hand, and the door opened onto a black chasm.

Still using the towel, Garrett felt his hand along the wall beside him, searching for a light switch. He found the plate, but when he flicked it, there was only an empty click.

The hair on the back of his neck suddenly rose, as if he were being watched from—not the cellar below, but right behind him. He twisted to look back at the door—

There was no one.

Garrett steadied himself against the wall in the dark and felt in his pocket for the Maglite on his key chain.

He switched on the small, powerful beam and shone the light down into the darkness. The staircase plunged precipitously, with narrow steps of unfinished wood opening into a cavern of cellar.

Garrett stood on the top step for a moment, and deliberately stopped his breath, listening . . . listening . . .

Again, he had an overwhelming feeling of being watched from behind . . . but a glance over his shoulder revealed no one at his back.

And there was no sound, no stirring, and more importantly no *feeling* of life below.

Garrett relaxed a tad, and began the descent down the stairs, sweeping the small, concentrated beam of the Maglite ahead of him. The light picked up glimpses of the cellar: pale drapes of cobwebs on the ceiling beams . . . a peeling, noxious pipe that was surely asbestos . . . a malevolent old iron boiler the size of a refrigerator . . .

There was a packed earth floor below, and sagging wood shelves with rotting junk hanging on the stone walls around him. The beam fell on another wall and Garrett froze . . . at the sight of the triple triangle sigil painted large on the plaster, and thick scrawls of other words. Then he shifted the beam lower . . . and what he caught in the light took his breath away like a savage punch.

There was a crude narrow altar against the wall, draped in black cloth with fat black candles atop it and more triangle sigils painted just behind it. And in the center of the altar was a candleholder that he had only seen in a crude and disgusting sketch.

A Hand of Glory. Erin Carmody's hand, a wizened claw, clutched around a black taper candle.

Garrett gasped, breathing in shallowly against the sudden recoil in his stomach.

The smell of earth was around him; that root-cellar smell . . . and again, something else . . .

Garrett shined the flashlight beam straight ahead. It took him a moment to register what he was seeing and then he staggered down the remaining few steps.

A triangle was traced on the floor in some phosphorescent powder . . .

And at the points of the triangle were three low stone pedestals, each holding a roundish basketball-sized lump that on some level Garrett recognized instantly, but was unable to admit to himself. But the smell was a dead giveaway.

Dead being the operative word.

The eyes were the next clue . . . filmed over, but unmistakable. The round lumps were human heads. Three heads, planted at three points of the triangle, long hair on two of them . . .

Garrett choked out some guttural version of a cry . . . it sounded harsh and inadequate in the cellar.

He barely had time to register details of the scene, the fat, burned-down candles surrounding each pedestal . . .

And then an enormous rushing and a hideous growl came from behind and above him, and something was barreling down the stairs, thumping on the thin wood. Garrett barely had time to spin before it was on him, a snarling, frothing hulk of a creature, with the horrible reeking smell of madness, raving in lunacy, inarticulate, bestial sounds. It smacked into him and threw him to the floor. Garrett fell backward and hit his head with a sharp crack on something hard and cold, a stone surface. For a moment he saw stars.

Then there was shrieking, and the huge foul thing was on top of him, mauling him, grappling, grasping his neck.

Garrett gasped for breath even as the alien sounds chilled his blood. The bulk on top of him was a good seventy pounds more than his own weight and there was more than ordinary heaviness, the weight of crazy.

Garrett suddenly went limp, made himself a dead weight, playing possum. His heart pounded out of control in his chest while he willed himself not to move . . . there was a horrible, suspended moment as his attacker paused, trying to gauge the change . . .

Garrett shoved his hand down his own leg and grabbed for his Glock, freeing it. But just before he squeezed down on the trigger, he hesitated—and instead jerked his arm up from between their bodies, up toward the ceiling, and slammed the metal weight of the weapon against his attacker's head with a yell, hammering him over and over as the madman shrieked and screamed.

The last thing Garrett felt was warm and sticky blood running down his fingers, his palm, his wrist, as the bulk on top of him finally, thankfully, collapsed into a dead faint, knocking Garrett's breath out as it pressed him hard into the stale and stinking earth.

What happened next was unclear.

His attacker stirred on top of him and Garrett shot back to consciousness with a jolt of lifesaving adrenaline. He thrashed on the dirt cellar floor to reach the plastic handcuffs clipped to his belt, and in a frantic race against time, he freed his hands to grasp the wrists of the body on top of him and wrest him into the cuffs.

Even as he did so, he was aware of something hideously, mortally askew. His attacker was reviving, starting to writhe and spit guttural obscenities, but the voice was horribly familiar, and the feel of the clothes he wore was terribly wrong; Garrett could sense the cut of a suit coat and matching trousers, and the size and shape of the man on top of him . . . too, too familiar.

Garrett pushed with all his strength to roll the body off him, and simultaneously rolled hard to his right in the dirt to get himself free. He scrambled up to his feet as his attacker began to rage, his shrieks echoing off the cellar walls and ceiling.

The cellar was black with just a splash of light from the beam of Garrett's fallen Maglite.

Garrett lunged and grabbed for the Mag.

The rasping words of his attacker behind him chilled his blood: *"Choronzon, acerbus et ingens! Te hoc ferto pectore flamman Choronzon—"*

With his heart in his throat, Garrett spun and trained the flashlight beam on the man who lay cursing him, his rants stripping his throat.

The light illuminated a face hideously distorted by madness and hate. And even though Garrett had known what he would see, the sight chilled him as no other moment in his life.

The frothing monster was Landauer.

Chapter Thirty-eight

It was an eternity before the crime-scene van arrived, and the ambulance. Garrett was running down the dirt road as soon as he heard the sirens and the approach of vehicles, running and shouting. "Don't touch anything!"

He strode to meet Lingg as the crime-scene tech emerged from the van, followed by other HazMat-suited crew. "The place is booby-trapped," Garrett rasped out. "I think there are psychotropic drugs painted on the doorknobs, maybe other places. Land touched them—I didn't."

Lingg looked at him questioningly for a split second, but then nodded. "You stay, Detective," he said, and his voice was kind. "Stay here."

Garrett was about to protest, but found his legs buckling underneath him. And as he braced himself against the side of the van, he saw something that turned his bowels to water.

In the long grass beside the van were burned footprints.

The EMTs carried a raving and cursing Landauer out in a strait-jacket. Garrett thought, half-consciously, that the shaken looks on the faces of the EMS guys must match his own.

As they muscled Landauer into the ambulance, a dark Lexus pulled up into the dirt road. Garrett turned . . . and through his numbness felt dull surprise to see Dr. Frazer emerge from the car. He crossed the drive to stand with Garrett. "Malloy wants this handled in-house," the psychiatrist said softly. "What happened?"

"The doorknob," Garrett said again. His voice shook. "He said it was sticky. Ten minutes later he was . . ." He looked toward the ambulance, where Landauer was still ranting, his voice by now bloody raw and hoarse from abuse, starting to fade, but barely. "Probably belladonna," Garrett said bleakly. "I told the EMTs so they don't give him anything that would react . . ." He slowed, and swallowed, trying to block out his partner's invective. He was sickly glad the words were in Latin so he wouldn't have to know what Land was saying.

A tech slammed shut the doors, mercifully cutting off the hoarse shrieks. Garrett and Frazer watched as the ambulance pulled away.

They joined Lingg at the crime-scene van and both suited up in white HazMat jumpsuits. "Don't touch anything," Lingg instructed the other men. "Even with gloves. Walls, doors, furniture—we have no idea what might be tainted." He turned to Garrett and Frazer. "Probably whatever psychotropic it is was mixed with DMSO for rapid absorption into the skin." He handed both of them helmets with respirators. "We don't know how much might be airborne, either. Detective Garrett, we'll follow your lead."

"Straight down to the cellar," Garrett said through a dry mouth.

Inside the house all walked gingerly, single file, careful not to brush against the doors or walls.

The cellar door still stood open; the stairs plunged precipitously into darkness. Behind Garrett, Lingg switched on a halogen lamp and shined it down the stairs to illuminate the musty cavern below.

The light was harsh, blue-white, and created stark shadows in the dingy basement. The painted triple triangle symbol was huge on the wall, and 333 was traced on the wall opposite, with more scrawls of text surrounding it. Garrett recognized some Latin words; others were unreadable. He flinched at the sight of the altar against the wall with its gruesome human candleholder, and turned his head away, though he knew there were worse sights in store.

238 • Alexandra Sokoloff

He reluctantly turned his gaze toward the triangle in the center of the cellar. It glowed with phosphorescence on the packed earth floor, the lines now smudged and blurred from Garrett's scuffle with Landauer. Garrett focused on the three pedestals, one at each point of the triangle in the dirt.

And he froze.

The heads were gone.

Garrett stared. Each stone shelf held three fat black candles—and a dark blotch, something dried and dark, but there was no sign of the heads.

Garrett's mind did a weird, nauseating flip. *But I saw them. Not candles.* **Heads.**

"Their heads were there," he croaked out. Lingg and Frazer looked toward him. "On the altars."

Lingg shined the lamp into the triangle. The stone pedestals were clearly bare, except for the candles and dark blotches on each.

"I saw them," Garrett insisted. "They were on the altars. Three heads."

Frazer and Lingg exchanged a wary glance. "Was there anyone else in the cellar with you?" Frazer asked, his voice maddeningly neutral.

Garrett was reeling. "I don't know, I . . ."

His mind was racing, out of control. *Was the killer here? Was he in the cellar with us? Did he take them out from under my nose?*

He had run, left Landauer and run . . .

Garrett suppressed a shudder . . . and remembered the over-powering feeling of being watched when he stood under the cellar door. He spun to look up the stairs.

No one in the doorway.

But there was another dark smear centered above the door frame, and something in the center of the smear: a small blackish rounded lump that appeared to be nailed to the wall. Garrett turned to one of the techs beside him and took his light from him. He shined the light up the stairs, focusing on the lump.

For a moment Garrett couldn't make it out, then his stomach

turned over. Beside him the tech squinted up toward the pool of light, and suddenly sucked in a breath. "Is that . . . Jesus."

It was a human eye nailed to the wall.

The photos of the crime scene were strewn all over the confer-ence table at Schroeder, and they were as bad as in Garrett's mem-ory: the triangle in the floor, with the stained pedestals; the sigils painted on the walls; the gruesome Hand of Glory; the eye nailed above the door.

"What the hell happened down there?" Malloy raged as he paced the room. It was a quiet, tight-lipped rage, which made it all the more ominous. Frazer sat in an armchair in a corner of the room, silent, watching.

Garrett was shaky from anxiety and exhaustion, and he had to fight to keep his voice steady. "Lingg thinks the perp mixed a psy-chotropic with DMSO for—"

"What the hell were you doing there to begin with?" Malloy's voice ran over him.

Garrett breathed in to keep his face from betraying his loathing of the man. "We got a partial plate from the homeless man who witnessed Amber Bright's abduction. The plate matched a vehicle registered to John McKenna, a foreman from the Pine Street land-fill where Erin Carmody's body was dumped. McKenna stopped coming to work on June fourteenth without giving notice and with no further communication with his employers." He paused, and was grateful that for the moment Malloy was silent, simply pro-cessing.

"The eye nailed to the wall of the cellar is human, and this is a severed human hand." Garrett pointed to the photo of the Hand of Glory with its burned-down black candle. "Officers are searching the scene for other human remains, but my guess is that we're not going to find them." He pointed to one of the photos of a stone pedestal. "Lingg confirmed that this is blood on each of the three altars." Malloy recoiled at his use of the word.

"The lab is running the DNA to check against Erin Carmody's

and Amber Bright's, but it's going to take days for the results." Garrett took a breath. "My guess is that the killer was using their heads on these altars."

Malloy looked even more affronted. "*Using* the heads?"

"I believe McKenna was taking his victims' heads to use in a black magic practice called necromancy—"

"McKenna?" The outrage was plain in the lieutenant's voice.

"Yes, McKenna," Garrett said. "I believe we should be shifting our investigative focus to him. It's possible that McKenna is dead, a third victim, but he doesn't fit the victim profile: two teenage girls and a middle-aged man? It doesn't add up. We'll need HazMat to okay us to go back in and process this scene, but in the meantime, I'm going to be delving into McKenna's personal life and employment history, and tracking him down from his last known whereabouts—"

"Detective Garrett." Malloy's voice was sharp, and he held up a hand to stop him. Garrett fell silent. The lieutenant's eyes bored into his face. "I understand that you claimed that there were human heads *in* the cellar. Yet no heads have been found at the scene."

Garrett stiffened, sensing danger. He glanced toward Frazer, whose face was a blank. After a moment, Garrett answered carefully.

"It was very dark. I was attacked only seconds later. A lot was happening—"

Malloy stared him down. "Dr. Frazer is of the opinion that the psychotropics could have been airborne as well as absorbable by touch-contact."

Garrett didn't know where this was going, so he waited.

"I'm sending you for a full physical exam and blood tests," Malloy said.

Every warning bell in Garrett's nervous system suddenly went off. "I don't think that's necessary—" he began.

"I do," Malloy cut through. "You're to report to Dr. Ramos at Mass General in one hour for a full tox workup."

Garrett stormed out of the conference room, cursing Malloy in his head, but in the end he stifled his rage and went to the hospital anyway, because that was where Landauer was. Once the initial fury had worn off he was operating in a daze, and the everyday chaos of Mass General, the milling families, the crying children and striding groups of medical personnel—wasn't helping him focus. He headed for the ER, and though he was not family, a sympathetic nurse who understood about cops and their partners told him what they knew: Landauer was unconscious, in critical condition. The chemicals in his system were atropine and a variety of other toxins that should have been lethal; it was only because Landauer was so big that he was still alive.

They weren't letting anyone see him yet, but the nurse promised to call Garrett as soon as they knew more.

Garrett thanked her dully. He turned away from the counter and felt grief and fury wash through him.

Landauer's words—some of the last sane words he had spoken— kept going through Garrett's head. *I don't know what she is, but she mighta saved my life.*

Or ended it, Garrett thought grimly.

Now it was Tanith's voice he heard:

"Do you know I could have booby-trapped the house, put a spell on the door against intruders, bound the book with toxins . . . so if you so much as touched a page you would die a slow death, untraceable—"

And what if she did? What if that was exactly what she did?

A rage began to build, a blind fury at Tanith Cabarrus.

Chapter Thirty-nine

This latest crime scene threw the media into a feeding frenzy, especially since no one at the department was talking. On his way back in to Schroeder, Garrett dodged a mob of reporters and bolted up the DNA stairs.

He knew there was something wrong the moment he stepped through the open door of Malloy's office. Detectives Palmer and Morelli stood in the room in front of the lieutenant's desk, and the sight gave Garrett's stomach an uneasy lurch. Granted, the case had suddenly expanded, and with Landauer down Garrett had not been expecting to work the case on his own. But Morelli and Palmer were an ominous sign, especially because Morelli seemed to be in the middle of a verbal report. Garrett stopped in the doorway, watching in disbelief as the older detective spoke. "We've put out an APB on McKenna, and a MP report. So far there's no trace of him. There was no regular mail delivery; he has a post office box that he hasn't visited since he walked off the job—"

"That's why McKenna is looking like the prime suspect," Garrett interrupted, giving Morelli a cold look as he walked into the room. "He disappeared from work without a trace, his basement was being used for rituals, he had access to and knowledge of the landfill where Erin Carmody's body was dumped. By his stats on his sheet he's five-eleven, two-thirty, a powerful enough man to have subdued these victims. His car has been identified by a witness to Amber Bright's abduction—"

Palmer cut in. "A homeless schizophrenic? That ID will never hold up in court."

Garrett turned on him, barely holding himself back. "Since the two of you have been such good do-bees in my absence, have you found a single witness who has seen McKenna since he disappeared from work? Have you checked his computer for satanic sites?"

Malloy spoke for the detectives. "We'll be able to get into the house tonight. If you could give me a moment, Detectives . . ." He glanced at Morelli and Palmer.

The two older detectives nodded briefly and filed out of the room, giving Garrett oblique glances. He felt his blood pressure skyrocket, an ominous warning.

Palmer closed the door behind him and Garrett turned to face Malloy, seated in front of his wall of photos of himself with various Boston luminaries.

"Detective Garrett, we are not looking at McKenna as a suspect at this time."

Garrett stared at him. "What's the alternative?"

"The alternative is that Jason Moncrief killed McKenna and was using his home for his rituals."

Garrett shook his head in total disbelief. "Jason Moncrief has been in jail since September twenty-third."

"And there is no evidence to indicate anyone has been in McKenna's house since then," Malloy said flatly.

"So where's McKenna's car?" Garrett demanded. "What about the witness who saw Amber Bright get into a car matching the description of McKenna's?"

"The witness is not credible. And even if the wit did see the car, Jason Moncrief could have been driving that car."

"For that matter, so could I have been," Garrett shot back.

Malloy's eyes were stone. "That's not necessary to prove."

"How does Jason Moncrief end up in McKenna's house?"

"Jason Moncrief has been placed at the scene."

Garrett felt a shock of disbelief.

"There were CDs with his prints in an upstairs bedroom of the house," Malloy said, with grim satisfaction.

Garrett was reeling. "You seriously think Moncrief killed Mc-Kenna and was using his house?"

"I think it's more likely they were working together," the lieutenant said.

"A cult?"

"A cult, quite possibly including Tanith Cabarrus."

Garrett stared at him, and then—he couldn't help himself. He started to laugh. And as the lieutenant glared up at him in disbelief, Garrett chortled, "That's beautiful. That is some magnificent detective work, there, L.T. You don't need me—you've solved it." Malloy was seething, and Garrett stopped, pulled himself together. "I apologize, Lieutenant. It's been a shitty day. I need some sleep." He turned toward the door.

"We're not done here," Malloy snapped at him.

Garrett turned back.

"Your lab results came back. You have atropine in your bloodstream. Only it's broken down, which indicates that you ingested it more than thirty-six hours ago." Malloy stared across the room at him. "What haven't you been telling me, Detective?"

Garrett felt a hard knot in his stomach. "I accidentally ingested the atropine in the course of the investigation. I didn't know that . . . some liquid was laced with the drug—"

"Some liquid," Malloy said contemptuously. Garrett was silent. Malloy shook his head, but Garrett saw the gleam of satisfaction in his eyes. "I know about the congress you've been having with that—woman."

Congress? Garrett felt himself bristling. *Oh, yeah? What do you know? The rituals? The flying? The fucking?* He forced himself to remain calm as Malloy elaborated.

"The one who identifies herself as a 'witch.' Who has a prior relationship with Jason Moncrief—"

Garrett countered, "I've found no evidence of a prior—"

"Who has a criminal record for fraud," Malloy overrode him, and Garrett stopped. "You mentioned none of this in your reports," the lieutenant finished grimly. "This woman is an occult practitioner. She should have been listed and investigated as a potential suspect or accomplice as soon as you discovered the connection. Why was this not done?"

Garrett used every ounce of will he had to remain calm. "I consulted with her about occult rituals that were relevant to the case—"

"Is that what you call it? Consulting?" Malloy's outrage had that tone of religious condemnation that Garrett despised. He pressed his hands into the desktop to keep silent as Malloy raged on. "Your conduct has been completely unprofessional, and your partner is now in a coma because of your negligent—"

"Coma?" Garrett interrupted, feeling as if Malloy had just hit him with a two-by-four.

"A drug-induced coma," Malloy elaborated, and Garrett felt there was a small and sadistic measure of satisfaction for the lieutenant in delivering the news. Too sickened to look at him, Garrett turned on his heel and strode for the door.

"Tell me, Detective," Malloy shot at him from behind. "Did this Cabarrus woman send you to that house? Is that where you got your tip?"

Garrett stopped in his tracks and turned back to look at him.

The lieutenant stared back, then nodded. "Just as I thought." His face hardened. "We're picking her up for questioning. Detectives Palmer and Morelli will be taking over the investigation. You're relieved of duty pending review. Surrender your weapon— and get out."

Detectives Palmer and Morelli led the team of uniforms to raid Tanith's shop. Their warrant was in hand and they wore HazMat gear: suits and huge impenetrable gloves. There was no answer when they rang the bell, then pounded on the door—and then they kicked the door in, bursting into the exotically scented shop.

No cat looked up from the counter; no one answered their shouted summons. They fanned out to search the rooms and the upstairs.

The altar room was empty: no Book of Shadows, no crystals, no daggers, no cards, no candles—just the empty cabinet and shelves and the heavy drapes on the walls and the pentagram on the floor. There was no one upstairs, either, and the closet looked sparse for a woman's room.

The police finally lowered their weapons and began methodically to tear the house apart.

Unseen by anyone, a mouse watched from a hole in the baseboard.

Chapter Forty

She was gone.

None of the neighbors questioned by the officers had any idea she was leaving. Her utilities and mortgage payments were on auto-pay; the mail had been stopped. Her car was gone. There was no forwarding message on her voice mail; there was no personal computer in the shop or upstairs; she had no e-mail accounts that anyone could find. The cat was gone; her desk and personal drawers had been cleaned out.

The detectives seized samples of belladonna from the shop. More ominously, a doll was found on the premises in the shape of Landauer: the same proportions, dressed in a suit, with a crude badge pinned to its chest.

Cabarrus's sudden flight confirmed departmental suspicions that she was involved somehow with Landauer's poisoning. The belladonna seized from her shop, the threat that the detectives had witnessed in the bull pen (*You're done . . .*), and the weird doll were enough to justify a BOLO: wanted for questioning.

But so far there were no leads on her. She was "in the wind," as was said in law enforcement, and Garrett thought that in this case the term was more literal than anyone might suspect.

He had more time than he wanted to think about all of these things as he camped out in the hospital beside Landauer's bed, where his partner lay with a machine breathing for him. So far there had been no improvement.

He watched as the lung machine inflated Landauer's chest in a slow and horribly artificial-seeming rhythm. *I'll find her, Land. I swear to you, I will.*

When Garrett heard about the Landauer doll, he had risked Malloy's wrath—and disciplinary action—to sneak into the crime lab to see Tufts. Tufts showed him the doll, and Garrett understood why the other detectives, particularly Malloy, had reacted so strongly. It was a crude and alien thing, burlap hand-sewn in the shape of a man and dressed in some doll-clothes version of a blue suit, with a metal badge pinned to the chest.

"What's inside it?" Garrett asked Tufts.

"A mix of herbs—"

"Belladonna?" Garrett demanded.

"No belladonna," said the criminalist. "Mostly common garden herbs—maybe a bit more common if you're a witch! Mugwort, hensbane, dragon's breath . . . and tobacco."

Garrett stared at him. "Tobacco."

Tufts shrugged. "And hair." He opened a manila envelope, and removed a glassine bag. "Dirty blond, curly."

Now, in the hospital room, Garrett looked at his comatose partner . . . dirty blond curls crushed against the pillow.

She'd made a voodoo doll, or whatever a witch would call it.

And yet, the tobacco in the doll . . .

In his head, Landauer's voice came to him, unbidden. *"I haven't had one since she walked into the office that day. Fuck knows I've tried. I just can't."*

Either way, she owed Garrett some answers, and he was going to get them.

He had an entirely different reason than the rest of the police for wanting to find Tanith. Whether or not she had put Land into the coma, she was the most likely person Garrett knew to be able to get him back.

And time was running out.

Palmer and Morelli had a whole new crime scene's worth of evidence to process. Garrett knew they'd be doing exactly what he'd be doing: tracking the missing McKenna, questioning his neighbors and the managers and owners and workers at the landfill, seeking out family; while they collected lab reports on the blood samples and eye, looking for matches with Amber and Erin and trying to determine the identity of whoever's blood was on the third altar and in the handprint on the front door.

But they would be looking at all that evidence through the prism of Malloy's directive: to keep their focus on Jason Moncrief as the killer. And beyond that, Garrett knew Carolyn would fight not to have any other murders tied into the Carmody case. Garrett had not seen her since she had hurled Tanith Cabarrus's arrest file at him that day, but he knew how her mind worked, and he had watched the song-and-dance the department was doing for the media to keep McKenna out of the papers. Trying to prove another murder would muddy the solid case the state had against Moncrief. Carolyn was not about to fall into the trap of bringing new charges that might jeopardize her existing case.

All of which meant that key evidence could be overlooked for political expedience.

Garrett sat holding his partner's calloused hand while his mind raced through possibilities. He didn't believe McKenna was a victim. The former foreman had intimate knowledge of the landfill, its entrances and routines, making it a natural dumping ground for him. He had an isolated house, perfect for the kinds of rituals (Garrett's mind shifted away from dwelling on the particulars) that someone had been doing in that cellar. And Tufts had let Garrett in on the fact that books and printouts on demonology, including volumes by the ubiquitous Aleister Crowley, had been found in McKenna's house. He fit Dr. Frazer's profile of the "Self-Styled Satanist."

Palmer and Morelli would no doubt try to question Jason to determine whether he had any kind of connection with McKenna, and also to try to pin down a connection with Tanith. Evidence at

McKenna's house would be cross-matched with hair, fiber, and DNA taken from Tanith's house and shop, and from Jason's room and car.

Yes, Palmer and Morelli would be doing it by the book. The problem was, they didn't have time for the book. Even expedited, DNA reports took a minimum of two weeks and it was October 28. Which meant just three days before Halloween . . .

Samhain, Garrett's mind whispered.

"Samhain is the eve, when those who love the lost will grieve. Three to die to do the deed . . ."

They didn't have time for DNA.

And there was another unease that Garrett didn't even let himself look at too closely. *He's holding them*, she'd said. *Their souls are trapped.*

He looked at his partner, attached to machines by tubes.

Trapped.

But Garrett had an idea of how to find her.

Chapter Forty-one

According to her psych file from McLean State Hospital, Teresa Smithfield, a.k.a. Tanith Cabarrus, had been released to one Selena Fox after she was discharged from that institution in 2000. Garrett had no idea whether or not Palmer and Morelli had decided to follow up, but his own calls to the DMV and the credit reporting companies and searches on AutoTrack turned up no such person as Selena Fox, so he doubted the other detectives would have spent much time with it. They had other things on their plate.

Garrett knew that the other detectives were following McKenna's trail, so he headed in the opposite direction, out of the city and off the map: to Salem. An absurd little chant looped through his head as he made the drive: *Takes a witch to catch a witch.*

All that damn rhyming of the rituals. He couldn't get away from it. But the theory behind the taunting little homily was sound, he thought. The witch community seemed tight-knit.

So he strode again through gusting wind and swirling leaves on the Essex pedestrian walk, toward the witch souvenir shop he'd gone into by mistake on his first trip up to visit Tanith.

The day had been warm, Indian summer, but the slanting light was most definitely autumn, with long evening shadows beginning to creep across the cobblestones of the mall, shifting cerily with the wind. As Garrett walked the mall it was impossible not to note the explosion of Halloween decorations. Now, upward of seventy-five percent of the people around him were already in costume, and the shops were festooned with lights, pumpkins, black cats, the cornstalks lashed to lampposts and pillars. The sight made Garrett cold, despite the warmth of the evening.

The same beshawled proprietor was at the counter of the shop at the heart of the mall, and she looked him over with that same greedy interest before her smile curled cynically. "Back so soon? I told you you didn't want anything to do with Tanith Cabarrus." News of Tanith's wanted status had hit the papers. Garrett imagined it had caused quite a stir in the small Salem community.

"You were right about that," he agreed neutrally. "It's someone else I'm looking for now, though. Selena Fox."

There was an uneasy flicker in the witch's eyes. She looked away. "I can't help you."

"Well, you see, I think you can," Garrett said. He kept his voice casual, but there was an edge.

She shook her head. "I have no idea where Selena is. She hasn't lived in Salem for some time. But I can tell you this. If she wants to talk to you, she'll find *you*. And if she doesn't, you won't."

Garrett looked at her, startled. She gazed at him intently—no, not at him, but somehow a bit above him, and to the sides. "Are you sure you don't want a reading? Your aura doesn't look good."

Garrett had to bite his tongue. "I bet it doesn't. Thanks anyway."

Though he knew it was pointless, he drove by Book of Shadows. The shop was itself a shadow against the darkening sky and there was yellow police tape crossed on the door.

For no reason that he could think of, he got out of the car and moved up on the sidewalk to stand just before the porch stairs.

The cornstalks were still lashed to the porch columns, and Garrett wondered briefly what Palmer and Morelli and the other officers had made of that.

There was a stirring of wind, and then he felt an unsettling sense of presence behind him, the visceral sensation of being watched. Garrett turned quickly—

—to see a flash of pale skin, a shock of fiery red hair, as a slight, agile figure darted toward the bushes beside the house, heading straight on toward the thick hedge. Garrett tensed and reached automatically for his weapon, before he remembered that it was in lockup at Schroeder; he'd had to turn it over.

And then, unbelievably, the figure seemed to melt into the greenery, disappearing into the hedge with no crash of branches, no rustle of leaves.

Garrett stared.

After a moment he strode toward the hedge. He pushed the branches aside where the figure had vanished—melted—and was startled to see a solid brick wall. There was no gate, no opening through which a person could have exited.

This is crazy, he told himself. *I saw him. Her. It.*

Garrett stood in consternation, then looked behind him. The street was deserted, no cars coming and no sound of any approaching vehicle.

Garrett reached up to put his hands flat on top of the wall and pushed himself up, swung a leg over.

The wall enclosed a luxurious garden, deserted and luminous in the twilight. Garrett dropped to the ground and looked around him, quickly taking in a landscape design laid out in a spiral, with a profusion of flowering plants: white roses and gardenias and some kind of big white daisy, and the large pale bells of deadly nightshade, all glowing under the moonlight. In one flower bed was a very feminine statue, draped in a marble gown so flowing that every curve of its body was revealed. One corner of the yard held a graceful white gazebo, a water fountain whispered from another corner, and the fragrance of gardenia and lavender and roses mingled in the cooling air, subtle and intoxicating. A line from some poem or play floated through Garrett's head: *"Soft moonlight sleeps upon the bank . . ."*

Then a living shape popped up in front of him so quickly he caught his breath—and stared, eyes widening. *What the hell is this?*

254 • Alexandra Sokoloff

The garden was dark, but he could tell instantly that the—*boy?*—standing in front of him was strange, small and slight, with fiery red hair and pale freckled face and pointed nose and pointed chin. The hair was longish, covering his—its—ears, but Garrett had to forcibly stop himself from imagining points on the tips of those, too. The boy wore thonged leather sandals and short tan trousers and some tuniclike open weave sweater of coarse cloth. It was impossible to tell—its—his—age.

The boy grinned and there were points on his teeth as well, as if the canines had been filed, and his eyes were slits of blue fire.

"Who are you?" Garrett managed. The boy shook his head, still grinning, and waved an index finger in front of his face. Then his hand moved so fast Garrett had no time to react, and he was whipping something out of the tunic, though the motion was such a blur that something white seemed to simply materialize in the boy's hand.

In his palm was something the size and shape of a business card, which he presented to Garrett with a mock bow. Garrett's fingers had no sooner closed on it than the boy turned and lifted his arms to his sides, spinning in a circle like a child, like a top. Then he suddenly broke into a run, straight for a hedge of night-blooming jasmine growing in front of the garden wall.

This time Garrett was anticipating the boy's move and grabbed for him. His fingers closed around nothing and he stumbled, nearly falling on his face on the path. He threw himself upright and looked wildly around him . . .

He saw a flash of white by the hedge and said sharply, "Wait"—but the branches had closed around the boy without so much as a rustle.

What the fuck?

And when Garrett shoved his way through the branches, he came up against the stone wall again.

He backed out of the branches, caught his breath, and looked down at the card in his hand. It was not a normal business card, but a bit smaller and longer, gold-embossed letters on heavy stock. *Calling card*, his mind said, and he had no idea how he really knew that. The card held an address in Cambridge, and the handwritten notation: 10:00 A.M.

Nothing more.

Garrett turned and looked around him. The garden was empty . . . he was alone in the light of the rising moon.

And once again he was left with the shaky feeling of reality crumbling around him.

Chapter Forty-two

The address was an elegant old Cambridge house, a two-story stone Tudor in one of those unattainable dream neighborhoods with lush backyard gardens, waterfalls and arbors, and trellises and terraces.

The tall woman who answered the carved oak door was as aristocratic as her house; at what must have been past seventy she was still as slim, upright, and graceful as a dancer, her years only slightly softening classic aquiline features. She wore a loose silk caftan in shimmering apricots, creams, and golds, and looked Garrett over with penetrating sky-blue eyes.

Garrett silently handed her the card.

"You're prompt." She smiled at him without introducing herself. "I like that." She stepped aside so that he could enter the hall. Garrett's eyes swept the rooms that he could see from the entry; they were large and light, and crammed with antiques, real oil paintings, silk rugs on hardwood floors gleaming with age.

"If you'll follow me," she said, and glided down the hall past equally elegant rooms toward a high arch of double glass doors. She opened a door for him and Garrett stepped into an atrium with octagonal walls of glass enclosing a jungle of exotic plants, from orchids to tropical trees and all manner of flowers with riotous colors and voluptuous blossoms. The atrium overlooked the garden, and autumn sunlight poured through the walls of glass. As Garrett followed the older woman through the greenery, they passed a waterfall whispering into a series of connecting pools; Garrett caught glimpses of fat pale fish through the green water, in the same colors his hostess was wearing. He half expected to hear the calls of tropical birds.

Sure enough, as they slipped through an arrangement of plants that opened up into a seating area of wicker furniture, he was confronted with a cream-colored cockatoo perched on a stand.

The woman indicated a wicker sofa with a wave of her hand and seated herself on one of twin wicker chairs with high arched backs. On the low table in front of her was a silver tray with a tea service and a plate of cakes. "Would you like tea, or something stronger?"

Garrett remained standing. "I'm sorry, I like to know who I'm eating with."

She smiled at him. "Oh, come now, Detective Garrett—surely we can dispense with the obvious."

"Selena Fox?" he asked sharply.

"That will do."

Garrett wasn't in the mood for word games. "Where is she?" he demanded.

"In time," Fox said serenely as she poured amber liquid into eggshell-thin cups. She lifted the cup and saucer toward him.

Garrett stared at her. "Lately I'm not so hot on drinking anything a witch hands me."

Fox lifted her shoulders, a smooth, lithe gesture. "I can understand your reluctance. Still, don't you find the end sometimes justifies the means?"

Garrett's mind wanted to rebel against the elliptical conversation, but he honed in immediately on what she was implying: the drugged trip Tanith had induced in him had led to the discovery of McKenna's house.

His face hardened. "My partner is in Mass General, lying in a coma. I don't think that end justifies anything."

The older woman's eyes contracted in sympathy. "I'm very sorry about that, Detective. I think you're misattributing the cause, however." The sound of water from the fountain echoed, a whisper against the glass around them.

Garrett finally sat, though he didn't reach for the tea. "What do you want from me? Why did you call me here?"

She raised her eyebrows. "I understood it was you who were looking for me."

His eyes narrowed. *You're not going to trip me out with these witch games. That shopkeeper called you and said I'd been by asking for you, that's all there is to it.* Then his mind flashed on the strange redhaired boy. "Who"—he'd almost said *what*—"was that you sent for me?" he asked abruptly. "The kid?"

She looked amused, as if she'd heard his mental correction. "Someone who does errands for me occasionally. Very reliable. Single-minded, one might say."

Garrett had the distinct sense that he was being toyed with. He spoke roughly. "I'm looking for Tanith Cabarrus. Are you going to help me or not?"

"She is easily available to you. It's a matter of intention and attention."

Fuck this New Age witch shit, Garrett thought grimly. He stood. "You can tell her that disappearing was a bullshit thing to do. There's a warrant out on her, now. Even if she wasn't involved with Jason Moncrief, she's looking at serious jail time. The whole department thinks she's complicit in the attack on my partner."

"And what do you think, Detective Garrett?" Fox looked at him with ageless, clear blue eyes.

The question stopped him and he found he could not answer smartly or facetiously. "I know she hasn't told the truth. I know she knows more than she's telling."

Fox lifted her hands. "Oh, certainly. But can you really blame her for that?"

"I know she's been arrested for fraud," Garrett ground out. "I know she's been institutionalized for paranoid schizophrenia."

"For seeing demons," Fox said pointedly.

"Yeah. For seeing demons," Garrett said.

"Perhaps you should ask her about that," Fox suggested. Garrett stared at her. Her gaze on him was steady, probing. "Do you know what I see, Detective? I see two people who are not at odds. Who perhaps have two different sides to a vital puzzle. A puzzle in which lives are at stake, and in which the clock is running out."

Garrett was not merely struck by her words, he was close to mesmerized.

She looked at him, and the sunlight behind her illuminated her pale hair. "So many lives at stake," she repeated softly. "And perhaps more than just lives."

Without realizing he was doing it he nodded, which she took as a sign to continue.

"Every life in the balance here—and each soul as well—deserves a little faith. And I believe that you are not a man who must follow the book to the exclusion of truth, or justice. I believe you are willing."

"Willing to what?" he said, and his voice sounded strangled.

"Willing to make a leap of faith. Willing to do things by a different book." Her blue eyes held his. "Three children killed," she recited, in muted tones. "Another imprisoned. A good man at the brink of death. And three more children to die, if someone does not intervene."

Garrett's stomach roiled, but he couldn't look away from her eyes.

"Your own department has banned you from the hunt, when even given what you are reluctant to believe, you know you are light-years closer to the truth than they are. This masculine jockeying will most certainly cost more lives if someone does not say, 'Enough.'" She opened her hands. "Are you willing to work outside your comfort zone?"

Through his confusion and gnawing anxiety, Garrett managed to speak. "What do you think I've been doing?" he retorted.

Her eyes twinkled at him. "You're quite right."

"I want the killer." Garrett's voice was suddenly harsh. "I don't care who it is. I don't care what gets me there. I want this to stop.

I want this guy put away for eternity. That's all I want. You're supposed to know things. You decide."

She was very stiff and still, her eyes boring into his. And then she suddenly went limp, some hidden tension relaxing. "So mote it be," she said, and the words were formal, with a regal import.

She took a deep, shaky breath . . . for a moment Garrett feared he would have to perform CPR. Then she glanced toward the other high-backed wicker chair across from her.

Garrett followed her gaze, and then shot to his feet, staring.

Tanith sat in the other chair, as if she had been there all along. He had not heard, nor felt her come. She sat very still, leaning on her forearms on the arms of the chair, barely breathing.

"Jesus Christ," Garrett muttered, and wondered crazily if she had been there, invisible, all along, until she—or Selena—had chosen to make her seen. "How the fuck did you do that?" he demanded, completely forgetting all manners.

"A trick." Selena shrugged. "But we will need more than tricks to achieve our purpose."

Tanith spoke, avoiding looking directly at Garrett. "I heard about Detective Landauer."

"You *heard* about him?" he responded bitterly.

Her eyes flashed. "You think I would ever *do* that?"

"How would I know what you would do?" he demanded. "You drugged me—why wouldn't you drug him?"

"I didn't hurt you," she retorted, but there was less fire in her voice, and Selena glanced at her.

"It was wrong," the older woman said, and Tanith looked away.

There was an icy silence, which Selena broke, her voice sharp. "There's no time for recriminations. There is one center of this investigation, and it's time to do what needs to be done."

Garrett looked toward her, confused. Tanith spoke warily. "Jason Moncrief."

"Of course," Selena said, with an impatient wave. "Have you ever even spoken to him?" she asked Garrett pointedly.

Garrett sat for a moment, stupefied at the simplicity of the suggestion, then he remembered. "Once. His attorney took out a TRO: a technical restraining order. No law enforcement officer is allowed in to talk to him."

"That won't do," the older woman said. "It should not have prevented you when you knew he was not guilty."

"I don't know that," Garrett countered angrily. He was about to continue arguing but she cut through him.

"Don't pretend you don't know what I'm talking about. You have the key, Detective Garrett." She suddenly reached forward and grabbed his wrist, a bony grip so strong Garrett drew in a startled breath. Her eyes were black, all pupil as she stared unseeing into his eyes.

"The book," she gasped, and she kept speaking, but Garrett didn't hear words. Images were blasting into his head: the hand-bound book of maroon leather, the rough paper, the twiglike lettering, the disturbing black-lined drawings.

He jerked his hand away from the older woman's grip and was shocked to find he was standing, but so shaky he was barely able to keep his balance.

Selena was also standing, rigidly, drawing deep, shuddering breaths. "Where is it?" she whispered.

Garrett stared at her, for the second time wondering if she was on the verge of a stroke. Tanith rose from her chair, and her dark eyes locked on Garrett's. "You know what she means. The grimoire."

Selena felt for the back of a chair and Tanith was there at her side, instantly, helping her to sit. After a moment, Selena lifted her head, looked up at Garrett. "There *is* a book, then. A grimoire. If you still think Jason Moncrief is guilty, perhaps you have only to read it to find all you need to set your mind at rest." Her eyes drilled into his. "Do you have it?"

Garrett was about to say it was in evidence and he was off the case, and then he remembered. Not only did he still have his copy, he had his copy in the trunk of his car.

"I think we might have a look at it, then," Selena said, and Garrett was not even surprised that she'd read his mind.

———

The two women set the copied book on a long oak table in what Garrett supposed was a dining hall. The chairs were medieval-looking, with lions' paws for armrests and feet, and tapestries and marble friezes were hung on the walls. The women stood over the table with the stack of pages in front of them and studied them, and Garrett could only think of priestesses, of sibyls, of goddesses. They reached for pages in tandem and communicated only with looks and once in a while by pointing to passages.

Garrett paced the polished plank floor impatiently until Selena looked up at him and said, "Detective, perhaps you would be more comfortable in a chair."

Garrett sat, and watched them, seven million conflicting thoughts in his brain. *It's easy enough to stage*, he argued with himself. *Cabarrus knew about the grimoire, and why wouldn't she have told Fox about it? There's no mind reading going on, it's simple con artist tricks.*

And then he remembered the steel strength of the woman's hand on his arm and the sizzle of electric shock when she—yes—*read* him.

At one point Tanith covered her face with her hands and the elder woman put her hand on her neck, comforting her. Garrett wanted to speak but felt rooted to his chair, felt like an intruder watching something intensely private.

After a long time they closed the book and sat down in the chairs with the lion-paw hand rests. Selena looked drained, her skin fragile as paper.

"Well?" Garrett demanded, looking at Tanith.

"He was doing rituals to summon the demon Choronzon."

Garrett tensed. "So it was Moncrief. He killed them."

Tanith said, "No," immediately, and Selena said simultaneously, "I don't think so."

Garrett looked from one to the other, focused on Tanith. "You said that was what the killer is doing."

Her voice was tightly controlled. "What Jason was doing was on a very elementary level. It is dangerous, and dangerously stupid, but there is no indication he was considering anything involving sacrifice."

Garrett bristled. "I saw the spell for the 'Hand of Glory.' And Erin's left hand was missing."

Selena frowned, looked to Tanith. Tanith shook her head impatiently. "The Hand of Glory is a spell that shows up commonly online. These kids who get involved in ritual magic for thrills . . . they collect spells like that."

"Oh, really, now?" Garrett lashed out. "That's convenient. Do you have some proof? Because a spell using a corpse's left hand and a dead girl missing her left hand is a pretty great match to me."

Selena clucked her tongue. "But if this young man kept such an incriminating spell in his grimoire, so openly, why would he not have kept spells of the actual sacrifice, of rituals using sacrifice?" she asked reasonably. She waved a hand over the book. "There's nothing like that here. Nothing indicating any intention to perform human sacrifice."

Garrett remembered that he had gone all through the book, that one long night, and studied all the sketches, and it was true that there was nothing drawn that resembled human sacrifice, and no spell titles that contained the word "sacrifice." The Hand of Glory had been the most ominous of the drawings by far.

Selena nodded, as if he had agreed with her. "You see, a grimoire, like a Book of Shadows, is as illuminating as a diary, really. The magician makes very detailed notes of his or her preparation for a major ritual—the cleansing, the fasting, the gathering of instruments, the position of the moon and tide. Come, Detective, and look." She lifted a graceful hand, beckoning him to her side, and Garrett rose, crossed to her. She pulled the book toward her and looked up at him. "We know the sacrifices were performed on Sabbats, do we not? Erin Carmody's murder was on the night of Mabon, the fall equinox, September twenty-one. The killing of that other poor girl was on August first, Lammas, or Lughnasadh. But look."

She opened the book and turned pages to the month of June. "The entries for June are spells of money, success, fame." She turned

264 • Alexandra Sokoloff

pages and stopped on the sketch of the hand with the candle. "Here, you have the Hand of Glory spell. A loathsome thing. But it is only after that, in August, that Choronzon's name and sigils begin to appear. A dangerous path, make no mistake." She turned more pages. "But then in September . . . ah, this is telling, I think. The spells are for attraction. Love." She turned more pages, to where the book went blank. "And after September nine . . . nothing."

She looked up from the book, into Garrett's face. "There is no indication here that he was preparing for major rituals. Moreover, there is no mention of Choronzon in September at all."

Garrett stared at her, trying to process what she was telling him.

"This boy has not been circumspect in his magical practice. He wrote down what he was doing. According to these entries, the obsession with Choronzon was waning, not increasing."

And maybe he just knew enough not to write about it, Garrett thought, and Selena smiled. "You think he was dissembling. Perhaps. But my experience is that a nineteen-year-old boy is not a paragon of control, including in matters of deception." Her eyes twinkled at him, and Garrett was uncomfortably reminded of his biggest doubt he'd had about the case from the beginning: that a nineteen-year-old could be capable of the kind of precision and control that he felt in this killer.

"Ah, you do understand," Selena said.

"So what else do you see in this—diary?" Garrett said roughly, resisting the pull to trust her.

Her twinkle disappeared. "A very troubled boy indeed."

"Stupid," Tanith muttered. "Stupid. Reckless. Arrogant."

Selena sighed. "Yes. All of that. And more." She glanced obliquely at Tanith. "Children—people—who feel powerless will seek power wherever they can find it. Even a power that tricks and traps and enslaves. And this particular darkness is very aware of the weakness of vulnerable people."

"I don't think I understand," Garrett said, even though on some level, he did.

"This is how he got caught up in all this. This is why he's in such peril," Tanith said impatiently. "You open a door like that with thoughtless experimenting and anything can come through. He invited the demon in, and it used him for its own purposes."

The words shot a chill through Garrett. He suddenly remembered his encounter with Jason: that stretched-tight face and guttural voice, the layers of babbling voices on the tape of the interview . . . "You're saying Moncrief *is* possessed?" He stared from one woman to the other.

"Not possessed . . . but infected, perhaps." Selena's eyes were clouded. "Evil is a contagion."

"It used him," Tanith said. "Found Erin through him. Even framed him."

"The demon framed him," Garrett repeated incredulously.

"Through its human instrument," Tanith answered. "So he would not be interrupted before the time came. Jason is being used as a pawn. A distraction."

Garrett felt prickles of doubt, like sandpaper scraping on his skin. *All this time we've had Jason Moncrief locked up, McKenna's been out there, completely under the radar . . .*

He walked in a circle on the Persian rug, and laughed. "If you believe Moncrief is *infected* with a demon, what would make you think he didn't kill these girls? Or at least was part of it with"—he almost said McKenna—"someone else's help?"

"The same thing that makes you think it," Selena said calmly. "The truth that you see. The fact that he didn't."

Garrett stopped his frenzied circling and looked at her.

Behind him, Tanith exploded, with raw nerves. "Talk to him. The point is, talk to Jason. He's communed with the demon. That's your most direct link."

"Exactly," Selena affirmed. "That's your most direct link. Go." She looked from Garrett to Tanith. "Both of you. Go now."

Garrett stared at the older woman. "Take *her* into Suffolk County? There's a warrant out for her arrest."

"Then if you're caught, you were simply bringing her in, weren't you?" Serena said placidly.

"Why don't I just arrest her now and save a step?"

Serena quirked an eyebrow at him. "Are suspended officers allowed to make arrests?" she inquired, the picture of innocence.

"I know for damn sure we're not allowed to sneak them in to see inmates in correctional facilities," he shot back.

"She can go in as a member of Jason's legal team," Selena said.

Garrett turned to look at her in disbelief. "No one would buy that."

Selena shrugged again, that irresistible lift of her shoulders. "Try it."

Garrett shook his head. "This is crazy—"

"Tanith is your best chance of getting in to see Jason Moncrief," Selena said.

Garrett looked to Tanith now, who sat watchful as a cat in the window seat. "You mean he'll confirm this attorney story because you know him already."

Selena sat wearily back against the medieval chair. "Detective Garrett, you do not seem the sort to resist a golden opportunity. Why are you resisting this one?"

He stared across the long oak table toward Tanith, who said nothing. "Because I don't like gift horses. Because I don't trust her."

Tanith's face blazed with fury, but Selena spoke calmly. "But you are not a stupid man." She found Garrett's eyes and held them with her clear blue ones. "You know what is at stake, and you will take this chance, because it must be done. And we have no more time to debate."

Tanith was like a statue in his passenger seat as Garrett drove the circular driveway out toward the street.

The calls had been made and astoundingly Jason had given consent to the visit. But just as the Explorer reached the front gates, Garrett saw something that changed everything.

A large dark man in overalls and a straw gardening hat stood beside the garden wall, with shears, trimming the roses that rambled over the stonework.

Garrett's eyes widened in recognition.

It was the Dragon Man.

Chapter Forty-three

Garrett struggled not to show his shock. He drove past the gardener, out the gates and onto the street, his mind going a million miles a minute.

Is this all an act? All of it? They're all in it, working together?

Waves of paranoia broke over him.

He drove ahead in silence, waiting until he had turned the corner onto another quiet street, before he hit the child lock so that Tanith couldn't get out, and jerked the Explorer to a halt by the curb. He reached out across the console and grabbed her. She instantly turned into a wild animal, her body writhing as she fought him. He took both her wrists and pinned her against the seat.

"I saw him. The Dragon Man. He works for you."

"He works for Selena," she blazed. "Of course he does. What were we going to do, put him back on the street?" She jerked her arms away from him, rubbed her wrists. "He needs a stable environment. He's healing. He even talks a little now, real sentences." She stopped, looked at Garrett, read his face. "What—you think this was all a setup? He's in on everything with us? We're a coven? A cult?"

Hearing her say it, he felt the same sense of absurdity he'd experienced when Malloy voiced a similar theory. "It makes more sense than anything else you've been trying to make me believe."

She laughed. "Oh, now we're forcing you. You have a mind, Garrett; you have instincts, you have experience, you have a consciousness. Why don't you use them? What do *you* believe?"

"I don't believe, I know. You lied about not knowing Jason Moncrief. That's why he consented to the interview."

"I don't know him," she retorted. "He did come into the shop."

Garrett stared at her. She shrugged, agitated.

"He didn't buy the books. He bought a wand. Cherrywood, with a quartz crystal at the top. And a censer. Not the Crowley books—I wouldn't have sold those to him. Those he must have taken."

Garrett was deeply skeptical. "Why would you hide that?"

She shook her head wearily. "What was I supposed to say, that I know he isn't the killer because I did meet him? Because I would have known if he were buying any of those things with the intention to kill? Would you have believed me for the slightest second?"

Not a chance, Garrett thought. *And I don't believe you now.*

He fixed her with his gaze. "I saw your file."

"I gathered," she said shortly. She stared straight ahead through the windshield, struggling with herself. "You heard Selena. People who feel powerless will seek power wherever they can. I have a— talent. I read people. I dream things. I see enough that people will pay for what I can tell them, and there was a time I was desperate enough to take them for all they had."

She finally looked at him, and for a moment he was unable to look away. "I'm not proud of it," she said, and her voice was bitter. "It was the first control I'd had in my life and it was addictive. In a way, I was looking for revenge." She didn't say revenge for what.

"I played around with darker and darker things. I . . ." She stopped, swallowed. "It did make me crazy for a while. I was going down a completely destructive path. And then Selena found me. She taught me how to use what power I have to help, when I can. I owe her everything." The look on her face was stark.

Garrett was unnerved to find himself wanting to believe her, on the verge of believing her. And then he remembered.

He took her hand back, this time turning it over and pushing her sleeve up to reveal the old scars: parallel vertical lines on her wrist, the shiny traces of random knife marks and gouges.

She stiffened, but didn't pull her hand away. Her face was pale and her eyes distant. "Yes, I was trying to cut the demons out of me."

"There were demons inside you," he said flatly.

"Yes," she answered defiantly. "I summoned them. They came. They wait in darkness, watching . . . hoping for an invitation. And time after time, we invite them in. It doesn't take much, to fall out of the light."

She is crazy, Garrett thought. But that's not what he felt. Hadn't he seen exactly that, on the streets, over and over again? An invitation to the dark, and a swift fall out of the light?

She bit her lip, looked out the passenger window. "So I know what path Jason has taken. And I know he hasn't gone as far down it as you think he has. He can still be saved." She hesitated. "You can call it schizophrenia if you want, or drug-related psychosis." Then she turned to him and looked him full in the eyes. "But what if I looked crazy because seeing demons makes you look crazy?"

Garrett had no way to answer this. But finally he sat back in his seat, turned the key in the engine, and drove.

As they walked through the triple-thick glass doors into Suffolk County jail, Garrett felt Tanith stiffen beside him, the same kind of tensing he was used to seeing in ex-cons who had to cross the threshold. He was none too easy himself with the idea of escorting a wanted fugitive into a maximum security facility. Then he saw her take a breath and her face smoothed out to perfect neutrality.

They stopped at the security check-in at the outer control desk, where Garrett sweated bullets as he presented his badge. The desk officer nodded briefly to Garrett and checked off their names on the approved visitor list without questioning them.

In the visitor processing area, under the gaze of surveillance cameras, one of the corrections officers instructed them to remove their belts, shoes, jackets, cell phones, and keys and place them on the table. Wordlessly, without looking at each other, but with excruciating awareness of each other's presence, Tanith and Garrett stripped themselves of the objects, emptied their pockets, and stood waiting while the officer examined their property.

Garrett felt there was something odd in the dynamic of the room, but at first couldn't identify it. Then all at once he realized the C.O.s at the security checkpoint were paying Tanith no attention whatsoever, even as she pulled off her coat, bent to take off her shoes. True, she had changed her clothes at Selena's house and had dressed more plainly than usual for the visit, in a boxy navy suit that was too large for her without calling undue attention to itself, and her dark profusion of hair was pulled back in a severe knot. But she would have had to have a bag over her head—a body bag—to conceal that she was a spectacularly beautiful woman.

And yet these male officers, who were not as a whole known for their feminist sensitivity, were acting as if she was not even in the room.

Garrett suddenly recalled a similar lack of attention by male patrons of the bar when he'd met Tanith at the inn, several weeks ago. *How the hell does she do that? What kind of trick is it?* he found himself wondering, and then pushed down the thought. No time for doubts. They had gotten this far.

They stepped through the metal detector, Tanith, then Garrett, and then the C.O. pushed their shoes and coats and equipment through to them to put back on.

The C.O. took them through a steel door and they walked past the officer's station, a cage in which more unsmiling C.O.s sat before panels of controls, and then down a long hallway with the hollow sound of opening locks echoing against the walls, as a series of barred gates opened before them and slammed shut behind them. At the end of the gauntlet their guide opened a metal door into the visitation room, divided by a scratched and dirty Plexiglas wall, with counters on both sides and phones at each seat.

Garrett and Tanith seated themselves at the counter in front of the wall to wait, in plastic chairs with annoyingly rounded bottoms. Now that they had stopped moving, Garrett felt his pulse elevated, sure that at any moment they were going to be busted and detained. Tanith sat completely still, a pillar of calm; he could not even detect her breathing.

Unable to contain himself, Garrett put his hand on Tanith's arm, leaned in close to her.

"How do you do it?" he mouthed, against her ear.

She stiffened slightly, said nothing.

"You know what I mean." His voice was low, urgent. "They don't see you."

She was silent, and his fingers tightened on her arm. She didn't look at him as she spoke; her eyes were fixed straight ahead. "Don't you know how to blend in? Can't you make people not notice you? Isn't it your job?" She paused, and then said flatly, "Isn't it survival?"

Garrett had worked his share of undercover, and she didn't have to explain further. "Not like that," he answered, finally. "I can't do it like that."

She turned her head and looked at him. "But you could."

They both twisted forward as a door on the other side of the wall opened and a guard led Jason into the room. He wore the standard toxic orange jumpsuit and his face was pale and hollow, the pallor of confinement, his features seeming sunk into his face. He was passive in the guard's grasp.

But his eyes, as he slumped down in the chair, were active and watching, and Garrett caught a glimmer of recognition as he took Tanith in. She reached for the telephone receiver on their side and Jason reached for his own.

The guard stepped away and assumed an "at ease" stance beside the door.

"Hi there, *Counselor*," Jason said from behind the wall, in a crawling, insinuating voice. "Long time no see."

Tanith just looked at him through the barrier for a minute. "If you ever want to get out of here, Jason, you're going to want to drop that act," she said, her voice low and level. "We are your absolute last hope."

Garrett glanced toward the guard at the door. "He doesn't see," Tanith said softly. Garrett saw that the guard was standing with open but unfocused eyes; he seemed asleep on his feet.

Jason's eyes shifted, and he licked his lips. "The Master will take care of me," he said, and the feral slyness of his voice shot adrenaline through Garrett's veins. The sound was not quite human.

Tanith looked at the teenager steadily. "That's a good trick," she said softly. "I can see that it's keeping you fairly safe in here. But your 'Master' is who dropped you into this shithole to begin with and he will leave your ass hanging out for any and all to use, if you don't pull yourself together and start thinking."

Garrett saw Jason flinch, and for a moment his face trembled. Then the sly cunning was back on his face.

"You dare order me, witch?" he hissed, with a sibilance that sounded like more than one voice, many voices.

Tanith's eyes blazed . . . Garrett felt her tension like electricity beside him. "Be gone," she commanded.

Jason blinked, and his face trembled again.

"You stupid child," Tanith said softly. "If you play with Darkness, the Darkness will play with you. You called on this monster and it used you for its pleasure and it will take more pleasure in watching you fry." Her voice cut like a steel blade. "Do you hear me, Jason Moncrief? Focus yourself *now* and come out of there, before it's too late."

Garrett felt his blood turn to ice . . . as Jason's eyes went dull and his face seemed to blur, like a wave of bad reception on a television screen. Then his face cleared and he looked human again, but disoriented. He swallowed several times, then rasped, "What do you want?" in a voice as hoarse as if he'd been screaming for days.

Tanith pressed the phone to her cheek, her hand clutching it so tightly her fingers were white, but her eyes never left Jason's face. "Erin's dead, do you understand that? You brought her into this and she was ripped to shreds by that abomination you've been courting. She was stabbed, mutilated. He cut off her head."

Garrett stared through the Plexiglas and saw Jason's mouth working, his eyes shifting back and forth. And then the young man shuddered through his entire body, and the look on his face was suddenly just a boy's, hollow-eyed and frightened.

"I didn't know. I didn't know," he choked out, and Garrett was startled to see tears in his eyes. "Oh, God . . . Erin."

Tanith whispered to Garrett, "Talk to him. *Now*."

Garrett leaned forward, and spoke in as low a voice as he could manage. "What happened that night?"

Jason swallowed. "I don't know. We were making out in the car . . . we were tripping, and we had sex, and then I passed out. When I woke up I was alone in the car. I didn't know where she was . . . I thought maybe she just took a cab home."

"You didn't see anyone, hear anyone?"

"We were so out of it—"

"You didn't go looking for her?"

"I was sick. I . . . I passed out again. I called her when I woke up, but her phone was off."

Garrett glanced back toward the guard, who was still standing, staring ahead. "Have you ever been to the Pine Street landfill?"

The boy looked confused. "No. Why?"

"Do you know a John McKenna?" Garrett asked him sharply.

"No."

"Your prints were at his house."

Jason stared at him.

"A farmhouse in Lincoln?" Garrett demanded.

Jason shook his head. "Lincoln? No way."

"All over some CDs?" Garrett snapped.

Jason stared at him, bewildered . . . and then something flickered on his face. "Someone took the band CDs. That night we were at Cauldron. I had a couple of *Current 333* CDs in the console of my car . . ." He stopped, lifted his hands helplessly. "When I got back to school, they were gone."

Garrett sat still, thrown. But there was a certain weird logic there that he could almost buy. If McKenna had been watching Erin at the club, if he had followed Jason and Erin out, and pulled Erin out of the car when the teenagers were passed out . . . and he saw the CDs on the console . . . the Choronzon CDs . . .

Wouldn't he take them?

There was an element of intention, of inevitability, Garrett didn't want to think about, though.

He shook his head to clear it and asked sharply, "Have you been practicing rituals with anyone else?"

"No," Jason said loudly. "It was just for the band, you know, and then . . ." His eyes darkened in confusion. "It started to feel . . ." He stopped.

"Feel what?" Tanith said beside Garrett.

Jason's eyes were bleak. "Bad."

Tanith leaned forward to Jason. "Then be still and listen. The true killer holds Erin's spirit trapped. If you want to save your own soul and hers, you will help."

"How?" the boy whispered.

"You will take me to her tonight."

Both Garrett and Jason looked around them incredulously, at the wall of Plexiglas, the bars at the windows, the whole weight of the jail around them. Tanith continued, unfazed. "Look at me, Jason Moncrief. Listen." She fixed her eyes on him, until he met her gaze. "You are Erin's only hope. You must tell me. What was her favorite place? Someplace she felt safe—somewhere she went often? Someplace you may have gone with her?"

The teenager was distraught. "I don't know . . . there were so many places . . ."

"Think," Tanith said sharply.

"Revere Woods," he answered on command. "There's a trailhead there that leads to a waterfall, with a pool."

"Yes," Tanith said. "I know it."

"We hiked there . . . to swim." He swallowed. "She said it made her feel whole."

"Good," said Tanith. "Good. I need you to help me now. I need you to be there tonight. When you lie back in your bunk tonight, focus your mind on the waterfall and the pool, and go there. Imagine Erin with you there. Call her to you. You must bring her there, Jason." Her eyes were black and Jason was fixed on her from behind the glass, his hand clutching the phone as she was, and

Garrett saw their reflections melded together in the sheen of the Plexiglas, like twins in a mirror.

"Do you understand?" she whispered.

"Yes . . ." Jason said, just a boy now.

"Then go," she said. "And pray to whatever goodness you believe there is in the world to save your soul."

Jason sat, unfocused, behind the blurry Plexiglas wall. Garrett swallowed through a dry mouth, motioned to the C.O., who blinked to life and gestured to the guard behind the inner door, who stepped forward to take Jason away.

The C.O.s on the way out were as unmindful of Tanith as they had been on the way in; it was as if she wasn't there at all. One even nodded at Garrett without acknowledging Tanith, while she walked in silence at his side.

By the time they got to the parking lot, Garrett was near bursting with impatience and confusion. He slammed his hands on the top of the Explorer. "Are you going to tell me what the hell that was? What the hell do you think you're going to do?"

"Just as I said," Tanith said calmly. "I will go to the spot he named and he will bring Erin's spirit to me. They had sex; he's bonded to her still." As she said it Garrett felt an uncomfortable pull between them. She looked quickly away from him. "It's our best chance of reaching her—our best chance of finding where her killer is keeping her and the others." She hesitated. "Including Detective Landauer, perhaps."

Garrett stared at her, incredulous. "What?" She didn't answer him. "I want to be there," he said roughly.

Her eyebrows quirked. "Are you sure?"

And for a moment she looked at him, into him, and he knew she saw his greatest fear.

"I'm going to be there."

She hesitated. "Come to Selena's tonight, then. Ten o'clock."

Chapter Forty-four

Garrett was outside the house, watching, by nightfall. It wasn't that he didn't trust them. It was that he didn't trust them at all.

He had seen no motion at the windows, no change in the light. He debated charging in, interrupting whatever they were doing. But the moon was nearly full in the sky, and there was something about that moon that made him think that if any ritual was to be done, it wasn't going to be done in the confines of a house.

He was not completely aware of thinking this through, but that was his thought process. So he watched the house, not from the front, but from the back, which he'd scoped out and discovered a back gravel alley behind the block of houses for trash pickup and delivery access, and at the end of the high cement wall surrounding the back garden there was a coach house big enough to have been converted into a garage. Garrett waited at a distance, down the access road, the Explorer camouflaged by trees and a shed that housed trash cans.

At 9:00 P.M., the door of the coach house rolled up and a car exited that could only have been Selena's: a vintage Packard, gleaming silver in the moonlight.

Garrett watched the vehicle drive down the access road, and after a moment he followed.

The Packard was easy to follow in the dark, so Garrett was able to hang well back on the highway. They were driving west, on a winding road through dense forest, which luckily was trafficked enough that Garrett's Explorer wouldn't stand out on the road. The Packard's windows were tinted so Garrett could see no one in the car.

Revere Woods was not a long drive. The Packard turned off on a side road of the state park before they were out of the city limits. Garrett slowed his vehicle to give them a lead, then made the turn himself . . .

. . . and tensed, staring ahead of him.

The road was straight, a tunnel through thick walls of trees, ending abruptly in a dead end against another wall of trees. The Packard was gone.

Garrett silenced his racing thoughts. *All right . . . all right . . . there's a turnoff. They aren't going to park out in the open.* He slowed the Explorer to a crawl and drove, staring out the windshield, scanning both sides of the road, looking for any break in the wall of trees.

He drove to the very end of the road. The dark green wall was thick, there was no passage for a car, but there was a wooden post with the number 42, indicating a trailhead.

Garrett had seen no possible place for the Packard to have turned off.

But it's here. They're here somewhere.

Garrett parked the Explorer, took his personal Glock from the glove compartment, holstered it, and got out. He walked to the post of the trailhead, saw the path leading into the woods, lit by moonlight.

All right.

He walked through the gate of trees onto the trail, his feet crunching softly on dry leaves, the cool scent of earth and pine enveloping him.

Moonlight shone through the pine branches, and Garrett felt unease. *Wherever they are, Selena can't have walked far,* he thought.

The wind whispered in the treetops. The path wound before him, giving no clues.

He walked, his shoes thudding softly on packed earth, the silky rustle of pine needles above him . . . with increasing certainty that he was going in the wrong direction. *What I need is a sign.*

He rounded the curve of the trail, and out of the corner of his eye he saw a flash of white.

He spun to his left. Trees . . . darkness . . . the faint whisper of wind . . .

And then a startlingly familiar face. Pointed chin, wild spiky hair, electric blue eyes. The red-haired boy, peering from a clump of ferns.

The boy laughed soundlessly and withdrew, vanishing into the undergrowth. Garrett crashed off the path after him.

He ran through the brush, dodging through tree trunks, straight in the direction the boy had gone. Once he thought he saw a flash of the brown tunic and bare feet, but he heard not a sound of running and was not entirely sure he was not imagining the whole thing, or dreaming.

He felt the ground sloping and instinctively slowed—some self-preservation instinct, obviously, because as soon as he stopped he realized he was four feet from the edge of a sheer drop. He caught a ragged breath . . . and then he saw it: the glimmer of moonlight on water below.

A clearing, with a natural pool in the center of a rock circle, and beside it, two slim feminine figures, like nymphs in the moonlight.

Garrett was as quiet as he could be, keeping low to the ground as he crept from one bush and fallen log to the next, working his way down the steep face of the hill. Below, Tanith had built a fire and was scouting for more wood, while Selena coaxed the flames with twigs. Garrett was no more than halfway down when Selena raised her face toward the hill and said, "Ah, Detective Garrett. Just in time."

Garrett straightened from the leafy underbrush and stood looking down on them.

"Funny, I had the feeling I wasn't invited." He glanced at Tanith, who looked back with no expression and dropped more logs beside the fire. Sparks flew up around her.

"Not at all," Selena assured him lightly. "No sacred space can be entered without effort. The journey is meditative, mental preparation." She lifted her hands. "And here you are."

Garrett was about to answer angrily, when again he saw the red-haired boy, hovering between the trees, with that sly smile. As soon as Garrett spotted him, he faded back into the dark greenery.

"I followed him," Garrett said, without realizing he was going to say it. He strode down the remainder of the hill, pointing. "The red-haired kid from her garden."

"Is that right?" Selena raised an eyebrow. "How interesting."

"Is he real?" Garrett asked, in spite of himself.

Selena half smiled. "What is real?" Before Garrett could bristle, she relented and explained, "He is a fetch. A servitor. A fetch is a thought form created for a particular task. He was made of my intention, and your expectation. There are unformed energies in the other dimensions which are eager to interact with the world of humans, and those energies can take on a supplicant's intention." Her face shadowed. "Demons are much the same: dark energies that gain power with human intention." She shook her head. "But the fetch—merely a playful energy. I must say I wasn't expecting such a Shakespearean bent to you, Detective—it's quite charming."

She glanced toward the woods where the boy had disappeared, then back to Garrett, with an appraising look. "Odd, though. I didn't summon him just then. Which means *you* must have."

Before Garrett could begin to wrap his mind around that, Tanith spoke behind her. "We should start." There was agitation in her voice.

"Yes," Selena said, still looking at Garrett. "Let's begin."

They cast the circle together, Tanith on one side of the moonlit pool, Selena on the other. Garrett sat on a boulder by the side of the water, watching as the trees around them rippled in the soft wind, and beneath the moon they called on the four quarters, the Elements, the Watchtowers. Garrett had thought the ritual powerful when Tanith did it alone, but watching the two women together was a whole other dimension; the entire primeval life force of the forest seemed to be with them: wind, fire, water, earth.

Then Selena took a lit candle and walked around the pool three times, while Tanith stood still at the edge, her arms at her side, turned away from the water, face tipped to the moonlight, her body outlined against the fire. And when Selena completed the third circle, she stepped to Tanith and turned her toward the pool, then placed the candle in her hand. Tanith moved obediently, like a sleepwalker. Selena raised her hands to the moon.

"Hecate, Goddess, Mother Night, give thy daughter perfect sight. This water a window through which she can see . . . as I say, so mote it be."

Tanith dropped to her knees beside the water with the candle clasped in her hands and stared into the dark shadow of her reflection.

Garrett suddenly recalled Tanith staring through the Plexiglas of the jail, at Jason's silhouette, the two mirroring each other.

Beside the pool, Tanith reached one hand toward the water, toward her own pale reflection. And in his mind Garrett heard her words to Jason in the jail: *I need you to help me now. I need you to be there tonight. You must bring her there, Jason.*

The older woman stood as if bracing herself against the wind, and spoke. "Erin Carmody, are you there? Erin, hear my voice and come to me. Come to the light I hold. We are here for you."

The candle in Tanith's hand flickered, reflected in the water . . . and Tanith reached down toward the pool, the hand of her reflection reaching up toward her . . . And as her fingertips touched her reflection, she closed her fingers, holding tightly . . .

Garrett watched, unnerved. Her arm stretched forward, as if someone were pulling her hand. She bent over at the waist, until she was folded over herself on the bank of the pool, her outstretched hand submerged in the water.

Tanith suddenly dropped the candle, jerked her hand out of the water, and sat bolt upright, as if she had been struck by lightning.

"*Help me!*" she screamed, in a voice too light and high to be her own. Garrett recoiled with the shock of it. "*Help me!*"

"Erin Carmody, hear me," Selena commanded in a voice that brooked no argument. "We are here for you. We are here to help you."

Tanith scrambled on the bank, her fingers digging into the earth at her sides; she was panting like a dog, her chest heaving, her eyes dilated with terror. "Help me help me help me help me—"

"We will come for you. We will come. You must tell us where you are. Erin. Do you hear me?"

"Dark. So dark, so dark. Can't move. Scared. Scared." Tanith writhed and scrabbled on the ground as if she were bound and fighting to escape. "Where are my hands? Where are my hands? Oh God oh God oh God . . ."

The young voice was shrill with panic. Garrett moved involuntarily toward the pool, toward Tanith, and Selena threw out a startlingly strong arm to block him. Garrett halted in his tracks, but just barely.

"Erin, open your eyes," Selena commanded, her voice resonating in the night. "Open them and look. You must tell us what you see, so we can come for you. Tell us."

On the ground, Tanith was hyperventilating, her breath coming in short, panicky gasps.

Selena's voice cut through the firelit darkness. "Erin. *Erin*. Calm yourself. Focus on what you see. Tell me what you see."

"Dark dark dark dark . . ."

"Focus in the dark. You can see. Tell me what you see. Tell me what you smell."

"Blood," came the voice. "Smells like blood. And dust, and fire. It smells like—garden."

"Like garden," Selena said sharply. "Like garden how?"

"Like moss," the young voice said. "Like soil . . . potting . . . clay . . ."

"That's good, Erin. That's very good." Selena darted a glance toward Garrett. "Now look. What do you see?"

"Big, dark, space. Glass. Glass everywhere. Big gray glass. Broken. Barn? Dirt, on the floor. Dirt floor. And a triangle in white," the young voice said. In his own mind, Garrett saw the triangle in the dirt floor of that dank cellar, the altars with the heads . . .

Tanith's breath shuddered in a gasp, and Garrett snapped back to the present. "Dead," Tanith whispered. "Everything's dead."

"What is dead, Erin?" Selena asked from the circle.

"All the flowers . . . all the flowers are dead."

Garrett felt a chill. *Choronzon. The sign of the demon.*

Tanith whimpered deep in her throat, like an animal. "Bad. It's bad."

"Erin, tell me. Are you alone?"

Tanith shook her head rapidly and violently. "Three of us . . . so dark, so cold . . . And one warm one."

Selena straightened. "A warm one . . . you mean, alive?"

Garrett felt a sick adrenaline charge. "A live one? What?"

Selena's voice never rose. "Erin, there's someone there with you?"

"Warm . . . warm . . . warm . . . He wants more."

Garrett's mind was spiraling, his thoughts out of control. *He's already taken one? But it's not time, they said we had more time . . .* Tanith suddenly writhed on the ground and screamed. "Coming! He's coming . . ."

Selena planted herself in front of Tanith, a pillar of strength, speaking over her frantic screams. "Erin, we will come for you—"

The older woman suddenly gasped . . . and pulled back, as if resisting something. She held up her hands to the moon and recited quickly, "Back to your body, child of my heart. End this journey, return from the dark."

Tanith's body jerked on the ground and she sat straight up with a huge intake of air.

"Yes, child, yes." Selena knelt on the wet leaves and took Tanith's face in her hands. "You're safe. You're here."

The wind rustled through the treetops, and Tanith collapsed in the older woman's arms. Garrett stood in the whispering clearing, looking down at the two women embracing by the pool in the shimmering moonlight.

Chapter Forty-five

Tanith was out like a light—there was no rousing her. Though Selena insisted she was fine, just exhausted, Garrett knelt to check her pulse and eyes. She was breathing slowly, but steadily.

He had to carry her out of the forest, holding her to his chest again, Selena climbing carefully before them, leading him a shorter way back to the Explorer through the towering shadows and whispering leaves and redolent smells of cedar and pine.

"What if I hadn't been here?" he demanded of the witch.

"But you are," she said placidly, never faltering in her steady ascent.

Back at the Explorer, he lay Tanith in the backseat, with her head on Selena's lap. "Your car . . ." he started.

"It's taken care of." Selena stroked Tanith's hair.

Don't tell me the Dragon Man is driving now, he thought, but all he wanted to do was get out of the forest, back to the city, to the light, and find out what all this meant.

Back at Selena's they settled Tanith on the sofa of a room he hadn't seen before, a sitting room, and Selena beckoned him forward into the connecting room, a small library, and pulled the door not-quite-shut behind them.

Garrett paced amid the glass-cabineted bookcases. He was having trouble processing any of what he had seen in the forest clearing; it seemed too much like a dream. His mind was bending in ways he didn't like at all. "How is this happening?" he demanded of Selena. "What happened?"

Selena lowered herself to a love seat. Her face looked drawn. "I suppose the easiest way to explain it is that Tanith removed herself from her own body so that Erin's spirit could come into it and use it to talk to us. It's channeling. Tanith has a facility for it. She allowed herself to be possessed by spirits at an early age and that makes her able to channel now . . . thankfully more judiciously, these days."

"Channeling Erin's spirit," Garrett said flatly, shaking his head.

"Yes. Erin is trapped between this world and the next. This man you seek has bound her soul to what he has kept of her body so that he can use the power of her spirit for his own purposes."

Garrett didn't believe a word of it. *But the heads . . . he kept the heads.*

He asked the first thing that came to mind. "She sounded afraid. Why is she so afraid of him if she's dead?"

Selena shook her head. "She knows not what she is. Part of her believes she's alive. She is in a dark and miserable place, with no peace, no light, no love, only a living presence of hatred and terror."

"Purgatory," Garrett said involuntarily, and then wondered where the hell the thought had come from. He had not been to mass in ages.

Selena smiled at him fleetingly. "Indeed." Then her face grew grave again. "That's why it's essential that she be freed—she and the rest."

Garrett felt everything in him rebelling against what she was saying. "I only care about what's real," he said roughly. "She—Tanith—said some things. Descriptions. An empty space. A barn with glass everywhere."

"Do you know it?" Selena said, suddenly keen.

Garrett paused, his mind racing. There was something familiar about it, something he felt he should be able to place, maddeningly elusive. He shook his head, frustrated. "I don't know. Maybe."

Despite her obvious exhaustion, Selena rose to her feet. "You need to know this, about Samhain—"

"It's Halloween," Garrett said, not wanting to use the witch words. "She already told me. Tomorrow." *Or was it already after midnight?* he wondered with a chill.

"It's more than a holy day, though," Selena said. "You must understand this. It's the most powerful night of the year, the night that the door opens between this world and the next. That is when—that monster—thinks he can let the demon through. He will do his magic on Samhain's eve, and he will kill to do it." She stopped her nervous pacing and faced Garrett directly. "But it is also the night when all souls who have passed during the year move from this world to the next. The door opens and spirits can depart—or come through. That means it is the night when the souls of those children he holds captive can most easily be freed to go on to the next world."

Garrett felt every logical thought in him rebelling against what she was saying. "I can't do anything for the dead," he exploded. "If I'm supposed to believe all this, he's about to kill three other people. I need details. I need something *real*." Selena had stopped still, and was regarding him quietly. He fought to compose himself, looked toward the door behind which Tanith lay asleep. "Will she remember any of—that?"

Selena gave him a veiled look. "She may, or not."

"Wake her, then."

Selena stiffened. "She's exhausted. You don't understand the ordeal—"

Garrett rode over her. "I understand that if you're telling the truth, if any of this is real, then three more kids are going to die tomorrow. So wake her or I will."

Selena gave him a look that would melt steel, but she rose and crossed to the door. She stopped in front of it and pushed it open.

Garrett strode past her into the room—and stopped in his tracks.

The room was empty. Tanith was gone.

Chapter Forty-six

Samhain is a festival at the time of the closing dark. For pagans it was the beginning of the new year, the time that is neither past nor future, during which the doors are open between worlds. It is believed that all the souls of those who have died during the year must wait until Samhain to pass through to the other side.

It was also traditionally a time of ritual propitiation: sacrifice, animal and human, and of the choosing of a sacrificial victim by lot.

Wind pushed through the streets of Salem, rustled through the brilliance of the autumn colors, swirled flurries of dry leaves on the sidewalks and driveways, swept through the cornhusk decorations and swayed the Halloween lights in the eaves and rafters and pillars of porches.

Children roamed the streets in costumed packs: pirates and aliens and princesses and goblins and ax murderers, followed on foot or in cars by parents who had long ago ceased to believe that it was safe to let their children out on this night or any other, even in the biggest pack.

Toward the town center the streets were closed off to accommodate the waves of revelers who had been flooding the town for the last few days, by train, by car, by shuttles from Boston and else-where. Every available parking space was taken and illegal parking was rampant.

The costuming on Essex Street was more elaborate than the children's. There were pirates and princesses and Pilgrims here as well, but others with hundreds of dollars invested in materials and makeup and special effects for their costumes, many with lights and sound effects and moving parts. The night was warm enough that fetish wear abounded: there were large men in leathers and chain-mail codpieces and women in no more than bits of lace, in addition to the green men and vampires and, naturally, every pos-sible variation of witch: maidens, queens, crones.

And there was a man who walked the streets, with no costume but a white mask and black cloak, and yet everyone who passed by him shivered away from him with the impression that there was something far more grotesque and calculated about his costume than they were actually seeing, like some troll.

And that was what he did; he trolled. There was one in his trunk already, chloroformed and trussed, and one he'd taken yesterday, secure in his ceremonial space. He had one more to find, now, and a banquet of victims was spread out before him; he reveled in the choice.

He walked on the cobblestone streets, clearing a path as other revelers moved subtly away from his presence, though none that looked at him really saw him; the glamour he'd conjured for him-self assured him of that.

The girl walked and weaved in the crowd a few yards in front of him, resplendent in her glittery dark fairy costume; dyed black hair and painted black nails and deep purple sequined bodice with yards and yards of tulle, a black half mask and high, high fetish boots. She had fallen behind her friends, like a hobbled antelope; it was, of course, the boots. Those boots would make her easy to take; she could not run, literally, to save her life. Add to that she was drunk already, as most of the revelers were, drunk and high, and adrenalized with the gaiety and sheer numbers of the mob that sur-rounded them.

The troll took her arm and mumbled to her, steering her toward an alley, asking directions. She had no time to think; the hypodermic was stabbing her in the neck before she had a sense of anything. Her eyes registered one moment of sheer terror . . . and then she was buckling, crumpling.

The killer swooped her limp body up into both arms in one deft gesture and she was gone, then, that quickly, hidden in his cloak, which fell over her body and only made the troll look more misshapen, more troll-like, as he pushed and weaved his way through the crowd toward his car and the sun flamed in the sky, a perfect Samhain sky, of orange and scarlet and shimmering gold.

Chapter Forty-seven

Garrett stood in the salon in stunned silence. There were no doors to the room but the one he stood in, and no windows, either.

He turned to Selena in a daze. "Where is she?"

Selena looked pale, but resolute. "I think we both know the answer to that."

"That's insane. She would go alone?"

"If she felt she had to," the elder woman said softly. "You must do what you must do, and so must she."

He took a sharp step toward her. She didn't flinch. He summoned all the self-control he had. "This is a killer, Ms. Fox. Whatever else you believe is going on, this is a man who will kill without hesitation, a man who has killed and beheaded three teenagers without a second thought. If you think that whatever 'talents' Tanith has are a match for that, that's one thing; maybe you think you know her well enough to allow her to go into that kind of jeopardy. But if you believe that this man is going to use three more teenagers as sacrifices to his demon, do you think you have the right to decide for three innocent victims?"

The older woman looked him full in the face and he could feel the conflict raging in her. He held her eyes and put his soul into his next words. "Don't let her try this alone. If you know something, help me."

Selena shook her head. "I am sure where she has gone. She will go to release the souls of the bound." She hesitated, then finished bleakly. "I've no idea where that is."

Garrett had had to surrender the murder book, with all his notes, to Morelli and Palmer when he was suspended. *But it's a new trail now,* he thought as he paced Selena's library, while Selena watched from the love seat. All he had to go on were the words Tanith had shrieked in the forest clearing, with a voice that was not her own.

"Glass panes, dirt floor, like a barn," he muttered.

There was something solid in this, after all, and he would focus on that. It was the *place* he had to find: McKenna had a new lair where he was taking his victims. And that was the question: where? He'd been using his own cellar, his own—well, his inherited house, because as it turned out, he'd taken over the house when his mother was killed in an automobile accident. (And if Garrett had not been racing against time, he would be looking into that death.)

The house was isolated, remote, McKenna's own: it had been perfect for the killer's purposes.

Now he needed a place that was even more private, if he was holding live victims, and planning a—Garrett's mind balked at the word—sacrifice.

"Glass panes, dirt floor, like a barn," Garrett mumbled. Was it a barn, or a greenhouse? He shook his head. "There must be thirty thousand barns in Massachusetts." Not to mention the surrounding states, New Hampshire, New York, Rhode Island . . . And there were no guarantees McKenna wasn't out of state by now. The Camaro was gone, and an APB had failed to pick it up for going on four days now . . .

"Detective Garrett, stop. Be calm. Breathe," Selena said placidly. "You know all you need to know."

Garrett stopped his frenzied pacing and looked at Selena, so still on the love seat where she sat.

This is a place that he knows, Garrett thought again. *He uses places that he knows. His own home. The landfill where he worked—*

Where he worked.

Garrett spun and stared at Selena.

"I need your computer." He hoped to God she had one.

Selena not only had a computer, she had a state-of-the-art system, and in no time Garrett had called up AutoTrack, a private database service that provided searches of all public records, including DMV, public utility, cable service, and credit reporting agencies. He punched in the police department's code for access and inputted McKenna's vital statistics to get a screen that provided McKenna's past addresses and what Garrett really wanted: his employment history. Garrett scanned the list, eyes moving quickly over the entries . . .

And there it was. Greenbrier Nursery, in Malden.

While Selena watched, hands folded in her lap, Garrett paced with his phone to his ear, listening to the recording telling him, "The number you have dialed is no longer in service." He punched off, and punched in information, asked for the Greenbrier Nursery. "No such listing in Malden or the greater Massachusetts area," the operator came back. Garrett punched off and stared at the address. He made one more call back to information. "Malden, Massachusetts—main post office, please."

And he was lucky; he got a chatty postal clerk. Five minutes later he punched off with the knowledge that there had been a Greenbrier Nursery in Malden, it had closed down over a year ago, and the property still stood vacant at the address listed on Garrett's AutoTrack printout.

An abandoned nursery where McKenna had worked. He'd caught a break.

Garrett shoved his phone in his pocket and turned to Selena. "I need you to call BPD and get them to this address." He circled the information for the Greenbrier Nursery, and shoved the page at her. "Call them and keep calling. That's where he is. That's where she is."

And he was striding for the door.

Chapter Forty-eight

Garrett drove like the wind on the country road under a darkening sky, wishing like hell he had Land with him. One hand on the wheel, he speed-dialed Schroeder and asked for Palmer or Morelli. Neither was in. Garrett left an urgent message.

Next he called Dispatch to connect him to the local police in Malden. "Detective Garrett, BPD. I have a possible hostage situation at the old Greenbrier Nursery. Suspect John McKenna, resident of Lincoln, whereabouts unknown. Suspect wanted for murder," he lied. "Request immediate assistance." He disconnected before he had to answer questions.

Just past the town of Malden, acres of dense forest had been cleared to make room for the fields of commercial trees, shrubs, and plants of the now-defunct Greenbrier Nursery. Garrett turned off the highway and onto the packed dirt road and looked out through the windshield over gently rolling slopes under dark and fast-moving clouds. Rippling on the hills were high canvas tents, erected to create a more sheltered environment for the less hardy outdoor flowers and plants, but now filthy and sagging and flapping in the strong wind.

Garrett rounded a curve and the main building came into view:

a barn with several attached greenhouse wings, the whole structure vaguely in the form of a star, or a starfish, with its arms being the long glass-paned greenhouses.

Garrett didn't drive all the way up to the nursery's front door, with its drooping sheltered porch. Instead he parked the Explorer beside a massive spreading oak tree. He killed the engine and his ears were immediately assaulted by the spiraling rumble of the wind outside, so strong it swayed the Explorer on its tires.

He looked back toward the dirt road. *Where the fuck are the cars?* There were no police vehicles in sight, no sirens either, and that was unnerving.

An uneasy thought flicked through his head.

A spell. No one's coming. He's keeping them away.

Then he dismissed it as nonsense. *Insane.*

Garrett turned back and stared through the windshield as the car shuddered. There was no other vehicle in sight, no sign of the dark blue Camaro. Maybe he'd gotten lucky and arrived when the killer was off the premises. Then again, he wouldn't expect the car to be parked anywhere immediately visible.

Wait for backup? Could he chance it?

And if Tanith is here, if she's really been so foolish and crazy to come out here on her own, with nothing but some belief in occult powers, and perhaps a ritual knife which McKenna will take from her and use on her without blinking . . .

Garrett opened the console and withdrew the Glock he'd taken from the drawer of his nightstand. He checked it and holstered it on his belt. He took out the Taser and put that in his windbreaker pocket for good measure. He already had the Kevlar vest strapped on underneath the jacket. His thoughts were racing, against his will.

It's beyond stupid to go in. But if they're in there . . . if he's in there . . .

He reached again to the console and took out protective latex gloves, several pairs of them. He pulled one pair on; the others he stuffed into his other jacket pocket.

He got out of the Explorer and started up toward the building, fighting the wind. It hurled dry leaves in his path, papery flurries, racing and rolling as the trees swayed precipitously, their branches shuddering and shaking. *Witch's wind,* he thought, not knowing if he'd made the phrase up. The sky was layered thickly with clouds, from steel gray to purple to black, and there was an eerie orange light.

Hell of a storm coming, Garrett's uneasy thoughts continued. *As if things aren't bad enough.* He looked back toward the road, hoping to hear the sound of sirens. There was nothing.

He tried to focus ahead of him as he walked. The property had been stripped and most inventory moved away, but there were still vestiges of ponds and waterfalls and fountains in the front of the building, and some statuary and concrete garden accessories, which Garrett wound his way through now: cracked and chipped bird-baths, urns, benches, sundials, forlorn stone frogs and rabbits and turtles that had been too damaged to bother moving out or looting: the discards, the left-behinds.

The greenhouses had been vandalized; there were shattered windows and some with rock-sized holes and spidery cracks, and ugly words spray-painted on the sides of the barn. The site had been utilized, most certainly, for timeless teenage rituals; Garrett saw scattered beer cans and broken bottles and limp condoms in the dirt. But there was a pall over the place now that had nothing to do with those hopeful drunken fumblings. The wind pushed through the trees, laying branches flat and swirling dead leaves in cyclones along the packed and parched grounds. Dark and layered clouds moved and gathered in silent waves, and lightning flared on the horizon, not close enough to branch, yet, but flickering feverishly, like a dying lightbulb. Garrett braced himself against the gusts, smelled the iron scent of rain.

And as he approached the barnlike door of the main building, he saw blackened footprints in the rippling weeds: scorch marks.

Choronzon . . .

No, a killer. A killer named McKenna. Remember that.

He drew his weapon and surveyed the door, a wide stable type. It was padlocked shut, but it had been opened recently; he could see the drag marks in the dirt.

His instinct was not to touch any of it. McKenna's house had been booby-trapped with lethal chemicals; it was a good bet that this location was equally contaminated.

He debated his options, with heart pounding. *Shoot the lock off?* If McKenna was inside, and wasn't aware of Garrett's presence already, that would seal it. And if he wasn't inside, but returned anytime soon, the broken lock would alert him to someone within.

Garrett stepped back and scanned the front of the building, looking for a less obvious option.

The greenhouse wing to the left of the building had several shattered panes of glass in the tall windows. As Garrett moved toward them, a tornado of dust and leaves spiraled up in his path; he had to sidestep it, turn his face away from the choking dirt.

On the way toward the wall of windows he grabbed a concrete pedestal, and as he reached the largest of the broken windows, he put the pedestal down. He took off his jacket and wrapped the cloth around his arm to knock out the remaining glass, then threw the jacket over the window frame and stepped up onto the pedestal to look inside.

There was just enough dusky light left in the sky to light the interior of the building in gray.

As Garrett's eyes adjusted to the dimness, he looked in on rows and rows of long wooden tables of different heights, laden with all manner of plants and trees and shrubbery. It was a maze.

There was no one visibly moving within, and he could hear no human sounds.

He boosted himself up on the window frame and hoisted himself inside.

From the window he dropped down onto the cement floor; the sound was a hollow thud in the long room. A puff of powdery dust floated up from the floor; Garrett felt the gritty sting in his nostrils. He straightened up, willing himself not to cough, and moved quickly out of the dust cloud, looking around him in the dim gray light.

It was an eerie, dead place, with withered vines and blackened plants and flowers—not just dry and dead; they'd been burned.

Choronzon . . .

No, an effect. It's an effect.

But the effect meant that McKenna had been there.

Garrett's grip tightened on his Glock. Instinctively he understood that for his purposes the killer would need more darkness than this wing of the greenhouse afforded. Garrett started down a long plant-lined aisle toward the wooden inner building, his whole body tense with listening and looking.

The greenhouse was quiet; Garrett's own breathing sounded magnified to him, labored. Then he heard rustling to the right of him. He spun, leveling the Glock.

On the table beside him, a row of green plants was withering in front of his eyes, shriveling and curling and blackening.

Garrett's pulse spiked with shock and disbelief. There was a whispering all around him, like the sound of voices overlapping.

This can't be happening . . .

And then he realized.

The dust cloud when he'd dropped from the window. There was some powder on the floor beside the windows. A hallucinogen.

He had a sudden flash of Landauer, frothing and raving and shrieking.

The demon causes mental chaos.

He forced himself away from the thought, forced himself to focus, take inventory through the wild pounding of his blood in his veins.

How bad am I?

There was a faint glow around the shapes of plants around him. The door in front of him seemed ever so slightly to be breathing.

Garrett had once done psilocybin mushrooms as a college student—it had been a reckless night, and recklessly he'd said yes to the drug that another student had offered him at a party.

The effects he was experiencing were like that trippy night: slightly off from reality. Physically he felt queasy, but not incapacitated. He took several strides toward the door, partly to see if he could . . . and found his legs were functioning adequately, although there was a heaviness to his limbs that was worrisome. The situation was not ideal.

He moved forward and leaned to listen at the door without touching it . . . and thought he heard a human whimpering.

He stepped back and lifted a leg and kicked open the inner door.

He darted through it, leading with his weapon and shouting, "Police!" Simultaneously a powder exploded from the top of the door, a pale cloud of granules, drifting down.

Garrett ducked away, covering his face with his sleeve, trying not to breathe.

He had just time to see a triangle inscribed on the floor in powder, gleaming whitely, and candles flickering at the three points—

Then something heavy came down on his head and everything went black.

He woke to a breath of air, like touch, gentle, urgent, and a voice whispering in his head.

Garrett. Wake up. You have to come around.

He forced his eyes open—it was an effort; they were crusty and gummy. His head was throbbing. He tried to sit up, but found he could not move. He flexed wrists, and then ankles, and realized he was bound. He could smell her, though, the scent of apple musk.

He blinked, staring through the dark—and suddenly Tanith knelt on the dirt floor beside him. Her skin glowed as if it were lit from within, and he started . . . then realized he was tripping; he could feel the drug roller-coastering in his veins, the lurching feeling of nausea. He swallowed and tried to focus. She seemed insubstantial, not merely glowing, but nearly transparent—but that was the drug, wasn't it, he was still hallucinating?

Untie me, he said, but heard no words.

She shook her head. *I'm not here.*

Garrett blinked, and tried to process. She was speaking, but not speaking; the voice was inside his head.

There are three kids in there; he has them trussed like you are now. Can you stand?

He opened his mouth to speak. *No,* she said sharply. *Don't answer aloud, just tell me.*

Drugged . . . he managed. It seemed a great effort to form the word in his mind.

I know. And your gun is gone.

Garrett's stomach dropped, and his pulse rate shot up, which brought on another wave of nausea, and a rush of colors, but she was speaking, and he tried to focus. He could feel the Taser was gone from his pocket, too.

There is a nail, in the wall behind you. Can you sit up?

Garrett fought the nausea, and jerked himself upright. In that sitting position he swayed, and fell back against the wall, wincing at the hollow thud he made, not because of the pain, but because of the sound.

He used his fingers to feel along the wall behind him and found it, a bent nail, rusty, protruding.

Hurry, she said, and faded away.

He felt the edges of the nail, getting a sense of it, and then began to saw the rope against it.

The barnlike inner room had no windows, no glass at all; it was a light-controlled space. Outside, the night had darkened, the moon was hidden behind the storm clouds, and the clouds finally dumped their rain, a thundering, splashing roar on the panes of glass. Water cascaded down from numerous broken panes. Now the room was as dark as a cellar, with just faint outlines of illumination along cracks in the wood. The floor was dirt, and a large triangle was inscribed on the floor in some powdery substance, lime or concrete, faintly glowing. A huge triangle, at least fifteen feet at the base, and black candles lit and flickering in a circle around it.

A man sat on the dirt floor at the highest point of the triangle, but outside the faintly glowing lines, and he faced away from it. He was cross-legged, surrounded by more fat black candles, and he sat in front of a large upright piece of black glass, at least five feet by five feet. He stared into it with fixed and dilated eyes and chanted, an ominous and repetitive muttering.

At the edge of the room, beside the door, Garrett stood perfectly still, not breathing, his eyes locked on the man. Thanks to the muffled roar of the rain outside, he had gotten through the broken inner door without drawing attention to himself, though now that he was in he realized that if the dark plate of glass had been a real mirror, he would be visible to the man at the head of the triangle right now, and probably dead.

But the reflection in the glass was so dark—just a faint glimmering of the candles and the insubstantial outline of the man . . . that Garrett realized it couldn't be a mirror, but something else. And that meant perhaps the killer might not be able to see him. Certainly he was deep into whatever bizarre meditation he was engaged in.

The sick-sweet smell of incense wafted from the altar and various other points around the triangle; the smoke drifted in the candlelight, swirling in eddies with the drafts. Outside, the wind was a dull roaring that shook the building.

The man at the point of the triangle—*McKenna*—was dressed in a black robe and his crossed feet were bare. He had unkempt, bushy hair, a beard covering most of his face.

Garrett's quick assessment was that he was medium-sized but powerfully built. A lethal-looking double-edged sword lay across his knees. *And he has your weapon*, Garrett reminded himself grimly. *Within reach somewhere*.

The bearded man stared into the black glass and muttered to himself, a barely audible chanting that sounded vaguely Latin, though Garrett could recognize no words from the old-style masses his mother had dragged him to.

Garrett's eyes quickly scanned the huge, dark room.

There were familiar dark smears on the wall, the sigils of Choronzon: 333 and the three triangles. Above him, veils of cobwebs hung from the rafters and Garrett saw gleaming red eyes watching him from the silk strands. *Hallucination*, he reminded himself.

He glanced to his right and his heart lurched. On a crude altar, three leathery heads were lined up, with lit black candles sizzling wax around and between them. They were pasty and unreal, they looked fake, but didn't feel fake, and Garrett knew they were not.

Two were barely recognizable as female; one had Erin Carmody's long blond hair; the other the waifish dark hair of Amber Bright. The other was vaguely male, from the angularity of the features.

Garrett felt a surge of fury, and tried to breathe in quietly to control himself. *Lose it now and you lose everything.*

He stood as still as a statue and continued to take visual inventory. Across the triangle from the altar with the three heads was another altar, lit by a candle the holder of which made Garrett's stomach turn again: another shriveled, waxen hand. A large book lay open on the center of the altar, with the rough pages Garrett recognized now as handmade, hand-bound: grimoire pages. The drugs made the pages appear to glow with a sickly pallor, the glow undulating upward like the heat from a candle flame.

Garrett's eyes widened as he took in the other items on the altar: a chalice—and a dagger, a shining eight-inch blade. So far his best chance at a weapon. But the altar was a good twenty feet from him, and the cross-legged man with the sword was only five feet from it. Garrett would never make it.

He held the thought of the dagger in his head and shifted his eyes to the phosphorescent triangle in the center of the floor, and of all the things he had seen so far, this sent his stomach plummeting. At each point of the triangle, a human body lay, each wrapped in coils and coils of rope, looking sickly like huge insects caught in spiderwebbing. All three were so still Garrett felt a stab of fear that he had arrived too late.

But then he saw one shift slightly and moan . . .

A small swirl of dust started at one of the points of the triangle. At first Garrett thought it was a breeze, but then a second began, and then a third, three dust devils rising at the points of the triangle.

McKenna's chanting grew louder, with a note of triumph. *"Choronzon, acerbus et ingens! Cede pectares alere flamman tuam. Ab Choronzon principium. Do et dus—"*

And the altar with the grimoire began to shake. A candle flipped over and thudded to the dirt floor. And then the entire altar slid four feet through the dirt, with a powdery scraping sound.

Garrett looked toward the dark mirror and froze. There was an insubstantial shape taking form, the outlines blurry but disturbing, behind the flickering reflections of the candles. First just a pale shape with dark crevasses of eyes . . . eyes that were living black holes. Then the paleness began taking form.

I'm not seeing this. It's the drugs, Garrett told himself, but his legs felt like water and he was unable to look away.

The face in the black glass was ivory, discolored as aged teeth; a skin leached of life; like a corpse, like a mummy. A feral, triangular head with a long narrow jaw, bony ridges above the eyes, and something like a ridge on the top, something spiny and inhuman . . . but it was no animal; there was a savage intelligence in the black eyes, in the snarled set of the jaw. The mouth was maybe the most frightening . . . it seemed either snaggle-toothed, or as if the mouth had been stitched together in crude, wide, triangular stitches and then ripped open in a gaping death's-head grimace.

It was huge, the face, at least three feet across, and the contours of the body were rapidly filling the entire five-by-five glass, the shape becoming clear. It was powerful, like a lynx, but bigger, horribly bigger, and it was crouched on haunches with talons extended— and as Garrett watched in paralyzed disbelief, it sprung, like a tidal wave of black water.

The shape was in the triangle now, a savage thing with red and demonic eyes.

Hairy, yet naked. Human, yet monstrous. Insubstantial, but vibrating with power. Yellowed fangs and lolling tongue.

Garrett felt a drowsy, paralytic terror, felt his mind shudder with denial.

McKenna leapt to his feet and spun, holding the sword up in his two hands, and began to chant deliriously. *"Choronzon, acerbus et ingens! Cede pectares alere flamman tuam. Do et dus. Date et dabitur vobis! Abyssus Abyssum invocat!"*

The creature in the triangle threw its spiked head back and roared, a sound that ripped through Garrett's whole being, in its wrongness, its essential negation. It strode on clawed feet toward the man in the robe but when it reached the phosphorescent line of the triangle, blue sparks flew from its hide and it roared in pain and rage. Garrett stood staring and stupefied, but then shouted at himself, *It's the drugs. You're drugged.*

The demon roared, a hideous snarl that sounded impossibly like infinite voices, layered on top of each other. *"Otref coh sutcam eaem eugueailiamaf omod siem euqsirebil ihim suoitiporp snelov seis itu, rocerp seceprp sanob obdnevombo otref coh et!"*

The killer stood above the first cocooned body with the sword and his voice was calculated, cunning, a question: *"Date et debitur vobis?"*

The demon snarled back in that impossible, layered voice: *"Otref coh et!"*

The killer raised the sword above the first webbed body, hilt clutched in both hands, about to plunge the blade.

At another point of the triangle, one of the bound kids came to life, thrashing in her trusses, and began to scream, a piercing, nerve-ripping sound. The thing in the triangle opened its jaws in a yawning growl of pleasure . . .

Garrett seized that distraction and ran headlong for the altar, pounding in the dust. He lunged past candles, sending them flying, but as his fingers reached for the dagger, McKenna spun and was upon him, brandishing the sword, bringing it down with a snarl of rage. Garrett let McKenna begin the swing and then viciously kicked out at his knee and connected. McKenna roared in pain and the sword crashed down into the altar instead.

Candles fell against the wall, black wax sizzling and splashing. The dry wood went up like tinder, flames licking up the walls, an orange glow. Behind them in the triangle, the demon shrieked, a hundred savage layered cries.

Garrett lurched for the splintered altar and grabbed the dagger, and while McKenna struggled to pull the sword from the wooden altar, Garrett whipped around and thrust the blade into McKenna's throat.

McKenna dropped to his knees, gagging hoarsely, eyes wide and staring as he clutched at his neck. Blood seeped from between his fingers. Behind them, the unearthly thing in the triangle paced and snarled, but did not move beyond the gleaming white lines . . . McKenna collapsed onto the packed dirt, convulsing . . .

Then Garrett felt screaming inside his own mind as the eyes of the first head on the altar opened and looked at him, then the next, then the next, until all three were staring with filmy, black gazes. The dead mouths opened and mouthed words, without vocal cords, voiceless. But Garrett heard them anyway: *Help. Help. Help.*

And as the thing in the triangle turned toward Garrett, with jagged teeth bared and red eyes glowing, McKenna rose to his knees, blood pouring from around the dagger stuck in his throat. But Garrett had heard the death rattle, the gag of breath; he could smell the stink of his evacuated bladder and bowels.

He's dead, Garrett's mind shouted . . . but McKenna kept coming, a shuffling stagger, lifting the sword.

Then there was a breath of wind, so soft it might have been a dream.

And behind McKenna, Garrett saw Tanith in the black mirror, standing pale and shimmering, with her arms raised. Three insubstantial wisps surrounded her, swirling and circling, as if drawn to her light. She stood and chanted, and Garrett saw the world open, a black universe of night, that shuddered and separated into dark and light. The three wisps swirled up and toward the light. Inside the triangle, the demon shrieked in rage. It crouched, coiling into itself, and pounced at the glass, toward Tanith. It hit hard and bounced back off it as if it had tried to charge a closed door.

Tanith drew her hands together, drawing the light into her grasp. And then she turned and hurled the ball of light at the mirror.

The light hit and the black plate of glass shattered. But instead of exploding outward, it imploded, inward. And the thing in the triangle was pulled into the explosion as into a vacuum, howling its rage in the cyclone of wind . . . a wind that pulled at Garrett, staggering him, pulled at the dust on the floor, pulled at the flames licking up the walls of the greenhouse, pulled at the very structure of the greenhouse until the beams and joists groaned . . .

And then was gone. The triangle was empty. In front of Garrett, McKenna's body dropped to the ground like a stone.

The walls around Garrett were pure flame now. One of the teen-agers bound at the triangle was screaming endlessly.

Garrett lunged toward McKenna's body and pulled the dagger from the corpse's throat. He bent and slashed the ropes binding the screaming teenager. "I'm Boston police. Can you run?" he shouted in her face. She nodded, wide-eyed and shaking. "Then go." He pulled her to her feet, turned her toward the door. "Get out."

She staggered a few steps forward, then bolted. Garrett seized the next bound body and began to drag it toward the door.

He pulled both bound bodies into the main greenhouse, one at a time. Smoke drifted blackly in the rows of shriveled plants, but Garrett's vision was clearing; the effects of the drug were wearing off, perhaps diluted by adrenaline. Garrett stooped and lifted the first bound body, registered that it was a boy, before he threw it over his shoulder and ran for the nearest door.

By the time he made it back in for the last teenager, the barn was an inferno behind them, flames reflected in a thousand panes of glass, blazing through the whipping wind and pouring rain. Gar-rett lifted the girl's body and clutched her to him as he stumbled forward, through the rows of shriveled plants, through the door . . . into the night, into the wet, into the wind.

Chapter Forty-nine

The Internal Affairs hearing was a formality; the media loves nothing so much as a hero and had elevated Garrett to such iconic status that no one in Boston or the free world would have dared suggest that he had broken every rule in the proverbial book.

Garrett sat before the suited panel and recited the barest facts with no inflection. "McKenna charged me with the sword that he intended to use to behead the hostage, and we fought. The fire began when lit candles on the altar were knocked over in our scuffle. I grabbed a dagger from the altar and stabbed him in the throat, and then dragged the hostages out."

Malloy was livid; Garrett could feel the force of his fury from across the room, but there was nothing he could do; Garrett was restored to duty with extraordinary honors. He could have run for Congress that month if he'd wanted to. Any such thought was the farthest thing from his mind.

Outside, the media swarmed on the steps, and Garrett allowed himself to be jostled and photographed as the press shouted questions. A CNN reporter shoved a mike in his face.

"Is it true that you were suspended from duty for pursuing this line of investigation?"

"The department was aware of this line of investigation," Garrett answered evenly.

"Then why were you alone at the scene, Detective Garrett?" another reporter called.

"My partner was incapacitated in a previous attack by McKenna. I arrived first on the scene and determined there was no time to wait for backup."

The shouts of the reporters started again until one voice rose above the fray. "Is it true you alerted three separate departments to the situation and backup never arrived?"

The shifting hoard of newspeople went silent, straining to hear Garrett's response. He stared at the reporter levelly. "It's my understanding that all departments arrived in due time after my call."

The crowd murmured and the same reporter raised his voice again. "You have *no* criticism of the way the department handled this investigation?"

Garrett looked into the camera with no expression. "I can only say I regret my own part in the arrest and detention of Jason Moncrief. We made the best determination we could based on the evidence we had at the time. I am glad the real perpetrator . . ." He hesitated for the first time, and on the monitors it seemed that he was looking far away. He finally finished: "Has been stopped."

As he turned away from the reporters, he saw Carolyn standing in the crowd of police officials, watching, as lovely and polished as ever. They looked at each other without speaking, and then Garrett moved on, jostling through the shouting crowd.

The small private room of the hospital was so crammed with flower arrangements and potted plants it could have been a florist's shop—or a greenhouse. Garrett winced unconsciously at the sight when he stepped through the door into the room, but all these blooms were fresh and colorful and alive, the plants a lush green.

Landauer lay propped up with pillows, a mountain in the bed. He had regained consciousness the night of Garrett's battle with McKenna. Garrett had checked the precise time with the nurses and in his estimation Landauer awoke at the same moment that McKenna died.

A woman sat beside his bed. She and Landauer turned to the door to look at the same moment. Garrett stared back at them from the doorway: his partner, and Tanith Cabarrus.

"What the hell took you so long?" Landauer scowled at him.

"I stopped to get you flowers but the whole city seems to be out," Garrett deadpanned, casting a look around the room.

"Too busy playing American Idol to check up on me, is more like," his partner accused.

"That and I.A.," Garrett agreed.

"Fuck 'em," Landauer answered. "What do they know?" And the men looked at each other.

Tanith rose from her chair beside the bed. "I'll leave you two to catch up."

"Thanks for stoppin' by," Landauer said, then visibly struggled with himself, and met her eyes. "My wife said to say thanks, about the smoking thing."

Tanith looked back at him. "If you go back to it, you'll be dead within a year. You get that, don't you?"

Landauer's grin twisted. "Funny, she said exactly the same thing."

Tanith smiled faintly. "All women are witches."

"I always thought," Landauer agreed. He hesitated. "So . . . if I don't, you know, start again, how long have I got?"

Tanith stepped toward the bed and looked at him squarely . . . Garrett could see Landauer holding his breath . . .

Then she shook her head. "I can't see that far into the future," she said lightly.

Landauer grinned like a little kid. Then he faked a yawn and looked at Garrett. "Awright, both of you out of here. I need my beauty sleep."

Tanith walked silently beside Garrett in the hospital hall, past a glass wall of windows overlooking the garden, while Garrett recited the facts as he knew them in a carefully neutral voice.

"McKenna had a sheet under the name Andrew Forsythe.

Cruelty to animals, sealed juvie record, drug convictions, psychiatric detention, questioned in the disappearance of a teenager in Maryland. No association with any organized satanic or pagan groups or cults, just a lot of Crowley and demonic stuff on his computer and in the motel room he'd been renting for a week. He fits the psychological profile perfectly. A lone satanic practitioner who uses the trappings of satanism to satisfy his own violent fantasies."

"That must feel good, to have things wrapped up so cleanly," she said, and there was no mockery in her voice.

"Yeah. Yeah, I'd like to close the book on this one," Garrett said, and didn't look at her.

She nodded, and bit her lip. Her voice was cool, with just a hint of a tremor. "I can understand that."

He stopped on the bridge, and now he did look at her. She was so darkly beautiful he had to look away again. "I couldn't do my job if there weren't some—underlying sense to it."

"Yes," she said.

"I want to thank you for your help, though," he said. "I know—" He paused, and struggled with himself. "Sorry—I—I'm still recovering from the drugs. I was dosed pretty hard."

Something flickered on her face. She nodded slowly, not speaking.

"What I know is, those kids would be dead if not for you." And finally he turned to her. "And I probably would be, too."

"No. You wouldn't have been there at all." She looked into his eyes, and her voice was gentle. "You took a big risk. You went farther than—anyone else would have. You went out on a limb and you saved four lives."

He shook his head. "Not four. Land would never have been in danger to begin with if I hadn't—"

"I meant Jason Moncrief," she said, without smiling. "Thank you for that."

She started to turn away. He caught her hand, but flinched back at the contact, as if it burned him. "I just can't . . ." He looked at her fully for the first time. "I don't want to live that way."

She smiled, with effort. "I know."

"I live in *this* world," he said.

"I know."

Her hand was still in his . . . neither of them moved. He could feel the blood pulsing in her wrist . . . and a sense of power beyond imagining . . . a sense of dark . . . and light . . .

And life.

Acknowledgments

My fabulous and much-loved agents, Scott Miller and Frank Wul-
iger, and Sarah Self for their fine representation and help.

My spectacular editor, Marc Resnick, who makes me glad every
day that I decided to try this novel thing, and the lovely and tal-
ented Sarah Lumnah, for her help and support.

Again, Marc and Sarah, and Sally Richardson, Matthew Shear,
Katy Herschberger, Talia Ross, Matt Baldacci, and the entire
St. Martin's Press team.

Michael Gorn of the Boston PD Crime Lab, for his extraordinary
willingness to share his knowledge and expertise. The mistakes I
have made and liberties I have taken are solely mine.

The awesome Beth Tindall, webmistress; and Michael Miller,
Sheila English, and Adam Auerbach for their art.

Sarah Langan, Sarah Pinborough, and Rhodi Hawk, dark soul sisters under the skin.

Kimball Greenough, for his extraordinary contributions to this story and my understanding of the forces.

Rhodi Hawk, Laura Benedict, Sarah Shaber, Brenda Witchger, Elaine Sokoloff, Franz Metcalf, and Jess Winfield for their early reads and phenomenal notes.

The whole gang at Murderati.com, for teaching me the business every day.

Heather Graham, F. Paul Wilson, Harley Jane Kozak, the Pozz's, and the Slush Pile Players—the best reward for *finishing* writing.

The Coven, because a girl just needs her witches.

The authors, officers, and staffs of Sisters in Crime, International Thriller Writers, Mystery Writers of America, Horror Writers of America, and Romance Writers of America, for creating these incredible communities.